The CRUEL STARS of the NIGHT

Also by Kjell Eriksson

The Princess of Burundi

The CRUEL STARS of the NIGHT

Kjell Eriksson

Translated from the Swedish
by Ebba Segerberg

THOMAS DUNNE BOOKS
ST. MARTIN'S MINOTAUR   NEW YORK

This is a work of fiction. All of the characters, organizations, and events portrayed in this novel are either products of the author's imagination or are used fictitiously.

THOMAS DUNNE BOOKS.
An imprint of St. Martin's Press.

www.thomasdunnebooks.com
www.minotaurbooks.com

Library of Congress Cataloging-in-Publication Data

Eriksson, Kjell, 1953–
    (Nattens grymma stjärnor. English)
    The cruel stars of the night / Kjell Eriksson ; translated by Ebba Segerberg.—1st ed.
        p. cm.
    ISBN-13: 978-0-312-36667-4
    ISBN-10: 0-312-36667-1
    I. Segerberg, Ebba. II. Title.

PT9876.15.R5155 N3813 2007
839.73'8—dc22

2007008353

First published in Sweden under the title Nattens grymma stjärnor by Ordfront

First U.S. Edition: May 2007

10   9   8   7   6   5   4   3   2   1

The CRUEL STARS of the NIGHT

Police Headquarters, Uppsala, September 2003

Has your father shown any signs of depression lately?"

Detective Sergeant Åsa Lantz-Andersson dropped her gaze as soon as she uttered the question. The woman sitting across from her had such a fierce expression on her face that it was hard to look at her. It was as if Laura Hindersten's eyes nailed her to the wall, saying, I don't think you will find my father and for this reason: you are a bunch of incompetent bunglers dressed up in uniform.

"No," she said with determination.

Åsa Lantz-Andersson unconsciously let out a deep sigh. The desk in front of her was overrun with folders and files.

"No signs of anxiety?"

"No, as I said, he was like he always was."

"And how is that?"

Laura Hindersten gave a short laugh. It was a quick, dry salvo that reminded the officer of a teacher she had had in elementary school, someone who had poisoned the children's existence. She had emanated pride mixed with embittered exasperation at having to put up with such thickheaded pupils.

"My father is a professor and researcher and devotes all his time to his life's work."

"Which is?"

"It would take us too far off track to explain it in detail, but I can summarize it by saying that he is one of the nation's leading experts on Petrarch."

Åsa Lantz-Andersson nodded.

"I see," she said.

Another dry cackle.

"So he left the house on Friday. Had he said anything about his plans for the day?"

"Nothing. As I said, when I came home from work he was gone. No note on the kitchen table, nothing in his calendar. I've checked."

"Are there signs that he has packed, brought things with him?"

"No, not that I can see."

"His passport?"

"Still there in his desk drawer."

"Your father is seventy years old. Is he showing any signs of confusion, that he . . . ?"

"If you're asking if he is senile or crazy, you're wrong. His intellect is completely intact."

"I'm glad to hear it," Åsa Lantz-Andersson said. "Is he in the habit of taking walks, and if so, where? The City Forest isn't so far from your house."

"He never takes walks."

"Was there any conflict in the family? Had you had a fight?"

Laura Hindersten sat completely silent, lowered her gaze for a moment, and Åsa Lantz-Andersson thought she muttered something before looking up again. Her voice was ice-cold, free of any attempt to sound agreeable.

"We had a very good relationship, if you can imagine such a thing."

"And why wouldn't I be able to do that?"

"Your work can hardly be very inspiring."

"No, you're right about that," Åsa Lantz-Andersson said with a smile. "It's depressing, banal work, but of course we will do everything we can to locate your father."

She gathered up her notes, but paused for a moment before getting to her feet.

"Thank you," she said and held out her hand.

Laura Hindersten remained seated.

"Aren't you going to . . ."

"Thank you," Lantz-Andersson repeated. "As I said, we'll do everything we can."

"He may be dead, murdered."

"What makes you think that?"

Laura Hindersten stood up. Her thin body didn't appear to want to hold her up. She teetered momentarily and Lantz-Andersson put out a hand to steady her.

It's a front, that haughtiness, she thought, and was suddenly gripped by a pang of conscience and pity.

Laura Hindersten was thirty-five, only a couple of years older than Lantz-Andersson, but she looked older. Maybe it was the clothes she wore, a gray skirt and an old-fashioned hip-length beige coat that gave that impression, for her face was the face of a young woman. There was no gray in the full, dark hair gathered into a ponytail—quite the opposite, in fact. Lantz-Andersson noted with a twinge of envy how shiny her hair was.

Her thin face was pale. The somewhat too-large front teeth led to thoughts of a rabbit especially when she laughed, but many would probably have said that Laura, with her mixture of forceful dark and delicate light, was an attractive woman. The eyes under the strong, dark eyebrows were light blue, and the small ears set close against her head had a classically rounded shape, like little shells.

On the desk, the photograph of her father taken a few years ago showed that Laura had inherited several of her features from him.

"One last question: was there any woman in your father's life?"

Laura shook her head and left the room without a word. Lantz-Andersson did not think they would find her father alive. Three days had gone by. After the first twenty-four hours you could still be optimistic, after two days the chances were fifty-fifty, but after three days at the end of September, experience told her that all hope was lost.

Lantz-Andersson tried to think past conventional explanations, but gave up. All rational explanations had been tested. Already on Saturday they had gone door-to-door in the neighborhood. A search party had combed the nearby City Forest, without results. The only thing they found, hidden under a spruce, were the stolen goods from a theft on Svea Street.

It was as if Professor Ulrik Hindersten had been swallowed up by the earth. No one had seen him, not his neighbors nor anyone in the few kiosks and shops in the area.

At the literature department, where Hindersten had earlier been an active member but of late had only visited once or twice a month, no one showed any concern over the disappearance. Lantz-Andersson had talked to a former colleague who made no bones about his intense dislike of the retired professor.

"He was a pain," was how the man summarized his opinion.

The impression from the door-to-door questioning in the area yielded the same weak results. No one actually expressed any regret at the old man's disappearance.

"The old man must have gotten lost in his own garden," the nearest neighbor said flippantly.

The latter was a professor of some subject Lantz-Andersson had never heard of, but she gathered it was something to do with physics.

She read through her notes. Ulrik Hindersten had been a widower for about twenty years and had lived alone with his only child during that time. Neither Ulrik nor Laura appeared in the police register nor did they appear to have any debts.

As far as she could tell the household was in good shape financially. Ulrik had a fairly generous pension and Laura's work yielded a monthly income of more than thirty thousand *kronor*. The mortgage had been paid off long ago.

There were three possibilities, according to Lantz-Andersson. Either Ulrik Hindersten had committed suicide, had lost his way and collapsed due to exhaustion or illness, or he had been murdered, perhaps during an attempted mugging.

If she were going to put money on one of these alternatives she would have to go with the second as the most probable. She shut the folder with the feeling that she would have to wait before finding out whether she had guessed correctly.

✦

One

"Manfred Olsson."

"Good morning, my name is Ann Lindell, I'm with the Violent Crimes Division at the Uppsala Police. I'm sorry for disturbing you so early."

She put the phone in her right hand and slipped the cold left hand in her pocket.

"I see, and what is this about?"

Manfred Olsson's voice was guarded.

"Routine inquiries," she started, in an unusually passive way.

"Is it about the car?"

"No, why, have you . . ."

"My car was stolen fourteen days ago. Have you found it?"

"It's not about the car."

Ann Lindell leaned against the wall. The rising sun warmed her frozen body. She had felt groggy when she woke up and it had not helped to be called out to a blustery front yard on a cold morning at the end of October.

The maple leaves glowed in shades of yellow-red, marred by tiny, black fungal spores, which, woven together, presented an impression both of the unending richness of the plant kingdom, but also of sadness and transience. Scoops of snow were evidence of winter having arrived early this year.

Ola Haver came out of the house, spotted her leaning against the wall, and nodded. He looked tired. He had mentioned something about both kids and his wife, Rebecka, having colds.

Or else it was because he had a hard time enduring the sight of a dead body. Lindell sensed it had to do with the fact that as a teenager Haver had seen his own father collapse at the dinner table—stung in the throat by a bee—and he had died within a few minutes.

"Do you know a Petrus Blomgren?" Lindell continued.

"No, I don't think so," Manfred Olsson said. "Should I?"

She heard voices in the background. It sounded as if a TV was on.

"What kind of work do you do?"

"Burglar alarms," Olsson said curtly. "Why?"

"We found a note with your number on it at the residence of Petrus Blomgren. He must have gotten it somehow."

Manfred Olsson did not reply.

"You have no explanation?"

"No, as I've already said."

"Are you acquainted with the Jumkil area?"

"No, I wouldn't say that. I know roughly where it is. What is this all about? I have to get going soon."

"Where do you work?"

"I work for myself. I'm going to . . . I guess it doesn't matter."

No, Lindell thought and smiled in the midst of the misery, it doesn't matter. Not now and maybe not later.

"Have you been to Jumkil recently?"

"I was there for a wedding once. That was maybe ten years ago."

"You install alarms, isn't that right? Have you had any requests for alarms in Jumkil in the last while?"

"No, not that I can remember."

"Thank you," Lindell said. "We may be in touch later and have you look at a photograph."

"He's dead, isn't he? That Blomgren man."

"Yes."

The conversation came to an end. A sudden gust of wind made the leaves dance at her feet.

"Nothing," Lindell said to Haver, who had come up to her. "He didn't know a thing, not about Jumkil and not about Blomgren."

"We've found a letter," Haver said. "A farewell letter."

"What? That Blomgren wrote?"

"It appears so."

Lindell sighed heavily.

"Do you mean he was planning to kill himself and someone beat him to it?"

Haver suddenly started to laugh. Lindell looked at him. One of their colleagues from Patrol looked up. Haver stopped just as quickly.

"I'm sorry," he said, "but sometimes it's just too much. You've got red on your back. You shouldn't lean up against walls."

He started to brush off her light-colored jacket.

"It's new, isn't it?"

Lindell nodded. She felt his forceful strokes across her shoulders and back. It was not unpleasant. It warmed her. She had an impulse to punch him playfully but restrained herself.

"There we go," he said, "that's a little better."

Lindell looked out at the surroundings. Here they were out in the field again. Yards, stairwells, basements, apartments, houses. Police tape, spotlights, screens, measuring tape, camera flashes, chalk marks on wooden floors, parquet floors, concrete floors, and asphalt. Voices from colleagues and crackling radio receivers. Footsteps in the darkness, in sunlight, in fall gloom and spring warmth. Objects that had been brought out, hung up, for decoration and joy, memories. Letters, diaries, calendars, notes, and grocery lists. Voices from the past, on videotape and answering machines.

Haver was talking about the letter but he stopped when he noticed her expression.

"Are you listening?"

"I'm sorry," Lindell said, "my thoughts were elsewhere."

"The view?"

"Yes, among other things, the view."

That was the first thing that had struck her. The view.

"He lived in a beautiful place," she said. "But tell me about the letter."

"It's short. A few lines. Somewhat oddly phrased."

"And Blomgren is the one who wrote it?"

"That remains to be seen," Haver said, "but I think so."

"If the murder was supposed to look like suicide it was an extremely sloppy job."

"Not with blunt trauma to the back of the head," Haver said and looked in the direction of the shed where Petrus Blomgren had been struck down.

"Fury," he said. "He is in very bad shape."

"Maybe it's Ottosson? Doesn't he have a summer cabin in this area?"

"Should we take a look?" Haver said and walked toward the hall.

They glanced at the building where the forensic team was working. One of Petrus Blomgren's legs could be seen through the door opening.

Lindell had already been in the house but had gone outside again to call the number they had found on a piece of paper. Petrus Blomgren had been a man of order, that much was clear. Maybe it's the number of Eldercare Assistance, Lindell thought, as she and Haver again went into the kitchen. Everything was in its place. No dirty dishes. A coffee cup and saucer, a serrated knife, a bowl, and several serving dishes neatly placed in the drying rack.

There was a saltcellar and a newspaper on the table. The waxed tablecloth was wiped down. A couple of potted plants in the window and a vase with the last flowers of the season, several twigs of goldenrod and orpine.

"Was he signed up to receive Eldercare?" Lindell asked.

"Maybe. It's nice and tidy, you mean."

"Yes, for an old man on his own. It normally looks a little different than this."

"Here's the letter," Haver said and pointed to an area of the counter next to the stove.

Lindell was surprised that she hadn't spotted the white envelope earlier. It was placed next to the coffeemaker, but partly blocked by the bread box.

She leaned forward and read: "It's fall again. The first snow. The decision is mine. That's how it's always been. I have had to make all of my decisions alone. You arrive at a certain point. I am sorry that perhaps I haven't always handled things as I should have. A final request: I beg you not to chop down the old maple tree. Not yet. Let it stand there until it falls. My grandfather was the one who planted it. It's not a pretty sight to hang oneself but I don't see any other choice. It's over."

The letter was signed "Petrus Blomgren."

"Why did he put the letter here and not on the table?" Haver wondered.

"Have you seen the leaf caught in the window?" Lindell asked and pointed. "It's like a greeting from the maple."

A yellow leaf had wedged itself into the woodwork of the window. The dark nerves were shaped like an outstretched hand. It wiggled a little in the wind, silently dashed a couple of times against the glass only to peel off and join the thousands of fall tokens whirling around the yard.

Haver looked at her.

"He wanted to die, but for the tree to live," she said. "That's strange."

"Could he have sensed that the killer was waiting for him?"

Lindell shook her head.

"But then he wouldn't have written like this."

"The neighbor who called said that Blomgren lived alone, had always done so."

"Where is she now?"

"At home," Haver said and indicated a house that could be seen some hundred meters up the road. "Bea is talking to her again."

"Did she see anything?"

"No, she reacted to the fact that the gate to the road was open. He was apparently very careful to keep it closed. She realized at once that something wasn't right."

"A creature of habit."

"A man of order," Haver said.

"Who couldn't get his life in order," Lindell said and walked over to the window. "How old is the tree?"

"At least a hundred years," Haver said, a bit impatient with Lindell's reflective mood, but well aware of the fact that there was no sense in hurrying her. It wouldn't make any difference to Blomgren anyway.

"Do you think it's a robbery-homicide?" Lindell asked suddenly. "Was he one of those old men with his dresser drawer full of cash?"

"In that case the thief knew where to look," Haver said. "The technicians say that nothing appears to be disturbed."

"Did he know that Blomgren was on his way to the barn? That's a barn, isn't it?"

Haver nodded.

"Or was he hiding in there and taken by surprise when the old man walked in with a rope in his hand?"

"We'll have to check with the neighbor," Haver said. "She seems to be the kind who keeps tabs."

They both knew that Beatrice Andersson was the most suited to handle the questioning of the neighbor. If there was anything Bea excelled at, it was talking to older women.

"Who stands to inherit?"

Sammy Nilsson's question broke the silence that had settled in the kitchen. He had come creeping in without either Haver or Lindell noticing.

Haver didn't say anything but gave him a look that was difficult to interpret.

"Am I interrupting?" Sammy asked.

"Not at all," Lindell said.

"Let's hope for a dead broke, desperate nephew," Sammy continued. Lindell tried to smile.

"Look over by the bread box," she said.

Sammy walked over to the kitchen counter and read the good-bye letter in a low mumble.

"I'll be damned," he said.

A gust of wind underscored his words. Their gazes turned to the window. Outside a rain of leaves whirled from the tree to the ground. Lindell had the impression that the maple tree had decided to shake off all its leaves on this day.

"Makes you think, doesn't it?" Sammy Nilsson said.

"I wonder how his thought process went last night," Haver said.

"We'll never know," Sammy said and read the letter one more time.

Lindell slipped away, entering the small room off the kitchen. If she had been forced to guess what it would look like she would have scored a nine out of ten. There was an old sleeper couch with dingy red upholstery, most likely from the thirties, and an armchair of the same color, a TV on a table with a marble top, a couple of chairs surrounding a small pillar table, and a bookcase. On the small sofa in front of the TV there was nothing except the remote control.

It was a very personal room in spite of its predictability. It gave Lindell the feeling of intimacy, perhaps because she sensed that Petrus Blomgren spent his evenings here alone. He must have favored the armchair; it was extremely worn and had threads coming out of the armrests.

She walked over to the bookcase, which was filled mainly with older books. She recognized a few of the titles from her parents' house. They had a coating of dust. No one had touched these books in a long time.

The left part of the bookshelf had a small cabinet. The key was in the keyhole. She pulled the door open with a pen and on the two shelves inside she saw what she thought was a photo album and a book entitled *The Uppland Horse Breeder's Association.*

Everything looked untouched. If this was a burglary-assault the per-petrator had been exceedingly careful.

"Allan will have to take a look at this," she said, and turned in the di-rection of the kitchen. She got up and looked around but could not spot anything out of the ordinary.

"He'll be here soon," Sammy Nilsson said.

Haver had left the kitchen. Nilsson was staring out of the window. Lin-dell looked at him from her position diagonally behind him and discov-ered that he was starting to go bald on the back of the head. He looked unusually thoughtful. Half of his face was illuminated by the soft morn-ing light and Lindell wished she had had a camera. She was gripped by a sudden feeling of tenderness for her colleague.

"What do you think about the new guy, Morgansson?"

"He seems all right," Lindell said.

Charles Morgansson had been working in Forensics for a couple of weeks. He had joined them from Umeå, where he had been for the past few years. Eskil Ryde, the head of the Forensics Department, had in-stalled Morgansson in the empty cubicle in their division and the northener had made a comment about it being like a row of boxes in the stables and had said little else since then. His reticence had irritated some, aroused the curiosity of others, but all in all the new recruit had acclimated well. This was his first homicide case in Uppsala.

"Have you heard anything of Ryde's plans?"

"No," Lindell said, who as recently as the other day had talked to Ryde about his plans of quitting the force and taking early retirement, but this was nothing she wanted to discuss with Sammy Nilsson.

"Anita thought his buns were cute," Nilsson said.

"Whose buns?"

"Morgansson's"

"Forget about his buns a while," Lindell said flatly, "we have an inves-tigation under way."

"I was just trying to . . ."

"Forget it. Can you take the upstairs? I want to take a look around out there. Tell Allan to go over the TV room."

The technicians Jönsson and Mårtensson had spent almost two hours going through the home. Now it was the detectives' turn but Lindell was finding it hard to remain in Petrus Blomgren's house. She couldn't exactly put her finger on it but it was something more than the usual oppressiveness she felt in the homes of those who had fallen victim to deadly violence. Perhaps a little fresh air will help, she thought and walked out into the yard again.

The mercury strip had indicated negative five degrees Celsius this morning but now there was milder weather approaching. The period of unusual cold would be followed by a warm front and the end of October would be marked by more normal temperatures.

She turned the corner and came out of the wind. A couple of black currant bushes, with withered leaves and the occasional, dangling dried berry, reminded her of a time gone by. It was always this way when she came out to the countryside. All the little cabins, woodsheds, and wood-piles with bunched-up twigs and grass took her thoughts back to Gräsö Island. This was her punishment, or so she felt. She had to live with it; she knew that. Everyone carried some painful memories. This was hers.

She sighed heavily, plucked a berry that she popped in her mouth, and looked around. There was nothing of note to see: a handful of old apple trees, a bed of wilted flowers, and a rusty ladder hanging on the wall. She took a closer look at it and the mounting hardware. The ladder did not look as if it had been moved in years.

Behind the house there was a pile of rocks that stirred the imagination. Large stone blocks pushed up against each other as if engaged in a wrestling match. From having been enemies once upon a time they had now made their peace and—weighed down with age, covered with moss and lichen—had stiffened, exhausted in their struggle, leaning heavily against each other.

Petrus Blomgren had planted a tree near this rock pile. Lindell rubbed its smooth, striated trunk. A single chair had been left out under its thin crown. Lindell pictured him sitting there in the coolness of the rocks, pondering the decisions he had to make on his own. Wasn't that what he had written, that he had to make all his decisions alone?

Where was the motive for killing an old man? Lindell stopped, took a deep breath, and drew out her newly acquired notebook. She was a little embarrassed about it. She had read a mystery novel over the summer, the first she had read in a number of years, and in it the protagonist had a notebook where he wrote down everything of interest. At first Lindell had thought it seemed silly, but after she finished reading she kept thinking about that notebook and so when it happened that she passed by a bookstore she had slunk in and bought a pad for thirty-two *kronor*. She always carried it with her now and she thought it had sharpened her thought processes, ennobled her as a police officer. Perhaps she was simply going with her gut here, but then, wasn't that a part of police work? At any rate, the notebook had not made things go any worse.

She had mentioned her new routine to Ottosson. He had laughed heartily, perhaps mostly because of the expression on her face, but had said something about how if she turned in the receipt for her expenditure he would gladly accept it.

Now she wrote down "motive" and smiled to herself. Thereafter she listed the various financial motives she could think of, skipped jealousy but wrote "conflict with neighbors," "a failed robbery," and finally "accident."

What the latter would be Lindell could not imagine, but she had enough experience to know that many crimes—even if they involved violence—were the result of unplanned circumstances.

She heard a car pull over on the main road and sensed that Allan Fredriksson had just arrived. This investigation is probably to his taste, she thought; he likes the country air. The Violent Crimes Division's own country boy.

Who was Petrus Blomgren? How did he live? She rounded the next corner of the house. The place suggested peacefulness, but loneliness even more, especially like this in the final days of October. May probably looked different, more optimistic. Now nature was switching off, dropping leaves, closing in around piles of rock and underbrush. She stopped and looked right into the vegetation surrounding the house. Static. The wind had died down. She imagined funeral wreaths. Fir branches. Bells that rang out in a doomsdayish way on a bare autumn day over a cowering congregation that tried to minimize its movements.

Don't let it get to you, she thought. There's no time to be depressed.

She had to create an idea of Petrus Blomgren's life in order to understand how he died. The good-bye letter was a fall greeting from a person
who had given up hope. The irony of fate meant he had not been granted
the time to take his own life.

Lindell crossed the yard at the same time as Fredriksson walked in
through the gate.

"Male, around seventy, not in our database, lived alone, killed in the
barn, no signs of robbery." Lindell summed up the situation for her colleague.

"Nice hill," Fredriksson said. "Have you seen the maple?"

"No, I must have missed that," Lindell said, and smiled.

"A lot of leaves. When I was a boy we weren't supposed to jump in the
leaf piles because you could get polio."

✦

Two

Dorotea Svahn suddenly got to her feet, walked over to the window, and looked out for a second before once again sinking down at the
table.

"I thought . . . ," she said, but did not complete her sentence.

"Yes?"

"I thought I saw someone I know."

The woman spoke in short sentences, forcing the words out, audibly
gasping for breath and it looked like such an effort that Beatrice Andersson inadvertently leaned forward across the table as if to help when
Dorotea got ready for another attempt.

"Petrus and I, we got along. I'm a widow."

She looked down at her folded hands. Behind her, on the wall, a clock
was ticking.

"Have been for many years now," she added and looked at Beatrice.
"Are you married?"

Beatrice nodded.

"That's good."

"How long have you lived here?"

"I was born in this house."

Beatrice could discern a streak of defiance, as if it were a strike against her to have been born in Vilsne village, in Jumkil county, and not ever to have gotten around to leaving.

"This is a beautiful area," Beatrice said.

"I'm the only one left." Dorotea sighed.

"Could you tell me a little more about Petrus?"

"He was"—Dorotea Svahn searched for the right word—"strict with himself. He didn't indulge himself in very much. He kept going as usual. For a while he worked in carpentry, in town as well. He got a lot of work. And that helped. But all that was long ago. The last couple of years he didn't come over as often. But I could see him sitting in that chair by the corner of the house. He sat there, philosophizing."

"About what?"

Dorotea smiled for the first time.

"It was mainly small things," she said, "things like, well, you know . . . small things. No big thoughts. It could be about that squirrel that disappeared or the firewood he had to get to. He picked mushrooms too. And berries. Could come back with buckets of it. I had to make jam and juice. My legs aren't so good anymore. For going in the forest, I mean."

Beatrice nodded. The clock struck a few peals.

"Was he worried about anything?"

"How do you mean?"

"Did he mention anything? Did he have any conflicts? People he didn't get along with?"

"Then he would have . . . He didn't say anything like that."

"Did he have any children?"

Dorotea shook her head. "No," she said flatly.

"Did he have many acquaintances?" Beatrice Andersson asked, although she knew the answer.

"No, maybe in the past. He belonged to the road committee and sometimes he might have gone hunting. But not very often."

Dorotea paused, glanced out the window. The begonias on the windowsill were still in full bloom.

"A long time ago the library bus used to come by," she continued. "He borrowed a lot. I did, too, for that matter. As long as the Kindblom's children were still at home it was more lively."

She made a movement inside her mouth, produced a smacking sound. She must have repositioned her false teeth.

"Do you remember him receiving any visitors out of the ordinary the past while?"

"Like in the ads, you mean, a tanker running aground in his garden?"

Beatrice laughed at the unexpected comment and could sense a younger woman's mischievous presence in Dorotea's eyes.

"No, he didn't get many visitors. The postman sometimes stops by. And then Arne, but that got less often."

"Who is Arne?"

"Arne Wiikman. He's an old friend. Their fathers worked at the mill together. One day Arne simply disappeared."

"Really? When was this?"

"Well that's a story in itself. He had inherited his father's temper. A real troublemaker who picked fights with everyone."

Dorotea smiled at some recollection and seemed to have collected herself somewhat. Her breathing was calmer.

"He was a communist. Everyone knew that, of course. But he was good anyway. A hard worker."

"Are you talking about Arne's father?"

"His name was Nils. Petrus's father's name was Karl-Erik, but they called him Blackie. They were always together. He was an edger working the saw. Nils was a lumber hauler. Of course, Petrus also worked at the mill when he was young. And so did Arne. Then he disappeared."

"When was this?"

"I guess it was the midfifties."

"But he came back?"

"Yes, that was about ten years ago. He bought Lindvall's old house and renovated it."

"And Arne and Petrus spent time together?"

"Yes, that's how it went. But so different. Petrus was calm, Arne fiery."

"Does he still live here?"

"Oh yes."

"Can you think of anyone who would want to take Petrus's life?"

"No, no one. He didn't harm a fly. He had no trouble with anyone."

"What was his financial situation?"

"He managed. He had a pension, of course. He lived frugally."

"Did he have any cash in the house?"

"You mean that someone would have wanted? I don't think so."

"Are you afraid now?"

Dorotea Svahn sighed.

"I'm afraid of getting old," she said. "What will happen if my legs don't carry me? I'm afraid of the silence. It will be . . ."

She looked down at the table.

"What a pity for such a fine man, to end like this."

Dorotea wept silently. Beatrice held out her hand and placed it on top of the older woman's. She looked up.

"It's strange that something so terrible is needed to stir things up," she said.

"Your son, where is he?"

"In town, but he travels a lot. Sometimes internationally."

"When was he here last?"

"It was a while ago."

"What kind of work does he do?"

"To be quite honest I don't really know what it is. Something with medical technology. Or that's what it was before."

"Is he married?"

"Divorced. Mona-Lisa, his wife, was . . . well, she got tired of him."

"Grandchildren?"

Dorotea shook her head.

"She had a child later. Afterward, I mean, long after. I think she is doing well."

"Do you like her?"

"I have nothing against Mona-Lisa," Dorotea said.

"If we might return to Petrus. When did he usually go to bed?"

"After the nine o'clock news, sometimes he sat up later if there was a good movie on. He liked movies."

"Did you see him yesterday?"

"We didn't chat or anything, but I saw him as usual. He usually brought in wood in the evenings. Before, when he had a cat then . . . well, you know. He really loved the cat. A little black one with white paws. She disappeared."

"So you saw him fetch firewood last night?"

"No, I don't think so. I must have sat here," Dorotea said thoughtfully, "with the crossword puzzle. And then I wrote the grocery list. Petrus was going to look in on me today. He did some shopping for me. There's always something you need."

Beatrice nodded and scrutinized Dorotea.

"You are the first Dorotea I've met."

"Is that so? Beautiful it's not, but you get used to it. The worst was when they called me Dorran, but that was a long time ago."

"Did you think it was strange when you didn't see Petrus last night?"

"No, not really. I saw that his lights were on. Then when I got up this morning I saw that the lights were still on, and that the gate was open. I mean the big gate. At first I thought an ambulance must have been here. Petrus always kept it closed. And then the door to the old barn was open."

"You were up early."

"It's my bladder," Dorotea said.

"You didn't see a car here last night?"

"No, I would have noticed something like that," she said firmly.

Beatrice looked down at her notes, a couple of lines, a few names, not much more. Just as she was about to end the conversation her cell phone rang. She saw that it was Ann and answered immediately.

She listened and then turned off the phone without having said a word. Dorotea looked at her with curiosity.

"I've just been informed that Petrus wrote a good-bye letter."

"A good-bye letter, what do you mean?"

"He was planning to take his own life," Beatrice said.

Dorotea stared at her.

"That's impossible," she said finally. "Petrus would never do anything like that."

"My colleagues believe he wrote the letter," Beatrice said. "I'm sorry."

"So you mean to say—"

"—that Petrus had made up his mind to commit suicide. Yes, that's how it appears."

"The poor man. If only I had known."

"It was nothing that you thought might happen?"

"Never! He was a little down sometimes but not in that way."

"I'm very sorry," Beatrice repeated and Dorotea looked at her as if she took her words to heart.

After a few additional minutes of conversation Beatrice Andersson left the house. At the gate she turned and waved. She couldn't see her but assumed Dorotea was standing at the window.

It's strange, she thought, that in Dorotea's eyes it would have been better if her neighbor had been killed without the complicating factor that he had already decided to commit suicide. On top of the tragic news that Petrus Blomgren was dead she now had to bear this extra burden, the knowledge that he was tired of life and perhaps above all that on his final evening he had not sought her support.

Lindell, Nilsson, Haver, and Andersson were standing in the yard. Lindell took the fact that she could hear the technicians talking as a sign that they were wrapping up their work in the barn. In her experience the forensics team often worked in silence.

"It's strange," she said, "how a place changes after something like this happens."

Perhaps this did not strike anyone as a particularly sensational or original observation and Haver was the only one who took the trouble to grunt in response. The rest were looking around. Beatrice looked back at Dorotea's house. She was probably bustling around the kitchen or sitting at the kitchen table. Beatrice wished she had been able to spend a little more time with the old woman.

"Yes," Sammy Nilsson said with unexpected engagement, "now it is the scene of a murder. People will talk about this house as the one where Blomgren was murdered for a long time. They'll walk past, slow down, maybe stop and point."

"Not a lot of people walk past," Beatrice said.

Allan Fredriksson joined the group.

"What a wonderful place," he said. "Have you noticed what a complex biological habitat the place is? It has everything: spruce forest, deciduous groves, open meadows and fields, dry hills, and even a little wetlands."

Lindell smiled to herself.

Fredriksson pointed to the other side of the road where a large ditch ran down to a marsh. The green moss glowed in the morning sun. Tufts of sedge grass looked like small rounded buns and a clump of reedy marsh grass swayed in the wind.

"I wonder if Petrus was interested in birds?"

"Petrus didn't have many friends," Beatrice said, "and he does not appear to have been a rich man who hoarded cash or valuables."

"The only thing I found was a letter from the Föreningsspar Bank," Fredriksson said. "There was not a single account book or any withdrawal slips, but perhaps he kept the papers hidden. We'll have to go over the place with a fine-toothed comb."

Neither the forensics team nor the criminal investigators had found the least trace of burglary or disturbance. There was nothing out of the ordinary in the house in Vilsne except for the fact that its owner lay murdered in the barn.

"Will you check the bank, Allan?" Lindell asked.

Lindell looked at their new forensics team member, how he carefully packed away his equipment. Anita's comment came to mind.

"Nice buns," she said.

"What?"

"Morgansson's," Lindell said and nodded in the direction of the barn.

Haver turned his head. It looked like he was about to say something, but he held back. Everyone was watching the technician.

A door opened and a light reflection from the glass in Dorotea Svahn's front door swept over the hill where the police officers were assembled, then disappeared into the thicket of alder and willow. The old woman looked out at her neighbor's house, took a slow step onto her porch, and gently closed the door behind her.

She stood there with a cane in one hand and the other on the wrought-iron railing. She walked down the stairs with an effort and moved toward the police. One of her legs didn't seem to want to come along.

She was wearing a gray coat and a dark hat. Beatrice had the impression that it was not Dorotea's everyday outfit.

"Is she on her way over here? Maybe she needs help," Haver said and took a step toward the gate.

She was not fast but she did seem to have developed a technique to compensate for her bad leg. A car approached. At first there was only a faint rumble behind the forest that surrounded Blomgren's property. Dorotea must not have noticed the engine sound that increased in volume and when she was halfway across the road the van from the Medical Examiner's Office rounded the corner. Fridh was driving. Dorotea stopped and lifted the cane over her head as a signal.

Ola Haver took yet another step forward but stopped himself. In his mind he saw the Greek shepherd he and Rebecka had once encountered, on a curvy mountain road in the north. The shepherd was moving his flock across the road. Like a wooly string of pearls they slowly streamed from one side to the other. Still, they brayed nervously, the lambs following the ewes and the flock keeping tightly together.

The shepherd had raised his staff like a weapon, or more likely a sign. He spoke deliberately, even though no one could hear him, with his gaze lifted to a point somewhere above the waiting cars. The stream of sheep seemed never to end, someone in the cue beeped, and the shepherd raised his staff a few centimeters higher. He spoke without ceasing. Haver stepped out of the car—he was at the front of the line—and he observed the timeless scene.

The same feeling now gripped him as he watched the old woman raise her cane at Fridh's van. Wasn't she also saying something? He thought he saw her lips forming words that no one could hear.

Fridh had stopped. Dorotea continued over to Blomgren's large gate, hesitated a moment as if she was unsure of where she was going, then turned into the yard. Beatrice walked over to her.

Dorotea Svahn was out of breath. She covered her mouth with one hand, perhaps wiping some saliva from the corner of her mouth.

"I want to see Petrus," she said in a strained voice.

Fridh had pulled up and Beatrice took the woman's arm and guided her to the side so that the van could drive in.

"He's badly beaten," Beatrice said.

"I realize that," Dorotea said.

"I'm sure you'll be able to see him later, I mean when they've had a chance to clean him up."

"I want to say good-bye. Here."

There was a faint smell of mothballs around her.

"Of course you can say good-bye. I'll come with you," Beatrice said.

Fredriksson turned away. Haver kicked the leaves at his feet. Lindell and Sammy Nilsson looked at each other. Lindell shook her head, turned, and walked up to the house.

Beatrice accompanied the woman up to the door of the barn. Charles Morgansson had finished putting away his equipment and he made way for them. He nodded to Beatrice who took it as a green light for them to go in.

"I think the very first blow made him unconscious," Beatrice said.

She felt Dorotea's thin body tense up. She freed herself from Beatrice, took the cane as support, and sank down next to Petrus Blomgren, mumbled something, and put her hand on his shoulder. Bea was glad that Dorotea had not walked over alone in the dawn and found Petrus, but that she had just called the police and forced them to come out and take a look.

"He was my best friend," Dorotea said.

Beatrice crouched down so she could hear better.

"My only friend. We pottered around here like ancient memorials, me and him. Petrus said many times that it wasn't right, 'They had no right,' was how he put it."

Beatrice didn't really understand what she meant.

Dorotea's hand caressed the wool sweater. She appeared oblivious of the blackened blood in the wound on the back of the head.

"Little Petrus, you went first. I could almost . . ."

Her voice was overcome with emotion. The bony hand went still, took hold of the sweater as if she wanted to pull the dead man to his feet.

"He came over with lingonberries this fall. More than usual. 'Now you have more than enough,' he said, as if he knew."

She braced herself on the cane and slowly straightened to standing.

"When you are as old as I am you see things, how it is all connected. Petrus would always say it would be better to turn life around, be old first and then become younger, leave the frailty behind but keep the wisdom."

"That would be good," Beatrice said.

The old woman sighed heavily.

"They had ten cows in here, maybe twelve. He sold the land later on."

"For a good price?"

"It was good enough. He didn't lack for anything, Petrus."

"It looks like he lived frugally," Beatrice said, taking the old woman's arm and helping her back out into the fresh air.

"That's how we were raised," Dorotea said.

"Do you know if Petrus had a special place for his valuable documents?"

Dorotea shook her head. "I don't know anything about that," she said.

The four police officers were still waiting in the yard. Beatrice had the feeling that she and Dorotea were leaving a church, as if after a funeral.

Fridh was sitting in the van and would remain there until after the old woman had left.

"Will you pray with me?" Dorotea asked. "Just a few words. Petrus was not a believer but I don't think he'll mind."

Beatrice interlaced her fingers and Dorotea quietly said a few words, remained motionless for a few seconds before opening her eyes.

"He was a magnificent man," she said. "With a good heart. May he rest in peace."

Far off in the distance, a horse neighed.

✦

Three

Had she ever liked him? She often asked herself this question. At times, perhaps. That time when he tripped outside the house and fell on his face she had at least felt sorry for him. That was what he had said, that he tripped, but Laura imagined that something else must have happened since he had scraped both his cheeks and forehead.

She dressed his wounds. She did this with divided feelings: part disdain for his whimpering when the disinfecting solution stung, part tenderness at his helplessness. The skinny legs dangling over the edge of the bed, the thinning hair growing still thinner, and the hands that gripped the soiled blanket.

At other times she could hate him almost beyond reason. If she was in the house and he was nearby she had to escape, out into the garden or even out into the town, in order not to strike him down with the nearest blunt instrument. This hate was indescribable, so dark and so consuming that she believed it deformed her physically.

Even after she managed to calm herself, it could take several days before she was able to address her father in a normal tone of voice.

"I see, you're that way now," he would usually comment on her state, unable to grasp what had upset her.

Once upon a time everything had been nicely ordered, then it fell into disarray. Books, manuscripts, and loose papers piled up and formed drifts on the floor. Laura sometimes had the feeling that she was out on the rocking waves of the sea. She had given up trying to keep things in order long ago. There was simply no aspiration for order. It was not part of her father's worldview and Laura had grown up in an accelerating chaos.

The house smelled a little odd and it was only now, a month after her father's disappearance, that she realized what it was. She had always thought it came from the discarded clothes that were heaped together on the floor.

She had detested him because of the mess. But while she was cleaning up after him she was forced to go into his bedroom, something she had avoided doing all these years. And there was the reading lamp, the one that had been there ever since she was a little girl. It had been bought in Germany at the end of the fifties, modern at the time and now again a desired object at flea markets and auctions.

When she stood close to the lamp the odor was more pronounced than ever. Against her will she sniffed closer and closer to the hateful thing. The plastic—the lampshade consisted of mottled plastic strips—emitted a stale smell when the sixty-watt lamp was on. He kept it turned on even at night. Laura suspected that some nights he fell asleep in the armchair next to the table, submerged in some problem that had to do with Petrarch or some chess game.

Her first thought was to throw the lamp out, but it still stood in its spot next to the table. She never turned it on and the smell slowly dissipated.

Most of the things in the bedroom were untouched. Even his reading glasses still lay on the nightstand. There was also an essay from the Humboldt University in Berlin. It was about Petrarch's Laura, about whether or not a newly discovered portrait was a depiction of her.

Laura was named after this woman from the fourteenth century who had become a literary concept and the object of research. Many times she herself felt like a concept. As a teenager she started to doubt whether or not she lived, if she even existed here and now. What did she mean to her father? She pinched herself, experienced pain, cried, and felt her cheek grow wet with tears, but did that prove her existence?

She started to think he only saw her as Petrarch's Laura, a shadow from the past, without human qualities. No daughter to love, but a re-born literary figure. Even so she continued to live, here and now, getting up in the morning, leaving the house, walking to school, walking home, growing up.

When she had her first period she immediately told her father. Her first feeling was one of shyness, perhaps shame, but suddenly she simply said it: "Father, I have to buy sanitary pads." It was as if an unknown voice spoke through her mouth.

He put down his knife and fork and looked at her with an expression that was difficult to interpret. Laura imagined he felt offended. She rarely used the word *Father*. He wanted her to call him by his first name.

After a pause he resumed eating. She understood that his worldview had received a blow. He didn't like it, she saw that.

Who will carry on after me?" he would sometimes exclaim, with that combination of pride and desperation that became more strongly reinforced in him over the years.

His contribution to research was incontestable. Or perhaps it was closer to the truth to say that those who may have had reason to question his earlier work saw no reason to do so now, thirty-five years after the dissertation. At one time he had been important, but now he was marginalized and excluded from the debate.

He himself contributed to this in large part. Like a boxer who relies more on raw strength and intensity than technique and calculation, he slugged his way through the academic world. At first he was successful, in part due to his renowned ability to tire out his opponents with masses of data, many times dished out in long, apparently incoherent tirades. But as time went by he became labeled a fossil who had become stuck in outmoded ideas.

But there were still those who allowed themselves to be seduced by his words, above all when he recited some of the more emotional sonnets. He did so with such feeling and in such perfect Italian that the words by their own power appeared to hover in their own rarefied space with no room for questions, objections.

Was he a genius? Or simply an overeducated lunatic? Or both?

He was never promoted to full professor.

"I am consistently overlooked," he said. "In Florence and Paris they realize my greatness but in this backwater one rewards mediocrity. Here inbred careerists from the land of Lilliput take the high seat, while the giants are forced to jostle just to get inside the door."

He dug through his stacks of paper, extracted letters from colleagues all over the world, waved them excitedly in the air, and shoved them under her nose.

"Here, here are the witnesses who shoot down the claims of the feebleminded."

He raised his voice, came up close to her, and forced her to study the letter, struck the signature with his index finger, and told her that the author of the letter was one of the world's greatest authorities on the poetry of the Italian Renaissance.

"He is a scholar, mark my words. *Scholarship*, not loose assumptions or flabby opinion."

His raised his voice a notch. Suddenly he could drop his arms, turn inward, retreat to his room. Once, after an outburst of this kind, she had followed him, had stood in the doorway to his room and watched him from behind. He had dropped the letter and it had fluttered to the floor and slid halfway under the bed.

Laura had also seen other sides of her father, sides that were only rarely revealed in public. His love of the words themselves. He could become intoxicated by a single phrase, a few tentative letters on a page, as if only hesitantly entrusted to the page, a spontaneous expression of the author's inner life. Sometimes it was quite moving, if a little tiring, when her father called her to him and read something to her, a couple of verses, parts of a sonnet, almost trembling, with his glasses perched on his nose. Often they were about love:

Tempo non mi parea da far riparo
contra colpi d'Amor: però m'andai
secur, senza sospetto; onde i miei guai
nel commune dolor s'incominciaro.

"Isn't it beautiful? So vivid, so expressive," he would always exclaim after he had let the words sink in. Laura was not expected to say anything, simply listen. Her father needed an audience. Someone who did not talk back, did not engage in sparring about the text. Someone who simply listened, enraptured. Listened to the words that intoxicated, that carried one away, transformed and gave life meaning.

"The sonnet is superior!" he could suddenly shout and then burst into laughter when he saw her expression of surprise and—sometimes—fear.

If only he had laughed more. That was what Alice, her mother, had said, that her father took life too seriously. He was an expert in the language of love but incapable of romance or tenderness, imprisoned in an environment where the beautiful words did not carry any weight.

Laura had noticed the tension between laughter and silence early on. Sometimes her mother would sing but she always stopped when her father approached. It was as if it was inappropriate to display joy over something as trivial as fair weather, the scent of the roses from the garden, or that a movement could be an expression of a joy in living and not simply a means to get from the desk to the dining table.

Laura's mother was from the country. He would use Skyttorp, the name of her village, like an insult. It became a synonym for stupidity and laxity. He loved to correct her country expressions and when she used a dialect word he pounced on her like a hawk. Her language shrunk. She swallowed the words and the songs of her childhood on a small farm between Örbyhus and Skyttorp.

Laura remembered one time when her mother had cracked, how she in a forceful attack accused him of being a hypocrite: he loved Petrarch's simple Tuscan language dialect but despised her own. Astonished, he listened to her barrage, her increasingly vulgar language, how she assaulted him in pure Uppland dialect, and finally burst out into a ringing laughter that seemed never to want to end.

"Hysterical," Ulrik called her and Alice slapped him across the mouth.

She grew silent and kept up her silence when her husband was around. She died eighteen months later. She had recently turned forty-four.

As her father's health declined and his isolation increased, as the world's scorn, the neighbors' pointed words and open disdain grew, Laura was erecting a strong line of defense around the house. She placed the ridiculously ugly white plastic furniture in the center of the garden only to taunt the nearest neighbor, the aesthete who edged his lawn every other week. The furniture shone, jumped out at the professor and his wife. Later she completed this arrangement with a sun umbrella that loudly proclaimed the superiority of Budweiser.

She fed pigeons so that they would dirty the surroundings, played senseless music at high volume outside while she lay inside reading, refused to do anything about the shared hawthorn hedge that was encroaching on the neighbor's carefully tended vegetable patch.

When the professor complained she was unapologetically rude. That worked, she knew. Insolence, an unwillingness to discuss things reasonably, vulgarity—that was what the academics in the neighborhood found the most distressing.

She flaunted her poor taste, dressed even worse than her father, entertained loud acquaintances who sat in the white garden furniture and carried on noisily long into the night.

Her father was oblivious to it all. He only went out into the garden a few times a year when he walked around and talked in a concerned way about the increasing state of disarray but without doing anything about it. Sometimes he would say that they should hire someone to help prune the old fruit trees but nothing was done. In the garden there were wild apple-oaks that blew down during fall storms, groaned under the weight of moldy fruit that was never harvested.

The state of disrepair both inside the house and in the garden became more extensive. Why did she keep living there? Sometimes her colleagues asked her this but she couldn't answer. She tried to explain it in terms of financial considerations, but that was a lie, everyone knew that. She offered reasons such as the need to take care of her confused father. That was more satisfying but was still not completely satisfying.

Sometimes she claimed she felt so comfortable in the old house that she could never get used to a modern apartment or townhouse. But people around her shook their heads, concerned that she was taking after her father.

She sat at the kitchen table with the same feeling of liberation she had felt a month ago. The radio had been on that time. The Swedish people had just voted no to joining the European Monetary Union and the kitchen was filled with commentary that did not interest her in the least. She had not even voted.

She looked out of the window, turned off the radio, and was overcome with the silence. The room shrunk. The dark green kitchen cabinets seemed to bulge out, to be coming closer. The kitchen counter—covered in dishes—seemed to expand with deep breaths.

A moment of regret, or rather, reflection, came over her like a tremor, but disappeared just as quickly. The way she had chosen left no room for doubt. Or rather, the path her life had taken was not the result of a conscious decision, was how it seemed to her. She had given herself up to a wave, a force that was now mercilessly carrying her forward, simply forward. No history, no reflection, simply a kind of quiet rush, hard as flint, that far exceeded her father's emotions at reading those beautiful words. His euphoria was relative and fragile. He was weak. She was strong.

Words, words, words, into infinity. She did not want them, the artfully arranged, duplicitous assurances that people surrounded themselves with. She silenced the words and eradicated their falseness.

Laura felt that she now commanded two worlds. Now she could step out into reality without anxiety or anticipation. She carried a shield, an armor against which the words bounced off.

"You seem happier," a colleague said in the lunchroom a few weeks after her father's disappearance.

"It's the only way," Laura answered cryptically.

The colleague was pleased, thought she could see a new Laura, convinced it was because her suffocating life with her father was over, that a new Laura was being born in the midst of longing and grief. Horrible, but true.

"Maybe we could go out sometime," the colleague had suggested.

Laura shook her head.

Kerstin was one of the better ones, but did Laura want a confidant? No, Kerstin would not understand the feeling of liberation. Laura was and would remain alone.

"My father may have been murdered and you think I should go out and enjoy myself?" she said and left the room.

✦

Four

The task of going door-to-door in the area around Petrus Blomgren's house did not take long. Sammy Nilsson and Bea Andersson, who were in charge of this, could afterward report that there were altogether some twenty properties. Fourteen of these were permanent residences and the rest were summer cottages.

No one had seen or heard anything. There was not even any gossip, no hints or speculation, simply disbelief that something so horrible could happen in Vilsne and that it was Petrus Blomgren who was the victim. No one had a bad word to say about the victim. Sammy and Bea listened to the testimony without being able to discern any criticism between the lines. Blomgren was well-liked, highly thought of even, in the area. Neighbors had only praise for his still life, his industriousness, and concern for his nearest neighbor, Dorotea. An older man talked about Blomgren's love of nature, another about how admirable it was that even though Blomgren was a bachelor he managed to keep everything as clean and tidy as he did, and a third, the Kindblom couple, told them that their children when they were young would go up to "Uncle Petus" and there be treated with candy and sometimes, on Thursdays, with freshly made pancakes and homemade jam.

"Jumkil's Mother Theresa," Sammy Nilsson summarized and glanced at Bea to see if she had anything to add, but she only nodded.

"I see," Ottosson said and turned to Lindell.

She and Fredriksson had spent the day trying to bring order to the state of Petrus Blomgren's paperwork.

"At the Föreningsspar Bank they were unusually helpful," she said after a moment's hesitation.

She and Fredriksson had decided that he was the one who would present their findings but he had not turned up.

"Actually Allan is the one who was supposed to . . ." Lindell began.

"Take us through what you know," Ottosson said, unusually brusque.

"All right, as you like. Blomgren had seventy-six thousand *kronor* in his savings account. There are very few transactions. He received his pension, took out a couple of thousand every month. The last withdrawal was six days ago. Two thousand. In the house we have recovered around nine hundred *kronor* in cash."

"No cards?"

"No, he only had one account and no bank cards."

"Could there be accounts at other banks?" Sammy Nilsson asked.

"No, the guy at the bank didn't think so. Blomgren had been with the Föreningsspar Bank his whole life, though it was called something else before."

"The Förenings Bank," Fredriksson said, who had just come through the door. "It became the Förenings*spar* Bank a good many years ago," he continued and sat down at the table.

"In addition, for many years Blomgren had a donation by direct deposit set up with Doctors Without Borders. They received four hundred *kronor* every month. He recently raised the amount. Earlier it was three hundred."

"That's strange," Ola Haver inserted. "I would have expected Save the Children or converting the heathens, but Doctors Without Borders is unexpected."

"The guy at the bank also asked about this, but Blomgren gave no particular reason," Fredriksson said. "Maybe he saw a TV program about them?"

"No large withdrawals recently?"

"No," Lindell said. "As we said, everything was in order. No unexpected transactions."

"He kept a will at the bank," Fredriksson said. "I talked to the lawyer who drew it up three years ago. It was at Blomgren's behest. He came alone to the lawyer's office and had a prepared document that he wanted the lawyer to look through. It didn't take long. All assets go to Doctors Without Borders, with the exception of twenty thousand to his neighbor, Dorotea Svahn, and ten thousand to Jumkil Church."

"Damn," Sammy said.

"It's hardly credible that Doctors Without Borders or the church board have death squads posted in the countryside," Haver said, "and Dorotea probably can't kill a fly."

"That was sweet of Petrus," Bea said. "I don't think Dorotea is so well off."

"The church is," Sammy said.

"Not in Jumkil," Ottosson objected.

The last maple leaves are falling right now, Fredriksson thought. No one will be raking Blomgren's yard today. As he often did, he fell into a few moments of thought. His colleagues were used to these short pauses and waited patiently for the continuation.

"I think we can rule out a planned financial motive," Fredriksson continued, "but of course it's always possible that a passerby had the idea to attack this old man in the hopes that there was money to be gained."

"But nothing in the house was touched," Haver said.

"The killer was scared off," Fredriksson determined laconically.

It seemed he felt there was no more to say on the topic.

For another hour the group discussed possible motives and how they should proceed with the investigation. They did this in an unusually calm manner, as if Petrus Blomgren's quiet and retiring lifestyle had influenced the assembled homicide detectives.

Everything went according to procedure. The drama that Ann Lindell had once thought she would experience when she started as a police officer fell away as the years went by. The difference was noticeable.

The first investigations in the Violent Crimes Division in Uppsala had thrown her into a state of intensity, had claimed her thoughts day and night. Many times it had rendered her unable to live a normal civilian life. It was, she now realized, one of the reasons that she and Edvard had never really become close. In spite of their mutual love and their longing for that intimacy. Now he was lost to her and she steeled herself not to let the bitterness and regret poison the rest of her life.

They had not been in touch since last spring. She had called him right before Pentecost, enraptured and almost completely convinced that a reconciliation was possible. But Edvard was no longer interested. She could hear it in his voice. All summer she had cursed herself, consumed with self-pity and distaste for her life. Only her son, Erik, could make her really happy.

The fall had started with a rape and a case of assault. No excitement, only routine, and a nauseating feeling of indifference.

Now it was October. Her blues month. A new murder. No suspense, only sorrow. She pictured Dorotea on the gravel road, struggling up the hill to Blomgren's house, on her way to say good-bye.

"Hello, Earth to Ann." Ottosson interrupted her chain of thought.

"Sorry," Lindell said quickly, suddenly intensely embarrassed at her distraction.

"I wonder if you could draft a media statement?"

"Of course," she said, "I'll talk to Lise-Lotte."

The meeting broke up.

"We'll fix this," Allan Fredriksson said to Lindell as they left the room.

"Think so?"

"Sure thing, Allan. After all, crime doesn't pay."

Sammy Nilsson was snickering behind them. Lindell turned around.

"What do you think?"

"Allan's the gambler, but I say two weeks. Are you in? I'll wager a hundred."

"Okay," Fredriksson said, who during the last year had won large sums on horses.

Ann Lindell left the group with a feeling of isolation. All too often she felt they simply talked past each other, that the indispensable feeling of teamwork was lost. She didn't know if this simply had to do with her or if the others felt the same way.

For Lindell this feeling had a physical manifestation. She would get warm, sometimes glowing red, her sight altered so that she saw the room as a sealed space where the objects and words were bent inward toward an imaginary center that was Ann Lindell, single mother and investigative detective. The walls in the room were at the same time protection and limitation.

At first she thought she was sick. Now she had accepted that her psyche played these tricks on her. She sometimes lived as if inside a container. When she spoke she heard an echo and was surprised when the people in her surroundings reacted to her words. And despite all this she went on.

She stopped, slightly nauseated, feeling sad and sweaty. At that moment Sundelin, a colleague from the policing division, came hurrying down the corridor. He halted and asked her how the investigation was going. Lindell replied that it was probably going to be difficult.

"You'll crack it," the colleague said confidently. "You usually do."

He smiled and Lindell smiled back.

Sundelin hurried off. She watched him and wished they could have talked for a while. Sundelin had been one of Munke's acolytes. Munke, whom Lindell had always thought of as somewhat of a buffoon, competent, of course, but not someone she particularly enjoyed working with.

They had worked during the spring on a murder investigation and that was when their mutual respect for each other's professional expertise had developed into the beginnings of a friendship. Munke had died of a heart attack at the tail end of the investigation and Lindell felt as if someone from her inner circle had passed on.

She had taken everyone by surprise when she gave a speech at his funeral in Vaksala Church, touching on the small connections that contained the large. Only very few members of the audience had probably understood what she was trying to get at. Berglund, the old dog, perhaps, and Ottosson definitely, who had afterward taken her aside and told her he was going to step down as head of the Violent Crimes Division.

"There are other things," he had said, and Ann sensed that behind his talk of his summer cottage and the grandchildren there was a fear for the direction society was taking and also, at a very personal level, of death.

"Ann, you are a sensitive soul," he had said, "but don't break down," and Lindell just wanted to fall into his arms. "In that case it would be better for you to quit the force," he had added.

"The force." How many people called it "the force" these days? It sounded like a brotherhood held together with a unified spirit. For better or for worse it had bound policemen together, for that was what they were: men. Men like Munke. Boorish, sometimes real pigs, many times recruited from the military, most of them politically conservative. From these some real police officers appeared. Like Munke. Lindell and he were rarely in agreement when talking about current events, but there was a genuine honesty in her deceased colleague that she had appreciated a great deal.

The unifying spirit was no longer there, she knew. Not so much because of the individual colleagues but more because of the pressure from above. Lindell thought it was mostly for the good—the homogenous group of men functioned fairly well in the old days but no longer. She was needed, Beatrice also. Ditto Ola Haver and Sammy Nilsson. They had seen themselves as young officers with a new way of looking at things and new insights. Now they had all entered middle age and soon they would make up the ranks of the veterans.

She continued on down the corridor, still very warm and aware of her own body.

"Am I sick?" she muttered to herself, heading to the cafeteria, aware that if she could only hear other voices she would return to a state of relative normalcy. The loneliness made her feel even worse.

The cafeteria was mostly empty. Four patrol officers of unusually strong build were sitting close together at the far end of the room. They resembled a group of black animals, pressing up against each other in a tight circle, united, encircling a fallen prey, on their guard at their surroundings but also against others in their flock.

Lindell watched the one who was currently holding forth. He was gesticulating, emphasizing his story with large movements and conscious of his own importance. The others watched until they all burst into a roar of laughter that filled the whole room.

Lindell did not need these thundering hulks, not now. She sat down behind a big green plant, curled up with a cup of coffee and a pastry shielding her from the world, took a bite of the chocolate-dipped marzipan treat, looked down at her watch, and sighed heavily.

"Doesn't it taste good?" came a voice from behind.

Lindell turned around.

"Mind if I sit here?"

It was Charles Morgansson from Forensics. Lindell nodded. Her colleague sat down. He also had a cup of coffee and an identical little pastry on his tray.

"Great minds think alike," he said when he noticed her gaze.

He made a very light impression. It wasn't simply his hair color and pale skin, he was also wearing a dazzling white T-shirt, with a Hugo Boss logo. A thin silver chain wound around his neck.

"How's it looking?" he asked.

"A bit complicated. Blomgren hasn't yielded many avenues of investigation and no one seems to have seen anything of interest."

"And we couldn't contribute much either," Morgansson said and halved his treat with one bite.

"I know," Lindell said.

Morgansson shot her a look, devoured the last of his pastry, and washed it down with coffee. Don't go, she thought.

He put down his cup and looked at her. "Want to go to the movies?"

"What?"

"The movies, you've heard of them."

He smiled. It was as if the police station did not exist, no investigations and no red-marked files, no bringing in for questioning, no preliminary investigations, everything that was Lindell's life. She couldn't answer.

"Are you okay?"

"Yes, of course, I was just a bit taken aback."

Ann felt that she was blushing and was suddenly furious. At herself, at him, at the whole situation, in fact.

"I was planning to go tonight, take it easy, but it's not as much fun to go alone. It'd be more fun if it was you and I."

"You and me. Not you and I," Ann said.

He smiled again. I don't like that smile, she thought.

"You and me," Morgansson repeated. "How about it?"

Is he hitting on me, she thought in amazement. It was as if a relay had kicked into place, admittedly in a system that was somewhat rusty but that nonetheless—after an initial resistance—started to function; energy pulsed into the cable network inside her and a fear-filled pleasure suffused her chest.

"Maybe," she said, "but I have a son who I would have to find a sitter for."

He nodded.

"But that shouldn't be a problem," she added.

Morgansson crumpled up the plastic wrap that had surrounded the pastry. He wore a metal band on the ring finger of his right hand.

"I don't ask my friends for babysitting favors very often, so it should be fine."

He nodded again.

"His name is Erik."

"I know," he said, "that you have a boy, I mean."

"What were you planning to go see?"

Ann wished he would start talking so she didn't have to say anything.

"I'll take a look in the paper," he said, "and give you a call. Catch you later."

He got up, picked up his tray, and left. She looked at his powerful body. When he had left the cafeteria, the fury inside her grew. Who did he think he was? He had gone to the trouble of asking her, of course, but he also took her for granted. "Look in the paper." "Give you a ring." His casual speech and attitude diminished her. As if it were a given that she would go with him, accept his choice of film, just give her a time, and voila! There she would be, picked up by the most self-confident northerner there ever was.

And anyway, she had a murder investigation to solve. It was typical. The forensic technicians could do their job and go home. In the Violent Crimes Division there were no such opportunities to rest. Should she go to the movies when Petrus Blomgren's body had just been deposited in the deep freeze a few hours ago?

Then it hit her: how many people had she made an impression on in the past little while? The past year?

She looked down at the table and arranged the crumbs in a long line.

Charles was the first man in a long while to take the initiative. The last one was "the abominable man from Svartbäcken" as she called Erik's father. He had asked her to dance when she was out once with some female colleagues. He was a good dancer but that was the only bright spot. The night they spent together was not particularly memorable. He had probably forgotten everything, an episode, perhaps one of many. For Ann's part the whole thing resulted in an unexpected pregnancy.

Since that night they had had no contact. The man probably did not even know he was Erik's father, and Ann had no particular wish to inform him of this. She knew he lived in Svartbäcken, that he was married and the father of two teenage children and that he was an engineer.

Charles Morgansson. She tried out the name. It was not particularly attractive, a little heavy and a mouthful. People would talk if they saw them together at the movies. Everyone would be surprised. Lindell wasn't someone you flirted with.

✦

Five

The parrot's name was Splendens. It lived in a cage in the living room. It was messy. And noisy, filling the room—no, the whole house—with its racket. It drove her mother crazy, and as often as she could she covered it with the dark cloth. It was called Splendens for Mussolini. Because it screeched in Italian.

"It's an endangered species in Brazil," her father would often use as an argument when the subject of getting rid of it came up.

"Then we'll send it there," her mother answered every time.

When it died, the house became quiet as the grave. They never found out why it happened. One day it no longer moved, made no noise, simply sat completely still on its favorite perch, comfortably propped up against a branch. It looked like it was sleeping. Maybe it was dreaming of the Amazon.

Laura was nine and did not really grieve. Splendens had never been tempting to cuddle or spend time with. Even giving it food was boring. It always looked displeased, even when Laura brought the tastiest morsels. It jabbed at her fingers.

It seemed as if her father could not accept its death. He was under the impression that it had entered into a state of suspended animation and that it would start its screeching again at any moment. Several days went by before he pulled the parrot from its perch and buried it in the garden.

Her mother was jubilant but her father stopped her from throwing out the cage. It remained on its pedestal like a threat that her father could at any moment drag home a replacement for Splendens.

He sometimes stood and stared somewhat foolishly at the empty cage, the floor of which still contained some dust-covered sticks.

When Laura entered the living room it was as if she were transported back twenty-five years. The cage stood in its place, and she thought she could hear Splendens run through its repertoire of curses and dirty words in Tuscan dialect, phrases that Laura sometimes used in the office. These were always a big hit. Laura as fresh-mouthed Italian hussy became a staple at the annual office Christmas party, even if she afterward felt dirty inside.

She walked over to the cage. It still smelled of droppings, she thought, but realized it had to be her imagination. The cage looked smaller and she tried to remember how big Splendens had been. In her childhood she had thought it enormous, frightening, its claws quickly scrabbling up and down the wires of the cage, life-threatening, its broad beak ever ready to hack, pinch so hard that Laura's skin was striped with blood. Only her father could stretch in his hand. Then the parrot put its head to one side and let out an almost loving sound.

Now the cage was on its way out. She put it in the driveway where mounds of junk had gathered the past few days.

The professor came walking by and condescended to say a few words. He asked her if she had heard anything about her father. Laura shook her head.

"Spring cleaning?"

Laura nodded. You hypocritical bastard, she thought but smiled.

"That always feels good," her neighbor went on. "Eva-Britt and I are thinking about ordering a container. One always ends up accumulating so much stuff."

Lies, Laura thought.

"Oh, what kind of things?" she asked innocently.

The professor was at a loss for words.

"I'm thinking about renovating," she said suddenly.

The thought hadn't even crossed her mind but when she saw how nervous her neighbor looked she continued firmly.

"Renovate. Perhaps knock out a few walls and make the living room bigger."

"So you're planning to stay here?"

"It's my home."

They said nothing more and he went back to his house. Laura remained outside although she was cold. The professor was at least talking to her. His wife hadn't said a word to her in several years, hardly said hello. Many times she pretended not even to see Laura.

The disdain, which sometimes grew to hate, surrounding "the Dream House" sent out sour puffs that enveloped the house in a permanent atmosphere of isolation and contempt.

Laura Hindersten was cleaning. A whole life, or rather several lives, lay at her feet. She was wading through decades of former thoughts and hopes as she picked aimlessly through the junk. Sorrow congealed around worn toys, birthday presents, and binders with school essays, stored between old tablecloths and lace-trimmed sheets.

A ceramic vase bought at the outdoor folk museum, Skansen, released a whole world. It was spring but still very chilly, with strong winds from the north. They were standing by the monkey hill. Her mother's hat blew off, bouncing, was lifted up and floated down to the monkeys who immediately threw themselves over it, pulling and chewing on the hat.

Her father broke out into one of his rare bursts of laughter. Her mother was furious. Laura, who thought the whole thing had been comical, did not know how she should behave. She offered to climb down and get it. Her mother grew quiet, looked at her daughter and said something that Laura didn't hear in the wind. Was it a yes or no? During the whole Skansen trip she thought about it and all expected pleasure trailed off in the wind.

Many years later Laura returned to Skansen, during a school trip to Stockholm, and she immediately threw up in the parking lot by the main entrance. The teacher hurried over. He thought her nausea was due to the bus trip. He crouched down in front of Laura, offered her his handkerchief, and spoke kindly in a very low voice as if he wanted to shield her from the world. Laura felt ashamed but was warmed by his unexpected warm-hearted manner.

Later in the day she bought the vase as a gift to her teacher but she couldn't bring herself to give it to him. Now it lay in a box in the garage. It was hard to hold it in her hand. The kindness burned. The sweet, sympathetic words from the teacher came back to her. His name was Bengt-Arne and he disappeared after a semester or so. The vase remained, ugly and a little damaged, meaningless to everyone except Laura. It went into the garbage bag, like a lot of other things.

She found a box filled with linen dish towels that she had admired so much as a girl, tracing the curlicue letters with her fingertips and fantasizing about the people who were concealed by the embroidered monograms. She asked her father about it but he didn't know, or he didn't want to talk about it. He didn't care, to him the towels were worthless. They came from his mother's family. "Those old bags," he simply said, "they had nothing else to do."

They were folded in bunches of twelve, wrapped up in paper string. Laura loosened a bundle, unfolded a towel. It was as if the initials spoke to her, as if there was a concealed message, but the unknown names were as foreign as the language her father always talked about, that language that was spoken before the time of the Etruscans. It was the subject of many and lengthy discussions on his part.

She threw away the towel and all the other packets followed.

Fourteen black garbage sacks in total, neatly lined up along the driveway. She tied them up carefully. Nothing could slip out.

Many times Laura imagined that there was a knot of life, a tidy little stump tied up in a bow. If you tugged on it all problems fell away. They unraveled. Dissolved.

Often it was a red bow that resembled those that decorate thoughtfully wrapped packages, but it could also be a sloppy knot with a couple of dangling ends.

Laura pulled on the thread and in a dream world a landscape emerged. It did not remind her of anything she had ever experienced. She stepped in among the blooming bushes where there were tall trees laden with delicious fruits and the breeze was mild, caressing her cheeks.

She became one with the pleasing surroundings, disappeared into the luxurious vegetation, was swallowed up never to reemerge.

Sometimes it could be frightening because she never knew what awaited her. It could be the realm of death; behind a cleverly alluring curtain there was a sooty and suffocating hellish realm of suffering. She did not want to believe it. Nothing ugly could exist behind the good-tasting fruits in the trees and the shiny nuts on the ground.

A cat slinked by, freezing in mid-movement when it discovered Laura, and then darted off through a couple of planks in the fence.

There was nothing here that in any way resembled a heavenly gate that she would be able to walk through. She closed her eyes and tried to will it into being but it did not want to appear. When she opened her eyes the cat was sitting in front of her feet. It had snuck back without a sound. The tip of its tail was moving slowly.

"I'm alone," she said softly.

The cat stared at her with eyes that looked like a concentration of hatred.

Laura Hindersten let them take away the old Citroën that had been in front of the garage for almost fifteen years. It had started to melt into the surroundings, had assumed a mottled shade of green-brown, hidden under ever-more lush and wild greenery. It was really only the wheels that signaled that it had once been a car.

The man who came to take it away laughed when he saw the wreck. Laura was upset at first but then joined in. When he had attached the hook and winched the car onto the tow truck she started to laugh again. The squeaking sound of the winch was like the most beautiful postlude over her father and the life she had lived. The man from the scrap yard smiled, unsure of her reaction. The old car protested, the steel frame creaked, leaves that had been lying on the roof slipped off reluctantly, and the deep cracks in the dried-up tires wailed.

It was when the wreck was settled on the tow truck that the absence came. The space it left in front of the garage became a void in Laura's interior. Confused, she went and stood where the car had just been. No person had stood in exactly this spot for many years. The last time might have been when she graduated from grammar school. The car worked back then. Her father had picked her up from the *Katedral* school. Even then the car was basically a wreck, a sorry sight, and she was embarrassed. Her classmates were picked up with horse-drawn carriages, leaf-adorned carts, and shiny American cars, driven through town in celebratory triumph and happiness.

But she had sunk deeply into the backseat and glared at the back of her father's head, listening to his disjointed conversation and irritated by his clumsy driving. The gears jammed, there was a rattling sound from under the hood, and she wished she were far, far away.

Now the car was on its way from here. She absently signed the piece of paper that the man held out to her. He looked at her in a way she knew well. There was wonder, mixed with ridicule and pity.

That was two weeks ago. Now there was a much fresher car in the driveway. To drive the Ford into the garage was a physical impossibility. The garage was full of discarded furniture, boxes with publications no one read any longer or even knew existed, empty bottles, piles of newspaper, and mounds of other junk.

Already the new car was her ally, sworn to loyalty. Her secrets were only shared with him. It was a he, she had felt that at once. He obeyed her, took her to the places she had decided to visit. He never doubted whether it was right to go here or there. She talked to the Ford, shared her thoughts and plans. He answered by starting willingly and following her orders.

Now he stood at the ready, heard Laura rattling the keys. She hesitated for a few seconds. There was still time to put the keys away and go back into the house. She knew that as soon as she got into the car there would be no turning back. The agreement with the Ford had to be upheld.

She counted silently in her head. When she reached the count of five she opened the car door and got in. The Ford shook itself and the outfit rolled out onto the street. Everything in Kåbo was calm. She turned onto the street that ran right through the neighborhood.

A child was walking on the sidewalk, a violin case in her hand. Laura slowed down, carefully rolling down the street, looking at the girl who was walking in the way that children do, a little dreamily with an eye for the small details.

Laura was very close now. The girl, who was perhaps ten, twelve years old, was dressed in a red parka. Her hair was held back in a ponytail with a white, broad hair band. It swung in time with the girl's step. She turned her head around, probably heard the sound of the car. Brown eyes, searching gaze.

Laura smiled. The girl smiled back, a little unsurely, but you're supposed to smile back when you are greeted with one. This way, Laura thought, you're supposed to smile, she's been raised this way.

She slowed down and lowered the window. The girl stopped, hesitantly waiting.

"I used to play the violin, too," Laura said.

The girl nodded.

"Is it going well?"

"Yes, pretty much."

"Even if it's difficult, you should keep practicing."

A new nod. She had probably heard this before.

"Good luck," Laura said and drove on, her gaze stubbornly fixed on the wet asphalt right in front of the car. With a hasty movement, she pulled the heating knob to zero. She wanted to look around in the rearview mirror, but that would be too painful.

The violin was still there. Laura had seen a glimpse of the case in the garage. For six years she had practiced and practiced, once a week walked—just like the girl on the street—the three blocks over to Miss Berg, the violin teacher, who lived in a house not unlike the Hindersten family's. It had the same smell and the same stale atmosphere.

The only public performances were at the end-of-the-year school events in June. The promise of summer holidays blackened into anxiety in the face of the thought of standing alone on stage, enduring everyone's looks and to play two pieces chosen by Miss Berg.

Every time in the wings she brought up her breakfast but was forced onto the stage by the teachers. Miss Berg was also there. Otherwise Laura might have found the courage to refuse. She played with a sour taste in her mouth, thought she was ugly, pitiable, and smelly.

Every time she received praise and applause. Her father was proud, Miss Berg hugged her, and the teachers patted her on the head. Stig-Björn Ljungstedt and Leif Persson sat at the very back of the auditorium and laughed scornfully at her. They would continue with this. Laura could sometimes see them on TV, the same mocking grin and derision as before. At home they were beaten but at school they were kings.

It was at the school graduation in eighth grade that she touched her violin for the very last time. Miss Berg had died that spring. In spite of her father's nags and threats she stopped playing. He had found her a new teacher but Laura refused with a stubborness that bordered on hysteria. The violin fell silent and disappeared into the junk in the garage, the family's sad archives.

✦

Six

She drove slowly through the streets of the city. She was on sick leave but was supposed to spend time with others, her doctor had said— meet friends, socialize, try to get over her father's disappearance.

That he had disappeared did not mean he was gone. In fact, he had become even more real now. She thought she had been freed but his voice echoed inside her head. Sometimes in Italian. A few stanzas of a sonnet or a stream of curses.

Laura's thirty-five years were arranged like a photo album where her father had taken and mounted all the pictures in the order that he wished.

———

She was forced to stop by the Flottsund Bridge. A wide cargo van appeared on the other side of the Fyris River. The driver held up his hand in thanks as he brushed past her car. When she was about to drive onto the bridge her car lurched and stalled. Immediately a car behind her honked. In the rearview mirror she saw a middle-aged man, how he waved his hand, how his mouth moved. She put the hand brake on, stepped out, opened the trunk, and took out a lug wrench.

As she smashed the man's windshield she came to think of her father. Was it all of his repeated lectures about Queen Kristina's life, above all the procession out of Uppsala, that made her think of her father? He never spoke of her arrival, when she and the whole court went from Stockholm to Uppsala in order to flee the plague. Surely they would have come to Uppsala on the same road, over Flottsund, through that which today is Sunnersta, over the fields by Ultuna with the castle on the hill in sight. No, it was the queen's sorti that interested him, how she one day in early summer put down her crown and regalia, spoke to the estates of the realm in order to leave the city that same day and begin her long trip to Italy and her father's beloved Rome.

"Sixteen fifty-four," she muttered, as she hit the car with the lug wrench one last time. "I remember, I remember all the dates."

Shaken, she returned to her car, started it, and drove over the bridge. Left behind was the broken Volvo with its shocked driver who only managed to call the police on his cell phone once the crazy woman had disappeared around the bend on the other side of the river.

Laura Hindersten took a left on the old Stockholm Road and drove back into town. She had thought herself south to the region where she and her father once spent a summer in a rented cottage. It was the year after her mother had died. Laura had the impression that her father for the first time experienced the house in Kåbo as the prison it had been for her mother.

It had been a happy summer. Their old Citroën took them twenty kilometers out into the country. Her father read as usual, most often in the garden, leaning over old manuscripts and reciting sonnets, so in this there was no difference to life in the city. But the landscape was different, the kilometer-wide view over fields and meadows that reminded her of the sea, or how Laura thought the sea might look.

The cramped house and garden of the city was far away. Outside the cottage there was space, a sky that Laura always experienced as light, even when it was overcast. On the other side of a little stream there were grazing cows. It seemed to her they were the luckiest creatures on the Earth. She could stand there for hours just looking at them. She was not allowed to crawl under the barbed wire—her father had ingrained that in her—but the cows often lumbered over to her, gawked at her. She fed them grass. Their muzzles and rough tongues, their indolence—as if they were full but still willing to accept another bite of grass since it was being offered—made her warm inside.

Even though they were plant eaters there was something carnivorous about the way they smacked and chomped. They did not eat like humans, who inhaled their food and chewed frenetically in order to swallow quickly and load up on more. The cows ground their fodder, sensually, slowly, and with pleasure, paused from time to time and goggled with dull curiosity.

Green-fingered and with the animals' dried saliva all the way up her arms, she walked across the slender plank across the stream and then ran home.

Did they themselves eat anything? She had no memory of her father making any food. He simply sat in the garden. Many times she got on the swing in the large pear tree. Her father had put it up. She swung in wide arcs. Sometimes he looked up, occasionally smiling slightly before he returned to his tomes.

In the evenings they played chess in the light from a hurricane lamp. Her father's hands looked sickly in the sharp, white-yellow light. He moved his pieces with great care, always with commentary. They never played with a timer and Laura was very thoughtful. Her father never hurried her.

Sometimes moths came in, fluttering around the lamp. Then her father would interrupt himself, go to some lengths to capture the visitor, and gently carry it out into the dark. She liked him a lot for the trouble he took to save the small creatures.

She would always remember his bent figure in the doorway, the pitch-black darkness outside and the lamp that generously cast its beam of light into the yard. She thought there was a limited supply of light, that the chessboard would get darker when the door was opened and the dark outside stole some of their light.

The contract on the cottage was not renewed. The owner, whom they rented from, said he was going to renovate it for a relative. Laura recalled how her father burned all the sheets and furniture in the yard the last evening. For a few moments she thought he was going to burn down the whole cottage.

Laura had looked around. It was still burning. Some of the joy and excitement of the summer holiday in the cottage had evaporated but it was with great sorrow that she took her final look at the red house, the outhouse and the woodshed, in the door of which she had carved her very own sonnet in Italian.

When Laura reached the roundabout in Nåntuna she became unsure. Should she turn around and go south as she had planned or turn around and drive home? The incident at the Flottsund Bridge had thrown her off kilter.

She knew the police must have been called in and that they were looking for her. She had no idea if there had been other cars or pedestrians at the bridge. Perhaps someone had made a note of her license plate number? She tried to think back through the events and did not think she had seen any witnesses.

She became convinced her father would have been proud of her. She fought back, didn't let anyone steamroller her, and she meted out a punishment at once. That the punishment was not in proportion to the crime would almost certainly not have troubled her father. He wanted so to strike back, but the powerlessness that increased with the years had reduced his desire for revenge to a displeased querulousness. He said on many occasions that he wanted to bomb the whole miserable lot.

His language could get very vulgar. He could talk of "the saggy boob conspiracy" when two women in his department had made a written complaint about his teaching to the chair.

"They're about as exciting as hollowed-out old trees whose caterpillars and beetles in their interior is their only life. One should plant a bomb under their fat arses."

But it was only words, at first some counter missives with rancorous attacks that inflamed the situation, later on harangues of invectives and insults.

She turned in toward Bergsbrunna after a sudden inspiration that there might be a patrol car by Lilla Ultuna, keeping lookout for a woman driver in a red car. Now she instead curved around past the Denmark's Church and came out onto Almunge Road. From there she found her way back in toward the city and its center.

The other drivers signaled to her, gestured and made angry and frustrated faces. She crept through the western parts of Uppsala. This was her city. The other side of the river barely existed in Laura's consciousness. She had an impulse to go there. It was only a couple of kilometers away. Maybe that would lead to something else, something better? But she dismissed the thought.

Her father had spoken of the "pölsa," or scrapple, city, which was how he referred to the eastern part. Laura had never eaten *pölsa* but had seen the brown meat-and-grain dish in the school cafeteria and so she imagined that people on the eastern side of the river slurped this unattractive mush while they followed some soap opera on TV.

"I'm burned out," she said suddenly out loud to herself at a stoplight by Norby Road.

They talked about that at work, how everyone walked around burned out. For her part she had felt burned out most of her life. All of her insides were a pile of ashes, black soot clung to her blood vessels, and from her mouth there came puffs of breath with the smell of singed flesh.

The light became green and she crossed the intersection and turned into the parking lot of the Botanical Garden. At this time of year there were not many visitors and there were only a few cars parked outside. She stayed in the car and let the engine run for a good while before she got out and steered her course to the entrance. As a child she had come to the "Botan" almost every week. It was her mother who took her, sometimes she had packed a basket with coffee, juice, and rolls, and they had spread a blanket on the grass and had a picnic.

They became friends with people who remained nameless, other frequent visitors who loved to follow the changes in the garden, many day by day. They fell into conversation with these nameless strangers. Here nothing else mattered, only the flowers and bushes.

The visitors crouched down, leaned forward and inspected the fine plants, drew in their scent and smiled. They came down to Laura's level, looked into her face as if she too were a flower, smiled and said something about her dark hair. They spoke with low and friendly voices. No adult raised their voice in the Botanical Garden.

Her mother encouraged her to get closer, to scrutinize some plant nerves or the petals of a geranium that had just bloomed, a daylily or a primrose of some sort. Even though her mother knew many species and kinds by name, many times she only mentioned them in passing. The names were not important, it was the shape, the color, and scent that filled her senses, that made her smile and speak with complete strangers.

She always wanted to see the new flowers, giving cries of delight, subjecting them to close scrutiny and inhaling their scent. Sometimes Laura felt embarrassed. Her mother never checked herself, let her joy bubble over like a child and laughed a great deal.

The garden around their own house was narrow, bordered with hedges and could be surveyed in a single glance. Laura had measured out its length in steps. Thirty-eight steps in one direction and twenty-six in the other. Everything was known.

"Botan" by contrast was gigantic. Here she could never manage to keep track of the figures the times she tried to count it out. Laura tripped over her own legs, fell over, and the number of steps spilled out onto the lawn.

Her mother used to sit down next to Laura, kick off her shoes and wiggle her toes, lean back and turn her face to the sun. Her dark hair tumbled back. Laura thought she looked like a statue.

The people who walked past slowed down, glanced at her, their gazes finding their way back to her mother's outstretched figure. They looked like they wanted to stop, turn back, and join this dark, beautiful woman and her daughter.

It was as if Laura sat in a force field where her mother was the power source, leisurely relaxed but nonetheless crackling with a vital voluptuousness that flowed together with the garden's strength and beauty.

There were no holds barred in the life joy that her mother expressed. The sight of this wordless satisfaction, resting in a sea of green and blooming flowers made Laura shake as if with cold. She wanted to scream, embrace the garden and the world, throw herself into her mother's lap, and laugh, cry, burrow her face against her mother's neck.

But nothing of this took place. Laura sat where she was, turned into stone, dazzled, and with only one thought left in her head: don't let Father turn up. But the chances were infinitesimal. Her father never set foot in the garden. But what if he all of a sudden decided to go there? What if he surprised his wife and his daughter on the lawn, partly concealed behind the area for North American perennials but still visible to the world?

The men who walked by liked to look at her mother, and although Laura could not completely identify with their gazes she understood they conveyed more than simply an interest in black-eyed Susans and butterfly weed. Her mother smiled back at everyone, including the men, and often exchanged a few words with those who walked by. It was as if she wanted to say: "Tell me something about the weather or the garden, not necessarily anything of substance, only a few words to show that we exist."

She found it easy to make contact with other people, looked those that she spoke to in the eyes and used only a few words but could still get people to converse and laugh. But this was only true in the Botanical Garden, it was like a preserve, a green oasis where her mother went in order to speak freely.

Sometimes she lapsed into a kind of dialect that Laura thought sounded strange and that she later realized was the North Uppland dialect from her mother's home region. It was particularly when she spoke with other women that the words came. "Jestanes," she could cry out, "endes" and "vurte" left her beautiful mouth and together with her gestures they created an aura of intimacy around her and her conversational partner.

Laura came to linger under a tree, the branches of which hung all the way to the ground. Someone had thrown a piece of paper on the ground and Laura picked up the dirty note. "Milk, horseradish, ricotta, soup-in-a-cup, chips" written in a handwriting that was barely legible, and at the very bottom a string of digits, perhaps a telephone number. The piece of paper, a list composed in haste, disturbed her. Not because it littered this area—it was insignificant and would soon crumble away—but the painful aspect was the quotidian message from a world where you bought horseradish and chips.

Laura crumpled it up, but then folded it flat just as quickly with an impulse to dial the phone number. It was a sign, it hit her, perhaps a coded message for help.

She stared at the note, had to steady herself against the tree trunk, and tried to imagine another person, one with soup-in-a-cup in front of her, sitting at the kitchen table. Or else she had, because surely it was a woman, lost this list before she went shopping and was standing in the grocery store right now trying to remember the items she needed to buy.

Laura tossed the scrap of paper, pushed her way through the branches, and stepped out onto the gravel path. It was as if her legs no longer had the strength to carry her farther into the garden. She remained rooted to the spot, indecisive. An older man was strolling around the alpine section. He cast a quick glance in her direction and smiled.

Laura hesitantly followed the path and after a couple of meters turned toward the scrubby remains of some tall perennials. Her feet sank into the lawn that was soggy after the rain of the past few days.

She didn't really find things as she remembered them. The organization of the flower sections had been changed. She had run around here as a girl, chasing butterflies, stood absolutely still behind bushes and spied on her mother.

Now it was different. It was like visiting the neighborhood of your childhood where the buildings had been torn down and the streets repaved. Laura looked around. Everything had withered away except a few asters that were clinging to the remaining autumn warmth.

She heard voices from the entrance of the tropical greenhouse. Several women in work clothes stood on the steps, smoking. One of them laughed. Laura turned away.

"What am I doing here?" she asked herself. She looked at the asters. Maybe they had stood there twenty-five years ago. Laura couldn't remember. Her mother would have known. At different times she took her daughter to the most colorful areas, told her about the flowers. Sometimes she used names other than those printed on the metal signs. "My names," she explained, "the ones I learned when I was a little girl."

Laura knew that her grandmother had been known for her flower beds. They had never met. Her grandmother had died a few years before Laura was born. Her grandfather, who shortly thereafter moved to Tierp, she rarely saw. Perhaps sometimes in conjunction with a birthday. He did not come when she graduated from grammar school and did not even send a greeting when she graduated from the university. Then he died as abruptly as her grandmother. Laura attended his funeral alone. Her father did not have the time, he said, but Laura knew he had never liked his reserved father-in-law. There had been many people in Örbyhus Church. She recognized a few faces. She spoke to Mårten Jonsson, who had been married to Alice's sister Agnes, and his three sons. It looked as if Lars-Erik, one of the cousins, wanted to say something to her but the others' disapproving attitude held him back.

After Agnes had died, only thirty-one years old, contact between the Hindersten and Jonsson families had become much less frequent.

Laura knew who a couple of the other funeral guests were, but most of them were unknown, men as taciturn as her grandfather, buttoned into suits that were too tight, women who spoke quietly but without ceasing in her mother's dialect, with turns of phrase that Laura had not heard in years.

She cried at his graveside. The people from Örbyhus, from Skyttorp and Tierp, shot glances at her but did not say a kind or comforting word. Many speeches were given in her grandfather's honor but they did not say anything to the woman from the city, the grandchild who only turned up to the funeral.

Laura was ashamed of her tears. She wanted to scream out over the churchyard that, in fact, she had liked her grandfather and she grieved for him, but she knew they wouldn't believe her. Her words were meaningless in Örbyhus.

She was starting to get cold but could not make herself go on. The unwelcoming and damp garden, that at this time of the year only breathed death, was her church. She was struck by the thought that she wanted to be buried here. Without ceremony and speeches, simply lowered into the ground and shoveled over.

Suddenly her thoughts turned to warmth, mild winds, and a life far from Uppsala. They sometimes turned up, these thoughts. She had never visited a country other than Italy and then always with her father but nonetheless she had a vision of a little hotel by the sea. A place where it was always warm, that had a sun-drenched harbor with a little restaurant that she was in the habit of patronizing, where she was known and welcome.

She had once told Stig about her daydream. At first he laughed but then he became serious, looked at her, and said something about there being other lives. One only had to take the opportunity, and he said those possibilities were open to Laura, free as she was.

Sometimes Stig figured in this daydream, in that idyllic hotel where it seemed so easy to live, but she never talked about it. She thought that if she told him about her fantasy she could get him to dream in similar ways.

"I'm tired of hotels," was all he said.

As the director of marketing he traveled a great deal and complained loudly about the boredom when he was forced to travel to promote the company abroad.

Laura was awakened from her thoughts by the women who had apparently finished smoking and were on their way back into the greenhouse again. She walked back and got into the chilled car. She could leave the country, drive out on the E-4 and go south. She was free, as Stig had pointed out, now more than ever before. Instead she took the Norby Road to the Castle, turned right toward the Academic Hospital, down the hill next to the hospital, and passed the swan pond. Since she had bought her car this was her new route to work. She looked at the clock on the wall of the toll house, as she had started doing. From here it was eight minutes to the office.

✦

Seven

She walked in the door with a smile, nodded to Ann-Charlotte, entered in the code, and took the elevator to her division. Barbro looked up from her desk in surprise.

"Oh my, Laura, how is everything?"

Barbro loved tragedies, which is why she smiled a little more widely when she discovered who the visitor was.

"How are things?"

"Fine, thank you," Laura said.

She heard Stig and Lennart's voices from the conference room. They were bickering as usual.

"Nothing new about your father?"

Laura shook her head.

"How awful for you," Barbro said sympathetically. She had stood up, walked over to Laura, and placed a hand on her arm.

Let go of me, Laura thought. Barbro's breath settled like a sticky membrane over Laura's face.

"How awful," Barbro repeated and her grip on Laura's arm hardened.

"I just want to talk a little with Stig," she said and smiled, disengaging herself.

"Of course, Stickan has been wondering . . ."

Laura left Barbro without listening to the rest, heading toward the open door of the conference room. She hated it when people called Stig "Stickan."

She stopped outside the door and listened. They were talking about the German affair. Lennart was dissatisfied with their approach, which Laura already knew. Stig's voice was calm as usual.

She opened the door completely and stepped into the room. Her colleagues looked up.

"But Laura, there you are! I have sent you three thousand e-mails."

"I've been having some problems with e-mail," Laura said.

"And you haven't been answering the phone. We were getting worried. But I'm glad you came by," Stig Franklin said and got to his feet.

He was wearing the sweater vest. It didn't suit him, looking—like most of his clothes—out of place, but that was Stig. His scent and his hand gripped her. Lennart remained seated and stared at Laura with a vacant expression.

"We're talking about our plans in Essen," he said.

He dropped her hand.

"I took the revised offer with me. I have added some of the missing information," Laura said. "It makes sense to attach a copy of a calculation for the second year. It will give them a better overview, and Hausmann likes that."

"Marvellous," Stig said enthusiastically.

She looked at him. Every day she thought she saw something new in Stig. His beard was freshly trimmed, which she liked. She had an urge to caress his cheek. The messy hair made him look boyish.

"Jessica ran a calculation on the second year," Lennart said, "and she thought the figures for education and training were on the low side."

Laura shot him a quick glance.

"She doesn't know what she's talking about," she said.

At that moment a woman walked into the room.

"Laura!"

"We were just talking about you," Lennart said.

"How are you? I've been thinking so much about you."

Laura didn't answer, just sat down and started digging around in her purse.

"Here is the new one," she said and threw a folder on the table.

"Have you been working while you've been at home?" Jessica Franklin said. "You certainly didn't need to."

Lennart snorted.

"But do tell, have the police said anything else about your father?"

Jessica's voice was pleasant, not at all as shrill as Barbro's, but it nonetheless made Laura shiver. She saw how Jessica's red lips moved and how her tongue ran over her lower lip. Her speech was well-groomed, just as her appearance. She was wearing a red dress that Laura would never have worn to work but on Jessica it looked completely natural and it fit her perfectly. She had a little ornament on a thin silver chain around her neck. Laura knew it depicted the love goddess from Bali, a woman who had given birth to twelve children.

Jessica's hair was bobbed, very blond, and rested on her shoulders. Sometimes she threw her head back and ran her hands through her hair, gathering it into a ponytail, especially when she was excited, and it was a gesture that Laura understood that men liked. She probably did not do it consciously, but the sensual movement revealed her beautiful throat. Laura glanced at Stig. He smiled.

Barbro had once called Jessica a slut. Laura had asked what she meant and Barbro had explained that the gesture with her hair was an invitation. She didn't say anything else. An invitation. Laura looked at Jessica's throat. It was shapely.

Jessica kept talking but Laura only looked at her with confusion and Jessica broke off.

"But here I am going on," she said.

Stig put his arm around Jessica.

"You believe in Essen, don't you?"

He smiled even more widely and squeezed her shoulders.

"If we get this, then the Dutch will come on board, too," Jessica said. "Won't they, Lennart?"

He shrugged.

"I don't believe in your model for B-One," Laura said.

Stig's smile froze.

"But my dear, we've talked about that," he said.

B1 was Jessica's part of the project. Stig had also been critical in the beginning but had changed his mind. Now B1 was included in the offer, with exactly the presentation that Jessica had suggested.

"We talked it through while you were on sick leave," Jessica said. "They'll lap it up, you'll see."

And then came the head toss. Laura wanted to stab her pencil into Jessica's throat, drive it in deep, and twist it.

"Maybe," she said.

"Which we should celebrate," Jessica continued with unperturbed enthusiasm, adding, "Torbjörnsson certainly won't be."

Torbjörnsson & Son Inc. were their greatest competitors. Jessica had worked there for four years before she joined the company. Most of them assumed there was a desire for revenge in her eagerness to land the Essen account. Apparently something had happened at her old workplace. No one knew what but there was talk of Jessica having had an affair with Torbjörnsson junior.

When you die we will celebrate even more, Laura thought and smiled at her colleague. She looked at the pencil in her hand. It was freshly sharpened. She looked at Jessica's throat. Right there, in that hollow, is where I want to put it and let out all the poisoned blood.

"How are you, Laura?"

Stig bent down and looked at her.

"Everything is fine," she said. "I'm fine."

She tested the point of the pencil against her index finger.

Stig put his hand on her knee. She gave him a searching gaze as if to ensnare him in her sphere. He smiled unsurely and tried to take the pencil out of her hand.

"You might cut yourself," he said.

"Perhaps you want a glass of water?" Jessica said and leaned over Laura. "You look pale."

Laura held up the pencil with the point vibrating only a few centimeters from Jessica's neck.

"You can hurt yourself," she said and smiled. "Wouldn't it be a pity to get blood on your pretty dress."

Jessica straightened up and looked anxiously at Lennart. Stig's smile had become a grimace.

"Would you like a ride home?"

Laura nodded. Stig got up, glanced swiftly at Jessica, and made a dismissive gesture with his head.

"I'm going home soon," Jessica said, and turned to Stig. "The tile layer is coming at three. Dinner's at six thirty."

"Okay," said Stig, and helped Laura to her feet.

"Do you have your car?"

Laura nodded again. She wanted to stay close to him, feel his hand under her arm, almost so it nudged her left breast.

"We can take two cars, but I want you to come home with me."

Lennart stood up, gathered some papers together, and left.

Laura placed her hand on Stig's shoulder. For a split second they stood there like a dance couple. Laura moistened her cracked lips with her tongue. Slowly, as if she was on the verge of losing consciousness, she leaned in toward Stig and rested her chin against his bristly beard.

"Help me, Stig," she whispered into his ear.

The last time Stig Franklin had visited Laura Hindersten was a cold and clear morning, after several days of heavy snow. It was in February, they were on their way to a conference in Linköping and Stig was going to pick up Laura.

The sun had just risen over the City Forest and shone through the trees with a strong yet mild light. The branches of the snow-laden trees and bushes sagged, conceded defeat, and bowed deeply. Hare tracks ran diagonally across the otherwise undisturbed property.

Now none of that beauty remained. He noted with consternation the garbage that had accumulated in the parking space. She clung to his arm, did not say anything, pulled him up through the bushes to the front door.

"That's coming loose," he said and pointed to the place where the front steps met the wall.

Laura looked at him.

"Help me," she said softly without looking at the stairs.

There was a pedestal leaning halfway into a gigantic rhododendron. He stopped and gently squeezed a dormant bud. It glistened with moisture. Laura looked at his hand fingering the fleshy bud. She pulled him close and leaned her head against his shoulder.

"What's wrong?"

He looked around as if to assure himself they were not being observed. Laura sighed.

"Everything is fine," she whispered. "It's fine when you are here."

"You should rest a little," Stig said.

She nodded and he led her up the stairs, took the keys out of her purse, unlocked the door, and shoved it open as he put his arm around her shoulders. A stale burst of air hit them in the face.

In the hall there was a pile of old bed linens and a stained mattress was leaning up against the wall.

"Is that your father's?"

She didn't answer, pulled off her coat, and dropped it on the ground.

"Would you like anything?"

He shook his head, picked up her coat, and hung it up.

"Have you talked to anyone? I was thinking if you . . ."

He stopped abruptly when he realized that Laura had slipped out of her skirt, let it slide down her legs, and now with a rapid movement pulled off her blouse. Everything went very fast. Suddenly she stood there in front of him. Her breaths were warm.

"I have to go," he said and cleared his throat.

She shook her head.

"Rest with me for a while," she said.

"I can't."

"I know that you want to," she said and stamped her foot to free herself from her skirt.

She was wearing black pantyhose and a light-colored lace bra. Her skin glowed with unnatural whiteness in the dim hall.

"My father isn't home," she continued.

"I know."

"No one will disturb us."

He tried to avoid looking at her. She was beautiful in a frail way and Stig had to fight against an impulse to pull her toward him. He was very warm but did not unzip his jacket.

"You know I can't," he repeated, much less convincing than he had intended.

"Admit that you want to," she said. "You can have me here in the hall if you like."

Without meaning to he looked at the mattress. She pulled off her pantyhose, took his hand and put it on one of her breasts. It just filled his hand. She let go and he stood there passively with his hand on her breast. It was getting dark outside and he could hardly make out her face. Her chest rose and sank.

He was sweating, felt a drop run down his face and it was as if he couldn't get enough air. He drew a deep breath.

"You want to," she filled in with the self-confidence in her voice that he knew so well from the office, but that now stood out in such contrast to her delicate body that he had to look closely at her. She is two people in one, he thought.

"Maybe," he said.

"There is no one here to disturb us anymore," she said and leaned against the wall.

He quickly pulled his hand back, turned around, tripped slightly on the sheets on the floor, and flew out of the door, ran down the stairs, and was greeted by the chill of the October night. He stopped and swore.

A cat ran off and disappeared between the bushes. He heard her call his name. He hesitated, stared into the thick vegetation, saw something between the bushes. He heard light steps and a voice calling him.

Then she stood there, a fairy-tale creature appearing out of the rose brambles, half naked, panting from her dash out of the house.

They looked at each other. They had known each other for eight years. She had never been more beautiful. The dark hair that framed the pale cheeks, the skin that glowed like ivory, the minimal panty, a little slip of cotton that made him think of whipped cream, the slender legs that were trembling with cold and arousal.

"I'm a virgin," she whispered.

Stig Franklin came home right when *Aktuellt,* the news broadcast, started.

"I'm home," he yelled.

His face in the hall mirror betrayed nothing of the events of the early evening. The worry he had felt in the car on the way home was gone. He had driven with the window down, letting the fresh air blow through the tension and slight nausea.

Now he was both hungry and thirsty and walked into the kitchen. A plate had been left out on the dining room table, also a dish with boiled potatoes and a pork chop with a congealed sauce. He opened the refrigerator and took out a Ruddles County, took a few sips, and sat down on a chair, smiled, and felt now for the first time how tired he was.

He heard the prime minister speaking on the television upstairs but could not tell what it was about. The voice of the reporter was heard from time to time. It was that woman he had never been able to stand.

"You're drinking strong beer?"

Jessica had come downstairs without him noticing.

"I was thirsty," he said, and smiled and gripped the bottle as if he was afraid she would take it away from him.

"How was it? It took a long time."

"She wanted to talk."

"About B-One, of course. I knew it. What did she say?"

"It wasn't that. She's not doing so well."

"No, anyone can see that. She didn't talk about the deal then?"

"No, I said."

"Then what did she want?"

"Nothing in particular. She just wanted to talk. She's lonely."

"Living with her father in that haunted house all those years would have broken anyone down. Has she never gotten herself a man?"

"I don't know," he said and drank the last of the bottle. "She doesn't reveal much."

"If she didn't talk about work, and doesn't reveal anything, then what did you talk about?"

"All kinds of things. Her house, that it's a lot of work. She's apparently cleaning up after her father. There was junk everywhere."

Jessica sat down across from her husband. He wanted to have another beer but hesitated. Jessica was a teetotaler.

"She has a crush on you," she said.

"On me! Never. I'm not her type."

"Then you're blind," Jessica said and stood up. "She hates me at any rate."

"Now I think you're exaggerating. She's just a little jealous of you when you do well."

Jessica let out a harrumph, left the kitchen, and went to the bathroom. Stig immediately got up and took out another bottle of beer.

The beer did him good. On an empty stomach the rush came quickly. He snapped up a potato and ate it with the skin still on, picked up the pork chop and took a bite. He felt strong in an unfamiliar way. Jessica was bustling in the bathroom. He assumed she was preparing herself for the night and getting ready to spend a few hours in bed with a book. As for him, he wanted to stay at the kitchen table and feel strong, in some way outside his normal life, together with a beer, potato, and a pork chop that tasted heavenly.

"Is there anything on TV?" he yelled, mostly to have something to say.

She didn't reply, perhaps she couldn't hear. He got the idea that they should watch a porn film. He had bought a videocassette but the first and so far only time they watched it together was a complete disaster. It made him horny but it only made Jessica mad.

She came out of the bathroom and looked questioningly at the second bottle.

"Tomorrow's a workday," she said.

He stood up hastily, but sank just as quickly back onto the chair.

There probably won't be a porn film tonight, he thought. It's a workday tomorrow.

Jessica disappeared into the bedroom. Stig remained where he was.

"I'm a virgin," he said quietly and found himself getting aroused as he said it.

Laura was a beautiful woman, but crazy, he had understood that much during the course of the evening. For a while he had even become scared of her. It was unlikely that she was a virgin. What kind of life had she lived anyway?

There was something alluring about her. As if she was a figure from a novel living in a house of horrors, surrounded by the wild and unkempt garden. The chaotic mess in the rooms bore witness to a life in disarray. Or had she only started to live like this now that her father had disappeared?

He had worked together with Laura for many years but had never really gotten to know her. She had always been an isolated and complicated person but it was only this evening that he had seen the extent of her problems. There was little to find fault with regarding her work, of course, quite the opposite, in fact. During their low period a few years ago Laura was the one who had contributed the enthusiasm and creativity.

He regretted the fact that he had followed her in, but at the same time it pleased him that he had seen and experienced something beyond the everyday, as if he had taken a step into the land of insanity and returned. The dark side was frightening but also tempting. He was making a guest appearance. Now he was back in his clean and well-ordered kitchen, lit up by an attractive lamp, cherry cabinets, and gleaming white appliances.

Laura's kitchen was the complete opposite: an interior from the fifties, as he remembered the kitchen from his childhood, dirty and dark, with a smell that was reminiscent of corruption and stagnation.

He thought about her body. Above all it was the delicate whiteness that he remembered, as if Laura was made of the finest china, light in his hands, pleasing to drink from but nothing to take out every day. She would shatter like a fragile, translucent cup if used too often.

He chuckled and took a sip of beer.

"What's so funny?" Jessica asked from the bedroom.

"Nothing," he said.

He felt found out, in spite of the fact that he hadn't said anything. He felt as if Jessica had seen through him and his thoughts, and it put him in a bad mood. She bothered him. Because what he had gone through was something extraordinary that required thought. He wanted to linger in the feeling of unreality and exclusivity. Laura was no casual hotel-room conquest, but rather a rare experience of a mysterious and original liquid that dissipated in his hands. At the same time as he touched Laura she moved, gliding away with a smile he had never before seen in a woman. He had for a few hours been transported to a human sanctuary of intimacy, a moment of magic.

Now he was going to shower and crawl into bed with his wife.

✦

Eight

"I can't," Ann Lindell said. "It's impossible. Another day we might be able to . . ."

Fear shot up into her mouth like sour porridge and silenced her abruptly. Erik was screaming, or rather, singing. In recent months he had started to sing more and more, long strings of unconnected words. Sometimes Ann could identify the sounds, songs she herself sang in a distant childhood.

In September a new preschool teacher had started in Erik's group and had made serious efforts to bring song and rhymes into the curriculum. Now songs were a constant feature.

"Wait a minute, I'm going to switch phones," she said, mostly in order to win time. She took the handheld phone, left the kitchen, and went to the bedroom.

"A concert," Charles Morgansson said.

"Yes, that's Erik. I have a lot to do right now."

"Petrus Blomgren is dead and we can't do much about that. Not tonight."

"I was thinking . . ."

Her objection stopped here. She knew he was right.

"What were you planning to see?"

"A crime film," he said and chuckled into the receiver.

It was the first time she heard his laugh.

"*Mystic River*. Clint Eastwood is the director. I've read the book and it's damn good."

She knew nothing about the film or the book.

"A detective story," she said doubtfully.

Charles Morgansson waited for her objection, but Ann knew she wasn't going to be able to think of another suggestion due to the simple reason that she didn't know what else was showing right now. The last movie she had seen had been a French production that she saw with Beatrice, probably a year ago.

She looked out the window. All snow had melted on the parking lot. The wet asphalt reflected the light from the streetlamps. She wiggled the blinds back and forth. Erik had started a new song that reminded her of something she felt was familiar: ". . . little bunny . . . oh, oh dear me . . ."

"One moment," she said quickly and put the receiver down on the bed, took several steps toward the kitchen but stopped just as quickly and stared at it. Now he was lying there, Charles Morgansson, on her sloppily made bed. He was breathing into the phone. He was waiting for an answer.

She picked it bak up.

"It may work out," she said.

They decided on a time and place. Morgansson promised to get the tickets. The only thing she had to do was show up on time and buy him popcorn.

She exhaled, stood absolutely still for a few moments with her eyes closed, before she dropped the phone onto the bed, picked it up again, and dialed Görel's number.

The clock in the kitchen read several minutes past five.

"Spaghetti," she said.

Erik looked up but kept singing. Ann crouched down.

"I love you," she said softly and stroked his head.

"Little snail," he said.

Erik was watching a video. Ann let her clothes fall in a pile on the hall floor.

"Mommie's going to take a shower," she yelled.

She closed the door, opened the bathroom cabinet, took out her razor and inserted a fresh blade, stepped into the shower stall, changed her mind, stepped out, and cracked the door. Erik was singing along to the song in the film.

With the razor in her hand, she scrutinized her body in the rectangular mirror. Sometimes she had the impression that it lied, made her look more slender than she really was. She often felt chubby despite the fact that Beatrice—the only one at work who ever commented on her appearance—nagged her about how she should eat more.

"You're as thin as a goat!" she would say.

Ann thought Bea's comments came from the fact that she herself was getting increasingly chubby. After her second child she had put on eight, nine kilos, remained there, and now had to struggle in order not to put on more weight.

She was right about Ann having lost some weight. She thought it was due to her changed evening routine. Not as many sandwiches and only one glass of wine a night.

She ran a hand down her breasts and stomach and felt a feeling of joy, a reminder of something long ago. She turned her body. Her thighs were still good. She twitched as if a hand had appeared on her buttock. She closed her eyes and tried to remember the feeling, but it wasn't the same.

"This is me," she said aloud, stepped closer to the mirror and looked at herself intensely, let her hand caress down her stomach, find its way lower down, but the feeling wouldn't come. Her hand was somehow too unrefined, too insensitive. It only signaled a longing for pleasure but someone's hand on your body meant something else, so much more.

Ann climbed back into the shower, studying herself and her own reactions. She wanted to emerge from the stall not only clean and fresh-smelling with a pleased smile and an attractive bikini line, but also purified, with anticipation. Sure of her own wishes and desires.

She wanted a promise, or rather a contract, regarding life.

She stepped out of the shower with a feeling that the past didn't have to mean anything. There was only this moment, with these thoughts, this body, this life. She put in a period, wrote a line, turned the page, sprayed deodorant under her arms, dressed in the clothes she had laid out: the completely new and expensive thong from Wolford, bought at Kastrup Airport, the just as new bra, the silky-smooth pantyhose from H&M that promised "to give your derriere a lift."

She laughed. That's what I want, she thought: to give my derriere a lift. She put on a black skirt, a red top, clasped the silver necklace and threaded the earrings through her ears, brushed her hair, applied makeup discreetly but with noticeable deliberation, and then went out to Erik who, when he saw her, immediately stopped singing and got stumbling to his feet. At that moment Görel rang the doorbell.

Ann Lindell was ready.

He was only ten or so meters in front of her. She recognized the worn, dark leather coat that he often wore at work. She continued scrutinizing him. He had solid legs, maybe he had been a soccer player, and he walked with a swagger. That's how her mother would have put it. Strong steps that echoed against the wooden bridge. His hands shoved into his pockets.

Ann glanced at the water, the Fyris River. She could still extricate herself from this. She could blame it on Erik, say that he had suddenly come down with something. She slowed down, hesitated, but knew it was theatrics for her own benefit. Or not? Was there a streak of masochism inside her, that would make her back out simply so she could later wallow in self-pity?

What she most of all wanted was to accompany Charles Morgansson into the darkness of the movie theatre, into *Mystic River*. She wanted to speed it up, run up to him, so that she wouldn't have a last chance to pull out of this.

Now he turned right, up toward West Ågatan, kept walking determinedly to the *Filmstaden* cineplex. She stayed several paces behind him. Yes, he did indeed have nice buns.

Ann smiled, suddenly extremely self-satisified. She felt light as a feather, if a little warm.

The theater was packed and Ann was happy about that. So far they hadn't said much.

"It's great you managed to get away," he said and held the popcorn container while she sat down.

"Remind me. What kind of movie is it?"

He started to tell her but was interrupted by the previews. The light was dimmed, the sound of people talking died away, and everyone's attention was directed forward.

Ann snuck a peek at her colleague. He smelled faintly of cologne. The light from the screen was reflected in his face. The whole thing felt otherwordly as if she had been thrown into a new reality. Was it really her, Ann Lindell, sitting here? She who never, or very rarely, went out for entertainment.

The previews ended and *Mystic River* started. At first Ann had trouble following the film but was swept up. The grief in the actor's face when he realized his daughter had been killed was almost unbearable.

Charles changed position, sagged down, and straightened up, shifting his weight here and there. Ann thought about how restless Edvard had been the few times they had gone to the movies.

They stepped out into a light rain. Morgansson guided her along the sidewalk, put out an arm to lead her right, helped make their way through the crowd of people.

"This is our *Mystic River*," she said as they walked over the New Bridge.

He stopped and looked at the river in silence. He had turned up the collar of his coat. His hands were again shoved down into his pockets. Ann thought for a moment that he looked like a very unhappy man.

"What's the name of the actor who plays the father of the girl?"

"Sean Penn," said Morgansson without lifting his gaze from the dark waters.

"We had a murder last spring," she said, "and he reminded me of the mother of the murder victim. She simply sank down, disappeared from us, from life."

"She drowned herself," Morgansson said.

"So you know about it?"

"I read up on the investigation. You want to know something about the place you're going to."

"You wanted to know what kind of colleagues you were going to get."

"Something like that," he said and smiled for the first time.

"Sean Penn didn't commit suicide. He transformed his grief into hatred and revenge."

"His wife egged him on."

"It's good to have a wife to egg you on." The words slipped out of Ann's mouth and Morgansson burst into laughter.

"Should we go get a beer?"

Ann nodded.

They ended up at a little establishment by the river. A few of the guests were having a late dinner. Ann suddenly felt ravenous.

"I just have to make a quick call," she said and excused herself.

Görel had everything under control. Erik had fallen asleep at around seven and she herself was reading a book.

"You're sweet," Ann said.

"Is he nice?"

"We've sat in the dark together for two hours," Ann said, "so I don't know."

"You don't have to hurry back," Görel said.

She returned to the bar. Morgansson was conversing with the man behind the counter. He let out something like a laugh, or a snort. Morgansson smiled, nodding at the cook who could be seen in the open kitchen.

"You come here often?"

"I found this place last summer and keep coming back."

"Why did you move here?"

"Same old story," Morgansson said, but made no further attempt to explain what the story was, and Ann didn't ask.

They each took a beer. Ann looked around. Morgansson took a couple of deep sips.

"What do you think?" he asked.

"You mean about the murder?"

He nodded.

"To be perfectly honest, I don't really want to talk about it," she said. "Don't get me wrong, I mean . . ."

"Are you prejudiced against forensic technicians?"

"No, not at all," she said and laughed.

"You're beautiful," he said suddenly.

Ann gave him a quick look as if to assure herself she had heard him correctly. His gaze was resting on her, did not turn away, and he smiled.

"Beautiful," she said and looked down into her beer glass.

"If you don't want to talk about work then why don't you tell me about yourself?" he said.

"It's just the same old story."

He accepted this answer, turned to the bartender, and asked if it was allright to order a bite of food.

She got up and went to the bathroom. Inside there was a poster by Botero: a voluptuous woman in the process of taking off her bra. In front of her is a man resting on a bed. He appears to be asleep, looks innocent, kind, with a thin tango moustache that hints at vanity. The man is miniscule, the woman so much bigger; robust buttocks and thighs dominate the picture. Ann had the impression that the Amazon was about to devour the man with ease and at any moment.

She sat down on the toilet seat and studied the scene. It appealed to her. The self-possessed and proud woman in the process of seduction, of spreading herself out across this lilliputian and taking her pleasure with the same sense of entitlement with which she allowed her breasts to burst forth. This woman doesn't make any excuses, that was how Ann read the picture, she acted from her own desires.

The pantyhose—that were supposed to give her derriere a lift—were difficult to pull back up. Now go out to the bar and vanquish this man, she thought and smiled, tugging at her skirt and scrutinizing herself in the mirror.

She pushed her hand against her crotch as if to get in touch with herself, her body, and her desires.

✦

Nine

Two words. No more. She sat up in bed. The blanket slid down and bared her shoulders and breasts. She looked around the dark room, for a few moments unusure of where she was.

Two words had been whispered by a familiar voice.

She listened but the house was completely quiet.

"You must." The words uttered with determination, sternly commanding, but also in some way quite mild. She recalled that she, just before the rude awakening, had responded to the gentle, almost sensual undertone and that she had smiled in her dream. Had she not stretched out after him, been happy for his visit, whoever he was?

For a split second she had felt a great satisfaction. It was a promise. She let out a sob in bed. Sure, it was a promise of something, she sensed, was almost completely convinced of, something that would grant her the greatest happiness.

Thereafter came the threat for her. Behind the illusory tender atmosphere conjured by the voice there was the hard, on the verge of physically painful. "You must." The voice contained no mercy.

Laura Hindersten pulled the blanket to her, slid out of the bed, and snuck over to the window, pulling the thick curtain to the side. It was still dark out there. The garden brooding as sorrowfully as ever.

Was he still in the house? The uncertainty made her take a couple of cautious steps, lean her ear toward the closed door, and breathlessly listen for the nighttime intruder.

Who was he? She tried to remember the details but the image of his face fluttered away like a veil of mist, dissolved, and disappeared. A warm smell came toward her, not at all unpleasant. It was the breath of the person who had stood leaning over her and who had pronounced the words with such authority and weight, certain that Laura would obey.

In vain she fished for signs of recognition in the muddy waters of her memory but the only thing she found was the feeling of a forceful power over her. And her own powerlessness.

She pushed the door open. Barefoot she fumbled her way over the cold wooden floor in the dim hall. She bumped against the telephone table, stopped, and listened. She thought she heard a car drive by on the street. I have nowhere to run to, she thought at once and the image of the little harbor restaurant from her daydream of the warm, foreign country appeared before her eyes. I have no valid passport to get me out of here. No ticket anywhere. Only a worn suitcase, with a sticker from Firenze, down in the basement.

A breeze swept up from the basement, a smell of raw clay and mold. She closed the protesting cellar door with care and turned the key.

With one hand clenching the blanket around her chest and the other trying to find a hold along the walls Laura felt her way around the large house. In the living room she saw herself for a moment in the large gold-framed mirror, like a shadow that flitted by in a landscape of giant book-cases, full of dust and tomes with texts that few knew or wanted to decipher, and thick draperies that closed around oak furniture, the chiffonier, the lead-heavy chairs with false decor and the pedestal table in the same grotesque style, cluttered with decades of withered knowledge.

In the kitchen she sat down on a chair. There was a knife on the table, a bag of grapes, and a chipped glass in the bottom of which some wine had dried into a dark spot.

She didn't dare turn on the light. In the dirt-brown blanket that she had decided to throw away but that was her only protection right now, she had decided to await the sunrise.

She curled up, pulled the blanket more tightly around her, pulled her feet up on the chair and pressed her limbs against each other, let her hair become an extension of the blanket, closed her eyes, and stone by stone she reconstructed her inner being.

That which was true, the multitude of the Botanical Garden and the laughter that rose up from the uncountable grass blades, the raspy tongues of the cows and the butterfly in the panting flame of the hurricane lamp, she put aside in a safe place, out of reach of the world.

Laura Hindersten's inner being was becoming petrified at the same pace as the day was dawning. Everything artificial pulverized and melted together into a massive piece of black shimmering diabase. For this, one needed a superhuman strength that was only possible under immense pressure and a minimal amount of oxygen.

To think a person can be this still, she thought. One doesn't need to breathe in order to live.

✦

Ten

The blows were delivered by a person in an uncontrollable rage."

And what would you know about that, Ola Haver thought.

"At least that's what I think," the medical examiner added.

"Were there many blows?"

"Perhaps a half dozen or so. Clearly in excess of the situation. One, at most two would have been sufficient."

Petrus Blomgren's pale body lay on the examiner's table like a shriveled radish. Göran Finn carefully peeled off his gloves. Haver stared at Petrus's feet. It was obvious that they had been put to good use. They were crooked, with thick callouses and several deformed toenails on the right foot.

"Apart from that the old man was in perfect health," Göran Finn said. "He could have lived twenty more years."

Haver looked at the murdered man's hands. They were of the same caliber as the feet.

"We believe he died almost at once, at about nine o'clock. He was bludgeoned in the back of the head, fell headlong, and as a bonus received several more blows. Traces of brain tissue were found on his neck, on his shirt, and even on his back. Fury, in other words."

I wonder where he comes from, with that dialect, Haver thought.

"Was the killer . . ."

". . . yes, he was probably right-handed, if that's what you were wondering. That's always the first question you ask," the pathologist said with something that was supposed to pass for a smile.

"Are you from Skåne?"

The doctor did not reply, simply removed his coat, grabbed the tape recorder, and walked away from Haver.

"You'll be receiving my report," he said and disappeared out the door.

Haver was left with a corpse on a stainless steel counter. He looked at Petrus Blomgren again. In many ways he reminded Haver of his father, or what his father would have looked like if he had been allowed to live as long as Blomgren.

The investigation into the small-time farmer and carpenter Petrus Blomgren's life had not yielded a single significant result, not even a detail that could stir up speculation or ideas.

Ola Haver walked once around the dead man. Seventy years of hard work, that's how one could summarize his life. Raised in Jumkil, with "diligent" parents according to those in the area who remembered them, he had worked on the farm, at the mill, and in his final employed years as a carpenter and a kind of handyman on construction sites. The most recent employment could be traced to a couple of years at the end of the seventies and beginning of the eighties at a company called Nylander's Construction and Cleaning, a modest operation whose owner had died about six years ago. Sigvard Nylander's only child, a son about fifty years of age who lived in Uddevalla, couldn't even remember Petrus Blomgren but in a phone conversation with Berglund he had said that there were usually three or four men hired on with his father's firm at any one time and that in general they worked on renovations and other smaller projects.

After his years as a carpenter, Blomgren had jumped in as a seasonal worker during planting and harvesting, worked in the forest, thinning and felling trees, mostly on jobs close to home. Here it was even harder to get any details. Some of the forest owners—all farmers—had been vague. Some of them said they had used Blomgren's help, others had denied it. Berglund thought they were afraid of the Tax Authorities. Blomgren had most likely been paid under the table.

The money he had received from the sale of his farmland, about thirty hectares, hardly an outlandish sum, had been deposited in the bank and been well-used. He had drawn on the capital at a slow but steady rate.

There were no unusual transactions on the account over the last few years, only a withdrawal for sixty thousand in connection with the purchase of a car five years ago.

Blomgren's will was clearly drawn up without any gray areas, the donation to Doctors Without Borders the only question mark. No one could explain why that organization had been favored, but in itself there was nothing strange about that, nothing to keep a murder investigation going.

The murder victim would only leave an absence in one way. Haver thought about Dorotea Svahn's words and sorrow. This woman was the one who grieved him, the one who would miss her neighbor and friend.

Blomgren was without contours but Ola Haver knew it was wrong to say that he had been or was insignificant. He had been a man who did not take up a great deal of space, no man to figure in the headlines, Haver thought and smiled to himself, catching himself about to place a hand on the forearm of the dead man in a gesture of respect, perhaps as an excuse for the fact that he in his thoughts had reduced Blomgren's significance.

He was a normal person and therefore an unusual murder victim. If people like Blomgren died a violent death it was because of an accident, in the forest, with a tractor or on the job, by a falling tree, a malfunctioning PTO shaft, or falling from a scaffold. Men like Petrus were not bludgeoned to death. Well, sometimes, but then the motive was almost always financial. Several youths, searching for alcohol or cash, a car perhaps, who knocked down some old person, very often brutally, but seldom thought out in advance.

The weapon was often something to be found at hand, a frying pan, a tool, or a piece of firewood. This time they had not found anything like that. They had not even isolated a footprint in the soft yard, no car tracks, and absolutely no murder weapon.

What spoke against the theory of a robbery was the fact that the house appeared so undisturbed. The general consensus when they had discussed the case that morning was that the perpetrator or perpetrators had become frightened and left without even entering the house.

Haver circled the gurney. He felt some peace in the company of the dead man. They came closer to each other. He was happy that the doctor from Skåne had left. What Haver was looking for was something no pathologist could reveal. It could not be fixed on paper in a report.

Petrus Blomgren had a heavyset, slightly sorrowful face. Perhaps this impression was colored by the tone of his good-bye letter, but Haver had the impression that the dead man had not had an easy time of it during his hardworking life. Perhaps a little joyless, and not even the beautiful nature around his house had been able to compensate for the feeling of sadness that characterized Vilsne village.

Now it was October, it was probably different in May. Then perhaps the optimism of the place was as deafening as birdsong in the springtime. Blomgren could sit in the garden with a cup of coffee, or a little drink even, feeling pleased at the thought of the shed filled to bursting with firewood, at the thought of Dorotea showing up for a chat, that . . .

Ola Haver built up a nicer existence for the dead man, gave him a different, more comforting life, reshaped the heaviness and the deep furrows in his face to signify wisdom, experience, and security. Under Haver's gaze, Petrus grew to a man who was unafraid.

It seemed as if there had not been a woman in his life, at least not for many years. That bothered Haver. There should have been someone, nearby. Then he would never have written such a letter.

Revenge, he thought, was that why Petrus Blomgren was murdered? The revenge theory felt too cumbersome even if the logic of violent crimes was not always that easy to comprehend.

General statistics gave most credence to a botched robbery, where the killer had become frightened and fled, but he could still not let go of the idea that the murder had been planned.

The phone rang. It was Sammy Nilsson. Haver told him the results of the autopsy.

Nilsson grunted. Haver had the impression that his colleague was displeased, that he had been hoping for some sensational find that could lead to simply having to go pick up the perpetrator.

"I think we have to look more closely into Blomgren's life," Haver continued. "The motive could be located far back in time."

"I don't think that's very likely," Nilsson said.

Haver smiled. Sammy was being true to form. He almost always dismissed Haver's theories and suggestions. Often they were like cat and dog. Sometimes it was simply tiring but often their bickering brought their investigations a step further.

"And what do you think, then?"

"Robbery-homicide," Nilsson said curtly. "You know what, maybe there was something in the house that we missed, or to put it another way, that we aren't missing on account of the fact that we didn't know it was supposed to be there."

"Like what, for example?"

"A wad of cash, gold watch, stamp collection, a painting Blomgren bought in the forties and that's now worth a bundle."

"How likely is that? The farmer as art collector?"

"Maybe the guy didn't even know the painting was worth its weight in gold," Nilsson continued.

Haver didn't say anything.

"We should maybe talk to the neighbor and that childhood friend—who should take that on?"

"Ann," Haver said.

"Okay," Nilsson said. "Are you coming in?"

"No, I'm going out to Jumkil."

"I see, take Allan with you. He needs some fresh air."

They hung up. Haver knew Sammy Nilsson was immediately going to call Lindell and present his theory about an art theft.

A man in front of her was laughing. He was dressed in a green waist-length coat. His pants were frayed at the ends. He walked quickly, deliberately, and efficiently turned the corner by the *Vålamagasinet* building. Ann Lindell caught up with him.

There was a white sofa in the shop window. He stepped closely up to the window, put his head to one side, and Lindell realized he was trying to read the tiny price tag that had been pinned to one end of the sofa. Then she recognized him. It was Rosander, who for a short while had been a suspect in a murder case, but who had been cleared.

"It's too expensive," she said.

Rosander twirled around.

"Well, look who we have here," he said. "The fuzz."

Lindell disliked the expression, but nodded and smiled.

"How's tricks?" Rosander asked.

Lindell's smile disappeared. She looked at him. He was the same as always. Tousled, you could say to sum him up, but still with a mocking expression on his somewhat puffy face. She nodded, tried to think of something to say, but only put her hand on his shoulder and then left. Rosander stayed behind, staring foolishly.

Ann Lindell broke into a half-run. To bump into Rosander was to confront memories that cut like a knife. She had met Rosander in the same time period that she had first met Edvard. They came from the same village. Edvard, the man she had loved and let slip away.

Maybe Rosander was still in touch with Edvard. What else would they talk about except people they knew in common? Lindell didn't want to know anything, to hear news about Edvard.

She turned around for a look. Rosander was still there. Lindell slowed down. It started to rain and after a while she became aware of the damp seeping in. The October haze that plunged Sala Street into a gray hell, an enduring dark that found its grip and held on.

She bumped into Ola Haver in the entrance to the police station.

"Have you talked to the neighbor?"

"I haven't had any time," Lindell snarled.

Haver stared at her. She wanted to tell him to go to hell. "I'm on my way over there now. How about you?"

"I'm just back from the autopsy," Haver said shortly.

"And?"

He shrugged. "Nothing much. A blow to the head, but we knew that."

Lindell stepped into the elevator.

"Are you coming along?"

Haver shook his head, but just before the elevator doors closed Haver put out one leg so the doors slid open again.

"Is there anything in particular?"

"No, I met an old acquaintance. You remember Rosander, from the Enrico investigation? He had won some money in the lottery and was going to buy a new bed."

"He buys lottery tickets? You mean the insect researcher?"

"Two million," Lindell said. "He was going to buy a bed for fifty thousand. He felt fine. He sends his greetings and I guess that means you too."

"I'll be damned," Haver said.

"I know."

Haver backed away and Lindell went up, studying herself in the mirror. That was fine she thought and smiled in a grimace. That should shut him up. Ola Haver hated the lottery. He thought it was deeply unjust for some people to win money by chance. And anyway, Ola was the one who knew her the best and he probably sensed how much Edvard still meant to her. She begrudged him the pleasure of knowing that the meeting with Rosander had knocked the wind out of her. Unfair and ridiculous, yes, and above all deeply fictitious—an invented lottery win—but the lie made her feel better.

When she walked into her office it was with a sense of calm and confidence that was light years from the agitation she had felt on the street. She threw herself into the investigation and pulled her notepad toward her.

At that moment the phone rang. It was Fälth. Ann knew that meant trouble. As soon as she heard his voice she turned to a fresh page and reached for a pen.

"We have something new," he said in his drawling, slightly laconic way, "as if this weren't enough. It's always like this—"

"I know," Lindell interrupted him. His preambles always had a tendency of becoming long-winded.

"Another farmer," Fälth said.

✦

Eleven

An apple fell, and then another. Muted, slightly squishy thuds as they hit the moss-infested lawn. The inside of the apple appeared green-yellow through places where the peel had split open. The consistency was mealy and the fruit was falling apart. Laura poked one with her foot. The apple broke entirely, revealing a mushy interior and the sharp smell of incipient decomposition made her pull back.

Laura walked surrounded by lilacs that grew in thickets with straggling branches whose bark had started to peel off and hung like dried strips of skin. Here, inside the bushes she was safe but felt the threat that lurked along the surrounding hawthorn hedge and through the somber treetops. The world around her made its presence known through sounds from the street, a car that slowly drove by, maybe a truck with a delivery to one of the neighbors. They seemed to be constantly renovating their houses, reinventing their gardens, and buying new furniture.

The professor's flagpole could be seen above the trees. It rose like a reminder that there were holidays, something to celebrate. Sometimes a yellow cross on a blue background fluttered over the neighborhood, smacked in the wind, got tangled up, or hung limp like a rag.

For some reason her father had hated the flagpole and had toyed with the idea of cutting it down, taking advantage of an opportunity when the professor was away. Laura knew it was all talk. He would never have dared to do anything like that and anyway, she had trouble visualizing him with a saw.

Now he was gone. The initial feeling of freedom was more and more turning into a sense of approaching danger. It was not simply the mean, rough wind but also the fact that time seemed to devour her. The days went by. Her father's existence started to blur around the edges, he sank more deeply into the corners of the innermost recesses of the house, transformed into dust around dissertations and loose papers. She herself went around half alive, half dead, through archways built up of repressed memories and suppressed pain.

She pulled some fruit from a spindle tree. The orange-yellow fruit capsules glowed like embers. When she was a child she used to gather them in the little cups of the doll china and pretend to serve her mother a colorful lunch. They could sit for hours at the dining room table, her mother watchful with an eye on the garden. Sometimes she glanced at Laura, or said something, but most often she was absorbed in herself, as if she was passively waiting for something, although it was not clear what it was. Laura bustled with her china. Her mother sighed occasionally, producing a soft sound.

Sometimes her father came home very late, from working at the department. Dinner was put in front of him. The stew meat had congealed and looked like dark animals captured in a gooey sauce, the potatoes had hardened and become unappetizingly chewy. The pats of butter softened, overcome with heat and strange smells, they gave up and sank into a heap.

Laura lived in a shadow world where the old radio's green front gave off a soft light while her mother listened to classical music. Laura read the names of the radio stations over and over, sitting like a little ball by her mother's feet, waiting for the light to come back.

Her whole childhood was about waiting. Laura waited for the light, her father for his professors' title, her mother for the man who would one day come into the house and save her. The light never came, the title was not forthcoming, but the man appeared.

Laura shivered. It was getting colder. It felt as if it was going to snow again. She looked down at her clay-covered sneakers.

Suddenly there was life in the house, in the form of a man. He was going to help with the garden, dig new flower beds, dig holes for trees, and patch the soil and put in stone landscaping.

His thoughtful voice, not at all like her father's virulent harangues, partly dissolved in the dark. She listened, at first up close, but later hidden behind drapes and half-closed doors. Her mother laughed and it sounded as if a stranger had taken possession of her body. The man spoke quietly. Laura rarely heard what he said, but it sounded friendly, wise in some way.

They discussed things, Laura learnt that word that fall. They presented things to each other, like small packages. Here you go. Thank you, this is for you. Thanks, that's a good idea. They went on in this way. Conversing endlessly.

He came back the next day with new packages and windows were flung open, dust was cleared away. He was given food, and he ate, chuckling a little, it seemed. She heard her mother say that the stranger ate like a real man.

A flurry of activity, and thundering noise. Laura had to eat alone at the dining room table. She set the table with her tiny china and cleared it away, invited imaginary friends to lunch and discussed things with them. She tried to laugh like the man did.

After fourteen days he disappeared, but her mother said he would be back in the spring. Laura waited. It would be a long winter.

Then one day at the beginning of April he returned. Now he spent most of his time in the garden, spreading a white powder on the lawn. Laura was allowed to help. He pruned bushes and piled the branches into large piles. The apple trees were trimmed. Laura picked up twigs and was praised.

The professor, who had recently moved in, would come over and talk across the hawthorn hedge. They discussed different kinds of apple. Laura stood nearby. She thought the man smelled like apple. His green pants, stuffed into red boots, had marks from paint and had holes that were roughly patched with black rubber.

The professor went on about the apples. The man rested a foot on a shovel. It looked so comfortable, as if they were close friends, him and the shovel.

The rain increased. She drew closer to the French window that faced the garden, but shut it with her foot and remained standing out on the crumbling flagstone, partly shielded from the rain.

She feared the approaching afternoon. Her body was completely limp and she didn't see how she would be able to pull herself together and call Stig.

✦

Twelve

Later on, when they laid the investigation about the murder in Jumkil next to the investigation concerning the murder of Jan-Elis Andersson in Norr-Ededy village in Alsike, they appeared almost identical.

Both of them were elderly men living alone in the countryside, who had been farmers in the past. Andersson, just as Blomgren before him, had suffered brutal blows to the head with a murder weapon that the police had not yet found.

In the search for a possible motive the results were the same: nothing. Both men had lived a retiring, peaceful life, they lacked the ready assets attractive to a murderer, and they appeared to be without enemies, at least of the order to lead to a murder.

There was one difference: Jan-Elis Andersson had resisted. To what extent this was so it was not possible to determine but the evidence in his kitchen spoke for itself: three chairs had been knocked over, and the table-cloth had been pulled to the floor, taking a bowl of oatmeal, a spoon, and a jar of lingonberry jam with it.

"There's someone out there who doesn't like old men who eat lingonberries," Beatrice said, remembering Dorotea Svahn's words about Blomgren being a champion berry picker.

Most likely the killer had crept up on Andersson from behind. The neighbor had said he had severely impaired hearing.

Lindell could guess how it had happened. Andersson had been struck hard on the back of the head, had been thrown forward, pulled the cloth with him down onto the floor but had managed to get up and grab a chair for protection. One of the chairs had two broken legs. Ryde, the forensics specialist who was not supposed to be working but who had jumped in, was firm on that point: the chair had been used in an attempt at self-defense.

But Jan-Elis Andersson had failed in his attempts and now he lay face-down in a mess of lingonberries and blood.

Ann Lindell stood with her head bent. The technicians had—grudgingly—cleared a thin corridor of floor space in the kitchen so that she and Beatrice could come in and take a look. Morgansson sat in a crouch next to the counter, trying to secure some fingerprints. He looked up at Ann.

"Same guy?" he asked.

Ryde muttered something. He hated speculation during the work process.

"It could be a coincidence," she said and looked out the window.

Out in the yard, Sammy Nilsson was questioning the nearest neighbor, a man of about fifty who looked noticeably upset. He paced around and

Lindell saw Sammy try to calm the shocked man, who was the one who had found the body.

Lindell called Sammy and watched him reach irritably for his cell phone.

"Check out any potential connection to Petrus," she said and Sammy groaned.

"What do you think I'm doing?"

"I was thinking of farmer associations and such," Ann said in a docile voice. "There are things like that, aren't there? Blomgren and Andersson may have met at some point."

"I'm a country boy, if you recall. I've got this covered."

The people gathered in the yard gave Lindell the same déjà vu feeling she had had in the kitchen.

"The question of whether or not we believe there is a real connection between the murders is crucial," Lindell said. "If we do then what we have to set our sights on right now is to turn up everything that potentially connects these two farmers."

She stared out over the landscape. A police officer in uniform was climbing over a barbed wire fence a couple of hundred meters away. He looked clumsy and out of place in the terrain.

The fields that bordered the farm lay fallow. Or at least that was what Lindell thought. She compared them to the Östgöta area where she came from with its wide expanses of fields and sturdy farm buildings. Here things looked paltry by comparison, thin strips of cultivated land between swathes of dark forest. The cottages that were dotted about were small, as dictated by the landscape.

"The neighbor hasn't seen anything." Sammy Nilsson interrupted her thought process.

"Can he see this house from his?"

"No. He lives behind that clump of trees up there. You can see the roof," Nilsson said and pointed.

"What was he doing here?"

"Nothing in particular. He would sometimes walk over and have a little coffee and a chat with Jan-Elis. The neighbor is on disability."

"At least we have a clue as to when the murder took place," Bea said. "Around breakfast time."

Lindell walked off to the side. Was it the same perpetrator? In that case what was the connection?

Again she let her gaze sweep over the area, as if the answer was to be found out there. Not a puff of wind, not a sign of life or movement. A static place, maintained by a retired farmer and a man on disability. A region that had sunk down into its own wasted and worn sparseness. Who would want to or even have the energy to think of killing someone here? Everything already seemed dead.

Why kill two seventy-year-old farmers?

Just as in Blomgren's home, nothing here was touched. Straight into the house, bash the old man's head in, and then leave just as fast. That's how the whole thing must have happened.

She caught sight of Morgansson through the kitchen window. His wide back looked monumental in the tiny window. The night before she had toyed with the idea of going home with him, only for a night, in order to feel the warmth of another human being. Now that thought seemed somehow absurd.

They had said good-bye and good night and then left, each in their own direction. As she was walking down East Ågatan she had the feeling of being in a foreign city, a foreign country, as if she were on holiday, on her way to the hotel.

Pleased with the evening, she had crawled into bed and decided she would like to see him again, if for no other reason than to see another movie and have another beer.

Today is another life, she thought, not without bitterness. It was as if two consecutive days of happiness were not possible. She watched Morgansson move around inside. Then something in her changed, she felt a welling up of pride. She was standing in the yard involved in a murder investigation, yet again. She didn't need to denigrate herself. First, she was a competent police officer and second, a pretty good mother to Erik. Her contract with life had been signed and she was going to make the best of the situation. She didn't need to apologize for the fact that she wanted to live, wanted to laugh or go to the movies with a handsome man, who also happened to be nice and had awakened something slumbering within her.

But for now she would have to put all thoughts of movies aside. Two murders. She would not be able to relax even for a second. She turned to Sammy Nilsson.

"You'll be responsible for charting these two farmers—you said yourself you're a country boy. I want the minutest detail. Not a single item can go unchecked. They're around seventy and have a past. Somewhere their lives run together. Find that point."

Sammy looked at her and smiled.

"Full steam ahead," he said, turned, and left.

Just then Morgansson stepped out onto the stoop.

"I think we have something," he said and went back into the house.

Of course, Lindell thought, you have something. She followed him in. When she was in the hall Morgansson pointed to the little table right inside the door.

"A letter," he said. "I found it in the drawer under the telephone. You don't have to pick it up."

It was handwritten and lacked a signature, but Lindell immediately had the impression it was written by a man. She read it. Bea appeared behind her.

"What does it say?"

"It is basically a threat," Lindell said. "Some unresolved affair that needs to be corrected, according to the writer."

"No envelope?" she called out to Morgansson.

"Not yet," he called back from the room next to the kitchen.

"We don't know who wrote it, not even if Andersson was the recipient."

"He may be the person who wrote it," Bea said.

"That's easy to check," Lindell said. "What do you think?"

" 'Make sure you pay up otherwise you'll be sorry,' " Bea read again.

Lindell sighed.

"You pay," she mumbled.

"The writer of the letter has apparently been waiting a few years," Bea said, "and now he wants to be paid for something."

"No dates, nothing really," Lindell said, disappointed. "It can have been in the drawer for the past ten years."

"Then why save the letter?"

"You know how people are."

Bea read the letter again.

"What about this," she said and read out loud: " 'When I heard that you sold I thought you were finally going to pay me.' What was it he sold?"

"The farm, maybe," Lindell threw out, "or the land. It has to be some bigger thing, it can hardly be a tractor or such like."

"Can Andersson have written this to Petrus Blomgren? Didn't he sell his land? And then it wasn't recorded?"

"Far-fetched," Lindell said.

"But we're looking for connections," Bea said eagerly. "Think about it, an older farmer doesn't have so many dealings, it's normally about farms and land, leases and the like."

"Our farming expert has just left," Lindell said.

"Blomgren owes money to Andersson, who doesn't get paid. Andersson kills Blomgren and then . . ."

"And then . . . Blomgren hits back," Lindell said. "The problem is that he's dead."

"That suicide letter, that could have had something to do with this. He wrote something about not doing things as he should have."

"We'll have to check the handwriting first," Lindell decided, "and check with the relative that's supposed to exist. The neighbor said something about there being a niece who sometimes visits. She may know what this is all about. Maybe it's an old story that we'll be able to rule out."

It had gotten dark by the time they were ready to leave Jan-Elis Andersson's farm. Everyone was taciturn and in the faint light from the outside lamp Lindell saw how exhausted everyone was.

She took a last swing around the house, like she usually did.

Fredriksson and Bea drove away. They had loaded up the car with boxes of old papers and letters, tax returns, insurance papers, and bookkeeping from the time that Andersson had been an active farmer.

Berglund, who had come out during the course of the afternoon, hung around. He had, together with a few others from the patrol squad, gone over the various sheds and outhouses with a fine-toothed comb. The old police officer stood thoughtfully by the freestanding garage. He pulled the door shut behind him, looked at Lindell, and walked over to her.

"I'm not crazy about the dark," he said.

Lindell nodded. They stood side by side and summed up their observations in silence. Or that was what Lindell thought Berglund was doing. She herself was thinking of Erik, who had been picked up at day care by the parents of his best friend. It was a solution that worked. Erik did not object, but Ann felt guilty. She wasn't like the other mothers.

"Should we mosey along?"

"You're the only one I know who says that," Lindell said.

"It's from my grandfather," Berglund said. "He lived like this, exactly like Andersson, though he wasn't really a farmer. He didn't get around much but he was a devil with horses. Have you seen that movie about the guy who could talk to horses?"

"No, I missed that one. I rarely go to the movies."

"Is that so?" Berglund said with a mocking smile. "In any case, we went to that one. I thought it was going to be something, but it was shit."

"It's often that way with films," Lindell said.

"Granddad would have done it better."

"How did you know I went to the movies last night?"

"Hultgren saw you," Berglund said, "and you know how he is."

Lindell went to pick up Erik. It still felt strange to leave her colleagues in the middle of a murder investigation. She knew that the others would stay down at the station in order to organize the material, look up databases, contact people, and do everything else that was part of the inner investigation.

She wanted to be there too, in the middle of the activity. Ottosson had brought it up as soon as she returned from maternity leave, that he didn't want her turning up at the station at all hours, that he wanted her to focus properly on herself and Erik. Ann Lindell had tried to joke it away but Ottosson had been firm. She sensed, from the way he formulated it that he didn't want her to repeat his own mistakes.

She played with the thought of letting Erik stay at his friend's place for a few hours—after all, this was a murder and it was only the shame of calling and asking the parents that prevented her from going back to Salagatan.

When Erik had fallen asleep Ann Lindell turned off all the electric lights in the apartment and lit a couple of candles that she put out on the table in the living room. A glass of Portuguese wine was already out there, half empty.

A cozy evening at home, she thought, chuckled, and pulled her legs up under her. The silence was deafening. Sund, one of the few neighbors that Ann Lindell had a fairly regular contact with, had popped in with a construction set for Erik. He had bought it on sale, or so he claimed. Ann had the feeling it had not been inexpensive. It was an airplane. As usual, the neighbor had overestimated Erik's abilities. He was simply too young for Sund's gifts but Ann was touched by his thoughtfulness.

They sat at the kitchen table for a while and talked. Sund's car, a more than forty-year-old Ford Anglia, was completely worn out. Sund was of two minds about what to do. Ann Lindell advised him to have the car repaired. The neighborhood would not be the same if the "Black Pearl" disappeared from the parking lot.

After about an hour, when it was Erik's bedtime, Sund had reluctantly said good-bye and gone home. The faint smell of pomade lingered in the apartment. She had come to realize there was some talk in the building regarding Sund's old-fashioned attentions toward Ann, an older man's concern for the single woman some thirty years his junior, and some had taken to calling him Sick—a play on *Sund*, which means healthy—but for her it was a source of joy. She had never noticed anything unhealthy in her neighbor. Quite the opposite. He was just thoughtful and a little lonely.

She thought about Sund and from there it was not far to Petrus Blomgren and Jan-Elis Andersson. Men, lonely men around seventy. Those times she had visited her neighbor she had been struck by how the loneliness shone in the orderly home. Everything was clean and nice, everything in its place, perhaps a touch pedantic. The coffee cup always in the same place on the counter, placed on a small crocheted pad, ready to be used, carefully washed and returned to the cloth after the coffee break was over.

Well-ordered but very lonely. This was also true of the two retired farmers. What had Sund worked with? Ann recalled that he had talked about office work, maybe at the mustard factory, since Sund had talked a lot about the "pickle plant," as it was called. Had he been married? There was so little she knew of his life. Sund talked mainly about the here and now and his plans for the short term.

Had Blomgren and Andersson had any relationships? This did not immediately communicate itself from their homes and none of those who had been questioned so far had said anything. But back in the day there must have been some love in both of the farmers' lives. Somewhere perhaps there was a woman who remembered her love for Petrus Blomgren. Maybe there would be someone who would shed a tear when she opened the newspaper tomorrow morning and read that Jan-Elis Andersson had been murdered in his home in Norr-Ededy village, Alsike.

Women were good at keeping track of the dead as well as the living and there was always the chance that someone would turn up when the two murder victims were buried. Ann decided to attend the funeral services. She did not expect they would be very large.

If there was a connection between the two murders she was not yet able to see it. But she was convinced the connection lay in their lives, perhaps far back in time. Two farmers are not murdered by accident within two days of each other, not in Ann Lindell's book.

She did not feel optimistic but still more confident than before. Perhaps it was the chat with Sund or the fact that she had now poured herself her second glass of wine that meant the outlook appeared brighter.

She studied the bottle's label that showed a hilly landscape dotted with grapevines snaking up the slopes. In the background there was a castle with turrets and spires.

"From shed to castle," she muttered.

When Ann Lindell crawled into bed she was slightly dizzy. Two glasses of wine were enough. The pillow felt like a dear friend and the warm blanket like a desired lover.

✦

Thirteen

It was reading hour at the Homicide Division, something both funny and frightening.

Upsala Nya Tidning had headlined their first page with the news of the second murder in as many days. They had managed to interview the nearest neighbor who described Jan-Elis Andersson as an "honorable man."

"It's an 'honor' killing," Ola Haver said.

Expressen did its bit by dubbing this the work of the "Country Butcher." They had even managed to get a statement from the Federation of Swedish Farmers' chairman, who was not, however, particularly concerned. Apart from that the papers were full of bloodthirstiness and "revelations."

"She lives more than a thousand kilometers from here," Berglund said and pointed at a photograph of the head of the farmers' association. "Of course she's not particularly worried."

"A chairman of the Federation lives at least a thousand kilometers from all farmers," Sammy Nilsson said. "Especially from guys like Blomgren and Andersson."

Aftonbladet had also jumped on the theory about a serial killer. A well-known criminologist had expounded in its pages with customary verbosity and gave an account of experiences from the United States. What this had to do with Uppsala was not clear. *Dagens Nyheter* had managed to mix up the pictures of Blomgren and Andersson's houses.

"That one," Ottosson said bitterly. He had bumped into the expert and had formed his opinion. Ann Lindell walked in with the chief of the crime information service, stepping right into the charged feeling that the assembled daily papers managed to create in the morning. They chatted almost cheerily. The rest looked up. Sammy Nilsson grinned.

"Have you been to the movies again?" he asked Lindell, who ignored him. She knew that was often the best tack.

Ola Haver pushed the stack of papers away.

"Should we get going?"

Ottosson started as usual with a brief overview of the situation in the city and also dutifully came with a report of the Tierp area. This consisted of a violent perpetrator who had smashed a couple of cars and then taken off in his own vehicle in a southerly direction, most likely under the influence of some kind of pills. According to their colleagues in Tierp the man was considered dangerous.

Berglund sighed. Ottosson glanced up from his papers.

"Okay," he said, "now we leave all dangerous Tierpians. Question number one: do we believe in a connection?"

"Yes," Lindell said firmly and argued according to the thoughts she had had the night before. "We have to bore back through time," she said in conclusion and looked at Sammy Nilsson.

"The country division," Berglund said, when Sammy didn't react.

"*Nada,*" Sammy said. "Both of them are former farmers. Blomgren on a smaller scale, back in the day he was a dairy farmer with a small stock of animals, de-registered as a supplier of animals at the end of the seventies, continued to cultivate grain for livestock feed but then stopped completely. Worked a lot on the side. Fredriksson knows more about this. Jan-Elis Andersson's farm was a little bigger, about sixty hectares, most of it grazing for his and others' animals. Dairy cows but also in later years beef cattle and even horses. He rented out stalls and supplied the feed."

"Does he still have any animals?" the head of KUT, the Criminal Information Service, asked.

"Only a cat. The neighbor is taking care of it. Both of them sold their land. Andersson was in fairly good financial shape with close to half a million in the bank plus a few shares and bonds."

"Who stands to inherit?"

"A niece, Lovisa Sundberg, in Umeå. Married to an architect."

"Have we made contact with her?"

The KUT director's questions rolled out like a string of pearls and created a song of harmonious alternating parts between him and Sammy Nilsson.

"Sure, the Umeå colleagues have talked to her. She's in shock, but collected, they say. She was still up north as of yesterday."

"And the architect?"

"On a business trip to Stockholm. I'm sorry but he was sitting in a meeting from eight thirty in an office on Kungsholmen."

"When do farmers eat breakfast?" Berglund asked quietly.

Sammy Nilsson chuckled.

"That depends," he said. "Now, Andersson had no animals to take care of so it could have been any time, but in his case probably on the early side."

"Can the architect have killed him and then driven to his meeting?"

"He had breakfast at Hotell Tegnér at seven. I've talked to the staff."

"Good," Lindell said with emphasis and Sammy gave her a quick look before going on.

"It also turns out he's confined to a wheelchair."

Allan Fredriksson continued the proceedings by giving an account of Petrus Blomgren's various jobs and earnings. The farm had initially been the center of his finances but its importance had gradually diminished. It appeared that he had not at first realized that a farm of thirty hectares isn't a particularly good affair. His last years as an active farmer were the most meager. Since he started working at Nylander's Construction and took extra jobs in the forest the picture changed dramatically, or so Blomgren must have felt, Fredriksson conjectured.

"He doubled his taxable income in a couple of years. The deposits to his savings account increased. He had money to spare. I have tried to map out his professional life to see if there was anything out of the ordinary but I can't find anything. Blomgren kept on going, living a retiring and calm existence, no trouble with the authorities."

Fredriksson flipped through his notes. Ottosson glanced at Lindell and smiled. Subdued meetings and proceedings were the chief's specialty. In this territory he moved with a lightness that came as a surprise to the occasional outsider. Ottosson had a rare ability to create comfort and an unforced feeling of unpretentiousness.

"His time as a carpenter does not leave any visible tracks," Fredriksson continued when he had found the right paper, "except for an injury in the fall of 'ninety-one. He falls from a scaffold and splits his spleen."

Berglund sighed.

"I've talked with two men who used to work with him. They describe Blomgren as being extremely timid. Except for being very punctual and hardworking he didn't make much of an impression. He claimed to only have been drunk once in his life. He had spent a week in Spain—Mallorca, the men thought it was."

"The most exciting thing about his life was that he died," Sammy said.

"Are you done?" Ottosson asked.

Fredriksson nodded.

"With regard to Andersson we haven't managed to find very much," Berglund said, "but tomorrow we will probably be able to present the exciting details."

"Sammy," Ottosson said.

Sammy Nilsson's account of the two farmers' involvement in the Federation of Farmers was also not particularly dramatic. Both of them had been members but in different divisions. There was nothing to suggest that they had bumped into one another on such occasions.

"What about the threatening letter at Andersson's house?" Lindell asked.

"Everything points to him being the author. The handwriting matches that on his own papers, but it will be checked into more thoroughly."

The conference room fell silent. Ottosson gave Lindell a look and started to sum up the main points but noticed that his colleagues' concentration was failing. Everything had been said and they were experienced enough to know what had to be done.

They broke up convinced that their working day would be long. Lindell gathered up her notes and exchanged a few words with the director of KUT before she went back to her office.

✦

Fourteen

The knee-length grass swayed as if a giant hand was stroking it. Laura Hindersten thought there was something comforting about the movement. It was as if the wind in a gentle gesture took leave of what was left of the summer.

A rotted apple landed with a thud on what had once been a gravel path but was now woven through with weeds. The path led to an oval sitting area, paved in slate and surrounded by some gangly roses that Laura's mother had planted. Laura could still remember the name of the rose: Orange Sensation. She remembered where and when they had bought them. It was at the nursery on Norbyvägen and Laura had just turned ten. Laura thought the talkative gardener was a distant relative because he used the same words as her mother and because the ends of his sentences disappeared and were replaced by a gesture or an expressive face, exactly like her grandfather's.

He took them to an earth cellar on the edge of the nursery where they were greeted by the smell of raw earth. The roses were arranged on shelves, packed into bundles and with tiny pale shoots coming up from the stems. He carefully chose a bundle, cut the string, and inspected each rose one at a time. He saw poorly but compensated for this with touch and stroked the stems with his fingers. He put roses with shrivelled branches to one side.

"Those are B-quality," he explained, "and that isn't what you want."

Laura got the impression that he was treating her mother very well. Few people were as polite to her as this old gardener.

"Is the young miss also interested in roses?"

Laura nodded. The man smiled at her. It seemed as if he enjoyed lingering in the earth cellar. He read the different names of the roses bundled on the groaning shelves. There was Poulsen rose, Alain, Nina Weibull, Peace, and many others.

"The Poulsen I only keep because . . ."

He smiled again and nodded.

"Well, you know, memories . . ."

She had watched the garden passively for an hour. She was so cold she was shivering but could not bring herself to go inside the house.

If someone had entered the garden and discovered her pressed up against the French windows, with the grocery bags at her feet, then Laura would have given the impression of a person without hope. Her inability to cross the threshold had imparted a strange stiffness to her pale face. Her gaze moved restlessly as if it was searching for a place to rest. The movement in the grass and the sound of the falling apple had of course not spurred her to open the terrace door and step into the warmth but it did wake her from her paralysis. She pulled her right hand across her face while the left one felt for the door handle behind her back.

Right here, a very long time ago on a warm summer's day, was where her father and mother had stood. For once very close to each other, perhaps even hand in hand for a moment, in the no-man's-land between her father's domain—the house—and her mother's, which was the garden.

The terrace door had been completely open. There was a great deal of traffic between the bushes and the trees, where small birds flew around with food in their beaks. The day before she had found a dead baby bird by the mock-orange bush and buried it behind the compost.

Laura had been sitting at the foot of the apple tree playing with a new gift. Happy voices had come from the house. The toy was uninteresting. It was the voices that meant something. She had fled out into the garden but not so far that she couldn't hear the exhilarated guests' avid conversation and the volleys of laughter that echoed like frightening bursts of thunder.

Her parents looked at her and smiled. Ulrik Hindersten was dressed in a dark suit and her mother wore a green dress with white lace around the neck. Laura thought they looked like a bride and groom.

"Dinner will be ready soon," her mother said.

They went back in and Laura tried to understand why they had walked out onto the terrace together, so close to each other and apparently enjoying each other's company.

Laura stared out over the garden and could see herself sitting under the apple tree. That was the day everything started. The previous conflicts between her and her father were nothing but outpost skirmishes compared to the drawn-out war that came after, a war that went on for over twenty years.

She finally opened the door and stepped over the bags in the dining room. The heavy chairs and table, the candelabra on the massive tabletop had been there that time. She sat down, letting her gaze go from chair to chair and called to mind, as her father must also have done many times, the different guests and their placement at the table. She even recalled the scent of perfume and food and the young student's sweat.

All books and folders were gone, the curtains pulled back, and the light created a whole new room. On the table there was a white linen tablecloth and it was laid with the china that was usually stored in the oak sideboard.

Laura was called in but remained standing in the doorway. Mrs. Simonsson, who Laura saw for the last time at her mother's funeral, was bringing out dishes and tureens. She wore a little apron and a white cap. Laura couldn't help but laugh.

The adults were already seated. An older man whom Laura recognized from her father's workplace was the one who talked most frequently and loudly. The women on both sides of him listened attentively.

Ulrik Hindersten asked for their attention and said he hoped the food would please them. He concluded his brief remarks by saying a few words in Latin—Laura thought they came from Livius, an author from whose work Ulrik Hindersten would often read aloud in the evenings. Many people around the table laughed.

It was the twentieth of July, Petrarch's birthday, a day that was always celebrated in this house. But this time it was a twofold celebration. Over the summer a rumor had started and stubbornly grown stronger: that this fall the long-awaited recognition of Ulrik Hindersten's scholarly contribution would finally be forthcoming. He was going to be appointed to the professorial chair.

Many of his colleagues were assembled at the table but also several acquaintances from the neighborhood, not the most immediate neighbors but two couples who lived farther down the street. There was also a literature expert from Stockholm among the guests and some older men who spoke Italian.

It was a real party. There was an abundance of food, made by Mrs. Simonsson from Tobo, one of the few of Alice Hindersten's childhood friends with whom she was still in contact. Mrs. Simonsson would come two, three times a year and clean the house. Always before Christmas, but also in the spring and in September. Sometimes her husband came along, a quiet man who Laura was afraid of, mostly on account of his enormous hands. He performed minor repairs around the house, fixed gutters, re-caulked the windows, and oiled squeaky doors. One time Laura had seen him kill a stray cat that Ulrik Hindersten found annoying. First Simons-son had lured the cat over with some herring, then he twisted the cat's neck without a word and buried it in a corner of the garden.

Mrs. Simonsson brought everything out, the guests ate and drank and became increasingly noisy. Laura was sitting between one of the Italians and a student from her father's department. The student was as pale and timid as Laura, and ate cautiously. It looked as if he was having difficul-ties with Mrs. Simonsson's food.

"Your father will become famous," was the only thing he said to Laura during the entire dinner.

Laura didn't know what that meant. She understood the word but not how this fame would affect her and her family. Famous, she thought, and imagined her father's voice issuing from the radio in the living room and how he would appear on television.

She also did not understand where all the strange people had come from. There were never guests at the table and all of a sudden the room was bursting with unknown voices and laughter. Laura knew it had to do with the approaching fame.

She looked at her father. He spoke with food in his mouth, gesturing with the knife in his hand. He looked as if he wanted to stab his dinner guests. A spot of gravy on his shirt stood out like a flower. Laura saw how her mother watched him closely. But there was also an unusual expres-sion around her mouth that could be interpreted as a faint smile.

Mrs. Simonsson carried out new tureens, dishes, and bottles. Every-thing disappeared at an incredible rate as if the guests were uncertain how long the hospitality would be extended. One of the biggest eaters sat directly across from Laura and she knew immediately who he was. Her father had talked about "The Horse," a colleague in the department, who at present was shoveling in mounds of leek gratin, veal steak, and gravy with great relish.

After several mouthfuls "The Horse" interrupted himself, wiped his mouth on the napkin, struck his glass, and called for silence. His exhala-tions came intermittently across the table. As the speech progressed his pale cheeks were transformed. "Livores mortis" her father later called those glowing patches. "The Horse" continuously turned his knotted hands with veins like living worms under the blotchy skin, as if he wanted to strangle the linen napkin in his hand.

He began by describing the heights that Ulrik Hindersten had set his sights on and thereby started a path where only very few had been able to leave a mark. This got a rousing response, especially from Laura's partner. He clapped and shouted something about the apt metaphor. Laura, who had been raised in the presence of Petrarch, figured that "The Horse" must have alluded to something in the writer's work.

The speech was long. He talked about the meaning of obstinancy and her mother's smile was extinguished. He talked about humility and several guests chortled. Even Ulrik smiled. "The Horse" spoke of Ulrik's taking on Truth in single combat and now everyone laughed.

The student began to fidget when "The Horse" started in on the situation at the department. One of the Italians burped discreetly into his napkin. Someone tittered nervously. Mrs. Simonsson made an extra clattering noise with the dessert plates. Ulrik Hindersten's colleague went on at full steam, apparently unaware of the reactions around him.

"There are powers," he said, "that do not have the will nor the intellectual capacity to completely appreciate our host's brilliant ability to shed light on Petrarch's poetry. The contradictory elements of the medieval fourteenth-century mind . . . the complexity of man's remorseful struggle for fusion with . . . for an understanding of . . . that Ulrik has already approached in a trailblazing manner in his dissertation . . . cannot be emphasized enough . . . with an envious pettiness the critics have put aside all scholarly . . . our hostess . . . charming daughter . . . a home that breathes . . . gathered . . . a pleasure . . . the fullest extent . . ."

He went on in this way. The horselike aspect in his appearance was reinforced as he became carried away by his own eloquence and neighing laughter. The guests squirmed nervously in their chairs; Mrs. Simonsson became more impatient as she was serving ice cream for dessert.

The colleague concluded his remarks with a toast. Laura felt a purely physical relief as the guests reached for their glasses. Her intuition signaled catastrophe.

Her father, on the other hand, sensed nothing. His good mood made him open a dusty bottle of Taylor's when the guests left. It was a gesture of goodwill to her mother, who loved port. They sat in the bay window. Ulrik Hindersten was optimistic. He talked about buying a house in Italy. Laura sat down on the floor by her parents and listened. Her mother sat and listened dumbstruck to how detailed the plans had become. Outside Arguà, not far from Petrarch's grave, her father had seen an old three-story house, admittedly in disrepair but fully functional. With the house came an olive grove and a garden that sloped to the west. He described almost passionately the knotted olive trees and the little terrace with a pergola where grapevines created a pleasantly filtered light and coolness.

"We can live there large parts of the year," he explained. "You can cultivate the garden and I can do research. Sometimes I will of course have to travel back to Sweden but I think the department will only be happy if I am not there so often," he said, smiling with rare self-irony.

Her mother didn't say anything, just stared out into the garden.

"You'll have to leave the apple trees, but you'll get oranges and olives instead," Ulrik said and placed his hand on hers.

Laura didn't know if it was the unexpected show of affection or the thought of the garden in Italy that made her mother suddenly burst into tears. Only later did she understand that her mother was more clear-headed than her father. She had known there would never be an olive grove.

"It won't present any difficulties for Laura either," her father continued. "Her Italian is as good as mine. She'll adapt. Don't worry."

Laura shivered. How many times had she replayed this scene in the bay window to herself? She remembered every line, every expression, and her mother's beautiful but sorrowful, almost transparent profile.

It was as if she did not have a body, as if her father were speaking to a creature whose veil-thin skin contained something immaterial.

Laura reached out and grabbed her mother's ankle. The answer was an almost imperceptible head movement.

Several months later—when the garden was blanketed under the first snow—her mother returned to the topic of the dinner and especially "The Horse's" speech.

"They're not like other people," she said. "When they say one thing they mean another. Remember how 'The Horse' talked, how he praised your father. Everything was a lie. Everyone sensed it, everyone except your father. If the decision to appoint your father to the professorship had been made, then 'The Horse' would not have said a single word, perhaps would not even have come for dinner. But he came, ate like a horse, and deliberately talked nonsense. He enjoyed it. He knew your father would never receive his title."

"But why did he say those things?" Laura asked.

"So the fall would be even greater. The higher he could get Ulrik the greater the disaster. It's like that china figurine," her mother said and pointed to the figure of a girl in the window. "If it topples out of the window it will break in two, but if you drop it from a great height it will smash into a thousand pieces."

Mother and daughter, united for a few minutes of conversation, knew their husband and father all too well. He would never make his peace, accept the way things were, and be content to end his career as an associate professor.

Laura allowed her gaze to glide from the figurine to the garden. A line of snow that rested on the lowest branch of the pear tree blew down at that moment and for an instant the air was filled with a whirling white smoke cloud.

There would never be a house in Arguà, never any day trips to Venice, never walks among olive trees. She knew this in the moment her mother got up from the table without a word of comfort. Not even when Laura picked up the china figurine and dropped it on the ground did her mother turn around. She walked into the kitchen. It was almost dinnertime.

Laura got up on stiff legs. Her body felt foreign to her. Her face flamed and grew hot, her limbs felt prickly, and she felt slightly dizzy. It wasn't just the lack of sleep and food; it felt like the time she had taken a medication that did not agree with her. It had given her nightmares and she had vomited violently in the morning.

She put a hand on her crotch, which still ached. Stig would return, he had said this several times. She smiled suddenly. He loved her, she knew that now. And only Jessica stood in their way, the only thing that prevented him from coming back to her forever.

"Ulrik!" she yelled, as if to convince herself that her father was not there.

She dragged in the grocery bags from the terrace. A jar of honey fell out of a bag but she left it there. The exertion made her sweat. She unpacked the items in a trance-like state. The kitchen was one big mess. Masses of unwashed dishes were piled up on the counter, as well as glasses, teacups, and pots. On the kitchen table there were newspapers and unopened mail.

She ended up standing in front of the refrigerator. Inside it some shriveled vegetables, containers of margarine without lids, and dried heels of cheese were living their own life. Several slices of salami were covered in a green film of mold.

"Mrs. Simonsson," she called out helplessly, but in an attack of will she pulled a garbage bag out of the pantry and filled it with all the leftover food.

Before replacing them with the newly bought items she had to sit down and rest.

She read the headline in the newspaper that was lying on top of the pile. The preamble talked about the "country butcher" who had struck again.

Laura unfolded the paper. The photograph on the front page made her wince. She felt that swinging sensation from her childhood. The stale air in the kitchen was replaced with the smell of freshly cut grass.

She put her hand over the picture and looked out through the window, and the longing for a diffuse sense of something, a possibility, missed many years ago, blocked her thoughts for a few moments as if a temporary electric error had created a short circuit in her brain.

✦

Fifteen

Someone had laid flowers by one of the fence posts by the entrance to Petrus Blomgren's house. Ann Lindell slowed down and stopped. There were fresias and something green. They looked frozen. A note was attached to the bouquet. "All the good ones die. Thank you for your solicitude." No signature. Ann reread the two sentences. "Solicitude" was such a beautiful word. Had Blomgren been a caring person? Many things suggested this, not least Dorotea Svahn's testimony.

The house already looked abandoned, as if it had aged a great deal in only a few days. The foundation appeared to have settled and sunk several inches and the roof tiles appeared to have taken on a darker shade, or so Ann imagined, and she had the feeling that the whole place was going to be transformed over the course of the winter into a gray, moss-clad boulder that rested in an increasingly wild terrain, that the vegetation was going to take over and erase all traces of settlement and human life.

She did not really find it that remarkable. The farmer Petrus Blomgren no longer existed so why should his house remain? Lindell stepped out of the car, struck by the thought that the house should not be touched, that no one should be allowed to step through a murdered person's door, taking control of the hall, kitchen, and room. Never ever. Everything should be allowed to deteriorate as dictated by nature.

She smiled at her own thoughts and realized that it was the absence of human voices and the quietness of the place that had made her reflective. She would not have been surprised if an animal had appeared out of the forest and communicated in some way.

Ann was searching for a complete picture and felt she sensed who Blomgren had been and what it was that had been lost. The hillside in Jumkil drew heavy breaths. Maple leaves floated to the ground. No creature emerged from the forest, not even a hint of wind altered the scene in any way.

It was with a feeling of melancholy grandeur that Ann Lindell knocked on Dorotea Svahn's door. The old woman opened the door immediately and Ann guessed she had been spotted a long time ago.

"Come in," Dorotea said. "I've put on coffee."

Ann made small talk while Dorotea poured out the coffee and filled the bread basket with half a dozen sweet rolls that she had warmed up in the microwave.

"I saw you linger at the gate for a while," Dorotea said. "It's easy to get caught up in one's thoughts."

"Yes, I was thinking about the silence," Ann said, "how it comes over you. I'm so used to stress and noise that the silence impresses me with another reality. I sometimes feel that I don't have the concepts I need to express what is happening when I experience silence. Does that make any sense?"

Dorotea nodded but didn't say anything.

"Did you leave those flowers by the gate?"

"No."

"Anyone you know?"

Dorotea shook her head.

"I don't know who it is," she said curtly and Lindell dropped it, not convinced she was telling the truth.

"I've read my colleague's, Beatrice Andersson's, notes on her conversation with you," Lindell said, starting over. "You and Petrus seem to have been very close. Maybe you were the person who knew him best."

Dorotea nodded again.

"You said something to her about Petrus going abroad once, I think it was to Mallorca. Do you know anything else about that trip?"

Dorotea took a sugar cube and mixed the coffee with a spoon before she answered.

"Not any more than just that Petrus was a changed man when he came home."

"How do you mean?"

"He was . . . happier," Dorotea said after a couple of seconds of hesitation.

"Tell me!"

"He never used to go anywhere and then suddenly he was off to Spain.

He was anxious about it beforehand, all the business with ordering his passport, but he got away. One week he was gone. The car gone too, he parked it at the airport. That cost him two hundred *kronor* right there. He said he had had fun down there. He managed with the language. They could almost speak Swedish down there."

"Did he go alone?"

The question caused Dorotea to squeeze her eyes together momentarily.

"I think so," she said and Lindell saw she was lying.

"Did he talk a lot about Spain when he returned?"

"Yes, the first while maybe."

"Did Petrus have difficulties sleeping?"

"No, I don't think so," Dorotea said. "Why do you ask?"

"We found an old package of sleeping pills in the house."

"I don't know anything about that."

"What year did he travel to Mallorca?"

"It was about twenty years ago. I don't think he had turned fifty? No, he didn't until the next fall, or . . . perhaps it was . . ."

"Was it 1981?"

"In May," Dorotea said and nodded. "After the spring planting season."

"The sleeping pills were prescribed in June 1981," Lindell said.

She paused for several seconds, letting the information sink in, before she continued.

"Can't you tell me? It's important to understand what happened to Petrus."

Dorotea suddenly stood up and left the room with surprising agility. She returned with a postcard in her hand that she placed on the table in front of Lindell.

The card showed a beach in front of a hotel. There was everything one would associate with a charter trip: a bar in the background shaped like a giant shell, sun umbrellas, and lounge chairs in the foreground.

Lindell flipped the postcard over. It was addressed to "Dorotea Svahn, Vilsne village, Jumkil, Sweden." The text was brief: "Hi Dorotea! I am so happy and having a good time." Signed, "Petrus."

Dorotea stood with her hand held out and as soon as Lindell looked up she took the postcard from Lindell's hand.

"I want to keep it," she said.

"Of course," Lindell said.

Dorotea left again and returned, sitting down and looking at Lindell.

"I think he met a woman."

"It seems like it," Lindell said. "He used the word 'happy.' He didn't say anything when he came home?"

"No, and I didn't want to pry."

"Were you upset?"

Dorotea shook her head.

"Then he got a prescription for sleeping pills," Lindell continued. "You didn't notice anything, like him being down or anything?"

"Nothing. Petrus was not the kind to talk about himself."

Ann Lindell trusted Dorotea's judgment. Even if Petrus had not said anything about a woman Lindell was convinced that Dorotea had reasons for her suspicions.

"Do you have any idea who the woman might have been?"

"I don't know anything else," Dorotea said firmly and Lindell understood there was nothing more to say on the subject.

Lindell stayed for another half an hour before taking her leave. On her way to her car, which she had parked on Petrus Blomgren's property, she wondered if he had met the woman in Mallorca or if she had been his travel companion from the start.

The possibilities of checking passenger lists from May 1981 were slim, but she would look into it.

Next stop was Arne Wiikman. With the help of Dorotea's directions she found the small freestanding house close to the highway between Uppsala and Gysinge almost immediately.

Arne Wiikman was standing in his garden with a rake in his hand. When Lindell parked the car he stopped working, leaning the rake up against a tree.

"What a pleasure," he said as Lindell came walking up. "I hate leaves."

He looked as if he meant it. He glared at his garden.

"It's these damn poplars. Soon I'll take down the damn lot of them."

Lindell smiled and started to explain the reason for her visit.

"Yes, yes," Wiikman interrupted her, "I know why you're here. Let's go in. Why stay around this shit."

He kicked at a pile of leaves and walked over to the front steps.

"You've talked to Dorotea, I understand," he said and opened the door, letting Lindell enter first.

"No, don't take your shoes off. Just walk right in."

He more or less shoved Ann Lindell into the living room, a small room that was dominated by a sectional pine sofa, upholstered in brown cloth. The largest elk head she had ever seen was hanging on one wall.

"Not so cheeky anymore," Arne Wiikman said with pride in his voice, when he saw her gaze. "Sit down. You want to talk about Blomgren, I assume. Do you want coffee?"

Lindell shook her head.

"Good! Well, have you gotten the murderer? No, of course not or you wouldn't be here. That's a pity, and a shame. It's probably some foreigner or drug addict who . . ."

He stopped and looked at her.

"What did it feel like to shoot that addict? Yes, I recognize you from the paper."

"It feels like hell," Lindell said emphatically.

Arne Wiikman grinned.

"Would think so," he said.

Lindell flipped open her notepad.

"Who would want to kill Petrus Blomgren?"

Wiikman's expression shifted quickly. The grin was replaced for a moment by something that Lindell read as surprise.

"I don't know," he said and coughed.

"About twenty years ago Petrus traveled to Mallorca and had a love affair there. Do you know who the woman was?"

Wiikman looked up.

"Is that the kind of thing you dig up?"

"We dig into everything."

The man leaned over the low coffee table.

"See that elk head? Blomgren was with me when I shot the bastard. We were positioned next to each other. I spotted the creature approaching but he was too far away for me. Petrus had the perfect shot. He had a clear field of vision, maybe fifty meters. He just had to raise his rifle. Hell, he could have shot from the hip, but he let it pass. Do you know why? He let it go to me. He wanted me to take it. That's what a good friend does. He had bagged a giant a few years before and now he wanted to give me the same pleasure. See?"

Wiikman glanced at the trophy above his head. Lindell saw the emotion and anger in the man's face.

"Who would want to club a man like that to death?"

"Do you know who the woman was?"

Wiikman shook his head.

"Petrus didn't tell you anything about his trip to Spain?"

"He might have mentioned it, that he had been to Mallorca, but I didn't live here back then. He didn't tell me anything in particular. I don't think he thought it was much to boast about."

Lindell decided not to say anything about Blomgren's farewell letter but asked if Petrus had appeared depressed over the last while. Arne Wiikman hesitated a few seconds before answering.

"He was a bit thoughtful," he said finally.

But he could not supply any reasons why. They hadn't seen each other for a few weeks. The contact between the two men had been limited to a phone call some weeks earlier. They had talked about an acquaintance they both had in common who had been run over by a bus in town and who was now in the hospital. During the conversation Petrus Blomgren had not brought up anything out of the ordinary or appeared despondent.

Before Ann Lindell got ready to leave she asked if Blomgren had ever talked about women.

Arne Wiikman smiled for the first time.

"He wasn't bad looking in his day, so I'm sure he had a lady friend at some point, I'm sure he did. Who hasn't, after all, but that's not something you run off at the mouth about, especially if things seem to have dried up."

"I thought that was when the talk really got started," Lindell said.

Wiikman chuckled.

"You want to hear some?"

"Let's do it another time."

Wiikman quickly became serious again.

"I wish he had found some peace."

"Is there anyone else who would be able to give me information about Petrus?"

"No," Wiikman said immediately.

"One last question: Petrus regularly sent money to Doctors Without Borders. Do you know why?"

"No idea," Wiikman said. "I don't even know what that is."

Back in the car Lindell took the Gysinge Road toward Uppsala, made a few phone calls, among others to Freddie Asplund, a new recruit, and asked him to check if it was possible to find twenty-two-year-old records of passengers on charter flights to Mallorca.

When she reached the roundabout at Ringgatan she made a turn in the direction of the Savoy, a bakery cafe. She needed to think.

✦

Sixteen

The murmur from the radio turned into music. Laura reached over and turned the volume up. It was a piece she knew so well but could not place. She turned the volume up even higher.

Should I prove to be weaker than those who have looked down on me all these years? she thought and hit the doorpost as she rushed out of the kitchen, away from the music. She stopped short, whirled around, and glared at the radio, at the shiny volume knob whose rounded slightly glossy, chubby surface seemed puffed up with self-satisfied smugness.

Should I be weaker?

"Never, never!" she screamed and leapt forward, grabbing the radio and throwing it to the ground, stamping on the gray-tinted cover. Albinoni's "Adagio in G Minor" was silenced. She continued assaulting the appliance until all that remained of it were broken parts. She left the kitchen panting, then ended up standing in the living room, listening.

"That was a close call," she muttered.

Her old life had tried to gain the upper hand.

What she feared most of all was to walk down the street and not exist, to step into the elevator at work and discover that the mirror reflected someone else, to exit the elevator and hear the poisonous tongues gabbing behind her back.

Never, never, never again. No one would ever trample on Laura Hindersten again. The music had stopped.

She swept her coat around her, opened the French windows as far as they would go, and then started to empty the bookshelves in the dining room. Fifteen books in each pile. Dust flew up. Some books fell on the floor and she kicked them out onto the terrace. Methodically she cleared case after case. There went the German collection, the early editions of Goethe, the beloved Voigt and the hated Kinz. Ditto two meters of filled bookshelves by and about Schopenhauer.

When Laura reached Virgil she hesitated for a moment but attacked the Roman classics with even greater determination.

Ariosto she tossed out with a laugh. Under "B" she had a difficult job with Bandella, Berni, Boccaccio, and Boiardo, and she was forced to sit down on the edge of the terrace to rest.

On the lawn in front of her feet lay the library Ulrik Hindersten had spent decades of labor collecting. At the very top lay Middlemore's English translation of Jacob Burckhardt's *Die Kultur der Renaissance in Italien*. Laura picked it up and skimmed through it absently. Her father's notes and underlinings indicated that he had scrutinized it alongside the original from 1860 in order to find errors and weaknesses.

She tossed it back onto the pile, stretched forward, and took up another that turned out to be a dissertation published in Zürich in the mid forties: *Cicero und der Humanismus. Untersuchungen über Petrarca und Erasmus.*

She remembered that one, as she did Mills's *The Secret of Petrarch* and de Nolhac's *Petrarch and the Ancient World,* which she also glimpsed in the heap of books. These, and many others, Laura had read in the eighties.

In June of 1987 Laura and Ulrik Hindersten had traveled to Italy. Laura was nineteen years old and had just graduated from secondary school. Her father had received a grant to write an extended research article on

Petrarch's epistolary exchange with Cola de Reinzó. It was intended that the text be included in a monograph published in honor of a professor in Lund who was to retire the following year.

Her father bit the sour apple—the professor was in reality one of his enemies—and set off on a two-month trip to Italy.

The first part of the trip they rented an old house outside of Florence. It sat up on a hill, surrounded by a neglected garden, and the city could be seen in the distance through a blue haze. Laura stayed on the upper floor.

Her father disappeared early every morning, sat in the archives, met with colleagues and old friends, while Laura read and took walks in the surrounding area. Laura liked the house and the little village and June was a pleasant time for walks. But she became depressed and sensed the reason why. June was a critical month. It was June 23—six years earlier—that Laura's mother had died.

Her father didn't notice her grief. Quite the opposite, he became more and more enthusiastic the longer they stayed in Tuscany. He repressed all thoughts of the Lund professor, started speaking only in Italian, and again brought up the idea of moving to Italy for good.

One day Laura decided to put him up against the wall. Why had he and her mother not been happy together? Her father put his teacup down on the rough-hewn wooden table, let his head droop with a despondent expression as if Laura had deliberately insulted him. It was an expression she knew well, from when he talked about his department.

"She didn't fight," he said finally.

She could tell he had chosen his words with care.

"Fight for what?"

"Pius II once said that a servant could rise to be king."

Laura stared at him. She didn't recognize the quotation, she didn't know what context it came from, but she knew this was a strategy on her father's part. He used the words in order to conceal the real conditions, or as a way to start a dialogue she did not want to have.

Her father loved to converse in dialectical play, in a labyrinth where nothing could be taken for granted, where all words turned out to be double-edged, carrying multiple meanings. It was an art he had mastered to the fullest extent.

"I am your daughter. I need simple, normal words," Laura said and tried to catch his eye without success.

"Words can be simple but when they are used in combination they necessarily become—"

"I need true words!"

"I wanted to protect you from everything unpleasant," he said with unusual mildness. "Your mother did not have this ability."

"You are no better than Petrarch," Laura said. "He went on about the pure and the divine but would fuck anyone given the chance."

Ulrik Hindersten was taken aback by his daughter's words. He had never heard her speak in such vulgar terms. He tried to interrupt but Laura went on in a frenzy that made her spit out the words.

"I am sick of all the words, all the empty words! You talk about love but when it comes to this life here and now then it's nowhere to be seen. Not even when Mom died did you say anything to comfort me. I have never heard you say anything nice about my mother."

"You know as well as I how Alice died," Ulrik Hindersten said, "but I choose not to talk about it. But if you want to, then go ahead.

"We loved each other," Ulrik Hindersten said after a long period of silence, "you know that. I have not met anyone after . . ."

"I am talking about the hypocrisy," Laura said. "On the one hand you valorize the Middle Ages, when you would find living then a hell. You have always wanted to be the best, despised by all colleagues and scholars. You have squashed students who have asked for guidance because you were afraid they would outshine you."

Unconsciously Laura assumed Augustine's role in close combat with Petrarch. She had read his *Secretum* and underlined long passages. Now everything was mixed up in a bitter concoction.

"A lack of inititative and indolence are names we today assign to modesty," Ulrik Hindersten countered with a smile where Laura discerned a streak of pride.

The battle raged on for a month. Ulrik Hindersten's *"Vallis clausa"* as he often referred to the little valley where they lived, was transformed into a battlefield. They clashed with increasing frequency. Ulrik was in his essence, this was his domain. Laura fought with the implacability and rebelliousness of youth, but she became worn down over time.

She started to imagine that Ulrik was fanning the flames of the conflict, that he loved it for its own sake but also because he wanted to make Laura in his image.

"You must be toughened," he said.

"I don't want to be like you!" she cried.

"You are like me. It's you and me. You are my blood."

"But also my mother's!"

"I don't think you should talk so much about Alice. You are stronger than that and you have the talents that are required."

"She saw beauty. You only see the dirt. You don't really see the olive trees, the cypresses and stone walls, they are only a stage set for a fantasy image. It is Petrarch's landscape, nothing more. You don't see the farmers who harvest the olives and struggle up the steep slopes to prune the grapevines, you talk to them but you have no words for their world. You laugh and they smile back but out of sheer politeness. You can't even climb a ladder without a quote by Cicero or Seneca. You think you can capture everything on a page but the sweat on a farmer's brow is a form of writing you can't read. For them the ladder is a ladder, for you it's a metaphor."

Laura moaned out loud and rocked from side to side. The memories from Tuscany were ambivalent: the upsetting discussions but also the unparalleled closeness she had experienced with her father. It was as if the endless debates had brought them closer than ever before.

He revealed things about his childhood, details about the grandparents she had never heard before. Ulrik's father, a high-ranking official at the National Customs Service, had been dead for many years. Laura had only a diffuse memory of a large man in a sick bed. Grandmother Hindersten had left the family when Ulrik was five years old. Why, and what became of her, was a taboo subject, but Laura did hear that she had gone to Denmark with a Dutch artist and had settled somewhere on Fyn. News of her death at the end of the seventies was received with indifference by her father.

She got up, stared at the mound of books. She realized that she could not set fire to them where they were, that it could spread to the house. She retrieved the wheelbarrow from the storage and started carting all the books over to the middle of the lawn.

It took a long time but Laura paid no attention to the fact that she was getting tired. To the contrary, she felt as if the soreness of her muscles freed her of a pain that had been too long in her life. The stack of books grew, and with it her conviction that the path she had chosen would lead her to freedom.

✦

Seventeen

On her way to the police headquarters in Salagatan, Ann Lindell walked past what was to be her new workplace come fall. A giant of a building was rising up at the end of Kungsgatan and it was already giving the city a new skyline.

It was not only a geographic shift. It also accorded police authority a more central position from a purely psychological standpoint. The building on Salagatan gave an uninspired and mundane impression. The first time she laid eyes on it, it made Ann think of disconsolate individuals at an unemployment agency. In contrast, the new creation with its provocative façade of glass and plaster promoted the position of the police in the city, gave them a more contemporary flair. Someone had compared it to a palatial bank or the offices of an insurance company.

Ann thought about the police headquarters in Malaga that she had visited on the job a few years back, an enormous building with an imposing exterior, but still with a relaxed atmosphere in the airy entrance, despite its location in an area with chaotic traffic.

In front of Uppsala's new police station the motorists now wound their way rather gingerly around the newly constructed and, according to many,

unnecessarily complicated roundabout. Several accidents had already occurred there and letters to the editor called it a new traffic disaster.

Several of Ann's colleagues had been by on study trips and admired the
view of the city they were there to protect. Sammy Nilsson said something
about Uppsala being enjoyed best from above and that the uppermost
floor was most likely reserved for the senior administration. From there
they could both look down on their fellow citizens and be close to heaven.

"The higher up you get, the smaller the problem looks," Sammy said.

"We're already cramped," Ola Haver filled in, "even before moving in.
The Recovered Goods department is moving to the Fyrislund industrial
area."

"That's only so people won't be able to find it," Sammy said. "Then we
can sell the loot and throw parties for the police club."

Ann Lindell smiled as she traced her way around the roundabout and
was still in a good mood when she turned onto Väderkvarnsgatan. She
was looking forward to leaving Salagatan. It would be a fresh start, she
imagined, kind of like leaving a rundown rental in some far-flung suburb
to a centrally located, sophisticated loft.

Whether their crime-fighting efforts would become more effective
was not as certain. She recalled Sammy's comment that it would be better to have ten, fifteen smaller stations scattered over town. That was his
alternative to "the fortress" as he called the new structure.

"And anyway it's built on such slippery ground that we're probably going to sink into the Uppsala clay."

Sammy's brother, who worked in construction, had told them about
all of the problems with the foundation. Marked heights changed from
one day to the next as if the ground was playing tricks on the workers.

"But they used piles," Haver objected.

"Piles," Sammy said with a snort. "Nature has her own laws."

Ann drove into the parking garage, parked the car, and took the elevator up to Violent Crimes, where things were almost completely quiet.
A copier was spitting out paper, someone shut a door, and another colleague was whistling the theme song from the movie *Titanic,* another
colossus that nature had taken care of.

She wondered who the building's Celine Dion was and deduced that it had to be Asplund, the new recruit, a young man who seemed as if he had recently stepped into the big world outside his boyhood bedroom. They should talk but he would have to wait. The work on the passenger lists was probably not done yet.

Ann Lindell knew that the investigation of the two murders was floundering. The conditions were not ideal. They had not found anything to lead them forward. Ottosson would talk about the "blindness of a lack of imagination." A good criminal investigator, or technician, had to have the ability to read the scene of a crime, and even be able to identify the victim's landscape.

Ann thought she had been able to come up with an idea of Petrus Blomgren. His landscape was known to her; she could articulate the connections that had directed Blomgren's life. With two exceptions: the intended suicide and the prescribed sleeping pills. These constituted a tear in the fabric that drew the gaze, that nagged at her.

She had encountered this before. It could be a person's dream, an old injustice, a humiliation that needled, itching like a stubborn mosquito bite.

Sometimes it was love, or the absence of love. Ann knew what that meant. Petrus Blomgren had lived a quiet life in an environment that he knew through all his senses. Everything was familiar and reassuring. Blomgren had had work, food, firewood and therefore warmth, and he could live, function as a citizen in Vilsne village, Jumkil county, Sweden, but something was missing: love, closeness to another person. Hadn't he written something about the fact that he had to make all of his decisions alone? There was the tear in Blomgren's life.

Ann wrote a few lines on her pad, got up from her desk, walked over to the window, and tried to link her line of reasoning with the second victim, Jan-Elis Andersson. He appeared just as alone but in this case the loneliness was of a different order.

"A load of shit," she said out loud and returned to her desk.

The primness of the Andersson household gave a different impression. Suddenly she thought of what it was: there was something calculatingly parsimonious about the house.

At Petrus Blomgren's the impression had been of something else, a kind of warmth that suffused the house in Jumkil. You could sense it in the small details like the occasional decorative items, the pictures on the walls, the little TV room, predictable in its simple, worn appearance, but nonetheless radiating a personableness that was absent in the house in Alsike.

At Jan-Elis Andersson's the bookshelves were the dominating feature, filled to bursting with light brown folders in hard-pressed cardboard, carefully arranged in chronological order. Why did one keep accounts, receipts and vouchers, ancient sale agreements and contracts with such meticulous care?

Money, Ann decided and doodled a little on the page. It was the concern about his own finances, need for order and a nervous cataloging of debit and credit that controlled Jan-Elis Andersson's life.

Perhaps he was happy with his folders, but there was probably also a source of concern and perhaps even anxiety. Was that the tear in Jan-Elis Andersson's life?

"BLOMGREN—LOVE" she wrote in capitals on her pad, followed by a heart. On the next line there was "ANDERSSON—MONEY" and a dollar sign.

The investigation into Andersson's life was in full swing. Sammy Nilsson and Ola Haver were the ones who were doing the digging and Ann believed they were going to verify her theory that money was the driving force in the murdered Andersson's life.

Lindell was speculating, she knew this, but from the swaying tower of loose theories that she was now constructing she would perhaps be able to provide herself with an overview.

She saw the process in an inner graphic, how she scrutinized the landscape, binding together Vilsne village, Jumkil and Norr-Ededy village, Alsike, and in the intersection between the imagined lines she would find the answer.

"It's that simple," she muttered, drew a few lines, and threw down her pen, suddenly aware of the fact that it was the first time she could see Uppsala and the surrounding area in her mind, exactly as she could with her childhood Ödeshög. She had become an Upplander.

With this conviction she left the office but returned immediately. It's not quite so simple, Upplander or not, she thought and opened the telephone directory. There she quickly found Birger Rundgren's name and number, and pulled the phone over.

The voice that answered betrayed the fact that Ann Lindell was speaking with an old man. He could not remember Petrus Blomgren, which did not surprise Lindell. Blomgren was not the one who ran to the doctor at the slightest twinge.

"But his medical entries are most likely still there," Birger Rundgren croaked. "My son, who has taken over the practice, can surely help you."

Lindell took down the number to Lars-Erik Rundgren, thanked him for his help, dialed the number, and smiled to herself as the phone rang.

It turned out that Rundgren Jr. sounded like his father.

"I have an upper-respiratory infection and shouldn't be speaking at all," he managed to squeeze out.

Lindell explained what she was after, gave the doctor her e-mail address, asked him to look for Blomgren's records, and then send her the information he felt was relevant.

The mail arrived in five minutes. Petrus Blomgren had, of his own accord, contacted Birger Rundgren, whose office was on Kungsgatan at that time, on the eighth of June 1981. They had never met before. Blomgren had cited sleeping difficulties as the reason for the visit. The reason for the problem was "that the pat. has felt anxious for a while." The doctor had noted that "not fin., wk, rel., loss."

Otherwise he appeared healthy, employed as a farmer and construction carpenter. He was prescribed Ansopal, one tablet per night. No follow-up visit was required.

Lars-Erik Rundgren concluded with an explanation of his father's cryptic abbreviations. According to his father there were four main reasons for poor sleep: bad finances, unhappy at work, love problems, or the loss of someone close to you. In other words, in Blomgren's case Rundgren senior had ruled out all four explanations.

What does that leave? Lindell wondered as she read the mail a second time. She surmised that the doctor's conversation with Blomgren had been short, that no real examination had taken place, that no diagnosis had been made, and that Rundgren had taken the easy way out.

✦

Eighteen

What surprised him was not Laura's pale skin that looked as if it never saw the sun, or the exquisite body that she had always managed to conceal beneath layers of clothing that betrayed a lack of attention to color and finesse. It was the abundance of hair.

He pulled his hand down her belly, his index finger tracing a dark line down to the luxuriant tendrils and swirling it around.

"Should I braid it?" he asked, turning his head and looking at her.

He had no idea what she was thinking and right now he didn't really care. He was still caught up in the physical rush, now mixed with a satisfied indolence, after the release of desire and a feeling of revenge.

Stig chuckled. She closed her eyes.

Laura had said at most ten words since he arrived. When he commented on the massacred bookshelves she shrugged and pulled him closer. She was dressed in a flowery dress that he imagined was very old. It reminded him of his grandmother's summer dresses.

The ghost-like house, Laura's silence, and the tense anticipation he felt made him talk. He talked about work, what the Germans had e-mailed and what he had replied. She did not seem interested.

Stig started to get cold.

"Laura," he whispered, "I have to go soon."

She opened her eyes. He saw the whites.

"We're going to have dinner," she said.

"I don't have time."

"Ribs."

"I have to go," he repeated.

Her eyes moved anxiously.

"Are you cold?"

He pulled up the covers and carefully draped them over her breast, got up on his knees and kissed her stomach and drew the covers further up over her body.

"You have to stay," she said.

"I can't."

He got out of bed. She stretched out and grabbed his elbow, looking him in the eyes.

"It's you and me, Stig, right?"

He nodded. She swung her legs over the edge of the bed, put her ear against his crotch, and started to talk.

"I'm cleaning out my old life. If you only knew how good that felt. I was no one before. I was half a person."

"You were a little depressed," Stig said. "That can happen to anyone."

"I held my tongue all these years but now I'm talking. I know many people don't like it. You should see how the neighbor watches me. When I carried the books out in the garden he stood there staring at me through the hedge."

"He must have been curious."

"He hates me. I think he's started a campaign in order to get rid of me."

"It's too bad about all the books," Stig said, and felt desire stir again. "You've been a little confused since your father disappeared," he continued and put his hand on her head.

"Maybe he's not my father," Laura said.

"What do you mean?"

She turned her head.

"Stay," she said.

"We can't keep going like this," he said and pressed her head to his crotch.

Jessica was waiting for him. He was sure she was sitting at their shared desk. He could see her clearly in his mind, illuminated by the globe-shaped lamp, how she put the last touch on the offer to the Germans, fine-tuning the wording and examining the numbers to the last little decimal.

He should also be there. More and more it felt as if the future of the firm stood and fell with the results of the negotiations with Hausmann.

Laura licked one side of his groin.

"I love you," she whispered.

He stared straight ahead. On the wall across from him there was a photograph of Laura and Ulrik Hindersten. He saw no details but sensed it had been taken in Italy. Laura was around twenty. Ulrik had his arm around her shoulders and smiled for the camera.

Next to it there was a framed picture of a little red cottage. It was the type of aerial photo sold in the forties and that no cottager, farmer, or householder could resist. The colors had faded of course, but it made even the humblest little cottage look grand. There was no indication of how extensive the grounds were. All sense of meagerness was gone.

Desire slowly drained away from Stig Franklin and he very gently detached himself from Laura. Her nails bored into his buttocks and he suddenly became afraid, as if he had missed his chance, passed up something of value, while he was making love to Laura, whose nails now scratched his buttocks and thighs.

"What are you doing?" he yelped and freed himself.

He pushed the curtain to the side and let in a little light in order to be able to hastily collect his clothes. Laura's pale face was blank, as if she didn't really understand what was happening.

Stig pulled on his pants and fumblingly buttoned his shirt but stopped when he caught her gaze.

"What is it?"

She didn't answer, simply pulling the covers around her.

"I have to go, don't you understand? We'll have to talk more later."

"We haven't talked at all," Laura moaned and Stig glanced at her quickly, tucking his shirt into his pants.

He fastened his cuff links and pulled his tie around his neck. Laura swiftly stood up, grabbed him by the tie, and pulled. Stig fell headlong onto the bed and Laura threw herself over him, still with a firm grip on the tie. The weight of her body across his chest and the noose that was being pulled increasingly tighter locked Stig to the bed. Laura neutralized his waving arms by scooting forward and pressing her knees across the tops of his arms.

She didn't say anything, released the pressure around his neck after a few moments, and pushed her crotch up toward his panting mouth.

"You're afraid," she whispered, "afraid of that witch."

"Laura," he croaked, "I can't breathe."

"Yes, you can."

He choked back a sob.

"You like making love to me, don't you?" she whispered.

He nodded eagerly.

"We have so much to catch up on," she continued.

Stig made an attempt to get away, braced his feet and pushed back while at the same time he turned his head to escape the noose around his neck.

"We have so much to talk about," he said and managed to free one arm.

Her forehead was burning as if she had a fever. He stroked her face softly and was overcome with a feeling of intimacy. Her heat radiated toward him, her damp and tensed body gave the impression of a hunted animal whose shiny skin did not offer any protection.

Laura let him caress her. She calmed down somewhat, her breathing slowed. Her anxious eyes closed briefly and she sighed heavily.

He stroked her face and throat, put his arm around her neck and drew her close and whispered words he had never said to Jessica. Rationally Stig knew this was madness and everything he said doomed his marriage to annihilation.

The scratches, the smell of her genitals on his shirt, the marks around his neck, and the fact that he came home so late spoke for him. Jessica would not believe a single word of his invented explanations, that only a few minutes ago had seemed so reasonable. There was simply nothing to say.

Did he love Jessica? He thought so, or wanted to believe it. His life was the firm and Jessica. When he thought about his life, she and the future of the company were the same thing.

"I wish I could step ashore," Laura said softly.

There was no desperation left in her voice.

"And where are you now?"

"On a stormy sea."

It was a good image. Stig had no trouble imagining Laura surrounded by a screaming sea with waves that crashed threateningly onto the deck and tugged on everything living.

"I always dream about a little harbor with a restaurant, you know, one of those charming little harbor pubs, where I can settle down."

"Then you should go there," he whispered.

Laura kissed his throat and pressed herself against him. He held her and felt great tenderness when he touched her frail back with ribs running down like a grate and the thin pillar of vertabrae he slowly traced with his finger all the way down to her buttocks.

"I'll stay for a while," he whispered. "So we can talk a little."

When they shortly thereafter sat on each side of the kitchen table, Laura with a cup of tea and Stig with a beer he had opened but not drunk, it was as if the intimacy from the bedroom and the feeling of shared vulnerability had been replaced by distance and silence. Stig tried to imagine them making love again but shielded himself. He looked at her. She looked naked, even though she had draped a robe around her.

He thought Laura looked as if she was constructed out of the most delicate glass and the fear that she was about to shatter made him hold back his words. He was not the protective harbor she was looking for. Not now, and most likely never. He intercepted himself weighing the possibility. Jessica would perhaps forgive a transgression, but he would have to break all contact with Laura. That would be the wisest course of action but at the same time he was tempted by the closeness they had felt for a brief moment.

Laura smiled suddenly and said something in Italian. Stig took a sip of beer.

She was something outside the norm, definitely something other than Jessica. He knew that a relationship between him and Laura was an impossibility, almost a laughable abnormality, but still he chose to stay in her presence.

She had lived with her father in this house for thirty-five years, now he was gone and she could breathe easily. Stig knew enough about Ulrik Hindersten to know that she must many times have been living in a hell. Laura seldom complained but there had always been an imprisoned animal's sorrowful and desperately wild look to her eyes. Now her father was gone, probably forever, but how free was she?

He caught himself staring at her throat and the breasts that peeked out from inside the robe. Laura smiled again and her beauty was like pain. She put down the teacup and laid her arms on the table. The open hands formed a bowl, a gesture that Stig had once seen a holy man do in a little village in the vicinity of Angkor Vat. That was before Jessica, before everything. The emaciated prophet rested with folded legs and by his side there was a little rice on a banana leaf. His loincloth was dirty, the legs extremely thin, and the stomach appeared glued to his spine.

Stig reached for the beer bottle and drained the rest of it, contemplating the bottle's elongated shape. He visualized Jessica's face against the dirty-yellow wall paneling. Her hair pulled back, the mouth open.

The desire to stay with Laura disappeared and left a bitter taste of grief paired with relief. It was as if he was saying good-bye to part of himself. He wiped some drops of beer from his chin. He tried to smile, but the more he managed the more the smile left Laura's lips.

Stig Franklin left the house in Kåbo at eight thirty. He ended up standing next to the car for a moment. He wished he would have been able to take off his clothes and be rinsed clean. The rain had increased during the evening. Now it was pouring down, whipping against the roof of the car and a small river was running burbling down into a drain.

He had an impulse to throw his car keys down the drain as well, leave the car, and simply walk, go as far away as possible. He turned his head and looked back at the house he had left. He could only see parts of the roof. Not so much as the light from the windows penetrated the bushes and trees.

But the neighbor's house was lit up. Small lamps, placed in two orderly rows from the street up toward the entrance, spread a dim light over the garden. Stig saw the shadow of a person flicker by in one of the windows. It was the odious professor that Laura had talked about. Stig had an idea of who he was. He thought they had bumped into each other once during a lunch at the Gillet.

Without a doubt the neighbor had noted the presence of the car in the street and perhaps even recognized him. It was not possible to be anonymous. To be a Rotary member and keep a mistress in Kåbo was a losing proposition.

He couldn't possibly return to Jessica in this condition. There would be trouble, he knew that, and not just that. He would in all likelihood be thrown out for good. It was Jessica's house, paid for by her former company, perhaps even by Torbjörnsson junior himself. Rumors had circulated but Stig had never paid any attention to them, nor asked Jessica how she could afford a house in Sunnersta, but more than once he had been made to feel that he lived there on her charity. He had offered to pay for half of the house, had even been to the bank and arranged the loan, but Jessica had curtly turned down his offer.

She wasn't one to let something slide. He would have to pack his things and leave. Stig Franklin shivered and sat down in the car.

The clothes that were soaked through reminded him of a canoe trip in Ströms Vattudal many years ago, when he had flipped the canoe and been convinced he was going to drown. That time he had managed to crawl up on a stony beach but his provisions and canoe were lost. Shaking with cold he heard the wind pick up and how the waves rose up out of the black water. He had the feeling that they were disappointed, furious that he had escaped them.

An old man, who lived very close to the shore, came walking along and led Stig to his cottage. They shared a bottle of grayish liquor in front of the fire and the old man entertained Stig with fantastic stories about log-driving, death by drowning, and the devilishness of the sea.

The man's love-hate relationship to the water seemed grounded in an ancient conviction that man lived off water but also under its curse.

"It is the same thing with fire," the old man went on to philosophize and spit into the fire. "It warms us, but devours us also. Like love."

Stig put his key in the ignition and at that moment Laura Hindersten's car rolled out onto the street. He saw it vanish around the corner before he realized completely that it was her. He backed up a few meters and saw that her car was no longer parked in the driveway.

Where was she going? She hadn't said anything about going anywhere. Stig followed her and saw her rear lights turn the corner at Artillerigatan. At Dag Hammarskjöld's Way she turned right. Stig got a red light and was forced to stop but now he had an idea of where she was headed.

He checked the traffic in the intersection. Everything was calm, there was only one car in sight and it was driving down the hill to the hospital. Stig drove on red and took up the chase.

Stig watched Laura park about twenty meters from his home, a "funkis" house at the end of a cul-de-sac. He braked and drove down the street very slowly. He was at a loss. Should he drive up, park the car, and go in, pretending he hadn't seen her car? The risk was great that she would make her presence known, perhaps call out to him, want him to stop and talk.

If he, on the other hand, parked on the street, chances were good that the neighbors would see his car and start to wonder what it was doing there. Even if he crouched over the Dahlströms would catch him, he was convinced of that.

He stopped but let the motor run. Laura's car was partly concealed behind a hedge but he could see her sitting inside.

The lights were on in the bottom story of his house. Stig could picture Jessica, how she sat in the study and went through the Hausmann document, with concentration but upset, always glancing at the clock in the right-hand corner of the computer screen. Many times he had admired her ability to set aside all worry and soldier on, effective and focused.

If Laura left her car and approached the house what should he do? Try to stop her? How could he do that without attracting attention on the street? She would most likely start to argue in a loud voice. Run her over? That would wake up the whole street.

Stig visualized Laura's pale body, crushed against the black asphalt. He sneezed once, twice. How would he explain it? That she ran out in front of his car and he hadn't had a chance to veer away? In Laura's current condition no one would consider that implausible.

Harder to explain the scratches to Jessica. She would be able to accept that he ran over a confused Laura, but she would never accept infidelity from him.

It started to rain harder. The Nilssons turned out the light downstairs. Gustav Rosén let out the cat. Poor devil, Stig thought, as he pushed the car into first gear and quickly drove up to the driveway, opened the garage door with the remote control, drove in, jumped out of the car, and pulled the door down. All done in the span of a few seconds.

He took out a knife from the toolbox on the workbench, tested its edge on his finger, and then cut the back of his trousers with four quick slices of the knife. There was a sting of pain as the knife went through the fabric and cut his skin, and he yelped. Before he threw the knife back he jabbed his right hand, then opened the door to the driveway, closed it as quickly behind him, and walked into the house.

"That fucking cat," he yelled as he shut the door to the laundry room and walked into the kitchen.

"What is it?" Jessica shouted from the study.

"Rosén's damn cat attacked me."

He poured water on his hand. Jessica came out into the kitchen and stared at him.

"The cat?" she said unusually stupidly.

"Yes, Rosén's damn tiger. He was sitting in the garage and when I got out of the car he attacked me."

"What was he doing in the garage?"

"How the hell would I know? It must have snuck in."

"Is it still there?"

"No, I kicked it out."

"You pants are ruined."

"I'll make that damn tree-hugger pay for it. And the cat should be shot!"

"Calm down. You must have scared it."

"Are you working?" Stig asked.

"Yes. Where have you been?"

"At Laura's. She called. She's dissatisfied with Hausmann. I think she's going a little nuts."

"She's been that for a long time. But why didn't you call?"

"It just didn't happen. I'm sorry, but she threatened to call Weber and tell him, well, you know, everything . . ."

"Call Weber!"

Stig was rejoicing inside. He had succeeded in diverting Jessica's attention and now he stoked the fire. The relief made him improve even further on his story, how he had stood in the rain at Laura's, anxious to get away, but how she had more or less attached herself to him, even pulling him by the tie, and kept arguing with him.

"She said something about there being sixty thousand euros reserved for extraordinary costs for phase B. Is that correct? It seems ridiculous."

"No, no, it's only half that," Jessica said.

"Can you check it?"

"I know it's thirty thousand."

"But could you check it, please? It's thrown me for a loop. She may even have gone in and changed it."

Jessica walked back to the study and Stig followed, pausing in front of the hall mirror to check if the marks around his neck were visible. He was red there but that sometimes happened when his shirts were too tight.

"It's thirty thousand!" Jessica shouted.

"Wonderful," Stig said with emphasis. "I'll jump in the shower and then we have to talk about what we're going to do about Miss Hindersten."

Laura saw Jessica get up from the computer when Stig went into the kitchen. She couldn't understand why he had arrived so much later than she had. Had he driven by the office?

Laura imagined them talking, how Stig told her everything, that he loved Laura and that his and Jessica's relationship had no future.

After several minutes Jessica returned to the computer. She looked calm. Her hair shone in the light of the desk lamp. Stig was nowhere to be seen.

Laura stepped out of the car.

She realized there had been no confrontation. He was too cowardly, afraid of that witch. Laura had been too, before, but all fear had disappeared when she realized how life should be lived. It was as if a voice had spoken to her: It's time to settle accounts with your old life, Laura!

She remembered how strong this voice had been and reminded herself that it was necessary because of how many difficulties she had had to overcome. Shattered, she sat at the kitchen table asking herself how she was going to carry on while the radio reported the results of the referendum on the European Monetary Union. Then, somewhere beyond the fear that twisted her innards, there came the sound of victorious music and a voice that rattled off confident proclamations: No room for doubt! Strike back!

Sometimes this voice was interrupted by a collage of Italian voices but it always returned even stronger, filtering out the static in her head. She laughed with relief, pushed away the knife, whose edge she had tested on some fruit, and walked out into the library, finally clear on how the whole thing was going to be done.

Laura walked closer to the house, bent some branches down, and stared at her rival. She had an impulse to step into the square of light thrown onto the dark lawn by the light through the window, which would illuminate her like a spotlight on an otherwise dark stage.

She stared at the hateful woman who seemed so self-sufficient in her blond beauty and her purposeful, measured movements in front of the computer.

Only one thing held Laura back. It was not yet time to strike back. It was something Ulrik had taught her, strangely enough: patience.

✦

Nineteen

There was a gentle knock at the door. Mr. Sund, Ann thought immediately, but remembered that he was at a lecture at the Gottsunda Library. He had mentioned that the day before.

She walked over to the door and listened. Who knocked at half past eight in the evening? Perhaps the lecture was over and Sund wanted to tell her something exciting.

"Who is it?"

"The police," said a voice on the other side.

Ann put on the security chain and gingerly cracked the door.

"Hi, hope I'm not disturbing you. I didn't want to ring the doorbell in case your boy was sleeping."

Charles Morgansson took up the entire landing, or so it seemed to Ann. How big he is, she thought, and unhooked the chain.

"Come in. No, you're not disturbing anything. Erik has been asleep a long time. I'm just looking over some papers. You shouldn't take your work home but sometimes I think better at home. It was nice of you to knock. I thought it was my neighbor, he usually knocks. Do you want anything?"

Morgansson smiled.

"That was a lot of info at once," he said. "And one question. No, thank you."

Ann felt herself blushing.

"Please feel free to hang up your coat," she said, staring into her apartment.

A pair of pants and a blouse were thrown over a chair and Erik had put together his wooden train tracks in the middle of the hall floor.

"I'll pick up a little. Erik makes these messes. He has a little cold."

She walked rapidly around the living room, picked up the wineglass and looked around uncertainly then put it down behind a curtain. The bottle, she thought, but at the same time she remembered she had tossed it into the trash.

"You have a nice place," Morgansson said.

"Oh, I don't know," Ann said and straightened the cushions on the couch. "When you live by yourself . . . well, you know. Do you feel like having anything?"

"No, thanks. I've just come from my cousin who lives nearby, just two buildings down actually. Svante Henriksson is his name."

"No, no one I know," Ann said.

"He was actually the one who lured me down here, to Uppsala I mean. He talked so warmly about the city so when . . . We played basketball together earlier."

Ann nodded. Why did he come here, she wondered, while she kicked some toys under an armchair.

"How are things at work?"

"You know that as well as I do," he said and laughed.

"Yes, I guess," she said sheepishly.

They sat down across from each other.

"Maybe you'd like a glass of wine? Or a beer?"

He shook his head. Make this easier for me, she thought, and got a little exasperated with her smiling colleague.

"There's something I've been thinking about," he said as if he had read her mind. "Why do you kill yourself? Blomgren wanted to, though he didn't have the opportunity. Do you think he would have gone through with it?"

"I do. He was the type of person who followed through on his plans."

"But why? Sick of life? I don't think so. There was something that weighed on him. Had he hurt somebody?"

"Who would that be?" Ann asked.

Morgansson laughed suddenly.

"It's silly to sit here and talk about work. You must think I'm totally crazy."

He stopped and looked at her.

"Should we do it again? The movies, I mean."

Ann nodded. Morgansson got up abruptly.

"It's time for me to go," he said and Ann barely had time to react before he was at the door, putting on his coat.

Then he left as quickly as he had arrived. Ann Lindell had the feeling that he was out on an inspection round to check out her place.

When she fetched her wineglass from behind the curtain she looked out the window and saw him walk swiftly across the courtyard. The unpredictable manner, the rapid changes, the short lines, and the flash of his smile that changed as quickly into serious reflection, confused her.

Morgansson reminded her of a thief, Malte Sebastian Kroon, whom Ann had come into contact with many years ago. "The Jewel" as he was called, was quick both in his thinking and with his hands. He stole with a restless energy, driven by a fire greater than that of most in his field. At a house search in Kroon's home on Svartbäcksgatan they recovered over seven hundred items that could be classified as stolen, among these over eighty pairs of shoes. In the interrogation sessions he denied everything, but with such humor and quick wit that his replies were still repeated among the officers at the station.

Charles Morgansson did not appear as humorous, but the quickness and the disarming smile were things he had in common with Kroon.

Ann remained standing in the window long after he was out of sight and looked out at a rain-hazy Uppsala. She held her breath and tried to perceive the faint whistling sounds from Erik's room and her own inner voice.

"I'm fine," she muttered.

The following days nothing happened to help further the murder investigations. Of course, Ottosson claimed that they drew closer to solving the cases with each detail that they added to the case files, even if none of them could see it themselves. It was a worn cliché that afforded them little comfort.

Sammy Nilsson's mapping of Jan-Elis Andersson's life constructed the picture of a stingy, if not greedy, man. His own pedantic documentation bore witness to this. The oldest item was a receipt for a toaster bought in 1957.

A disagreeable man, Nilsson said in conclusion, who himself put all his important documents in a box, pushed into the bookcase with all the photos he was someday going to put into an album that he had not yet managed to buy.

It took him two working days to go through the folders but he had not found anything eye-catching, nothing that awakened interest or gave any clue to why the man had been clubbed to death in his own kitchen.

When Andersson's financial assets were added up the final sum was around one million *kronor*. On top of this was the value of his property and all the inventory. Strangely enough there was no will and his niece was most likely the one who would inherit it all.

Lindell decided that Sammy Nilsson should go to Umeå and question the beneficiary, Lovisa Sundberg, and her husband, the architect who was confined to a wheelchair.

Nilsson took the morning flight to northern Sweden, returned the same day, and then reported back on his excursion in a meeting late that afternoon.

"They live in an area called Pig Hill," he told them and sounded as if he thought it fit them perfectly.

"Were they pig-like?" Lindell asked.

"Stuck-up, if you like. If I had just been made a millionaire so painlessly I wouldn't be so damn sour."

"Painlessly," Lindell objected. "We're talking about a murder."

"They weren't grieving a whole lot, that much was clear. I got the impression that they only kept in touch with the old man because of the inheritance that was coming their way."

"Were they sure of it then?"

"Hard to say. They asked if there was a will."

"Did they know Petrus Blomgren?" Ottosson asked.

Sammy Nilsson shook his head. He told them that Lovisa Sundberg had lived in Uppsala for a short time in order to study. She was a teacher and had studied French at the university in order to expand her competency. During that time she had lived in a small cottage on her uncle's farm.

For a while she had thought about staying on in Uppsala but then she had met the architect, who was not disabled at that time, and he had a well-paying job in Umeå. So when she was done with her studies she moved up there.

Jan-Elis Andersson was both angry and disappointed. He would have liked to have seen his niece stay on, probably with the thought that he would get help with the horses he was taking care of on the farm.

"Cheap labor," Ola Haver said.

"She was allowed to live there for free in exchange for helping out in the stables," Sammy Nilsson said. "From what I can understand that was a lot of work."

However they twisted and turned the case of the niece and her husband they couldn't find anything that made it likely that the Umeå couple had any connection to the crime. Both of them had excellent alibis and it was at the very least improbable that they would have hired a killer.

Ann Lindell was finding it hard to concentrate. She was completely convinced of a connection between the two murders and the niece appeared less interesting. She let her thoughts run away and internally summed up the advances of the past few days, or rather, the lack of advances.

Checking the passenger lists to Mallorca had turned out to be impossible to do. The records simply didn't exist any longer. Lindell considered whether or not it was worth the effort to try to gather information on the hotels in Mallorca. Perhaps they could find Blomgren's name in some register, but it was likely that even these had been destroyed or were unavailable after twenty years.

Contact with a dozen or so members of the Federation of Farmers who could possibly give information about both of the men's activities within the farmers' co-op turned out to be a waste of time. There was nothing that spoke for the fact that Andersson and Blomgren had ever met in the context of the organization.

No witnesses had stepped forward to say anything about a suspicious car or any unknown persons who had moved in the murder victims' circles, either in Alsike or Jumkil.

The cases were slowly going cold. Lindell didn't like it. Or rather, she hated it. Two unexplained murders were simply too much. She could also see it in Ottosson. He was becoming increasingly tense as the days went by. His former cheeriness had been replaced by an irritable impatience.

Even the newspapers had stopped writing about the murders. The first few days' fat headlines bore witness to the journalists' excitement. The "Country Butcher" became an accepted concept. Now everything was quiet. Lise-Lotte Rask, who was responsible for press information, said that a few isolated reporters diligently called to see if there had been any breakthroughs. She thought she could almost discern a sneer to their pointed questions.

Lindell caught herself thinking about Charles Morgansson. Since his brief visit they had bumped into each other, said hello, and exchanged a few words but nothing had been said about another movie date.

She decided to give him a call. Maybe they should go out Friday?

"What are you smiling about?" Sammy Nilsson interrupted her thoughts.

Lindell glanced at Ola Haver, the one in the assembled group whom she thought best knew her thoughts, before she answered.

"Pantyhose." She smiled sweetly at Sammy. For once he was rendered speechless.

Back in her office she discovered that trainee Asplund had been in again. There were two reports on her desk. One was a report on who had lived in Vilsne village the last two decades. Lindell had asked the trainee to assemble this information. It involved about fifty people altogether. Ann looked through the list without really knowing what she was after.

The second report was a compilation of all the people who had gone missing in the district over the past year. She was surprised at the number, ten people, but knew that most of them would turn up again of their own accord. Most of the ones who disappeared without a trace did it of their own free will and were really no case for the police if they didn't involve underage individuals.

Two names on the list interested Ann more than the others and only because they were older men: Helmer Olsson, eighty-two years old, a former rubber worker from Rasbokil who disappeared in August. His wife thought he must have gotten lost but search parties that had been undertaken in the deep mushroom-filled forests north of his village had not yielded any results. Helmer Olsson's mushroom basket had been recovered at the edge of a swampy area. Perhaps he had gone down in the bottomless quagmire that was locally referred to by the name of "Oxdeath."

The other name was Ulrik Hindersten, a seventy-year-old professor, reported missing at the end of September. The person who reported him was the daughter, Laura Hindersten, with the same address as her father.

The results of the investigations added up to zero.

Ann checked who had taken down the information, looked at the time, and lifted the telephone receiver in the hopes that her colleague was still at work. Åsa Lantz-Andersson answered immediately and told her what she knew about Laura Hindersten, a woman she remembered very well.

After the conversation it was time to pick up Erik. Lindell went into Ottosson's office and told him that she had to bring Erik in for a medical checkup the next day, and that after that she was going to go see a woman whose father had disappeared.

"You think there's a connection?"

"I don't know, but we have to dig into everything."

Ann Lindell left the police station feeling unusually happy. Maybe it was because the sun was shining for the first time in several days. Admittedly the sun was only able to break through a small gap in the cloud cover but she took it as a good sign.

When she got home she was going to call Morgansson.

✦

Twenty

The flames reached almost as high as the snowball bush. Laura had to retreat because of the heat. For a few moments she was worried but told herself the damp grass was not flammable.

To burn books, she thought and remembered how her father, during a trip to Florence, had lectured her about Savonarola who had incited people to burn books during Carneval.

Ulrik Hindersten was divided in his opinion of this Dominican, who was a "devil" in that Petrarch's and Livius's books were on the bonfire. He took this as a personal insult and expressed genuine sorrow at how many antique texts had thereby been lost.

But her father also admired Savonarola as a speaker and for his ability to engage his audience. There was something attractive about his popularity. Her father appreciated strong personalities who were able to motivate the masses.

Savonarola ended up much like the books he had banned. Her father had taken her to Piazza della Signoria in Florence, the square where the monk was humiliated and burned as a heretic. With his Italian friends he discussed whether or not it was right to declare Savonarola a saint.

These debates were very much to Ulrik Hindersten's taste. Laura remembered how she had admired his ability to find arguments in the hour-long disputes.

Now Livius and Petrarch were destroyed in her own bonfire, and they burned well, the new dissertations as well as the old volumes, bound in calfskin and representing centuries of learning.

She followed the black flakes with her gaze and noted with satisfaction that many of them were blowing in the professor's direction. She bent over and picked up a slim volume of Capablanca and tossed it onto the fire. The pages flipped nervously in the wind before they were caught by the flames and were transformed into sooty confirmations of Laura's decree.

With tense anticipation she stared into the fire as if against the black paper there would appear the glimmer of a message about what her new life was going to look like. Laura crouched down, leaned forward, the heat brought tears to her eyes, and she was gripped by a feeling of solemnity as if at a graduation or funeral. She was so moved that she did not hear the car that parked on the street, nor the light steps across the mossy lawn.

"Excuse me, are you Laura Hindersten?"

Laura had to steady herself with a hand against the ground in order not to fall into the dwindling fire, and she turned toward the woman who was standing a few meters away.

"I'm sorry if I startled you. My name is Ann Lindell and I'm with the police."

Laura looked at her sooty hand and then gazed at Ann. Clearly, Laura could see her but it was as if her unsteady gaze could not bear to bring her into focus. Several seconds went by before she answered.

"Yes, my name is Laura Hindersten. What is this about?"

The voice was pleasing, completely devoid of concern or surprise. Ann saw how the woman in front of her changed from emotionality to coldness, as she stood up calmly and smiled.

"It's about your father, as perhaps you've guessed."

Åsa had forewarned her. Laura Hindersten was snobby and treated the police as if they were idiots and therefore Lindell unconsciously wore a stern expression.

"Because of some other cases we are checking on the individuals who have gone missing recently, and your father disappeared in September."

Laura Hindersten looked watchful. Lindell discovered that there was something mocking about her smile and had the thought that her father had returned. What if this woman was pulling something over on her? Was Ulrik Hindersten having a cup of coffee in the kitchen?

"Have you heard from him at all?"

Laura shook her head.

"What are you burning?"

"Old junk."

Ann Lindell bent down, picked up a book, and read the title on the spine.

"That's Livius's first book," Laura said.

Lindell hesitated in the middle of dropping the book back onto the ground. Laura took it out of her hand.

"Who was Livius?"

"A Roman."

Lindell was satisfied with the answer. Laura threw the book onto the fire, which was giving off a pleasant heat. Fires invite reflection and neither of the two women felt it was strange that they stood silently for a while side by side and watched Livius's words go up in flames.

"That was that," Laura said.

"Is it a series?"

"Series," Laura giggled, "Ulrik should have heard that. Yes, there's maybe some hundred and fifty books."

"And you're burning them all?"

"No, most of them have disappeared and there are only a few that have been translated into Swedish."

Lindell looked at the woman next to her. She hadn't noticed any of the heralded snootiness; instead Laura seemed to have more of a thoughtful, almost meditative aspect. Laura met her gaze and smiled introspectively.

Lindell wished she was a smoker. Then she would have taken out a cigarette, lit it, and then smoked it in peace and quiet while the fire so eagerly licked up the rests of Livius and all the others.

"Sometimes I think Ulrik is here," Laura said quietly.

"Do you think he's alive?"

Laura shrugged.

"Do you know anyone by the name of Petrus Blomgren or Jan-Elis Andersson?"

"No."

"Do you read the paper?"

When Laura made no attempt to answer, Lindell continued.

"Maybe you've heard about the two farmers who were murdered last week? They were the same age as your father."

Laura smiled at her and Lindell's feeling that the woman in front of her was unwell was strengthened.

"I'm thinking of going away. There are beaches that . . . my father . . ."

She stopped in the middle of a sentence, her mouth half open as if the

words didn't want to leave her mouth. Lindell had an impulse to shake her so they would fall out.

"Can we go in and talk? The fire looks like it will take care of itself."

They sat down at the dining room table. Lindell noted the mess but decided not to ask more about Laura Hindersten's cleaning project. Instead she tried to get her to talk more about her father.

After a moment of hesitation Laura became more animated. Lindell could listen, study her features and shifting expressions as the narrative progressed at a comfortable pace. She had the feeling that she was listening to a public radio lecture, the type of program that she all too often turned off, but that at those times when the tempo around her were conducive to listening, were an invitation to closeness to another person and a restful reflection.

Ann recalled how she had listened to a conversation between two women who had both been abused by their husbands and how that dialogue had taught her more than all of the seminars, arranged by various lecturing professionals, that she had participated in.

She fairly soon developed a kind of understanding for why Laura was burning her father's possessions and although she found it wasteful and unethical to burn books as if they were junk, she could identify with Laura's feelings and motivations. She used the word "free" on several occasions and then her voice took on a special quality, like a chord that a newcomer to the guitar has just learned and strums again and again with pride and wonder at the harmonious sound.

"You see," Laura said and brushed her hand across the table, "love and knowledge, Augustine's words. Ulrik had ideas, but most of them were borrowed."

Lindell looked at the hand on the dark tabletop. Laura sighed and the hand stopped.

"You didn't want to walk in his footsteps?"

"For a while, maybe. You saw the books; I've read most of them. When I was twenty I knew three languages, besides Swedish and Latin, and a little colloquial French."

She laughed a little.

"But I don't have any words for the simplest things."

"I can speak Eastern dialect pretty well," Lindell said.

"Stick with that," Laura said.

Lindell again looked at Laura's hand on the table, thin, almost transparent, with well-groomed nails, a round smudge of soot on the back of her hand that spread into a fine-veined pattern when she balled up her fist.

"Would you like a glass of wine?"

Ann shook her head

"No, of course not," Laura said with a smile.

She got up, walked over to a small table in one corner of the dining room, and took out a bottle of red wine.

"One of best things about Ulrik was that he taught me to appreciate wine. Only the best was good enough. This is a La Grola from 1990."

She put out the half-empty wine bottle.

"Bought in a small place north of Verona," Laura went on, and pulled out the cork. "Smell it! Produced by Allegrini. They became our friends, like many others in Valpolicella. We traveled around the vineyards and wineries. Ulrik could really charm people."

Ann leaned forward and positioned her nose over the bottle. It smelled different than the cheap red wines she usually drank.

"We were often guests of the Alighieri family. One of Dante's sons bought the property and it is still owned by the family. The thirteen hundreds," she added when she saw Ann's quizzical expression.

"You have to spend more than one thousand *kronor* for this, maybe more, I don't know. The cellar is full of bottles."

Laura stopped and looked at the bottle.

"I think my mother knew more about life and love than Ulrik," she continued more thoughtfully.

"Do you miss her very much?"

Laura didn't answer immediately.

"My mother came from the countryside and had a language for it. It worked. There weren't many who could talk and laugh like her, but she couldn't do it here, not in this house. It feels as if all of that has been lost. I sometimes imagine that there are people somewhere who speak like my mother, some dying population that is hanging on in a forgotten landscape."

"Don't you ever see relatives on her side?"

"No. I have three cousins, but I never see them. Their mother was Alice's sister. I don't even know if their houses are still there. I'm not sure I remember their language."

Ann thought about Vilsne village.

"My life has always been driven by others," Laura continued, "but now I've decided to change all that."

"Do you have any idea why your father disappeared? Do you think it may have been voluntary?"

Laura shook her head.

"He was too much of a coward to take his own life."

"He might be alive."

"No!"

"You seem very certain."

"He wouldn't leave this life voluntarily," Laura said in a voice that was barely audible.

Ann Lindell suddenly had a feeling of claustrophobia but squelched her impulse to get up and leave the house.

Laura retracted her hand from the table. She whispered something that Lindell couldn't hear. If Laura had seemed like an open and reasonable person only a minute or so ago, with even a touch of humor in her comments, her sunken posture and tightly clenched hands resting in her lap testified to a woman in the grips of enormous confusion and anxiety.

She glanced at Lindell who could sense both helplessness and fury in Laura's gaze. It reminded her of a prisoner, someone who all at once becomes aware of the massive walls and the closed door.

"What was your mother's maiden name?"

"Andersson," Laura said quickly as if she had been expecting that very question.

"Where was she from?"

"Skyttorp."

Lindell tried to place the name. It was an area north of the city, she knew that much but no more. She stood up and Laura flew up from her chair.

"Thanks for the chat," Lindell said and stretched out her hand. "I have one last question and you don't need to answer if you don't want to. Did your father abuse you?"

Laura let out a short laugh, a dry, sharp laugh.

"Is that what you think? Yes, he abused me, every day."

Lindell wanted to take hold of Laura, who noticed her impulse and took a step back.

"He abused me with words. And now I'm burning all the words," she spat and gestured with her head to the garden.

When Ann Lindell had left Laura remained standing for a moment in the middle of the room.

After reassuring herself that the policewoman's car really had left the street and that the fire had died down without setting fire to the grass, Laura went back in, opened the basement door, and walked down. She took the thirteen steps very carefully, turned the lightbulb so it would go on, and looked around. Everything looked normal. And who would have been down here?

It consisted of a storage area that, like the garage, had served as a storage place for a variety of unused items, a laundry room that had not been used since her mother's death, and a boiler room where the old wood-fired boiler rested like a surly animal from the past. Next to the boiler room there was a poorly lit section where the wood was stored.

The policewoman's visit had made her talk. It was the first time she had spoken of her father in that way. It was as if the outspokenness had delivered her, as if the words became more true once they were out in the open. They had been thought so many times over the years, now they had been uttered and were thereby legitimate, that was how she felt.

The visit had also set off an uncertainty in her that now forced her to go down into the cellar. She had been tempted to crack the door to her inner life and afterward had had the thought that there was something secretive about the policewoman's visit, that the police knew more than this Ann Lindell had wanted to say. She had of course not asked to inspect anything but there was something about her questions that had worried Laura.

Checking the cellar calmed her. She sat down on the stairs even though the bad air made her feel sick. It was laden with memories. On the worn concrete in front of her was where her mother had lain in a crumpled position, her arms outstretched as if she had thrown herself from the top step in order to fly but had never gained air under her wings and had crashed to the floor.

Laura made herself stay put and she felt as if she was paying a vague debt, unsure of to whom, and that with each payment she was lifting a portion of the suffering from her shoulders.

She wished she could get up, leave the cellar, and emerge as a new person, clean and brave in the way the world demanded.

"I want to be normal," she muttered. Many times she had cursed her life as the daughter of a man who saw the ordinary as a weakness, a sickly defect.

Now she was paying back but she knew deep inside she would never be debt-free.

A memory from Italy surfaced in her mind. It was early spring, the cherry trees in the mountains above Verona had just blossomed. Ulrik and she winding along the hairpin roads. He was driving jerkily, unused to the rental car, sweaty and stressed because they might have taken a wrong turn.

Laura didn't care. She admired the view and the trees, with shiny trunks as if they had been polished with rags, and the intense flowering that was flooding the valleys and hillsides, and Laura thought it looked as if God had laid out all his bedclothes for airing.

In a little village that only consisted of six or so stone houses, above Negrar, Ulrik stopped to ask for directions. Laura also got out, a little dizzy from the hairpin curves and walked into an orchard, sitting down on a low wall whose stones could hardly be seen because of wild cascades of yellow-flowering runners. Bees were buzzing in the trees. In the background she heard Ulrik's voice. She got up and started to walk down the hillside between rows of trees. The buzz became louder and created a sound weave of low, contended activity.

Laura turned and looked back. The houses of the village could no longer be seen. A valley that cut down between the steep hillsides reminded her of a fruit, whereas the occasional house resembled dark seeds in the green-white flesh. She paused and experienced a couple of seconds of absolute silence before a dog started to bark somewhere in the valley. Angry, aggressive. She turned around but caught sight of movement between the trees. It was a woman and a man. No longer young, perhaps in their forties, they sat leaning against a tree, talking eagerly. The man laughed and the woman joined in, bopping him lovingly on the head. He grasped her arms, sort of winding himself around her and they rolled onto the ground, tightly entwined.

Laura looked away and started to walk back to the village but then stopped and looked back at the couple. They did not seem to have noticed her presence. The woman's pale shoulder stood out. The man kissed her neck. Her hands moved under his shirt, pulled it out of his pants, and exposed his back.

Laura curled up. She was perhaps twenty meters away from the couple. Their excitement, accompanied by the bees' zealous industry, was carried through the air by a warm, sweet breeze. Laughter, a few words, but above all the passion in the lovers' movements. Enchanted by the timeless scene she watched them take each other's clothes off, how the man with a few quick moves arranged their clothes into a kind of bed for their lovemaking.

When he entered her she cried out. Laura ran off, tripping between the same trees where she had experienced such peace and tranquility only a few minutes ago.

Ulrik was standing by the car looking displeased. He complained about the farmers and the fact that she had disappeared. Now they would definitely arrive late to the Allegrini family.

Laura stared into space, panting after the quick run, indifferent to her father's reproaches and exhausted by what she had seen. She felt as if she was bursting inside in a remarkable mixture of fear, anger, and excitement.

She had to turn around, away from her father, and stare out at the hill on the other side of the road where the grapevines tied to supports resembled people hung up on a cross, holding hands in a ring dance on an enormous Golgotha.

She wanted to stay in the village, but when Ulrik shut his car door she got in on the passenger side, gathering up her body into a little package that was going to be transported down the hill toward Fumene. Nothing of the landscape lingered on her retina. It was as if she was traveling through a tunnel. Before her she only saw the woman's naked skin, her oustretched throat, and the passion that had joined her with the man.

Allegrini welcomed them and Ulrik's apologies with his usual hospitality. Marilisa Allegrini had opened a bottle of Amarone in advance that she immediately poured into some unusually beautiful glasses. They raised their glasses in a toast and drank. As usual when wine of the best quality was involved, Ulrik was amiable in that chivalrous way that all Italians appreciated, especially from a foreigner.

The somewhat bitter cherry note in the wine reminded Laura of the village and the orchard. She stared down into the dark wine. One of the Allegrini brothers was watching her, their eyes met for a second, and she tried to smile.

"What a spring," he said.

Laura stood up, took a deep breath, and then walked with heavy steps up the stairs. She lost her balance once and had to steady herself with a hand against the wall. Perhaps it was the wine, perhaps it was the flood of memories that streamed through her, that caused her misstep.

She tried to set Italy aside and instead think about the policewoman who had come to see her. Ann Lindell was not someone who, if you met her on the street, you would react to in any particular way, Laura thought, but the deliberateness with which she practiced her profession appealed to Laura.

She had asked about Petrus Blomgren and Jan-Elis Andersson. Laura smiled to herself. The police could search all they liked, it didn't matter to her. They didn't know about Ulrik Hindersten's life and her own secrets. How could they understand anything about real life?

✦

Twenty-one

Mirabelle was not an ordinary mare. Everyone who saw her jump realized this. The combination of unruffled calm combined with the explosiveness at the obstacles, which never ceased to amaze Carl-Henrik Palmblad, made her one of the most promising three-year-olds that he had ever seen on the track.

When Ellinor rode her he was sometimes worried. Mirabelle was so powerful in her approach and takeoff that Ellinor seemed at the mercy of powers that she had no hope of controlling. But it always went well. It was as if the mare considered her movements so precisely, in the closest coordination with the rider's qualities, that he never really had to fear that his grandchild would come to any harm.

Mirabelle was very strong and tireless, with a competitive spirit that promised a great deal for the future. Carl-Henrik Palmblad's greatest source of joy was perhaps not Mirabelle herself but the fact that Ellinor spent so much time in the stables. She came more frequently, and those times he wasn't able to give her a ride she took the bus from the city. Of course it was the jumping that attracted her and above all the fact that Mirabelle had become her best friend, as she put it, but it had also meant that the two of them, grandfather and grandchild, grew closer.

Ellinor was his darling. He would never have thought that contact with her would mean so much. His time as a father, when Magnus and Ann-Charlotte were young, appeared in hindsight as one big haze. He could not recall many times during their childhood when they actually did things together, but now every day that Ellinor came to the stables was a celebration.

They talked about all manner of things. He was able to take part in her everyday dreams, the conflicts with her parents—where Carl-Henrik almost always took her side—and how things were at school. When she started seeing a boy he was the one who heard about it before anyone else. And when it ended, he was the one who had to comfort her.

Ellinor had a knack with horses. Ann-Charlotte, her mother, had also done a lot of riding but without the same burning interest and conviction.

Now she would ride occasionally when she came out to the stables, mostly to get away from Folke, Ellinor's father, who was the one who paid for everything. He had bought the farm, paid for the fences and renovation of the stables. However, Carl-Henrik was the one who had bought Mirabelle, and he was grateful for that. Even if Folke got tired of sponsoring his daughter's and father-in-law's thing for horses, Mirabelle was there and Carl-Henrik was never going to let her go.

Sometimes he imagined that his son-in-law was jealous of him because he had the best contact with Ellinor. But other times he didn't think Folke cared much for either his wife or his daughter.

He had felt something in his back as he dragged out the hard-pressed bales of hay. He had enjoyed an inactive lifestyle and he had to pay for that now. His joints were stiff and despite many years of riding he was not particularly strong. On the other hand Lindberg, who helped out every other day, was just as broken down, and he had been physically active his whole life: orienteering, the Vasa race, and swimming in Vansbro.

He decided to do the exercises that his chiropractor had recommended, and he laid down on his back on the floor. The movements were difficult at first but after a few minutes the stiffness started to give way and it felt much better.

It was strange to see the room from below. Lying on the floor changed the objects in the room and distorted the perspective. Once Lindberg had found him lying here and the old engineer had looked completely different. Not only because of the surprised expression on his face but also because of the altered proportions. Lindberg, who normally looked very timid, made an almost demonic impression. The highly ordinary nose appeared enormous; the mouth, which normally had a little smile, looked frighteningly cavernous; and the eyebrows stood out like black brushes on a wild animal, as Lindberg gaped at him on the floor.

Palmblad bent his knees and pressed them up against his stomach, rested, and then repeated the maneuver. He felt his spine crackle and his lower back relax.

Suddenly he heard the door at one end open. It gave off a characteristic creak. Palmblad sat up. If it was Lindberg he didn't want to be found on the floor again. It was a bit like being caught with your pants down; he didn't want to appear to Lindberg as an old weakling.

But it was strange. Lindberg had very established habits and never came in on Mondays. Carl-Henrik Palmblad stood up, brushed off his backside, and cracked the door. The corridor down the middle of the stables was still and deserted. No one was to be seen. He craned his neck. The door at the end of the stables was closed. One of the horses neighed. Another kicked a stall door so it rattled.

I was mistaken, he thought and went back into the room and picked up a bridle. The fact was that he was worried about his hearing. Many times he didn't hear what Ellinor had said and had to ask her to repeat herself, but what was even more serious was that he heard things, voices and foreign sounds, that no one else perceived. He could be completely alone and still hear someone speaking. In the evenings he had a buzzing sound in his ears.

"Tinnitus," Ann-Charlotte said when he complained of it, "it's all the opera arias that have ruined your ears."

He smiled to himself when he thought of his daughter. She had inherited his determined manner and his predilection for categorical statements. Now he had been tempered somewhat, and expressing himself so harshly and self-confidently no longer appealed to him. If his body had become stiffer, then his mind had softened in his old age. And that was among others thanks to Mirabelle, and Ellinor, of course.

He smiled even broader when he thought of his grandchild. She was coming out after school. He would muck out the stalls and take out some of the horses, but he wasn't going to ride them. He would go home for a few hours and then be back in time for her arrival. Maybe he could pick. her up on the way?

He walked out into the central corridor and was again hit by the feeling that he wasn't alone. There had been a "visitor" about six months ago, someone who had broken in late one evening. It had frightened Ellinor but Palmblad had reassured her with the fact that it was probably just some teenagers out having a good time. Nothing had been stolen but some of the equipment had been thrown around and the stall doors had been covered in meaningless graffiti.

But burglars in the middle of the afternoon? Palmblad walked silently down the corridor, pushed on a storage room door, and peeked in. The smell of apples wafted out and he remembered that Ellinor had brought in a couple of boxes of winter fruit.

The break room was empty, just like the room where they stored the saddles, and this eased his mind somewhat.

Then he heard a scraping sound, as if a stall door was being opened. I'm hearing things, Palmblad thought. It's the horses moving around. Get a grip on yourself, he told himself and walked over to Mirabelle's stall. She neighed. Justus, an ungovernable stallion on the other side of the corridor, answered. Carl-Henrik Palmblad said something soothing, opened the stall door, stepped in next to Mirabelle, and patted her on the side.

Carl-Henrik died with a smile on his lips. The last thing he felt was warmth, a burning sensation down his back that radiated down to his legs. He fell headlong. Mirabelle had to receive his body and she shied away, neighed anxiously, circling the box but managing—as horses do—to avoid stepping on a prone human.

Justus became all the more nervous and egged on the other horses. The whole stall seemed to vibrate with restless hoofs. The nervousness only died down a good while after the stable door had creaked and shut again.

Mirabelle tossed her head and looked down at her caretaker. He was lying curled up with his right arm stretched out and the hand clenched around a few stalks of hay. The horse walked carefully around the box. She knew that something was wrong, Her nostrils widened, the muscles under the shiny skin vibrated, and she poked Palmblad's lifeless body tentatively with her muzzle.

Ellinor Niis walked into the stables at a quarter past four. She let out a whistle as she usually did, a shrill signal intended as greeting: I'm here. It was as much directed at the horses as her grandfather.

Mirabelle neighed. Otherwise silence reigned.

✦

Twenty-two

Once more Berglund stood over a corpse. For which time in his professional life he was not sure. He had worked as a police officer for thirty-five years, the past fifteen in the Violent Crimes Division.

"Can someone cut the music?"

His voice echoed in the stables. One of the horses in the box next to them answered with a whinny. Berglund turned and looked at the mare whose eyes were fixed on him.

"Poor bastard," he said and Ola Haver didn't know if he meant the man at their feet or the horse.

Ola Haver hadn't even registered the soft music playing from the loudspeakers in the ceiling.

"Thanks," Berglund said when the music stopped.

"Could he have been kicked to death?"

Berglund made a gesture with his head and shoulders to show that it was perhaps possible but that he personally thought they had a new case of murder on their hands.

"You sure got that horse out easily."

"I grew up with horses," Berglund said, still in the somewhat whiny voice that Ola Haver found increasingly irritating. It was hardly his fault that the guy had kicked the bucket, murdered or not.

"Don't you like Britney Spears?"

Berglund stared at Beatrice, who came walking down the corridor, as if she had insulted him.

"I hate Muzak," he said, with equal emphasis on each word, "regardless of whether it is in an elevator, in a department store, or at a crime scene."

"Maybe it calms the horses," Beatrice said lightly and smiled.

I can't believe they have the energy for this, Haver thought and gave Beatrice a look that clearly said: give it a rest.

She smiled at him but it was a sad smile. Haver suddenly saw that the wrinkles around Beatrice's eyes and nose did not simply testify to a temporary fatigue but also to a continuing aging process. The freshness that had always been Bea's signature was disappearing. The earlier always-so-healthy skin was no longer youthfully smooth. The rosy glow had been replaced by a hint of gray.

Bea's expression revealed that she had noticed his searching look and she tried to maintain her smile, adjust the sadness to a superior confidence that was not, however, there. The smile became a grimace and she looked away.

Ola Haver was both embarrassed and distraught over his unchecked examination of his colleague and friend. He had the feeling that he had betrayed her but knew at the same time that it could not be undone and that there was nothing to say to assuage Bea's apparent discomfort over being looked over in that way.

"I'm calling Ann," he muttered and pushed his way out of the box.

Haver ended up standing with the phone in his hand out in the yard, watching how a couple of crows were picking at a plastic bag lying on the ground. They pulled and tugged, each from their own side, paused for a second or so but continued with an energy and drive that was in marked contrast to his own state of mind. Even the crows are cooperating, he thought, and engaged the speed dial to reach Ann Lindell.

"Of course it's murder," Ryde said. "You can see that yourselves! A horseshoe would not have made this kind of imprint."

The pathologist grinned. Up yours, Berglund thought, but kept quiet.

"Only one blow was needed," Ryde continued, who had spent a couple of hours together with Charles Morgansson and three other technicians combing the stables.

Now the body was to be taken away. As usual it was Fridh who was taking care of this. His slow and mild manner made him suited to this task, everyone was in agreement about this, and when he came walking down the corridor the police officers grew quiet and pulled back.

Fridh nodded, took a first look, and then went to work.

"This is getting to be a regular occurrence," he said laconically as he bent down over the dead man. "Who is this one then?"

"Carl-Henrik Palmblad," Berglund said. "Born in 1936, dead today."

"The Berlin Olympics," Fridh said.

Berglund would have wanted to go home but knew it would be a late night. The others looked as if they shared his feelings. Only Lindell seemed to be in a good mood. She had taken the initiative directly and assigned the tasks.

Now she was outside talking to a couple who lived a few hundred meters away. The man spoke unusually loudly and Berglund couldn't help hearing how vividly and wordily he talked about the car he had seen parked in the woods.

"I thought it was mushroom pickers," he said with a thunderous voice. "There are a lot of people running around these woods."

"The car, what color?" Lindell shouted and Berglund realized the man was hard of hearing.

"Red, I think or . . . maybe . . . a little thing in any case . . ."

Berglund walked out. The man was still hesitating. Lindell was patiently waiting for a continuation but instead it was the woman who spoke.

"It was blue," she said firmly. "One of those that Agnes has."

"No, no!" the man yelled. "They have one of those Japanese."

Berglund turned away, walked around the corner, and kept going aimlessly. He heard the waffling continue. He knew he would be getting a report on this before long.

All at once Berglund was gripped by an anger that almost made him return to the woolly-headed witness, take hold of him, and shake him until he could at the very least decide what color the car was. "The color, for the love of God! Is it so damn hard to remember a color!" he wanted to scream so even a person hard of hearing could understand.

It was a surprising, unfamiliar feeling for Berglund, who was otherwise quite timid in his interactions with others.

I need a holiday, he thought, and remembered, not without some bitterness, how he had bumped into a smiling Riis in the city the other week. Riis was on sick leave because of vague abdominal pains. A load of shit, Berglund had thought uncharitably when he heard the colleague's friendly chatter about a boat he had bought for a good price and was renovating. That bastard is healthy as a horse.

Now the thoughts of Riis returned. A boat. Sure, don't we all have something we would like to buy cheap and fix up?

But what would he do with a holiday? What would he do?

A car came down the small road to the stables. It was Sammy Nilsson. Berglund raised his hand in greeting, walked with rapid steps even farther away from the crime scene, and sat down on a rock at the edge of the forest. He knew that a few minutes alone could cure him—at least temporarily—of the paralysis of hopelessness.

✦

Twenty-three

She couldn't stop shaking. Never had she experienced such inner fire, it was as if her blood were heated to its boiling point and ran through frozen veins to muscle tissue of ice. The pain pulsated through arms and legs, creating an almost freezing chill that resisted all willful movement.

The blankets and covers didn't help. Laura tensed her body in an arc in order to force away the evil that had possessed her but her body did not obey, only curling up and transforming her into a shivering bundle.

In her distress she let everything be, let go, and sank into a river of confused images and memories. The fever chills ebbed away and she could passively float along. Then she was caught up in a whirling anxiety, was washed up on rocks whose sharp edges razed her limbs.

Under half shut lids she glimpsed a shoreline of moss-covered stones, a clump of reeds here and there, and small, rickety docks, sunk down in the mud, that looked as if they had been abandoned for a long time.

She passed a deserted country without human life. She was caught in a river that rushed by more strongly. In the distance she heard a waterfall. The water became rapidly more shallow, there were more rocks on the bottom, and she was helplessly bumped between the white cliffs that now replaced the bands of reeds and abundant meadows.

The current was stronger than before and the thundering noise was overpowering. She came to her senses and just before the falls she was washed onto, or rather thrown onto, a cobblestone beach. She was blinded by a strong light, realized the stones were made of pure gold, and caught sight of a plaque with an ornately inscribed text in Latin. Before she sank into unconsciousness she read the inscription aloud to herself but could not make any sense of the words.

Laura Hindersten woke up with the taste of blood in her mouth. Her lips were chewed up and her thighs scratched by nails.

A thick layer of dried sweat covered her thin body and she was cold, but now in a more human way than before. The blankets were on the ground and she reached down and pulled them up again.

The fever dreams lingered in her consciousness like a veil of mist over a deserted landscape. In her memory she looked for the source of her nightmare, because it was certainly somewhere in the literature. She was, after all, Ulrik Hindersten's daughter. But she found nothing. This was her own river journey.

Ulrik would have loved the story and would have encouraged her to write it down, but she only wanted to bury the nightmare in forgetfulness.

After an hour she got up and, wrapped in a blanket, walked to the bathroom on unsteady legs. She knew what had to be done. The visit of the woman from the police had shaken her more than she first had realized. There was something in Ann Lindell's gaze that bothered her, as if she had grasped more than she had let show.

But mostly it was Lindell's ease that worried Laura, who had found herself during the conversation enjoying her time with the policewoman. She liked her voice, her slightly careful movements, and the little smile that was so well suited to self-irony.

Laura did not want to be disarmed by conversation. She feared the friendly words that could at any moment be transformed into their opposite.

She had been deceived so many times, had paid friendship premiums which, when the insurance policy matured, turned out to contain nothing but unpaid deductibles. Now was another time—the time of freedom— and no police officer in the world, however well-meaning she seemed, was going to be allowed to alter Laura's plans.

A couple of days, then she would conquer that little restaurant by the sea. A small pub, whose crooked doors never closed properly, with one table that leaned worryingly, and where the staff never asked if you wanted the check. An establishment that at the next severe fall storm risked being pulled out to sea and churned into firewood.

This pub existed. Laura knew it. She had seen it once.

✦

Twenty-four

Gusten Ander had no blood ties to the infamous murderer, the one who was the last man to be executed in Sweden. The fact that they shared the same name was something that Ander had had pointed out to him many times, but more so before. Now it was rare that anyone joked about his name. It was because of the worsening school system, he believed, or because oral storytelling traditions had changed. One hundred years ago the hunt for Alfred Ander and the dramatic execution was the climax of a thrilling tale. Now it was everyday fare. Who reacted if someone was executed? That happened on TV every day.

Therefore he was amazed when his young opponent, after some hesitation, posed the question. Gusten Ander smiled enigmatically and continued setting up his pieces.

"Could be," he said after a while.

The young man, Tobias Sandström, who Ander judged to be about nineteen years, gave him a quick glance, dropped the black queen on the floor, and blushed.

"How old are you?"

"Twenty-two."

"I'm amazed you've heard the story."

"We read about it at school and of course it's a pretty exciting thing," Tobias said and overturned both of Ander's theories in one blow.

"White or black, that is the question," he said and held out both hands.

Tobias pointed to the right one and got black. Ander made a move immediately and Tobias started by thinking and that made Ander thought-ful in turn. Is it really so much to think about? he thought irritably.

Then Tobias made his move and Ander countered at once.

"Are you new to the club?" Ander asked and broke one of his own principles: never to begin a personal conversation during a game.

Tobias nodded and moved.

"Recently moved," he said curtly, leaned back in his chair, and closed his eyes.

Ander smiled quietly to himself and made his move.

The unexpected attack came at the eleventh move. But perhaps it wasn't so unexpected, Ander had seen almost everything, but the way in which the young player proceeded bewildered Ander for several moments.

He countered immediately and was convinced the game would be over in a dozen more moves. He sighed, another strike against his own rules, and waited for the next move, which was what he had foreseen.

A couple of minutes later he lost his second piece. Sandström attacked with a pawn and left the board free for a bishop that now threatened a white knight.

Ander bounced off his chair.

"I have it!" he cried.

All the players in the room looked up in terror. Afterward Jonasson would tell over and over again for those that could be bothered to listen how the silence after Ander's outburst had felt intensely frightening.

"You are trying the variant from Barcelona!" he said loudly.

Ander looked around the large room. He could not complain about the lack of attention.

"You remember it, right?"

Everyone looked blank except Lind, who was a chess historian of a high order.

Lind left his game, came over, and stopped to study the board.

"Do you remember the name of that Basque?" he asked.

"Sure," Ander said absently.

"In the middle of a raging civil war. Do you remember what Lundin wrote?" Lind continued, and lost himself in a discussion of the late

nineteen thirties. He had written an article about the world champi-
onships in Argentina that started on the same day as World War II. As
the only member to have played against the legendary Gideon Ståhlberg,
and to achieve a draw at that, he felt justified in launching into old anec-
dotes at any moment.

"You will have to excuse me," Ander said and turned to his opponent,
"but I give up the game."

"Give up?" Lind said, baffled. "But you have it in the bag!"

"There's something else that's more important. Thank you," he said
and stretched out his hand to the astonished Sandström, and immediately departed.

Doubt came as Ander was turning the key in the ignition. Suddenly
the idea seemed completely preposterous. How many were familiar with
Antonov's exhibition match from 1937?

He himself had read about it during the sixties and been completely fascinated. Not only the frame of civil war and gunfire in the streets between
the different factions on the republican side—the process of the tournament itself and especially the match between Antonov and Urberuaga.

From what he could recall Antonov was as old as the century and had
been a grand master for many years. He had played all of the greats. The
Basque, who came from Ea, a small coastal village outside Bilbao, had recently turned twenty and was completely unknown in the chess world.

Ander rolled out from the Fyris School's parking lot, driving past the
half finished new police building, and checked the time. He knew that it
was Lindell's investigation. But could he call her this late?

He and Lindell had not had much to do with one another. Of course
they had met on occasion and had collaborated to some extent on some
previous cases, but not more than that. If it had been an older, male colleague he would not have hesitated. As it was it felt strange to call a
woman at half past nine in the evening.

He decided to call Ottosson instead. He knew the old wolf well. They
had even played bandy together, thirty years—and almost as many
kilos—ago.

He called the communications exchange and got Ottosson's home
number. If his chess theory was correct Ottosson would have nothing
against getting this call so late.

Luckily it was Ottosson himself who answered.

"Hi Otto, this is Ander. I'm not disturbing you, am I?"

He realized how idiotic the question was. To call a policeman with a work-related question was to disturb him, it was that simple, and he corrected himself right away.

"Of course I am, but this is important. It's about the serial killer. I think I know who the final target will be."

"This sounds like something," Ottosson said and Ander could not tell from his voice how imposed upon he felt.

"It's Queen Silvia."

Ottosson reaction to Ander's explanation was unanticipated. Ander had to hold the cell phone ten centimeters from his ear in order not to be deafened by his colleague's peals of laughter.

"I'm serious," he said when Ottosson had collected himself somewhat.

"Have you been drinking?"

"You know I haven't," Ander said sharply, "do you want to hear me out?"

"Okay, I can tell this at the club later. I never have any good jokes to contribute."

Ten minutes later Ottosson was bent over in the hall clumsily tying his shoes. Asta Ottosson stood behind him, looking at her husband with a mixture of irritation and tenderness.

"Is it the Queen's Lifeguards coming to the rescue? Do you want any help with those laces?"

Ottosson straightened up, red in the face.

"Ander is no court jester," he said. "Certainly the idea sounds completely crazy, but what if it's true?"

Gusten Ander laid out his hypothesis as methodically as he could. Ottosson immediately explained that he didn't play chess, so Ander started with the basics. He described the tournament in Barcelona, the commotion the game between Urberuaga and Antonov had caused, and he also summed up the remarkable life of the Basque player.

"You mean that this game is world famous, like Beamon's long jump in Mexico?" Ottosson asked. "That in my ignorance I've overlooked this?"

"Not exactly," Ander said. "It's famous in chess but not among the general public."

"Among chess nerds, in other words."

Ottosson looked thoughtful. Ander knew that everything weighed in the balance in this moment.

"Is it described in any books?"

Now Ander knew Ottosson was hooked.

"Yes, I've probably read about it in six or so articles. There are probably more. I can ask around. You can probably search the Web."

"Let's do this," Ottosson said. "You put together a report about this game, where you can read about it, what's been written recently. No long history. Can you have it ready tomorrow morning?"

Ander nodded. He would start at once.

"It's urgent, of course," Ottosson said. "She'll be here in three days."

"What is she doing here?"

"She's going to open some home," Ottosson said distractedly and Ander understood that he was thinking about which directions the investigation should now take.

"But can anyone be so damned crazy?" Ottosson burst out suddenly. "It seems so unbelievable, so, what can you say . . . ?"

". . . so deliberately calculating," Ander filled in.

"It's like it's been taken from an English television series."

"I never watch crime shows," Ander said.

"No, you're too smart for that." Ottosson chuckled. "You figure everything out twenty moves in advance."

"Don't we have to get in touch with the Royal Court?"

"Maybe not just yet. This is such a delicate thing, a slightly daring analysis. We're going to proceed with this all calm and collected."

They went their separate ways outside the entrance to the police station. It was close to eleven o'clock in the evening on Tuesday, the twenty-first of October. On the twenty-fourth Queen Silvia was scheduled to come to Uppsala.

After several hundred meters Ottosson stopped short. Vaksala Square lay deserted except for a young couple walking diagonally across it. Ottosson could tell at a glance that they were newly in love. The man had his arm around the woman's shoulders. They laughed from time to time. Ottosson followed their stroll until they turned the corner by Bodén's Bicycle Shop in the Gerd block. A block that was now in danger of being torn down because a majority in city government had gotten the idea of building a House of Music right there. It was doubtful if they fully represented the district's citizens. Ottosson was convinced there would be protests.

Just the other day, outside the bicycle shop, he had run into a scarred social democratic politician who had complained. His career was over but he couldn't keep from expressing his concern over the state of affairs.

"I'm too old to be told what to do," he said with a crooked smile and made a sweeping gesture with his cane. "It's worse with the young ones who have to vote against their conscience."

"The party whip," Ottosson said.

The old politician nodded.

"The ones who think differently are forced to go on sick leave when it's time for a vote in parliament," he snorted. "Prestige has come into it. I was also behind the House of Music, but now when the costs are getting out of hand you have to say no."

They parted and the old man was swallowed up by the masses on the square. It was Saturday morning and the shopping rush was on. Ottosson remained standing in his spot for a while and wondered how the old man would have voted if he had still been sitting in city government.

Ottosson suddenly heard a shout from the corner toward Väderkvarnsgatan and Hjalmar Brantingsgatan. It came from a collection of youths approaching each other from opposite directions. He actually felt a sting of fear. He was alone and would not have a chance if they decided to knock him on the back of the head.

Nothing happened, as it turned out. They met in the middle of the square and the youths went noisily on their way. Ottosson walked slowly home, reflecting on Gusten Ander's theory and what it would mean if they decided to accept it.

Ottosson had a great deal of respect for Ander and his judgment but on the chilly October night it was as if his mind cleared. The unlikely aspect of his colleague's reasoning—that a serial killer was acting out an old chess game, and moreover had the queen as the ultimate target—was suddenly self-evident.

He realized that he had taken Ander's theory seriously for a few moments simply because they had so much trouble finding any motive in the three murders. It was no advanced conjecture to think that they were connected, but the question was how? Two single, old farmers and a retired bureaucrat from the university, with horses as his passion, what did they have in common?

That question had been argued back and forth and Ottosson had noticed a certain desperation behind all the contributions.

Ottosson decided to sleep on it and to discuss the question with Ann first thing in the morning.

Asta was reading in bed but lowered her book and gave him a searching look. Ottosson knew he had to first try the idea out on his wife. For decades they had discussed police cases without Ottosson feeling as if he was breaking any code of silence. He knew she would never pass anything along.

Asta Ottosson had almost the same objections that he had raised and that he knew Ann Lindell would come up with.

After Ottosson had taken off his clothes and brushed his teeth, he sat down heavily on the edge of the bed and let out a sigh. Asta put her hand on his back. He turned his head and looked at her. It would be wrong to say she was as beautiful as a lily—that might have been true thirty years ago—but at that moment he fell in love with her all over again.

"You're something, you," he said and smiled.

"Come on, you old lug, get into bed," she said.

They lay as close to each other as two people can get.

Before Ottosson fell asleep he thought that Asta and Silvia were probably the same age but that was the extent of their similarities.

Sammy Nilsson refused to look at the clock but he knew it had to be close to one.

His brain was rinsed as clean as a dead tree root at the edge of a northern reservoir. Sometimes he got this image in front of his eyes when he associated something decayed and joyless. It was a childhood memory from the time when he and his father would go fishing in southern Lappland. Once they had gone past a dammed-up lake and stopped for a break. The artificial shore was littered with tree corpses. Hundreds of twisted, white-yellow tree stumps stood out as horrifying as dead animals whose bones bore witness to a slaughter of inconceivable proportions.

These stumps often returned to him in nightmares. The three murder cases that, reasonably speaking, had to be classified as one, appeared to him as something equally terrifying.

Everyone tried in their own way. Sammy's way was to be systematic. He had an instrument, just like the ViCLAS coordinator at the Uppsala Police. He had long been skeptical about the system but in time the resistance had weakened and now he tried to view the system as the support it was intended to be.

ViCLAS was a Canadian model developed in order to aid in the collection of data so that the investigators could discover similarities in different crime cases. It was thought to deepen and help the investigative work.

When, according to his own application of the ViCLAS system's extensive format, Sammy Nilsson now at this late hour made a data search in his clean-swept tree-stump brain, four factors came ticking out: access to a car, local knowledge, rapid chain of events, and the absence of a traditional deadly weapon.

The access to a car implicated a large portion of Uppsala's population, but most likely the killer was not an eighteen-year-old who had borrowed his dad's Volvo in order to go off on a murder rampage, nor was it a retired person. Probably the perpetrator was between thirty and sixty.

It was most likely a man; few women were serial killers. Sammy Nilsson had seen the statistics.

None of the cases involved a robbery. The motive must have been revenge. But revenge for what? The driving force must have been enormously strong in someone who systematically clubbed three elderly people to death. Three older men, none of whom were known to have an extensive love life or any financial difficulties. He bit his pen and stared out in front of him.

Motive? He stared at the six letters. An honor killer, he thought. Someone who had been deeply humiliated? By two farmers and an academic? Could it have been in grade school? Sammy made a note to check where the three men had gone to school. He thought that Jan-Elis Andersson and Petrus Blomgren were from the area, but what about Palmblad? Could an old wrongdoing some fifty, sixty years back in time be part of the background?

Sammy Nilsson approached the second point on his list, local knowledge. The facts that he was in possession of indicated someone who had lived in Uppsala or the surrounding area for a long time. He had trouble imagining a newcomer scraping together motive enough for three murders. Again a sign that this was old debris that had finally risen to the surface.

An amateur, he determined. In all three cases the murderer could have availed himself of a gun or even some kind of knife. Instead the victims were clubbed down with an unknown object. Ryde had hazarded a heavy iron tool but had ruled out a hammer. The murderer had been forced to come close and had surprised the victims. It was a moment that involved an element of risk.

Or perhaps the murderer was so sure of himself that he felt invincible? A perpetrator who ruled out any form of resistance. What did this say about his profile?

He shuffled the papers together into a neat pile, got up from the table, and looked at the time. In five hours he would have to get up.

Ann Lindell stared out into the darkness. She had fallen asleep shortly before midnight but had been awakened by a strange sound, turned on her lamp, and discovered that it was two o'clock.

The sound had returned several times. At first she had lain in a half daze, then she had awakened. It was a scraping, slightly squeaky noise, impossible to stand.

Her first thought was that Erik had gotten out of bed but when she checked he was sleeping peacefully.

She listened intently. Now it was completely quiet. It was pitch black in the room. She had bought new curtains that effectively kept out all light.

The image of Laura Hindersten came to her. An unusual woman. In some way Ann felt something in common with her. Perhaps only for such a trivial reason that they both lived alone.

Laura Hindersten wasn't exactly a dime a dozen. Her apparently senseless method for closing a chapter on her old life by burning up a valuable library attracted Ann in a strange way. It indicated a consistent and merciless attitude that Ann felt was lacking in herself. Everything she undertook was half-hearted. Even in something like raising Erik she proceeded without plans or deeper intentions. But Erik seemed completely normal in his development. He was happy and social and linguistically advanced. She was surprised at how easily and quickly he could orient himself and adapt to the most diverse situations. And she wasn't just a little proud when she heard how other parents at the day care worried about this and that.

Ann smiled to herself in the dark, but the thought of Laura Hindersten wouldn't leave her. The pillow was starting to feel more and more uncomfortable and her thoughts circled around the remarkable house in Kåbo. What had really happened to Ulrik Hindersten?

Laura had denied any knowledge of Jan-Elis Andersson and Petrus Blomgren and there was nothing that argued in favor of there being a connection between the three men. But it was also not a given that Laura would know her father's complete history and all acquaintances.

Shortly before three she hit on what the sound was that had woken her up: the skirt that she had hung out on the balcony to be aired out. It was swinging on its hanger and dashing against the window. That's what it had to be. And so it was that Charles Morgansson was the last thing she thought of before she fell asleep.

✦

Twenty-five

The morning meeting was magnificent. It was the largest in the history of the Uppsala Police. Even those who had no real reason to be there, including all commanding officers, had turned up, on time no less.

The chief of police came down in uniform and no one would have been surprised to see the national commander himself sail in. District Attorney Fritzén, who was formally in charge of the investigation into the three murders and was dressed in a suit and brightly colored tie, had three thick binders with him, that he dropped onto one of the tables with a bang.

Ann Lindell walked up to Ottosson.

"Have we contacted all of Palmblad's relatives?" she asked.

Ottosson was too nervous to reply. He had tried in vain to catch the eye of the chief of the crime divisions, who in turn was trying to get the police chief's attention. The latter, however, was busy reading a document that had come from Kungsholmen in Stockholm that morning, and trying to understand what was meant by the questions in the fax.

It nonetheless fell to Ottosson to begin the meeting since none of the others wanted to take the risk of making a fool of themselves.

As anticipated, the resulting discussion was animated but very little was said that was of concrete help to the investigators. Fritzén spoke at length about the media's image of the murders. Attention was at a maximum and cars from the press buzzed like bees around the police station in Salagatan.

Several calls had come in from Jumkil and Alsike, where people living close to the murdered Blomgren and Andersson complained of the unusually intense traffic and all the curious people who were invading the area.

The assembled group was losing concentration but when the attorney started in on his thoughts about it being time to turn to Stockholm, the silence thickened.

"In light of things I would not advise bringing in National Homicide even if it would perhaps mean a certain relief. Uppsala is such a large district that we should be able to handle this on our own."

Several investigators nodded. The higher authorities wore a becomingly neutral expression.

After Fritzén the chief of police took the stand. He spoke for a long time about nothing. Sammy Nilsson coughed meaningfully. Lindell felt the level of irritation rising and Ottosson longed for the conference room with the small group of investigators.

Is this what it's like to wage war? Ola Haver thought, and felt like a subordinate officer who had arrived at the front in order to take part in a commissioned officers' strategy meeting. He got up and left the room. Sammy followed him. Ottosson stared wide-eyed at them and gave Lindell a look as if to say, I want to go too. Lindell nodded but Ottosson just smiled and stayed put.

After about an hour the meeting was concluded. Now everyone felt informed and above all, involved. This was probably the only positive result.

The investigators met with Ottosson. It was crowded but Berglund brought in a couple of chairs so everyone could sit.

"This is like morning prayers," Ottosson said when everyone was assembled. He tried to set a jovial tone, but failed since his body language indicated something very different.

"Otto, what are you hiding?" Sammy asked.

Ottosson looked up from his notes, embarrassed.

"What?" he asked.

"You look constipated," Berglund said.

"I've received a tip," Ottosson said quietly.

"From who?" several people asked in unison.

"Gusten Ander. It's something that has to do with chess."

"—Mate," Sammy Nilsson added.

Ottosson gave him a grumpy look. Then he quickly summed up his conversation with Ander the night before.

The silence was deafening.

"Silvia," Fredriksson said finally. "I'll be damned."

Sammy Nilsson burst out a ringing peal of laughter.

"This is completely insane. It's like a tip from 'Crazy Beda.'"

"Crazy Beda" was his nickname for all of the—mildly put—fantastic tips and ideas that were called in to the police.

"Has there been any threat?" was the first thing Fredriksson wanted to know.

"Security has nothing," Ottosson said, having checked that morning.

"Nothing concrete, in other words, just a chess fanatic's—what should we say—fanciful concoction," Berglund said. "But I know Ander well and he doesn't normally let himself get carried away."

"That's my considered opinion as well," Ottosson said in a formal tone, as if he wanted to compensate for the outlandishness of the investigative hypothesis with his proper formulations.

"Who could be thought to have the motive for a serial killing with the queen as the final target?"

Fredriksson's question made Ottosson sink back into his chair. Until then he had been sitting leaning forward, as if about to spring into action.

"We'll have to consult upstairs," Berglund said, "however much it hurts."

"And who would set this up like a chess game?" Fredriksson continued.

"And a relatively unknown chess game at that," Ottosson said.

"We can do a Gallup," Sammy Nilsson said. "Is there anyone here who knows about even one game somewhere in the world?"

"I lost to my brother once," Ola Haver said.

"Which one?"

"My little brother."

"I see why you still remember it," Nilsson said, grinning.

"Well," Ottosson said, "that's how it is, but it restricts our search. Ander was going to come by with a memo. He'll be here presently."

"Is this it?" Lindell asked and picked up a green folder. "It's lying on your desk. Antonov versus Urberuaga, and the date is 1936."

"That's the Basque," Ottosson explained. "How the devil could he be so fast?"

"It's at least fifteen pages," Lindell said, who had opened the folder.

"Read it and then let me know how and if we can proceed with this thing."

"You mean," Lindell said, "that the victims have nothing more in common with Silvia or each other, apart from the fact that they have been selected more or less at random in order to coincide with moves in a chess game."

"Read it and weep."

Lindell looked far from amused. Ever since she got up that morning she had had the feeling that there was something about Petrus Blomgren that she had missed. It was a thought she had had last night that had whirled by without gaining a foothold. Since then it lay working in her subconscious but she couldn't get ahold of the loose thread.

Now she would have to put Petrus aside in order to study chess history.

Sammy Nilsson told them about his night activities at the kitchen table with the ViCLAS method. He read through his list: "access to a car, local knowledge, rapid succession of events without excessive complications, and no use of a conventional deadly weapon."

"What does this tell us?" he asked rhetorically and acknowledged Ola Haver's smile. "Yes, I know, we're constantly asking ourselves this question, but it's the pattern we have to detect. I don't believe in the chess idea, it seems too unbelievably sophisticated. Stuff like that only happens in books. No, I think this is a local guy with a number of enemies who pops them off with a weapon he happens to have near at hand. Is it the same weapon? I think so, and what does that tell us? The weapon itself may have a symbolic value for the perp. Or else it's simply a lack of imagination."

"But it's also smart to bring the weapon with him," Berglund said.

"True," Sammy Nilsson said emphatically.

He who normally was not particularly active at these meetings was now overflowing with energy.

"We're looking for a man, in fair physical shape, with a relatively non-descript car, maybe someone with a country background, and I don't think we'll find him already in the database."

Edvard, Lindell thought, and couldn't help but smile.

"It's not a clerk at the Department of Agriculture," Haver muttered, "that much is clear."

"Or else that's precisely what he is," Beatrice said in an unexpectedly sonorous and forceful tone of voice. "A little dry, flabby man, balding, with a townhouse in Valsätra, wife, dog, a Volvo 760, half-grown children, and troubling sex dreams at night."

"There, we have him!" Haver burst out.

Ottosson coughed.

"What do you say, Allan?"

Fredriksson pinched his nose, as he usually did when there were too many questions.

"I can buy two farmers," he said after a short pause, "but throw in an academic on top of that, that changes things. The motive must be very complicated. It can't simply be someone out to settle a score with farmers, as we initially believed. It's true that Palmblad was out in the country a lot as the owner of some stables, but is this significant? Neither Andersson nor Blomgren were involved in any trouble such as land disputes, unpaid debts, or anything else that had to do with their main line of support, right? I don't think Palmblad did either. If this is about chess, then yes, the horses are important: a knight is forced from the board. Then he could be replaced by any man with horses. Even a teenage girl could have been the intended victim."

He stopped but everyone saw that there was more and waited from him to finish.

"I believe in an irrational motive," Fredriksson said, "something we won't think of in the first instance. This could be the work of a sick mind with an *idée fixe*, something that doesn't have anything directly to do with the victims."

"Give me an example," Sammy Nilsson said.

Fredriksson pinched his nose.

"Someone who doesn't like seventy-year-old men," he said. "I'm thinking like this: it could be a woman who in her childhood was abused by dirty old men. At that time, perhaps twenty, thirty years ago, she was quiet, but now she's taking her revenge."

"Do you mean that all of the victims are pedophiles?" Bea asked.

"No, not necessarily. Perhaps none of them are. But they are seventy-year-old men and represent their gender and age group. Perhaps the real pedophile is dead but would today have been seventy."

"I see you've really thought about this," Ottosson said. "That's good! We need to consider this from all possible angles."

"We're completely in the dark, in other words," Haver said.

The discussion continued for another hour. Berglund reported on all of the telephone calls that Blomgren and Andersson had made over the last while but so far there was nothing that looked out of the ordinary. It was a short list, in Blomgren's case sixteen outgoing calls a month, and none made to any numbers that could be considered surprising.

Beatrice had checked out the alarm company, whose phone number they had found in Blomgren's kitchen, but it had not led to any discoveries. The only thing that was somewhat noteworthy was the fact that he had declared bankruptcy four years earlier and that eight years ago he had been charged with unlawful threat. That case was laid down.

Fredriksson made an overview of the murdered Carl-Henrik Palmblad's career. Born and raised in Härnösand, his father a pastor, his mother a deaconess, moved to Uppsala in order to attend the university, studied history of religion, French, and Nordic languages, later taught at the university, and the last ten years before his retirement worked as a bureaucrat in the university administration.

He had two children, his daughter Ann-Charlotte who was a grammar school teacher and had lived in Erikslund for twenty-five years, and a son, Magnus, who sold cash registers and other equipment in a retail business and lived in Täby, north of Stockholm.

Palmblad did not appear to have had any financial difficulties, at least not according to his daughter. After his divorce fifteen years ago he had not sought out any regular female companionship, as far as she knew, and certainly not in the past five, six years. Palmblad seemed to have spent most of his time in the stables.

That was the outer picture of Palmblad's life. Now Beatrice and the two investigators brought in from Criminal Investigations continued to work on filling in the details.

Lindell felt as if she was sitting on pins and needles, even though she knew it was important to hear all of the thoughts of the group. But Haver was right when he said they were fumbling in the dark, without having a single true lead.

The first thing she did when she came back to her office was to open the chess folder.

Ander began with a look back at the history, describing the two combatants from the tournament in Barcelona. He had apparently dug down properly in his sources, because the background was substantial, with the Spanish civil war as a backdrop and the feeling of euphoria that apparently characterized Catalonia and Barcelona during the beginning phases of the war. To arrange a chess tournament was a way of upholding civil life—Franco was not going to be allowed to disturb something as important as chess—and also, Ander wrote, it was an expression of international solidarity with the republican government in Madrid. Especially after the failure of the alternative sport competition held in 1936 as an answer to the Olympics in Nazi Germany. Ander described how the boxer Henry Persson and the other Swedish competitors had to turn back in Paris after getting the news that civil war had broken out.

Antonov was at that time a celebrity in chess circles, with legendary matches against stars such as the cautious Dutchman Euwe, the antisemitic Russian Alekhine, and the Cuban, Capablanca, who was the world champion in the twenties and had only lost thirty-five out of almost six hundred matches in major tournaments. Anders had also made a note of several matches against Swedish masters such as Lundin, Ståhlberg, and the uneven Stolz.

The Basque player, Urberuaga, was, however, relatively unknown but immediately received attention as the one who, although he had not perhaps been able to shake the great Russian, had nonetheless made a little history.

Ander had also attached a short biography of the Basque. Lindell was at first irritated over the extensive nature of the report but soon found herself drawn into Urberuaga's later fate. How he enlisted in the republican army, taking part in the struggles in Teruel and Belchite, was wounded on two occasions, and then fled together with a hundred thousand others to France when Franco's troops surrounded Barcelona. There he ended up in a camp, escaped, and participated in the underground resistance against the Nazis during World War II, fled once more, and eventually ended up in Mexico where he lived until his death in 1966.

In Jalapa he started a chess club that got the name "No pasarán," apparently a battle cry during the civil war, and he frequently took part in tournaments, even internationally.

"A pretty decent player," Ander commented. "Uneven in both his temperament and his strategy, and who with time developed severe alcoholism."

Antonov's fate was even worse. When he returned to the Soviet Union he was immediately imprisoned. The list of accusations included spying as well as traitorous activity. In all likelihood he died in a camp somewhere beyond the Ural. Whether he had had the opportunity to play chess in the camp was not known.

The next part of the report dealt with the literature available on the subject. There was a list of eight titles. "There are probably many more," Ander wrote, "but it is these that are somewhat known in Sweden. To this one should add a large number of print articles and information on the Internet."

Lindell sighed, eyed the list, and continued with part three of Ander's report, the part that described the actual match: "The Basque was black and Antonov white. The beginning was not sensational. At the midpoint, black's center was weakened and he almost landed in a forced-move situation, but defended himself decently with the sacrifice of a pawn. Antonov believed himself to be secure and saw Urberuaga's weakness as a sign of fatigue, possibly thinning patience, and he moved the queen to De8 followed by several quick moves that also increased white's position. The Basque lost yet another pawn. Two surprising and poisonous moves by Antonov, whereupon black reflected for a long time, countering but thereafter losing a knight. Normally this match could only have gone in one direction but Urberuaga astonished everyone, including the Russian, with a three-move combination that threatened the white queen. Slowly but surely Antonov came to realize that what he had taken for weakness had been an extremely clever trap. White lost the queen. It had cost him some pieces but in one stroke black immediately emerged much stronger."

Good god what nerds, Lindell thought and read on.

"In spite of this, white eventually came out the winner and thereby the Barcelona exhibition match was the display of a youthful drive to shine but also of the older man's (Antonov was thirty-six) superiority when it came to calm strategy and tactical adaptability."

Oh really, Lindell thought, what does all this have to do with our murders? Ander pointed out what everyone in the investigative team had discussed that morning, that the murders appeared so deliberate but that it was impossible to find a reasonable explanation as to why specifically Blomgren, Andersson, and Palmblad had fallen victim to the serial killer. "The motive must still be on high," as Ander put it, "somewhere beyond the three victims. They were chosen at random to fit a pattern. Each of them was cleverly chosen in that they lived isolated and that the perpetrator could approach them without being intercepted."

To hell with it, Lindell thought and shut the folder, getting up and standing at the window.

"The sun shone on the bones of the dead," she recited out loud while she tried to gather herself for something that would sound like a counterargument when she now had to report to Ottosson. She was convinced that he had already read the report and had simply pretended not to know that Ander had delivered it. He had apparently wanted her to make up her own mind first.

She took the folder and went in to see Ottosson, who was speaking on the phone. He waved to her to sit down. Lindell heard that it was a higher-up on the other end. Ottosson always had a special tone in his voice when he spoke to higher command. It rubbed Lindell the wrong way but she sensed that she probably did the same thing.

Ottosson hung up with a sigh.

"The top dog," he said in a tired voice.

"Which one of them?"

"The absolute highest," Ottosson said. "The chief. Yes, well," he continued quickly, apparently unwilling to comment further about what had transpired on the phone, "what do we think?"

Lindell shook her head.

"It's doubtful," she said. "It sounds a bit science fiction-y."

"I was just talking to outer space," Ottosson inserted and smiled in that kindly, sad way that only he could, "so it fits a little with science fiction."

"I don't believe in the fact that the murder scheme has been dictated by a seventy-year-old chess game," Lindell started and listed all her reasons.

When she finished, Ottosson sat quietly for a while.

"Fredriksson believes it," he said suddenly. "He can't say why and he agrees that it sounds implausible, but something tells me we are dealing with someone this crazy."

"Is that what you said to your superiors?"

Ottosson immediately looked embarrassed.

"No, not exactly."

"Not even indirectly, I take it? I really don't want to learn more about chess," she said and cursed her unusually passive tone.

"I understand," Ottosson said.

"Put Fredriksson on it then. Oh fuck," it slipped out of her, "I was supposed to talk to Allan. I knew there was something."

"What?"

"In Blomgren's house I thought I saw something like a photo album, but then Fredriksson was the one who examined the room and I forgot about it in all the activity."

"And now you want to look through it? Don't mention it to Allan, he's sensitive about things like this."

"Don't worry," Lindell said, "I'll just go out there. I know where the key is."

Lindell stood up but before she left she couldn't help asking Ottosson: "What did the top dog say?"

"He had apparently spoken with the professor who lives next door because he said that we should, and I quote, 'remove all bicycle officers and rookies from the investigation.'"

The maple outside Blomgren's house was now completely denuded and the leaves lay strewn across a large portion of the lawn like a thick rug. The pale sun was filtered through the tops of the fir trees in the west and reflected across the red and yellow shades of the leaves, creating the illusion of an impressionistic painting.

Lindell felt that Dorotea Svahn had noticed the fact that she had come by and she decided to visit the old woman after she had examined Blomgren's bookshelf.

The TV room looked even more ordinary this time. Everything was in the same place as she remembered. She opened the little cabinet next to the bookshelf. The album was still there. For the first time in this investigation, Lindell felt a certain excitement.

The photo album was an old-fashioned model with a gray linen cover and stiff pages with glued photographs. The first one was of the house. An older couple was posing in front of the entrance, a couple that she guessed was Petrus's parents. Then a large number of snapshots followed where the farm appeared to be the center. There were only a few pictures that she thought were taken outside Vilsne village. Quite a few people appeared in them, the parents regularly and a young Petrus also, stacking hay, standing at the gate or outside the barn in a pose that was supposed to be humorous.

The photographs seemed to be taken during a fairly narrow time frame. She guessed from the middle of the forties and about twenty years forward.

Ann flipped through the pages, as she believed Fredriksson had also done, but there was nothing that could reasonably have any meaning for the murder and the investigation.

A few captions had been written. One that Ann found slightly touching was written in pencil under a picture. "Me and mother" was written in spiky handwriting. Petrus, who in the shot looked to be in his thirties had his arm around his mother in a slightly awkward way. You could see that the old woman was smiling behind the hand that covered half of her mouth.

The last three pages were empty. Ann closed the album with a feeling of disappointment. She should have known better. If there had been anything to find here, Fredriksson would have spotted it.

She pushed the album back into place and was about to close the cabinet when her eyes slid to the book next to it. It was a thick volume from the Uppland Horse Breeder's Association. She pulled it out and looked at the cover, which depicted a farmer plowing. The horse was struggling on an imagined field.

On the flyleaf, on a dotted line, it was written that the book belonged to Arthur Blomgren. She opened it and absently turned the pages. It was mostly text with statistical tables, but also several pictures of horses, among them one from a plowing competition in Rasbo, 1938.

When Lindell shut the book she caught sight of a white corner that stuck out in the back. She opened to that page and a snapshot tumbled out. In the brief moment when it swooped to the floor she knew she had found something valuable. It landed facedown so the first thing she saw was the inscription on the back: "To my beloved Petrus."

She waited a second or so, then bent down to pick it up and turned it over. It was a picture of a woman. What else? she thought with a pleased smile. It was clearly a studio portrait but without identifying business markers.

The woman was in her forties, a brunette. The most eye-catching aspect to her was the beautiful hair pulled back into a ponytail. A girlish touch. She smiled, not an exaggerated grin, rather tentatively.

Ann thought she was beautiful and the first thing that struck her was the contrast to Petrus. But she immediately corrected herself. She had seen him dead, brutally slain, at seventy years of age. She pulled the photo album back out and looked up the picture of Petrus with his mother. Sure enough, he had been a handsome man, a little angular perhaps but that may have been the result of the circumstances. Styled in a photographer's studio he may very well have been able to hold his own next to this woman.

Lindell turned the card over and read the dedication again, perhaps written by the companion to Mallorca and the reason he had gone to the doctor and gotten a prescription for sleeping pills. This was the tear in Petrus Blomgren's life.

But was she also the reason he was murdered? Undoubtedly this photogenic woman was the absolute best thing, not to say the only thing, that they had found so far and that Fredriksson had missed. How would she tackle the fact that he had been sloppy? The photo had to be brought forward and the woman's identity established. Should she lie and say that Dorotea had produced it? But why on earth would she be hoarding the picture of someone who was most likely the lover of the man she herself had probably been hoping for, at least at some point back in time?

No, that would be wrong, Lindell decided. Fredriksson would have to stand there with the shame.

Lindell laid the photo on the coffee table and then started flipping through all of the books in the small library. If he missed one clue there might be more, but the result was zero.

One photo, one woman, was the day's yield. Lindell locked the door behind her, very satisfied, and steered her course to the neighbor's house.

Dorotea Svahn looked at the picture for a long time and then shook her head, but kept it in her hand and Lindell hoped that the old woman wouldn't turn it over.

"You don't recognize her?" Lindell asked and took the photograph out of her hand.

"No, I've never seen her before."

"Are you sure?"

The old woman nodded.

"So this is what she looked like," she said. "I've always wondered."

✦

Twenty-six

The stovepipe chimney howled. It usually did in gusty weather, but only if there was a westerly wind. The whistling sounds from the fireplace sounded like someone was sitting in there playing a variety of out-of-tune instruments.

When Laura was little they would make fires there. It was always Alice who arranged the wood to make sure it caught fire. When the flames were well established she would pull out an ottoman cushion and sit so close she grew red in the face after a while. Laura would lie on the floor, not quite so close but still close enough that she would grow warm, which one otherwise seldom did in this drafty house. Sometimes she stretched out an arm to feel her mother's bare underarm.

One day a chimney cleaner came for an inspection. He declared the stovepipe unfit. It was cracked, not functionable, and if they kept making fires there was a chance the house would burn down. Down to the ground, as he put it. Ulrik grumbled, but her mother knew better than to argue with the chimney sweep. She was raised in the country and knew about chimney fires.

"To the ground," Laura repeated to herself.

She sat in the armchair at whose side her mother's basket of wool and knitting needles usually was. It was called the resting chair but Laura never saw Alice rest there.

"Down to ground." It was a child's phrase. She didn't know then what the ground of the house would be exactly, but sensed it meant that everything would be destroyed, all furniture and books, her toys, her mother's collection of seeds and pressed plants, yes, she saw everything before her and could even touch it. It was a dizzying thought. Frightening and alluring at the same time.

She had dozed off. These last few days sleep seemed to come and go as it pleased. She was becoming more and more tired but blamed it on the work with cleaning all the junk out of the house. She was unaccustomed to this much physical labor.

The chimney whistled. She stared into the open mouth of the fireplace. Now there were no sticks there, just a brass candelabra. It glimmered like gold against all the black.

She had been dreaming. A strange dream that she had traveled to a foreign land in order to find out about their old habits and customs. Laura had brought several older women together in a cobblestone yard, perhaps it was in front of a barn because you could hear the rattling of chains, the thump of hooves, and the occasional melancholy mooing. The women tried to explain what their lives had been like seventy, eighty years ago. They gesticulated and spoke with an intensity that made their wrinkled and weather-beaten faces appear youthful. The problem was that Laura had trouble with the language. Admittedly she had studied this foreign tongue, taken several courses, and could even adequately understand written texts but here she came up short.

The old ladies chattered on. Laura strained herself to her breaking point but was only able to snap up fragments of their vividly related narratives.

Laura picked up a pad and pen from her bag and the torrent of words slowed somewhat. The group grew completely silent when she asked one of the women to write down a few words that Laura had understood were central to the context. It had to do with when they let the animals out onto the lush and thickly herb-sprinkled fields, she understood this much, but she wanted to get it right, with the correct expressions.

The woman grasped the pen clumsily. She formed an *A* with a great deal of effort, thereafter an *L* and an *O*. Then she stopped.

"ALO," Laura read. The woman handed the pen back without a word and pushed the pad away. The letters were printed in a sprawling, childish style, like that of a first grader. There were several centimeters between the letters, it was hardly a word, and looked more like three squiggles that were leapfrogging across the white paper.

There was shame, anger, and repudiation in the woman's actions as she, with the help of a knotted stick and with labored movements, stood up and pointed out over the landscape. Laura, who did not understand what she meant, quickly got up and looked out over the exquisite valley that surrounded the village, but the woman waddled off without a word.

Laura woke up at this point and she, in her half-wakened state, searched in front of her with her hand, as if to convince the old woman—messenger from a bygone age—to return.

She closed her eyes and tried to remember anything like this from her real life, but in vain. She had never worked with documenting old habits and customs in the countryside, quite the opposite. She had been focused on the future and her academic research had concerned theoretical models for the direction of companies with a high innovation capacity but with faltering sources of capital. Her dissertation was something that few people had the ability or interest to even try to understand.

When the dissertation arrived from the press Laura had given her father a copy. After having read some ten pages of it he had put the book away without commenting on it.

She got up, stretched into the fireplace and took out the candelabra, walked into the hall, and put it into a trash bag.

The cleanup of the house had slowed down. The whole upstairs was left. She glanced at the staircase but did not go up. She knew what was up there. It looked like the garage, a storage facility for old clothes, furniture, books, and other things.

Ulrik and Laura Hindersten had almost exclusively lived on the first floor the past twelve years. It was as if their energy had not been sufficient for two floors.

Driven by a gnawing ache in her gut she walked out into the kitchen. She had not eaten breakfast or lunch and it was almost two o'clock in the afternoon. The refrigerator was empty except for some shriveled tomatoes and a package of ricotta.

Suddenly the doorbell rang. Laura jumped, returned to the hall, and stared uncomprehendingly at the door. The sound was so unfamiliar that she thought she must have misheard. But then there was a new ring.

She took a couple of hesitant steps with her hand outstretched but then paused. A third ring, short this time, made her pull back. The door handle was pushed down but Laura always locked the door from the inside.

After half a minute she heard someone walk down the exterior steps. It struck Laura that it might be Stig. She hurried over to the window and apprehensively peeked out between the curtains, but saw the back of the policewoman Lindell disappearing between the bushes.

For the first time Laura felt an anxiety that she would not have time to do everything that she had planned. Time was running out. Everything was required of her. Everything. She was the one who had to do everything alone.

A sudden flash of inspiration had her throw open the front door, but then she heard Lindell's car already driving down the street. It would have been better if she had received answers to her questions and would then be gone for good. Now she would most likely turn up again.

There was only one thing left to do: follow through. She had an idea of how it should be done, but she wavered. Stig had not been in touch with her. Laura imagined him standing in front of her with that hopeless look he had when Jessica turned on him. Jessica did not use many words but her whole body signaled superiority and Stig adopted the posture of a subordinate.

How she hated the sight of a brightly smiling Stig, for in that smile there was no real joy only a desire to please. It affected the entire office. Everyone knew that Stig was a pushover. Barbro would joke about Stickan who was Jessica's little lap dog and Laura had often wished ill on Barbro because of her taunting laughter and deadly comments.

Laura lifted the receiver, dialed Jessica Franklin's number, and heard with rising anticipation how the call was connected and the phone rang. When Jessica finally answered Laura smiled and hung up. The sudden elation when the realization sunk in that that voice was going to be silenced for good made Laura teeter, steady herself on the telephone table, and laugh out loud.

Jessica would be allowed to realize that Stig was lost to her, that life was lost, that it was Laura's time.

"Laura's time," she muttered and it sounded unfamiliar, as if she was saying an unknown person's name.

The mirror above the table reflected a figure who lifted a fist against her own head and struck. The blow landed on her temple and Laura collapsed to the floor. Not so much the force behind the blow but more that the feeling of falling filled her with great happiness.

"That's how it is," she said, while she stared out across the naked wooden hall floor, in whose deep cracks decades of grime had gathered.

She sat in bed, naked except for panties and a camisole. Daylight filtered in through the gray-streaked window. She tried to counter the dizziness by chewing on some pieces of crisp bread that she had found in the pantry. They tasted like summer.

An untouched glass of wine stood on the bedside table. She absently brushed the breadcrumbs from her stomach and thighs. The dark scratches stood out on her pale skin.

This was the bed where she and Stig had lain the other night. The bedclothes were unchanged and she thought she could pick out his scent. She was no longer so certain that he was going to come back. He hadn't called her like he said he was going to. No one called.

The silence in the house was unbelievably dense, as if she lived in a vacuum. She chewed in order to produce some sounds.

She had decided to take a shower but when she walked past the cellar door she had instead gone down to get her suitcase. Now it was in the hall. There was still a tag from the Linate Airport in Milan on the handle. It looked like a good friend who was waiting for her. Without fuss, secure and stable, there it was.

She liked it. Everything else was expendable, everything else could be stuffed into sacks and heaved into garbage containers but this suitcase was going to take her to the sea and the little harbor pub.

Stig would come later. When everything had calmed down he would be standing there one fine day, smiling, the way he did when he was in a good mood.

"Let the final arrow fly," Laura said softly and reached for the glass of wine.

She spilled a few drops on the already stained camisole.

✦

Twenty-seven

The Brain Squad was assembled. Morenius from the Criminal Information Service was talking to the chief of criminal investigations and the chief of police. Ottosson came walking along carrying two thermoses. The security chief was standing on his own, leaning against the wall with a paper in his hand that he was reading with a perplexed look on his face.

On one side of the table there were Ola Haver, Sammy Nilsson, and Allan Fredriksson. Fredriksson was a deep red color and looked painfully tense. Lindell saw how he was trying to sort a file of loose papers, but apparently he couldn't get the pages under control.

Gusten Ander, called in as an expert, looked almost frighteningly focused, as if he was working out his next move, as he stood leaning over a slim booklet. Lindell thought it was a chess magazine.

At the short end of the table two colleagues from Investigations were leaning over a map. One had a pencil in his hand and Lindell watched him put an X on the map.

Eskil Ryde from forensics sat waiting next to Lise-Lotte Rask who was in charge of disseminating information and who was talking with a secretary. Two women who Lindell liked to exchange views with and not only about police-related matters.

More colleagues came in, as did Fritzén and another person from the DA's office.

Everyone filled the room with talk and the sound of scraping chairs being pulled out. Someone poured out coffee. Another downed an energy drink in a can and smothered a burp behind his hand. It was Jern from the Security Police, one of the few coworkers who had shown an interest in Lindell. He was known for spending a great deal of time on his fitness training and he was generally known as Superman.

He didn't look too bad and seemed unusually sensible for belonging to the felt slipper brigade, but Lindell was not going to let herself be charmed by someone from Sec.

Morenius looked at his watch and it was infectious. Soon more people were doing the same thing, as if to synchronize the time.

Ottosson coughed and spoke up since it was in Violent Crimes that the case was based.

"It's Wednesday today. Has everyone got their coffee?" was his magnificent opening.

A simultaneous humming rose from the group.

"All right. In that case, our queen is going to dignify us with her presence on Friday. She is going to open a home for something that's not quite clear to me. But in any case it is a new organization that is going to be set to sea with a great deal of pomp and circumstance. The location is the Academic Hospital. That doesn't make this any easier."

"It's not a home," Lise-Lotte Rask interrupted, "it's a new ward for the treatment of children with cancer."

"You've done your homework," Ottosson said with a half smile, and continued. "We have to make up our minds if this so-called chess trail has any merit. We are probably somewhat doubtful, even if our colleague Ander's report has been exemplary and stripped of any overly wild speculation."

Jesus, Lindell thought. She glanced at Sammy Nilsson, who was sitting directly across the table and made an almost imperceptible grimace.

Ottosson drew a breath and consulted his notes.

"Two farmers and one knight in the form of Carl-Henrik Palmblad, who was killed in his stables—all this is the setup for, according to Ander, a famous chess game from the late thirties. You have probably had time to read all this in his report. The interesting part of the game was apparently an extremely unexpected and bold attack on the white queen, if I have understood the matter correctly."

Gusten Ander shrugged but then nodded.

"Anyhow," Ottosson continued. "If this is true we have a delicate task, which is to protect Silvia from a lunatic."

He rounded out his concluding remarks by describing how the investigation had been organized thus far, how the absence of any motive, technical evidence, and witness accounts had brought them to three dead ends, as he put it.

Lindell leaned over the table and gave Fredriksson a quick look. He was still a glowing red color. She got ready to speak but was forestalled by Birger Åhs, the chief of Security.

"We have of course been preparing for the queen's visit for the past several weeks and have taken the precautions that we feel are necessary. We have procedures for celebrity visits where there can be a threat in the picture."

"Who is threatening Silvia?" Ottosson asked.

"It will take us too far afield to get into that now," the security officer said. "But what I can say is that we have nothing on the table. This took us by surprise, I must say. We have had some indications about some youth groups, but . . ."

"You mean AFA and that gang?" Sammy Nilsson asked.

Åhs flinched as if reacting to a physical irritation.

"Wasn't Silvia's dad a Nazi?" Sammy went on.

"Let me take issue with that," the security chief said, now as red in the face as Fredriksson. "He may have been associated with the party for a shorter time but that was solely for business reasons, ideologically he was a democrat, everyone agrees on this point."

"Whatever you say," Sammy said. "But of course he joined the Nazi party in the early thirties, earlier than—"

"Okay," Ottosson interrupted the exchange. "It's unlikely that a group of masked youths are behind these serial killings, definitely not if the design follows a chess game."

In the long and intense discussion that followed Lindell only participated infrequently and the longer the meeting went on the more difficult she found it to say anything about the photograph.

Should they cancel the royal visit? That was the DA's considered opinion. The chief of police and Ottosson argued against it. Morenius weighed in that he thought the court should be contacted at once and that they would have to make the final decision.

Lindell tried to meet Sammy Nilsson's gaze. He looked tired but smiled at her. She took it as a sign and decided to wait with the photo, talk to Sammy, and hear him out. There was still time.

"But what if the media gets wind of this?"

Morenius's tense voice made everyone else stop talking.

"You can imagine the headlines. I think we pass this along to the court," he continued, "that way we're in the clear."

"Yes, perhaps we should inform them," the police chief said.

"And look absolutely ridiculous," Ottosson objected with unexpected vehemence.

Ander coughed and waved his hand.

"I know that many of you think this hypothesis is absurd but my intuition tells me it can't simply be coincidence. Lindell, do you have something else?"

She realized that Ander sensed her doubt and now he wanted to hear her say that they didn't have a single other lead to pursue. She was again tempted to bring up the photo but resisted. She didn't want to embarrass Fredriksson in such a public setting.

"That someone out to kill the queen would first perpetrate a whole series of murders I find, mildly put, very unusual," she said cautiously, "but stranger things have happened."

Ander accepted this as a half confession and smiled at her.

The final decision was to inform the court but that they would not at the present time take any additional measures. Nothing was allowed to leak to the media. If the papers got wind of a possible threat to the royal family then the resulting situation would be chaotic.

✦

Twenty-eight

The container had been picked up and yet more cubic meters of the family's history had been carried away. Laura had asked the driver where he dumped everything.

"It can be burned, and in that case it'll end up in the furnace in Bolän-derna," he answered, casting an indifferent eye into the container.

She had an impulse to follow the container truck, and see all the junk tumble into an enormous burning inferno, catch fire, and literally go up in flames.

Now a new container stood in the driveway. Laura dragged out several bags from the garage and furniture from the house and the container was already half full. Her activities attracted a certain attention on the street. Many of the neighbors had already found a reason to walk past "the Dream House," they slowed their pace and stared with curiosity at what the Hindersten woman was tossing out.

There was talk. Some speculated that she was on her way to leaving the neighborhood. Others believed she was cleaning up after her father. A rumor had arisen that she was going to do a large-scale renovation of the house. Someone had seen her run half naked from the house to the garage. Another could tell that she had heard mysterious, shrill sounds from the upper story.

From having been relatively quiet for a time, the gossip had now gained new momentum and the house stood in the center of the neighborhood's attention.

Laura noticed her neighbors' interest but ignored their curious looks and questions. She worked on purposefully. Where this drive came from she wasn't sure. She was still going to leave everything—the house, Uppsala, and Sweden. But she didn't want strangers to touch the objects, books, and furniture. It was up to her and no one else to settle the score with her former life.

The upper floor was the hardest, not because she had to carry everything down the stairs but because that's where the most painful memories were.

Two rooms were full of Alice Hindersten's belongings. They were of little value and would only fetch a couple of thousand at an auction, Laura thought. The objects of the greatest value were most likely the old Jugend-patterned flower vases and a shaving mirror with a light wooden frame, probably birch. These things had been stored upstairs for as long as Laura could remember. The last few objects had been carried up shortly after her mother's death. A great deal had probably been thrown away.

For the first time since she had started to clean, Laura became hesitant. She could hardly stand to touch anything, much less throw them into the container.

She sat down on a stickback chair and looked at that which had been Alice's life. Laura knew that the gigantic America-trunk that took up almost a square meter contained dolls and other toys. Once she and Alice had looked through the trunk together. What had attracted Laura the most that time were the paper bookmarks from Alice's childhood. Some worn and frayed at the edges, others well-preserved and carefully packed into different envelopes, depending on their theme. What Laura remembered above all was the envelope with angels.

She opened the lid and breathed in the smells of her childhood. Numb with the pain of longing she picked aimlessly through the objects. The old doll with the lace dress had belonged to her grandmother and was probably one hundred years old. The dress looked moth-eaten and in addition it had a large tear on the front, a "skorsa" as Alice would have said. Laura wrapped the doll in her arms, rocked it, and mumbled some words of comfort.

Laura lingered in the room for over an hour, unable to carry anything down and throw it away.

It was getting dark when she returned to the first floor. Her hunger had somehow strangely abated, but her throat was dry from all the dust and she opened a new bottle of wine.

When she had downed half a glass there was another ring at the door. She put the glass down with care and tiptoed into the hall.

"Hello," she heard someone call out in a low voice and she ran up, turned the lock, and threw the door open.

"You came," she whispered.

Stig Franklin brushed past her into the hall.

"We have to talk," he said and scrutinized her half-naked body. "You're not wearing very much. Aren't you cold?"

Laura shook her head, elated and smiling.

"Are you hungry?" she asked and in that moment became ravenously hungry herself. It was as if his visit had awakened her from a kind of sleep mode and now when her bodily functions were switched on the hunger immediately returned.

"No," he said curtly.

"Surely you can have a glass of wine."

"I can't stay long."

"That's what you said last time," Laura said with a smile.

"Have you been drinking?"

"Only half a glass."

She was familiar with his views on alcohol. Jessica had inculcated Stig with ambivalence and guilt.

"It's a Valpolicella that you have never tasted, I promise."

"No thanks, I'm good."

Laura immediately went into the bedroom.

Stig remained standing in the hallway, unsure about how to proceed with what he had to say. He looked around in the increasingly bare house.

"What are you doing?" he yelled. "Are you getting rid of everything?"

He received no answer. He had an hour, then he had arranged to meet Jessica in town.

Laura returned, now in an old dressing gown.

"I have to shower," she said and before he had time to react she went into the bathroom.

Stig walked into the living room. He sat down in the only armchair left but got up again just as fast and walked into the kitchen, looked until he found a clean glass, poured out a little wine, and sat down at the kitchen table.

He felt it would be easier to talk to Laura here. He took a sip and had the feeling that Jessica saw him. He took another sip. How would Laura react? He prepared himself for the worst but it had to be ended. Jessica was no dimwit. She would soon find out about his visits and then things would be untenable when Laura returned to work.

He heard splashing from the shower and again felt desire stir in his body but he told himself to be strong and resist the temptation to be seduced. He had made his choice and in all honesty it was not even a difficult one.

He poured himself more wine and had a bite to eat. He could see her, soapy, her head tilted back and the dark hair hanging down. What fascinated him most—which was making him feel more and more uncomfortable on the hard kitchen chair—was Laura's complete abandonment in bed. She didn't seem to have any restraint.

He and Jessica had a pretty good sex life but Laura was something extraordinary. Jessica was controlled, it almost seemed as if she could press different buttons to regulate her emotions. Even the timing of her orgasm seemed to be something she had a button for. She always had one, as if she ran a program where the end point was a given. Afterward she washed herself fastidiously. Now he was used to it, but in the beginning it had felt a bit strange that she never lingered in bed. No, up like a spring and into the bathroom for the obligatory and scrupulous body wash, as if she wanted to scrub away every particle that came from him. It was rare that she came back to the bedroom. Instead she often went off to the computer or even to the laundry room to start the dryer or put a load in the washer.

I wonder how she will give birth, he asked himself and couldn't help smiling a little. She probably has some program for that as well. Into the delivery room, plop, and then out again. Not that that was happening any time soon. Not yet, she said. She probably had a time plan for that as well, he thought, not without bitterness.

Stig drained his glass, stretched out, and opened the refrigerator but it was as bare as the rest of the house. The sound from the shower had stopped. Stig got up, adjusted his pants in the crotch, and sank down on the chair again.

The door to the bathroom opened and suddenly Laura was in the kitchen. She smiled and Stig found himself smiling and felt very much at ease.

"Was it nice?"

She nodded. Her hair gleamed black, scented with an unfamiliar shampoo. Laura leaned against the fridge.

She grabbed the bottle in order to fill her glass and discovered that it was a little less than half full.

"You did want some after all," she said. "Didn't it taste good? It should actually be aired for an hour or even more."

Stig marveled at her calm. She again placed herself with her back to the fridge.

"We have to talk," he said and decided to look at her. He wanted her to sit down. It would feel safer with a table between them but Laura didn't move.

She nodded and Stig launched in.

"We have to talk," he said with unnecessary hardness and immediately regretted it when he saw her expression. "Don't get me wrong," he went on. "I like you a lot. You are attractive, very attractive."

He looked out the window, unable to continue, swallowed and made a new attempt.

"Jessica watches me like a hawk. I think she senses something."

"She isn't a problem," Laura said.

"Yes, she is."

"Stig, we love each other, it's that simple. We always have."

He stared at her.

"It won't work," he said flatly.

Laura smiled.

"Don't worry about Jessica. She's a bitch and you know it. It's me you want, isn't it? Look at me!"

Laura tugged on her belt and the dressing gown fell open.

Stig stared at her half-bared body.

"What have you done to your thighs?"

"I dreamed about you and I scratched myself in my sleep."

"I have to drive," he said, sniffling, rising on unsteady legs.

"You're not driving anywhere."

✦

Twenty-nine

"Could it be the bananas?"

Ann Lindell shook her head.

"I don't think so," she said with a worried expression.

Damn it, she thought, not now, not today.

Erik had vomited after snacktime.

"He was droopy for a while," Gunvor, the preschool teacher, went on, "but after that we didn't notice anything else. It was full steam ahead all afternoon."

"It must have been something that passed quickly," Ann said, who was finding it harder now to hang on to her expression of concern.

"He normally eats a banana," Gunvor continued.

"He seems happy now," Ann said and checked in his cubby to see if she had missed something.

"There's a meeting next Tuesday, did you see that?"

Ann hadn't seen it but nodded. She guessed that there was a paper pinned to the notice board.

"A lot going on at work right now?"

"You could say that," Ann said with an attempt at a smile and took aim for the exit.

"It's stressful here too, I have to say. Pernilla is sick and Lisbeth is at a workshop and we're not allowed to take in any substitutes. Luckily we have an intern and he's wonderful. Have you met him? He's only seventeen."

Lindell shook her head.

"Thanks for today! See you tomorrow," she called from the door.

There didn't seem to be anything much wrong with Erik. He walked quietly by her side to the car. Ann strapped him into the child seat and gave him a kiss on the cheek.

"Banana," he said and giggled.

"Mommy's going out tonight. Görel's coming over. That will be fun, won't it?"

Erik didn't reply, but there was nothing remarkable about that. He talked, and could be a real chatterbox but only when it suited him. For long periods of time he was completely silent only to explode into a torrent of speech.

Ann Lindell told herself she had no reason to feel guilty. How often did she ask Görel to babysit and find something to do of her own accord? Once a month, not more, and then it was often about work or a parent-teacher meeting.

Now she was going to meet Morgansson for a second time, but they were not going to the movies. Instead they were going to have dinner down by the river. He had called and asked her out. Ann had accepted without hesitation but had immediately called Görel as if she wanted her friend's approval.

Ann felt less nervous this time. She had gotten to know her colleague somewhat and could relax. But at the same time it was more serious now because this was date number two. It felt as if tonight would determine whether it would go any further.

Görel was going to come as early as five thirty. Görel was great. She had her own children, two girls, and she was straightforward in a way that Ann appreciated. No empty chatter, a sense of closeness without intrusive curiosity, and sometimes a raw humor that took Ann by surprise but made her laugh out loud.

Görel lived with Leffe. He was a carpenter and had helped Ann install windows to enclose her balcony. This was the only luxury she had permitted herself and she didn't regret it. It was fantastic to be able to sit out on the balcony as early as April and experience the first warmth of spring, or set the table for a Sunday dinner there in September and have the illusion of living in more southerly climes.

Erik started to talk once they were in the stairwell and continued without interruption when they reached the apartment. Ann had to bring him into the bathroom when she was going to shower, because if he didn't get answers to his questions he became inconsolably grumpy. Now he was perched on his stool, philosophizing. Ann commented on everything in a seasoned manner and from time to time threw in a counterquestion.

Ann couldn't drop the thought of her find in Petrus Blomgren's house. It was as if the photograph had imprinted itself on the mirror in the bathroom.

"To my beloved Petrus," she said.

"What?"

"Mommy's talking to herself," she said and continued brushing her hair.

Who was the woman? Did her existence even have any significance at all for the case? Ann decided to call Sammy.

"Too bad for Allan," Sammy said when Ann told him about the snapshot. "That's a real oversight. But why didn't you bring it up? I don't get it."

"I don't know," Lindell said honestly.

Of course she had thought about it. It wasn't simply because she didn't want to embarrass a coworker who had been sloppy. There were also other motives.

Erik appeared dragging his snowsuit.

"Play," he said.

"Wait a minute," Ann said to Sammy, lowering the receiver. "It's too late to go to the playground. Görel will be here soon. Mommy has to work."

Erik didn't say a word, looked at her with his wisest expression and lumbered off with the gear.

"It may not even be important," she said as she continued her discussion.

"I guess," Sammy said but Lindell heard his doubt.

"What should we do?" she asked.

"What should *you* do?" Sammy shot back, grinning.

They discussed the matter for a long time. Lindell felt a growing sense of relief. Her judgment and decision to keep this information to herself had been hers and hers alone and she was the one who would perhaps end up taking the heat for it but talking about the problem made her feel better.

"I don't believe in this queen plot," Sammy said for a second time.

"Who does?"

"Ander and Allan," Sammy said. "They sound like a circus act. 'Come and see tonight's act: Ander and Allan!' "

He made her laugh. Erik stood by her feet and laughed along.

"We'll talk more later?"

"You bet we will," Sammy said, and Lindell was touched by his words.

Thirty seconds after she put the phone down the phone rang. She picked up, convinced it was Sammy who had thought of something else, but the call came from Ödeshög.

"Hello Ann, I just wanted to see how you were doing. I've seen on the television how things are going there in Uppsala."

Ann sat down at the kitchen table. Yet another thing she felt guilty about. Ann called her parents all too seldom and she visited them even more rarely. Since Erik was born they had of course come for several visits but the contact between them was getting thinner and thinner. She didn't know why. Odeshog was a finished chapter. She had no ties there anymore other than the fact that her parents still lived there.

Ann had no siblings and felt some pressure to be a good daughter. Erik's birth had done some good in deflecting her mother's at times intrusive though well-meaning intentions, even if her mother had a great deal to say about the circumstances. She touched frequently on the fact that the boy didn't have a father.

Ann talked about the murder case for a while, shooting down the worst exaggerations of the media and trying to present the work in as sanitized a form as was humanly possible. Her parents were never curious in a positive way. They lamented the fact that Ann had such a depressing job. Ann was never quite clear on what profession they would have been pleased with. Most likely they would have complained about any job that she had had.

Her mother was in good health, her father somewhat unwell as usual. He had not stopped smoking despite his doctor's orders. Bertholdsson's youngest had moved away from home. The nearest neighbor had chopped away at the spirea hedge they had in common so it would probably never flower again.

That was, in short, the information that Ann received. Why don't you tell someone who gives a damn, she thought unkindly, but tried to sound attentive.

They ended the conversation with the usual exhortations from her mother's side, directed mostly at Erik's well-being, and Ann's half promises to visit soon.

Görel turned up and while Ann finished getting ready they chatted about this and that. Görel was like that, she mixed up big and small things into a single conversation. It could be the Prime Minister Göran Persson, discussions about the House of Music, or a new laundering technique.

"You can use regular dishwashing liquid," she claimed and pinched Ann's skirt at the same time. "This one is really cute. Where did you get it?"

"I can't remember," Ann said truthfully.

"It'll be coming off quick tonight," Görel said with a guffaw.

"What are you talking about?"

"This is the second time you're seeing him. And you aren't exactly a nun."

"But Görel, I don't want to . . ."

"Don't worry, I'm not going to embarrass you. Bring the man home if you like and I'll sneak off without a word. I promise! But I do want to see what he looks like."

At exactly eight o'clock—the cathedral on the other side of the Fyris River announced the time—Ann Lindell stepped into the I & I Kitchen and Bar.

Charles Morgansson was sitting at the bar, but could just as well have been sitting in the kitchen since he was involved in a lively conversation with one of the cooks.

He broke off at once when he saw Ann, stood up, pulled out a bar stool, and made a gesture of invitation. She had certain problems getting up there in her tight skirt.

"So, here we are again," Morgansson said in a knowing tone, after she had managed to get herself up.

Lindell looked around. There were many more customers tonight than last time. Two cooks were busy in the open kitchen and someone that Lindell assumed was new. He looked desperately young but was chopping vegetables at a frenetic pace and with a seriousness that demonstrated that he intended to make the mark.

"So are you done scoping the place out?"

A tall ungainly lug of a bartender towered over them from the other side of the counter. He would have looked rather forbidding had it not been for his eyes which revealed a more congenial personality.

"Perhaps a glass of white wine for the lady?"

Lindell got the impression that he didn't like to be contradicted and she nodded obediently.

"This here is Tall Per," Morgansson explained. "He graduated from Örebro Grammar School with a C in comportment."

"But a B in organization."

They bandied words back and forth while the Närke native poured out a glass of wine and drew a couple of glasses of beer.

Lindell smiled to herself, tasting the wine and peeking at her colleague from the side. He looked comfortable. She felt relaxed and a surge of anticipation. Her life had all too long been a series of disappointments and duties, with Erik as the only real source of happiness. Her work, which had earlier meant so much—not in terms of a career, which everyone always seemed to talk about, but rather the feeling of being able to make a difference—had slowly but surely changed character. Or was she the one who had changed?

Let it be like this for a while, she thought and took another sip of wine. When she turned to Morgansson he was looking at her.

"This feels good," he said and Ann was pleased at the straightforward comment.

She nodded. Tall Per retreated and disappeared into the hidden regions behind the kitchen. Morgansson put the menu in front of her. She was ravenous and decided to get the gambas to start and the anglerfish as a main course.

"Great choice," Tall Per said when she had communicated her order, and she felt as if she had finally received his approval.

They sat there for three hours. Ann called home once and everything was fine. They said almost nothing about work. In part this was because they were out in public, in part because neither one of them was interested in engaging in a form of overtime at the restaurant.

Ann told him about her background, but skipped Edvard. She imagined her colleague had heard that story anyway. When she started in on Erik, Morgansson looked more distracted.

"You don't have any children?"

He shook his head but said nothing and Ann let the subject drop.

Charles told her about his thirteen years at the Umeå Police. They found that they had similar experiences. Both of them had come from smaller towns and ended up working in large cities.

"I felt as if I knew everyone back home in Storuman, but in Umeå I didn't get to know very many people," Charles said. "I don't miss Umeå but I am homesick for Storuman."

Ann thought about whether there was any place she missed but she didn't think so, definitely not Ödeshög. She caught herself starting to think about Laura Hindersten but did everything to push those thoughts away.

Charles paid as he had offered to do, and Ann did not object.

When they got up from their seats she was gripped by anxiety. They hadn't said anything about the rest of their evening. Maybe he took for granted that he was going to go home with her? He knew she had a sitter.

They walked out onto the street together accompanied by Tall Per's thunderous thanks but then Morgansson ran back inside, said something to the owner, and returned just as fast.

"I've called you a cab," he said. "I'll pay," he added when he saw her confused expression.

She opened her mouth to protest but he held his hand up.

"No buts. I said I was going to treat you and that includes transportation."

So her evening ended with her sitting alone in a taxicab chauffered by a chatty young man. Ann sat in the backseat and watched as the buildings and people swept past outside and she didn't know what to think. What she felt very sure of, however, was what Görel would think.

When she entered the apartment there was just a lone lamp on in the living room. The soft sound from the loudspeakers sounded like whispers. Görel must be reading, Ann thought, and was suddenly upset about how the evening had ended. It would have been better if she had stayed home.

"Hello, I'm out here!" she heard Görel call out, and Ann heard a nuance to her voice that betrayed she thought Ann had company.

"It's me," Ann said.

Görel came out into the hall.

"Alone?"

Ann nodded.

"What kind of a man is he?"

"It feels fine this way, really," Ann said.

"It feels fine?" Görel sniffed.

Ann turned around, hung up her jacket, and pulled off her boots. Görel waited silently behind her back. Ann wished her friend would keep talking.

"Has everything been calm here?"

"Here? Sure. He fell asleep like a little pig."

"I think I . . ." Ann started, but she didn't finish her sentence.

All at once she became very sad, not angry, just sad. She accepted the glass of wine that Görel had poured out and was now grateful for the silence and the low light in the apartment. Chet Baker's voice almost made her cry. It was Edvard's music.

She sank into the couch, exhausted. Görel sat down next to her and at first said nothing, letting Ann taste the wine and run through the evening in her mind. After a few minutes Ann told her that everything had felt good until they were standing in the street and she realized he had called her a cab.

"What I regret the most is I let him pay. It's humiliating! As if I was a piece of luggage with no will of my own, that you can just send home."

"Maybe he's shy?"

"Shy," Ann sputtered, becoming more angry. "He's going to get his money back."

"He said nothing about a next time, if you were going to see each other again, or . . ."

"Nothing! It was as if it was on his terms, as if I didn't have any feelings. When he doesn't want to go out alone to the movies or the pub then I'm supposed to come through as company for him. And then get sent home."

"Has he had problems with women?"

"I don't know. He said almost nothing about his life in Umeå."

"He's gay," Görel pronounced in her incomparable way.

Ann tried to smile but couldn't manage more than a wry grimace. She was ashamed, for herself and her own weakness and because of what she must look like in Görel's eyes. She felt rejected. He hadn't even asked her if he could go home with her.

She didn't know herself what hopes she had had. Confused, sad, and angry, she drained her glass and immediately refilled it. She shouldn't drink more. But what does it matter, she thought, the bitterness burning.

Görel moved closer, put her arm around her shoulders, and whispered something comforting that Ann didn't hear.

"He didn't even give me the chance to say no," she sobbed.

She knew Görel needed to go home. She had to get up early. Leffe was probably wondering why she was so late. But at the same time it felt good to have Görel there. Her kindness made Ann feel somewhat less miserable and worthless.

She reached for her glass but Görel put her hand over Ann's.

"Don't drink any more," Görel said. "Tomorrow is another day."

Ann knew she was right but felt her anger return.

"You have to go home now," she said. "Tomorrow is another day for you too."

"It's not a problem," Görel said. "I have the night shift tomorrow."

Ann put down her glass and looked at her.

"Am I . . ." Ann started but then hesitated.

"You are beautiful," Görel said. "Don't think anything else. That Charles," and she made his name sound like an insult, "he's a bad egg. Forget him. Yes, I know," she said when she saw Ann's expression, "it's easy to say, but there are other men. Men who would give everything for a chance to cuddle up to a girl like you. And you know it."

Ann shook her head.

Görel went home shortly before midnight. Ann returned to the couch, stared at the half-full glass of wine but didn't touch it, got to her feet, and decided to try to sleep. She was not drunk, but intoxicated enough to stumble and knock over the standing lamp in the hall. The green glass cover shattered and the bulb went out.

She stared at the remains of the heirloom lamp that her grandmother had bought sometime in the twenties. For the first time she realized that she was perhaps not going to be able to manage, with work, with her loneliness, with being a good mother to Erik.

Without having removed her makeup or brushed her teeth she collapsed into bed with a feeling of regret.

✦

Thirty

Laura stopped at the point where all the paths came together. Granted, the sun was shining, but a sharp northerly wind that howled down the slopes of the Alps, sweeping past Lake Garda and striking the Valpolicella district in the back of the head, and the little village in the stomach, forced her to take shelter behind some jutting cliffs.

She was not equipped for a hike in challenging terrain; it felt particularly difficult when the wind grew in force.

She curled up there like an infantry soldier coming under fire. If she had had an axe or at least a knife, and for that matter something to kindle it, she would have gathered up some twigs and made a fire.

She searched the skies to see if the rain clouds were piling up the way they often did this time of day if the winds changed direction from the southwest to the north, but the sky was still an almost metallic blue and that calmed her somewhat.

Suddenly the wind carried a waft of fish. Laura sniffed and looked around. It was an improbability, it had to be at least twenty, thirty kilometers to Lake Garda as the crow flies, but the fact was that the stench was growing stronger. It smelled like the fish market in Venice that she had been to many times.

How could I go so wrong? was the question that she kept turning over in her mind. They had stopped in the village, Ulrik wanted to have a bite to eat and rest a little. Driving on the steep roads outside Fumene had taken its toll and he had become more and more cranky.

Laura had nothing against stopping but did not go with him into the small restaurant that lay very close to the road. She decided to take a walk instead. It felt good to get out of the car and even better to leave her father's muttering behind.

Now she was lost. She curled up in order to escape the wind, but also to gather her strength. She was convinced that Ulrik would be done eating by now. Maybe he would take a short nap in the car but he would wake up soon and wonder where she was.

He wouldn't leave the car but simply get more and more angry over her tardiness.

When she had sat sheltered for ten minutes she thought the wind was starting to die down and she braced herself to go out on the path again.

At once the stench returned and this time it was even stronger. After a curve in the trail that rounded a thicket of honeysuckle tangled up with iron oak, she made a horrible discovery. Lying on his back in the middle of the path, covered by a swarm of flies, there was a man. His mouth was wide open, his arms outstretched as if crucified, and his pants pulled down around his knees.

He must have been there for a while because his body was in an advanced state of decomposition. The open mouth was what still lent the face a somewhat human impression. It looked as if he was giving a shout of great surprise, or was it pain?

The knees were eaten down to the kneecaps and the thighs were badly mauled, probably by foxes, and a knife had been sunk all the way down to the hilt in his lower abdomen.

Laura turned and ran. Where her energy came from she didn't know but she ran at breakneck speed down the mountain, crawled on all fours up a ravine, and once she was up on the crest she saw the village. She could even see the car.

What had happened? Laura did not know. Perhaps it was a nightmare?

She told Stig everything. They lay next to each other. He raised himself on his elbow and looked at her.

"What did you do?"

"Nothing."

"Nothing? You found a murdered man."

"Perhaps it was the animals."

"Who had stabbed him?"

"It was a young man."

"How do you know?"

"He had white patent leather shoes."

"Oh my God," said Stig and sank onto his back.

He had gone out into the garden, dialed Jessica's cell and told her that he was at Laura's, that he had been forced to stay because she was threatening to take her life.

"Have you been drinking?"

"I had a glass of wine to steady my nerves. She's had almost a whole bottle, at least. She's in a bad way, I can't leave her, that's just the way it is."

"Call the hospital," Jessica said.

"I suggested that, but that made her completely desperate."

"We were supposed to meet."

"I know, but then I had to stay. She's really depressed. It wouldn't be good for the company if she killed herself. Hausmann wants her on part one. We can't just say: 'Unfortunately that won't be possible, she hanged herself last week.' "

"Do you want me to come over?"

"I don't think that's a good idea. She's calmed down a bit and we have agreed that she will try to cool it and try to sleep tonight. I'm going to get in touch with Severin tomorrow."

"Severin isn't a psychiatrist."

"I know, but he's a doctor."

He kept talking and lying so that he believed it himself, elaborating his conversation with concrete details that made Jessica buy it. Or so it seemed to him.

That was three hours ago. Since then he and Laura had made love with such intensity that Stig had never experienced anything like it.

Laura had fallen asleep but woke up after about twenty minutes, told him that terrible story and fallen back asleep.

He had remained awake and stared up at the ceiling. Was this what he wanted?

What had she said as they made love? Something about "Jessica will never fuck you again." And then that talk about the restaurant by the sea. She had brought it up before and at that point he had thought she had been there before, that it was an experience she was retelling but now he wasn't sure.

She wanted to escape, that was clear. Her efforts in the house were no ordinary cleanup, that much he understood. Apart from the bedroom, the kitchen, and parts of the dining room the house was basically empty.

Laura was going to escape and she was convinced he was going to come along. He had only realized that now. In a way it didn't bother him. It was as if their crazy relationship, or rather, their amazing shared ride in her macabre old bed, had pushed him into a landscape where the old, familiar value scale no longer applied.

She fucked for her life with a heat that exceeded all human behavior, as if life itself was the shared movement of their bodies.

Stig liked it. Laura boiled. Jessica's embrace was so cool he sometimes felt as if he had made love to the freezer box of an old refrigerator.

Laura licked and sucked, rode and bit. Jessica guided him in and made measured, controlled movements.

If that had been the only thing, but Stig had caught sight of the harbor with the little restaurant, that was on its way to sliding into the sea and splintering into firewood in the first big fall storm, and with a waitstaff that smiled and took you for granted and never asked you if you wanted the check.

Laura woke up and stared at Stig in confusion.

"Did you dream again?"

He felt more than saw how she waved this away with her hand.

"Were you really a virgin?" he asked, "I mean before . . ."

She smiled, and he was happy at her smile.

"I was," she whispered, almost inaudibly.

"How can that be?"

He rolled onto her. The room was so dark he could only make out the contours of her face.

"I didn't want to," she said finally, "but with you it's different. Am I good?"

"You are fantastic."

He saw her eyelids flutter and after a few seconds she fell back into sleep.

Stig Franklin stood outside Laura's house. The effect of the wine had faded but he still felt cut off from himself as if he wasn't really standing in this dark garden late at night, physically satisfied but perplexed about the turn that life had taken.

He stared at the wall as if he could see through the plaster, the bricks, wood paneling, and the striped brown wallpaper. Laura lay in there, slumbering, whimpering like an animal, afflicted by dreams and a desire that never waned. She was like an animal, stripped of human checks and possessed by the resolution to live out life completely, as if in the last days of a destructive war.

Convention and the old loyalties had to make way for her will for a devouring physical intimacy. She didn't appear to care about anything. She threw everything into the trash.

He was sickened by the filth in her house, the bad-smelling piles of old clothes and soiled sheets, the stench of molding food scraps in the kitchen, and the dishwater that only drained reluctantly from the sink and left behind a film of grease and a ring of grayish dirt.

Water was dripping from the rusted gutters. A couple of cat eyes glimmered and were gone. The rope ties on the neighbor's flagpole snapped weakly a few times. The faint burnt smell from the remains of Laura's book-bonfire made Stig feel as if he was in a strange place in a foreign land.

He should be going home but he knew that before he did so he had to make a decision. Should he tell Jessica what he had really been doing at Laura's or try to construct an even more advanced lie?

It was just before one o'clock. He took several decisive steps toward the terrace door but stopped abruptly. Did he want to return to his old life? That question was too big. The fatigue made his thoughts jump from one thing—running away with Laura—to another: leave her for good and try to puzzle his life with his wife back together. If she even wanted to. Stig realized that Jessica was going to find out what had happened, Laura would see to that if he betrayed her.

He stared at the outside of the house. It was probably worth a great deal and he knew it was paid off. What would Laura get if she sold it? Three million, maybe more. He could only come up with a couple hundred thousand at most. The house in Sunnersta was in Jessica's name and his own shares in the company weren't worth much.

Three million, he thought, and tasted it. Maybe Laura had money in the bank and other assets? He had the idea of riffling through her desk. He could probably find some ATM receipts.

Where would they go? How would they live? A life with Laura, he thought, and the thought was overwhelming.

He returned inside only to find that Laura was still sleeping. In the faint light from the lamp in the hallway he studied her features. So relaxed, the dark hair fanned out over her pillow, one leg pulled up, her right hand on her stomach and the left one straight out from her body as if she was waiting for him to lie down and rest on her arm. So beautiful, with the pale skin and the consummate beauty of a woman who has made love and thereafter fallen into a deep sleep.

Stig Franklin made up his mind, walked out into the kitchen, found a piece of paper and a pen, wrote a few lines, and left the note on the floor outside the bedroom door.

✦

Thirty-one

Ann Lindell was awakened by the sound of the phone ringing. She reflexively threw herself over the phone and at the same time registered the time on the clock radio: 01:03.

Twice this angry signal had woken her up in the middle of the night. The first time it had been work related and on the other occasion, about a year ago, it was her mother calling at half past two in the morning to say that Ann's father had been taken to the hospital because of heart problems.

This time it was about Ann herself. She answered sleepily and the first thing she heard was music.

"Hello?"

The dryness of her mouth made her wet her lips.

"Hi," a voice said on the other end, and Ann immediately knew it was the voice of a drunk person, "it's me, Challe."

Challe, Ann thought, drawing a blank until she realized who it was. She sat up in bed. Her mouth was like a desert and she felt the throb of a headache.

"It's one o'clock in the morning," she said.

"I'm sorry, but I had to call," Charles Morgansson said and Ann heard him straining to sound somewhat sober.

"You're drunk."

"I had to call," he repeated, "everything went so wrong. You understand . . . it went wrong. I . . . we have to talk."

"Now?"

"Can I come by?"

"Are you still at the restaurant?"

"I stayed," Charles said and suddenly Ann was wide awake.

"You call me up in the middle of the night, drunk out of your mind,
and you want to talk. What the hell about?"

"Can I come by?"

Ann got up out of bed. Never, she thought, I'll never let in a drunk
Morgansson, a man who has treated me as if I were an escort.

"I don't think so," she said, at the same time pulling away the curtain
and looking out at the parking lot. The electric lights were reflected in the
roofs of the cars. It had rained. A lone person came walking along the
street and turned into the parking lot, stopped, and lit a cigarette.

In the receiver she heard Frank Sinatra's voice and the clinking of
glasses. The man in the parking lot stood in place while he puffed once
on his cigarette and looked around. For one moment Ann thought he was
going to steal a car but the man continued his lonely walk, walking diagonally across the parking squares, and aiming for one of the building en-
trances. As he came closer she recognized him as one of the neighbors.
They had exchanged a few words outside. Ann knew he lived alone but
sometimes was visited by his teenage son.

"Charles," she said, and she could imagine him sitting on a high bar
stool, leaning over his glass with the tall bartender on the other side of
the counter. "I don't know what you want. You invited me to dinner and
then sent me away like a piece of mail. Now you call me at one o'clock
in the morning and you want to come over. What kind of a person do
you think I am?"

"I'm sorry," Morgansson said again, "I just want to talk. I know I've
behaved like an idiot but sometimes I get stuck."

Stuck, Ann thought and shook her head.

"I like you," Morgansson said, "but things went a little wrong. I chick-
ened out and . . ."

Ann heard a voice thundering in the background.

". . . I have to stop now. I'm not allowed to talk anymore. I'm disturb-ing you . . . ?"

His voice sounded incredibly sad.

"We'll be in touch," he said. "My apologies . . ."

"Wait," Ann said quickly. "The code downstairs is four-three-one-one."

"I know it," Morgansson said and Ann realized his cousin must have given it to him. "Does that mean I can come over?"

"I can't fall back asleep immediately anyway," Ann said and hung up, afraid of more words, tired of excuses, and amazed at her own compliance.

Charles turned up twenty minutes later. During that time Ann had brushed her teeth and washed her face, looked at herself in the mirror, pulled on her robe, had time to figure out her approach, and had time to change her mind several times.

"Thanks," was the first thing Morgansson said.

She let him in and walked without a word to the living room, where she had turned on the lamp in the window.

He had sobered up somewhat but looked like a sad dog. They sat qui-etly for a moment before he started to talk.

"I left a woman in Umeå," he started.

Ann closed her eyes. I should have guessed, she thought tiredly. Why do I let this happen?

"I liked her but I couldn't stay there, and she didn't want to move. She is a researcher at the university."

"Why did you have to leave?"

Morgansson lifted his head and looked at her. Now he looked com-pletely sober.

"I ran over a little girl," he said. "Every time I went downtown I re-played it over and over again. It became a nightmare."

"What girl?"

"She ran out from between two cars. I didn't have a chance to brake or veer. She died after half a day. It was ruled an accident but for me it was . . . she was eight years old."

He stopped.

"Do you want anything?"

Morgansson shook his head.

"Her mom was standing on the other side of the street."

"I'm sorry," Ann said.

She was struck by the thought of checking into the story with an Umeå colleague that she knew.

"It became impossible for me to work," Charles continued. "I thought about that girl all the time. Ronja was her name, like that robber's daughter in Astrid Lindgren's book. And about her mother's scream."

"So you left Umeå?"

"I had to, so I wouldn't go crazy."

"And your girlfriend?"

"She stayed. I think she was a little tired. I dreamed a lot at night. Went a bit cuckoo. She was working at home on her dissertation and I was on sick leave. It didn't work. In the daytime I walked around like a restless spirit and at night . . . well, you know."

Ann stood up and moved to the couch.

"Let's go to bed," she said and saw him tense up.

"We can hug but nothing more, okay?"

He looked at her quickly and nodded.

"Okay," he said, his voice cracking.

✦

Thirty-two

The wind grabbed hold of the large evergreens and shook them. After a few gusts, everything was calm again. Jessica Franklin leaned forward and peered out. The dark, pillar-shaped trees stood like sentries outside the kitchen window but Jessica thought they looked more threatening than protective. She had wanted to remove them and plant roses instead.

Once they had been little. The man at the nursery had said they wouldn't get bigger than two meters. Now they were twice that. Stig thought it a pity to cut them down.

She looked at the clock. For which time she didn't know. She had driven home right after Stig's call, made a simple dinner, and then anxiously walked to and fro in the house, unable to do any of the things she had to.

She didn't know what to think. His story about Laura was plausible for all its outlandishness. Laura was unstable and Stig was thoughtful and gullible. Was Laura trying to use him to change the course of the Hausmann deal? She had been forced to give in on several points and had been upset and mortified. Now perhaps she was using the nice and understanding Stig to alter the plans.

The longer the evening went on the more upset she became. Several times she decided to call Stig but changed her mind each time. Her pride forbade her. If he wanted to sit there and coddle Laura then that was his decision.

When it was close to twelve o'clock she first started having thoughts that Stig was having an affair with Laura. Jealousy bored in and spread like a cancerous growth. Again she wanted to call but did not want to give either Stig or Laura the satisfaction of appearing like a spurned wife who was anxiously calling for her unfaithful husband.

Jessica sat down at the computer, opened one of the Hausmann documents, and tried to work but the letters and numbers on the screen had lost their meaning. She left the study and walked around the house, furious and beside herself.

When she heard the car on the street she ran to the desk, sat down, and logged in again on the computer.

She heard the garage door open and shut. The door to the kitchen opened. Stig poured himself a glass of water and brought it down forcefully onto the counter. He must have had wine. That always made him thirsty afterward.

He called out but not how he usually did. She sat absolutely still and read a sentence in German, reading the words quietly to herself. An early memory of a German lesson at school came back to her. The lesson was about the Müller family visiting some relatives in the countryside. The thought was that the schoolchildren should learn words that had to do with farming. When Jessica had recited all the words she could remember in this context she heard Stig walking up.

"Hi," she heard him say.

She didn't turn around, but sensed he was standing in the doorway.

"You're working," he observed.

He sounded normal, but wasn't there a mocking tone in his voice? She turned around and got a shock. Stig's red-flushed face bore witness to what she had feared. He could look like that sometimes after they had made love.

"Are you proud of yourself?" she asked and made an effort to keep her voice from breaking.

He shook his head.

"We have some things to sort out," he said in a mechanical voice.

He told her calmly what had happened and that it was best if they separated. What scared Jessica the most was his control as he told her his reasons. It was as if he was making a presentation about the marketing of a new product.

There were none of his usual apologies or the awkward tiptoeing when he came to subjects that he felt were difficult or that he knew she didn't like to speak about, instead there was simply a methodological analysis of their life together and the conclusion that it was time to bring it to an end.

When he had finished she turned off the computer, stood up, and threw herself on top of him. The attack came without warning and he fell backward with Jessica on top of him. She hit him in the face with her fists and on his chest. He tried to shield himself, grabbed her wrists and held them in place. She spit in his face, bent over, and tried to bite him but Stig pulled away and managed to throw her off.

"You're crazy," he managed to get out.

"Says you, you bastard," Jessica screamed and Stig caught sight of features in her face he had never seen before.

She resembled an actress he had seen in a play on TV, wild, with distorted, naked features that radiated hatred and a bottomless sorrow. But for the first time he also saw fear in her eyes.

He jumped up from the floor but sank down again on his knees almost at once when he realized she was crying.

"Jessica, I'm so sorry," he said, "but we're no good together."

She curled up, writhing, pulled her arms in front of her face while her body was wracked with sobs.

He put his hand on her shoulder, unable to comprehend what was happening. He had expected many reactions, but not this.

The sobbing stopped after several minutes.

"Please, Jessica," Stig tried again.

She turned and looked at him with swollen eyes.

"Why?" she said.

"I've already explained."

"I love you."

Stig stared at her. It had been years since they had said those words to each other.

"I'd rather die than get divorced," she continued.

"Don't say that," he pleaded. "That's sounds so terrible."

Jessica pulled herself into a sitting position. Stig stood up. It looked as if they were in the midst of a choreographed dance routine.

"That woman!" Jessica suddenly burst out. "What do you see in her? She's crazy, you've said it yourself."

"I don't want to talk about Laura," Stig said. "We have so much else to talk about."

"That damn whore!" Jessica screamed. "She hates me. That's the only reason. She doesn't love you, she just wants to hurt me, don't you get it?"

Stig saw how this idea took root in Jessica. He realized it would become her interpretation and that Jessica's artillery would now be directed at this point in their shared terrain and that she would bombard him with explanations, stories about Laura's years-old hatred of her, her treachery, and how Laura would dump him when she had achieved the goal of separating the two of them.

"Don't you understand? She wants to get to me. That's why she keeps going on about Hausmann. It's not about phase B, it's me. That was my suggestion and that's why it had to be shot down. When she couldn't do it, when you backed up my idea she had to think of something else."

Stig pulled himself away. The unpleasantness increased as he observed the frenzy with which his wife presented her arguments.

"I'm having a beer," he said and walked out to the kitchen.

Jessica got to her feet and followed him and kept talking with an intensity that made him draw back from her.

"We'll have to talk more tomorrow," he said in an attempt to interrupt her.

She stopped for a second and stared at him.

"We have to straighten this out right now."

"We're exhausted, both of us," Stig objected.

"So you think we're going to go to bed as normal, sleep soundly, and then eat breakfast tomorrow morning as if nothing has happened?"

"I know it won't go back to normal," he said calmly and sipped his beer.

"Did you get drunk over there?"

"No."

"You drank wine."

"A couple of glasses. To keep her company."

"To keep her company! She got you drunk in order to get you in bed. You are so damned gullible!"

"Calm down, Jessica, nothing is gained by us screaming at each other."

"Calm down," she spat.

"I'm going to bed," he said and put the beer down on the counter, changed his mind and shoved it down into the garbage pail under the sink instead, struck by the thought that the beer bottle could become a weapon.

He walked toward the bedroom and awaited a physical or verbal attack from Jessica, but she had sunk down onto a chair and was staring unseeing at the new tile above the stove.

It was three o'clock, the night leading to Thursday, the twenty-third of October.

✦

Thirty-three

It had been several years since Ann Lindell had woken up with a man by her side. The last time was Edvard. Erik's father had left her in the middle of the night and gone off home to his wife and kids, leaving behind a used pillowcase and a pregnant woman.

If I get pregnant this time it will be a biological miracle, Ann thought and looked at the sleeping Charles. "Challe" he had called himself, and why not?

He was sleeping on his back. His chest was covered with curly hair. She didn't like hairy men, especially if the back looked like a shag carpet.

They had been lying close together. He had pressed up next to her but had not tried anything. Ann couldn't decide if it was because she had so explicity declared her position or if he didn't want to. She finally decided he simply wasn't horny. It bothered her a little because she had, when the evening began, had a thought in the back of her head that they might hook up. But now she was grateful that there had been nothing more involved than a hug.

Charles had fallen asleep after half an hour. She had not fallen asleep until around three. It was now seven o'clock and she should be more tired. Erik would wake up any second.

"Challe, it's time."

So damn ordinary, she thought and couldn't help smiling at his bewildered expression when he opened his eyes.

"It's probably best if you leave before Erik wakes up."

After he had left Ann got in the shower. She had the door open a crack but hoped it would be a while before Erik came shuffling in.

As the water streamed over her body Ann felt her suppressed desire return. She wasn't sure if she and Charles were going to share a bed again, or if she even wanted to, but the thought that it was actually possible made life feel brighter than in a very long time.

She smiled as she soaped up and thought about what Görel was going to say. That was the best thing: surprising Görel. It felt like restitution.

✦

Thirty-four

A rough-legged buzzard sailed over the fields at the Krusenberg farm. The ease of its flight made Allan Fredriksson smile joyfully to himself. He leaned forward, searching the sky through the windshield. For a few moments the buzzard couldn't be seen but then it returned and swooped very close to one of the ash trees at the edge of the road. It was almost the death of him.

As the car cut down into the ditch he was thinking about smews. Ingemar Andersson, the ornithologist from Buckarby, the most inbred village in Uppland, as he himself put it, had called the night before. He had spotted a couple of hundred resting smews at Lake Tämnaren and more were expected. Perhaps the record from 1978 would be broken?

The car dashed into the ash tree, made a quarter turn, flipped, and spun around on the newly plowed field.

Fredriksson flew forward in the seat belt, put his hands in front of his face, and the only thing he could later recall was the sound of metal buckling.

In the ambulance he said a few words that the emergency technician thought were "common barrow."

"That's a hybrid," Fredriksson whispered, half unconscious.

In his coat pocket there was something that would come to alter the investigation of the three murders. That morning he had dropped by Jan-Elis Andersson's house in Alsike and he was on his way back to Uppsala when the rough-legged buzzard turned up and played this trick on him.

Now, he had seen quite a few buzzards in connection with the spring and fall migrations as well as the occasional wintering bird, the last one in a field outside Åkerby Church in February, but a buzzard is a buzzard. Or rather, a bird is a bird, and Fredriksson couldn't get enough of them.

Fredriksson's early morning visit in Alsike was not due to his work ethic but his forgetfulness. The last couple of days he had been missing his cell phone. However much he looked he was unable to find it. It was embarrassing. It was the third phone he had lost recently. The first was in a washing machine and the second during a hunt for chantarelles in Lunsen. His sloppiness had become a refrain at work, not to speak of the caustic comments from his wife.

He knew that he had used his phone when he was at the home of Jan-Elis Andersson. It was his last chance. If it wasn't there he would yet again be forced to buy a replacement.

He had not found his phone but he had found a small object that had made his heart skip a beat. Gusten Ander's theory immediately took on a new light. Fredriksson jumped in the car in order to drive to the station. He had already forgotten about the phone.

Then the rough-legged buzzard came sailing by and now Fredriksson was lying on a stretcher at the Emergency Room entrance at the Academic Hospital. He was conscious. The ceiling fluttered by above his head.

"Am I paralyzed?" he mumbled and pulled off the oxygen mask.

A woman leaned over him.

"What is your name?"

"Allan."

"Hi Allan, my name is Ann-Sofie, and I'm a nurse. You have been in a car accident and have some injuries."

Fredriksson thought it was strange that she was smiling.

"What's your date of birth?"

"Alsike," Allan whispered, and threw up.

Nurse Ann-Sofie started to cut Fredriksson's coat while the others examined his body. Someone washed the blood from his head and carefully cut away the clotted tufts of hair.

"Is there anyone we should call?"

"Ottosson at Crimes," Fredriksson got out.

"Ottosson, as in the police?"

"My boss. He knows."

Allan Fredriksson felt as if a thousand hands went over his battered limbs. The pain in his back and neck were the worst, or rather, the fear that he was so seriously injured he would have to spend the rest of his life in a wheelchair.

"X-ray," he heard someone say.

The words dripped onto him. Some he understood, while others only conjured up pain and confusion.

"My coat," he said, between the waves of nausea.

"It will be allright," he heard a voice say.

"This will hurt a little," another one said.

It was a man with a beard.

". . . blood . . . we have to . . ."

"I can't move."

"You're restrained," the man with the beard said.

Fredriksson thought he smelled strange.

"I'm a police officer."

"Okay."

"There's something I have to . . ."

"It was a simple car accident, wasn't it?"

The bearded man's breath wafted over him.

"I mean . . ."

"I was thinking about a bird," Fredriksson said and had an image of hundreds of smews. He and Ingemar Andersson had been at Lake Tämnaren that beautiful October day. The twenty-third of October 1978, to think he still remembered the date. Fredriksson tried to figure out how many years ago that was, and failed. It was a long time ago. The children were young. Ingemar and he . . . to think that he called. There ought to be more like Ingemar. Pity about his wife. Ellen was her name.

The coat! He tried to get up. Someone put a hand on his shoulder. His head spun and he felt the mask over his mouth again.

His left arm was broken in two places, and the blow to his head had given him a strong concusssion and an open wound on his forehead.

He had woken up again but the pain in his back was so unbearable that when he tried to say something he fainted for a third time.

The breaks in his arm were complicated. The bone in his upper arm was protruding. Fredriksson had lost a great deal of blood. The injuries to his back and neck were not visible but would soon be determined with the help of an X-ray. His whole body would be X-rayed and every little fracture would be documented.

The bones in his arm received a preliminary adjustment and were bandaged. That had to be sufficient until they received a complete picture of his injuries.

The staff, a whole team, were both methodical and experienced in their work. Fredriksson embarked on his long journey back.

His coat had been tucked away into a plastic bag under the stretcher.

✦

Thirty-five

Even though it was many years ago she was sure she would find it. In her inner image, or rather, a rhapsody of many different images, she saw the houses, the fields, and the narrow, curving gravel road.

It ran through a sunny landscape. From what Laura remembered it was always beautiful weather when she and Alice traveled those thirty, forty kilometers north.

Once they had stopped in a clearing in the forest and picked wild strawberries.

"This is the landscape of my childhood," Alice said and smiled. "Of course I know where the wild strawberries are."

She used words like that, like "landscape," and dialect words for things such as *pastures, paddocks, hay-cutting,* and *hay-drying racks.* The landscape of childhood.

For Alice, the word "landscape" took on a magical meaning. It wasn't simply the word used to refer to districts like Uppland, Västmanland, Dalarna, and the other brightly colored patches in the school atlas, no, landscape became something completely different, a scent, a few words uttered in passing, a smile, and some wild strawberries threaded on a stalk of grass.

The road followed the same course as before but had been widened. The forest had changed, as had the houses. It looked deserted. Alice's landscape had grown more naked and cold. In part this must be due to the time of year but Laura had the impression that an illness had befallen the area. A slow-working virus that turned even the young spruce trees brown, and that bent the smoke from the chimneys, spilling a milky haze over the gardens and yards.

There seemed to be fewer people now, and they looked smaller, more afraid, barely looking up when Laura went past. It was as if they no longer cared. Back then they would straighten up, meet her gaze with curiosity, and hold up a hand.

She couldn't find the clearing with wild strawberries and suspected it had been planted with trees.

The old school was still there but it had been converted into a private residence. A jeep was parked in front of the entrance. The old schoolyard had been replaced by a gravel display area for *Entreprenad* machines.

Alice often talked about her teacher Miss Olsson, a woman from the Dalarna district who taught Laura how to prune fruit trees, plant and thin vegetable beds, and how to make heaped rows of earth for potatoes.

"That's its Latin name," was something Alice would say, "and that's what it's called in Uppland dialect, and Dalarna dialect." "Trifolium" became "bee bread" and "red clover." "Genum" became " three-flowered aven" and "prairie smoke."

All manner of thought-provoking names of herbs flew from her tongue like beautiful butterflies.

For each kilometer that Laura clocked, new memories returned to her. It was like opening an old photo album and making a trip back in time. She drove slower and slower with a feeling of solemnity and grandeur, aware of the fact that this was probably the last time she'd be seeing her mother's landscape.

Lars-Erik Jonsson came toward her with a wry, but nonetheless welcoming smile. Laura stifled an impulse to hug him. It was not a good idea. He wiped his hands off on his work clothes.

"After so many years," she said, suddenly embarrassed at his inquisitive gaze, "you still recognize me."

"You look the same," her cousin replied and held her hand in a firm grip.

Lars-Erik was five, six years older than Laura. She thought he looked worn. The skin in his face was loose and gray and when he walked across the yard, he limped.

"Do you have aches?"

"Yes, but nothing to worry about," Lars-Erik said. "It's my joints."

Laura knew that Agnes, her aunt and mother to Lars-Erik, had suffered greatly from rheumatism. Her aunt had died young, thirty-one years old, and Laura had no memories of her. She had only seen pictures of a woman who reminded her of Alice.

Lars-Erik had grown up with his father Mårten and two brothers. Alice would always tell Mårten what a fine job he was doing raising the three boys. A couple of times a year Alice and Laura traveled out to Skyttorp to visit them.

Mårten had a soft spot for Alice. Perhaps mostly because she reminded him of her sister, but also because Alice always remembered his sons' birthdays and namesdays, a Swedish tradition of celebrating the name assigned to each day throughout the calendar year.

"Will you have a cup of coffee? That thing's not going anywhere," Lars-Erik said and nodded his head at the tractor that he was in the middle of repairing.

The kitchen looked like before. The smell that came at Laura was also the same.

She wanted to talk, or rather, to hear her cousin's voice.

"How is everything with Jan and Martin?" she asked.

"Oh, like always," Lars-Erik said with a smile. "Janne is still up in Forsmark and Martin has married, divorced, and remarried."

He warmed to her question and spoke at length about his brothers. Since they had lost their mother so early they had become very close. Laura had never heard them quarrel or say a harsh word about each other.

Lars-Erik measured out the coffee and poured water in the coffeemaker. Laura looked at his gnarled hands.

"And you? Are you married?"

Laura shook her head. She considered telling him about Stig but didn't. Maybe Lars-Erik wouldn't understand.

"What about Ulrik?"

"Do you know about what's happened?"

"Well," Lars-Erik said, "I did see in the paper that he's missing."

"He's still gone," Laura said.

He looked searchingly at her before he silently set out cups and plates.

"Perhaps I should have called," he said finally, but they both knew it was an unnecessary comment.

He took out a loaf of bread, cut about half a dozen slices, set out butter, cheese, and a packet of smoked ham. Laura made sandwiches, they drank coffee, and talked about people they knew in common. To Laura's surprise the conversation flowed well. But Lars-Erik was the most communicative, more open than his younger brothers. He had a streak of nonchalance that both irritated and attracted Laura. He smiled often, quick in his thinking and conversation, putting her at ease with a frankness that she wasn't used to. She wished she had visited him much earlier.

In the office everyone talked past each other, used euphemisms and carefully chosen words that—behind their apparent innocence—could hurt. Not even praise could be taken at face value. Behind acknowledgements and fine words there could be jealousy and barbs.

Sometimes Lars-Erik paused before giving her an answer to her questions, became thoughtful and silent, replying briefly but with an unspoken signal that he would return to the topic later. It was a habit she knew so well from Alice.

"So, you don't have a man?"

"No, it didn't work out that way."

"Not for me either. Rose-Marie lived here for a while, but then she got a job in town. She thought it got too far to keep driving back and forth.

"It can be lonely sometimes but I have the house," he added.

She couldn't bring herself to say that she was preparing to leave Sweden. It would feel wrong. Lars-Erik wouldn't understand, he who couldn't even imagine moving to Uppsala, but she couldn't help asking if he didn't sometimes long to go away.

"You are so like my mother," he said. "Not just in your appearance but . . . everything," he continued, and now there was a hesitation in his voice that had not been there before. "She was an anxious soul. My father said later that she had gypsy blood in her and of course she was dark, just as you are."

"We have gypsy blood?"

"No, but that desire to travel, to get away."

"I've lived in the same place for thirty-five years," Laura said, feeling ill at ease.

"But are you happy?"

Laura looked at him, startled, then looked away, confused.

"I don't mean to say . . ."

"I know what you mean." Laura interrupted his attempt to try to cover over his unexpected question.

No, I am not happy and I never have been.

"Alice should have stayed here," Lars-Erik said and looked at Laura with an expression as if he was testing the limits for what he could say.

Now she could tell him! She knew that her cousin, and perhaps above all his father Mårten, had never liked Ulrik.

"It's going to get better now. I am . . . I have met a man.

"He's married," she added and made it sound like a bonus.

Lars-Erik did not appear to be interested in a continuation.

"I have to ask one thing," he said and drew a deep breath before going on. "It's about Alice. This is a hard question to ask but I have to know. She died in the basement. No one really knows what happened. Father said something a long time ago that maybe you pushed her down the stairs. He said that. That Laura was not an innocent child."

"It's a lie! Ulrik made that up."

"Ulrik came here once after Alice died. They argued, almost so it turned into a fight. It was probably something Ulrik said. Father wasn't himself for a long time. He was so fond of Alice."

Laura looked at him but Lars-Erik avoided her gaze. He kept talking as if to himself.

"It's not always how you think. I know that Alice and my father were close."

"Mårten never said a mean word to me."

"No, it was probably just something Ulrik tossed out."

Laura gazed at her cousin.

"Did you think, *do* you think that I pushed Alice?"

"No, why would you do something like that?"

Lars-Erik started to clear away the coffee cups and the plate of sand-wiches.

"Are you moving?" he asked suddenly, his back turned to her.

Laura didn't answer but he took this for a yes.

"Far?"

"Yes."

"You can move to Skyttorp. There are houses for sale."

Suddenly her plans appeared so paltry. All calculation and planning was in vain.

"Even though we're cousins," Lars-Erik continued, "I don't know you very well, but there are bonds that make us receptive to the same wavelengths. I saw that as soon as you got out of the car. At first I was shocked because you looked so much like Agnes. It's almost spooky. As if she had come back, for a couple of moments."

Laura stretched out and nudged his hand with hers.

"You looked so lost," he said, and Laura saw how he steeled himself to maintain his calm. "You gave me a look that said 'Save me!' "

"I have to do that myself."

Lars-Erik smiled.

"Where did Ulrik go?"

"He disappeared."

"And that made you happy?"

Laura nodded. He looked at her and she expected more questions but her cousin left the kitchen. She heard him walk up the stairs to the upper floor and suddenly felt abandoned, as if he had left her for good.

He returned with a small cardboard box in his hand, placed it on the table, and gave her a look that said, this is important. Don't say anything to ruin this moment.

Laura kept quiet while he untied the string that kept the lid in place. The box smelled like closet.

When he removed the lid she saw that the box contained letters and photos.

"Your mother wrote letters to my father," he said and took out a thick bunch of letters tied up with paper string. When he undid the knot she immediately recognized her mother's handwriting on the uppermost page.

"There's about thirty-something in all. The first one came about a week after my mother died and last one was written the week before Alice died."

Laura stared at him.

"Why did she write to Mårten?"

"She needed someone to talk to," Lars-Erik said. "I know it may feel unpleasant but we're adults now. I read some of them for the first time two years ago, after my father had died. I learned a lot about him. Everything may not have been so fun but that's life. Why I should I judge others?"

"Why did he keep them?"

Lars-Erik didn't answer.

"Are they love letters?"

"No, not really, but there is a lot of love in them. I've arranged them in chronological order. Do you want them? They are yours as much as mine. More yours, really."

Laura held out her hand and pulled out an envelope from the bunch, but hesitated in taking out the letter.

"Your mother was unhappy," he said.

"I hate him," she said.

"I thought as much," Lars-Erik said. "Do you think he's coming back?"

Laura shook her head. She couldn't tear her gaze away from the envelope with the neatly printed address. She experienced the divided feeling of both being close to her mother and being betrayed by her. She had written to another, and although Laura had only been a child when the letters were written she wanted all her mother's confidence. But the letters were also a greeting from Alice. The almost physical sensation of her mother's presence that seeped from the stack of envelopes filled Laura with sadness. Alice was still talking to her.

"May I . . . ?"

"Of course," Lars-Erik said.

"I won't read them now," she said and put the letters away, carefully retying the string and putting everything into her bag.

"You can get them back later," she said.

Her cousin's expression conveyed that it didn't matter.

Both he and Laura had trouble finding the thread again. The carefree conversation, the light talk about what had been, and the gossip about people in common did not want to restart.

Lars-Erik picked up the cardboard box, got up, and walked up the stairs. Laura looked out the window. Dark rainclouds were piling up on the horizon and gliding together into gigantic formations that threatened the sun.

So much sky, so much space and life, Laura thought. A movement on the other side of the road caught her attention. It was an old woman who with great effort came out of the woodshed with an old-fashioned woodbin in her hand. She stopped halfway, put down her burden, and rested.

"That's Elsa," Lars-Erik said, having silently slipped back into the kitchen. "She is my only neighbor. She's turning eighty-seven this year."

"I remember her," Laura said. "It's a wonder that she's still alive. I thought she was ancient twenty-five years ago."

"She still keeps chickens. Her grandmother was called Egg-Magda, her mother Egg-Karin, and now it is Egg-Elsa. But it stops there."

"Egg-Elsa," Laura repeated quietly. "A whole life connected to chickens."

"There are worse titles," Lars-Erik said.

"My closest neighbor is a professor."

"A remarkable woman," Lars-Erik continued. He had walked over to the window. "She's phenomenal at solving crossword puzzles. I usually see her when she's sitting at the kitchen window. Sometimes it happens that she comes over and asks about a word, but it's rare because most of the time she cracks them on her own."

The old woman resumed her walk and went into her house. There was smoke rising from the chimney.

The sun went behind clouds and the kitchen immediately became almost dark.

"I collect clouds," Lars-Erik said and leaned forward, looking up at the sky. "It is like an enormous art exhibition. I like to stand out in my yard and watch nature give me fresh exhibitions every day, and to top it off it's free. Have you ever thought about how the sky can give rise to the most unbelievable formations?"

Laura was watching her cousin, how his gaze and posture completely changed as he spoke so lovingly about the clouds, unaffected and surprisingly poetic.

"But the beautiful formations vanish immediately," she interjected, mostly to get him to keep talking.

"That's true, but it doesn't matter to me. I live in the moment, happy for each second. In town people hurry around, running to galleries and throwing their money away on art. Here everything is free. Sometimes Egg-Elsa comes out into her yard and we stand there on either side of the road looking up at the sky. There are worse forms of entertainment, wouldn't you say?"

"I have to go," Laura said abruptly.

They stood there facing each other. His shirt was spotted with oil. The dark stubble took on a metallic gleam in the dim light from the window. The brown eyes were Alice and Agnes. He opened his mouth to say something but stopped in the attempt.

Suddenly he looked taken aback and frail. The face that had earlier seemed so open, his cloud face, now seemed to hold many unspoken questions. She understood that his speech about the free art of the sky and finding joy in the moment were veils of loneliness.

Laura again felt an urge to hug him but held out her hand instead and he took it with such force and an intensity that bewildered her. She was used to neat, short handshakes.

"Come back," he said, "before you go anywhere."

Laura nodded, but knew they would never see each other again.

He didn't let go of her hand.

"Whatever has happened, you have to like yourself," he said. "Everything is not your fault."

What is "everything," she wondered.

"You saw the tractor out there," Lars-Erik went on. "For close to two years I have been restoring it. Egg-Elsa sometimes teases me and says I'm married to a fifty-year-old tractor. It'll be finished soon. I drove it out of the workshop yesterday. But what then?"

Laura didn't really understand what he was getting at with his question. She pulled her hand from his.

"You know that . . ."

"I know," Laura said.

The letters from her mother to Lars-Erik's father were in her purse. About thirty in all, written over a ten-year period. Three a year. That wasn't very much but Laura only had only received one letter and two postcards from Alice.

The letters weighed on her. As if she had a bomb in her bag. She didn't know if she would be able to bring herself to read them. Not right now. Maybe later, by the sea. Read them out loud to the staff and the other diners who would not understand a word but would listen and smile anyway.

The visit to Lars-Erik had made her despondent. Not that she wished she hadn't done it, because if she hadn't gone back to her mother's landscape one last time she would have regretted it. Now it was over. The next to last stop behind her.

She was happy to have come into these greetings from her mother, but a fear of what the letters might contain and her jealousy toward her uncle—who had had such a lengthy and almost intimate contact with Alice—soiled the landscape and Laura's own memories. The visits, together with Alice, to Mårten and his three sons, now took on a different meaning. Had Mårten and Alice been in love? The letters would perhaps provide an answer.

Again she stood outside and peeked into Alice's world. Instead of putting the landscape behind her as she had thought she would be able to accomplish with her visit to Skyttorp, the letters gave rise to new questions.

She felt Lars-Erik's gaze on her back as she got into her car. The smoke from Egg-Elsa's house billowed thickly. In the ditches the ferns were wilting and creating a yellowing edge to the green spruce curtain.

She pulled out onto the the road behind a lumber truck, whose heavy load made the ground tremble, followed it a kilometer or so before she overtook it but then immediately regretted it since the forceful vehicle had seemed to guide her through the terrain of memories.

It had felt safe to lie behind it and let the truck set the speed. Now she was driving along much too quickly.

✦

Thirty-six

How small he is, Ottosson thought. He stood there looking at
Fredriksson from the foot of the bed, feeling somewhat at a loss as he always did with hospital visits.

Ann Lindell felt guilty. She had not yet shown the picture of the unknown woman to anyone. If she were to pull it out now it would be like
adding yet another stone to the burden of her defenseless colleague.

"The question is what he was doing in Kusenberg," Ola Haver said.

"Jan-Elis Andersson in Alsike," Lindell said.

"Maybe he had an idea," Ottosson said. "You know how Allan is."

The bouquet of flowers in his hand was drooping.

"Should I get something to put them in?" Lindell asked.

Ottosson nodded absently. Lindell was glad to leave the hospital room
for a few moments. When she returned Ola Haver was leaning over
Fredriksson.

"At least he's breathing," he said and Lindell couldn't help smiling as
she arranged the flowers. They were not beautiful but Ottosson had insisted that they should bring something with them.

Suddenly Fredriksson opened his eyes. Haver jumped and grabbed
Lindell's arm.

"He's awake!"

"Allan, can you hear me?" Ottosson asked in a loud voice.

Fredriksson's eyes glimmered in response but then he appeared to sink
back into the fog.

"The coat," he said, almost inaudibly.

Opening his mouth appeared to be an incredible effort. There was a
smacking sound as some dried spots of saliva stretched like rubber bands
between his cracked lips.

"What did he say?"

" 'The coat,' I thought," Haver said. "Did you say 'coat,' Allan?"

Fredriksson nodded very slightly. He was as white as a sheet and Lindell was afraid he was about to throw up.

"I'll check with the staff," she said and left the room.

They found Frediksson's coat in a plastic bag in a nearby room. It had been cut to pieces and stained and Lindell shivered when she realized the dark spots were blood. She put it back in the bag and returned to the room.

Fredriksson appeared to have sunk back into his dormant state.

"Here it is," Lindell said and pulled out the coat.

"Check the pockets," Ottosson said.

"You'll have to do that," Lindell said.

In the left pocket Ottosson found an evidence bag containing a chess piece. A white pawn.

All three officers stared at the sleeping Fredriksson.

"Chess," Lindell said stupidly.

"The question is where he found it," Haver said.

Again they looked at their colleague.

"Check if he has the keys to Alsike on him," Lindell said.

Ottosson shook the coat. There was a rattling sound.

At that moment a nurse entered the room. Her name was Beatrice and Lindell took this as a good sign.

"Is he going to make it?" Ottosson asked.

"Is he going to make it? What did you think, that he was dying?"

Ottosson became noticeably embarrassed.

"Allan is a good friend," he said. "I was just worried."

"He has broken his arm, injured his neck and back, and banged his head pretty hard but he'll be watching birds again in a few weeks."

The three police officers looked inquisitively at her.

"He's been raving about smews and buzzards the whole time."

"And chess?"

"No, just birds, birds, birds."

She adjusted the IV tube that was connected to Fredriksson's arm, patted his cheek, and swept out as swiftly as she had entered.

"Ola, you stay here and when he wakes up you'll ask him how and why."

"Ask him what?" Haver said with an uncomprehending look.

Ottosson stared at him.

"I was just joking," Haver said and laughed.

He liked the idea of sitting at his colleague's side when he regained consciousness.

Ottosson's eyes were moist. Lindell knew that it was in response to the nurse's friendly chatter and care of her patient. Her boss had a soft spot for TLC.

Ottosson and Lindell went separate ways in the hospital parking lot. Ottosson had to meet the district attorney and Lindell answered evasively when Ottosson asked what she would do.

She drove through the hospital area, came out onto Dag Hammarskjöld's Way and turned onto the road to Kåbo. She couldn't get Laura Hindersten out of her thoughts. There was really nothing that indicated that this strange woman had anything to do with the three murders but this morning she had studied a self-drawn map where Jumkil, Alsike, and Skuttunge were marked with crosses. Between these points she drew straight lines and they intersected in Kåbo. Lindell did not put much stock in coincidences, and when the September disappearance of a seventy-year-old man was followed in October by the murders of three men around the same age, she did not believe it to be a coincidence.

Certainly, Ulrik Hindersten could have disappeared from natural causes, gotten lost, or simply run away of his free will, but in spite of intense searching he remained swallowed up by the earth. The City Forest was not that big. He would have been found, especially since police dogs had been used. The police had received help both from the military and the Uppsala Kennel Club. As far as Lindell could tell every square centimeter had been searched.

That he had left of his own free will was more implausible. His passport was still in the house, no personal effects were missing, and no withdrawals or purchases had been made with his bank cards since the disappearance.

Lindell played with the idea that Ulrik Hindersten was the perpetrator and that perhaps his daughter either sensed it or was even party to it.

Her behavior was odd, to say the least. To burn up all his belongings, especially the valuable books, implied a degree of feeling out of the ordinary. Was it a kind of grieving or was it the expression of hatred and revenge?

Lindell had to get an answer to these questions before she could let go of Laura Hindersten.

She turned onto the street and kept her fingers crossed that Laura would be home. The driveway was full of garbage bags but there was no car.

She parked on the street and got out. A woman peeked out of the window of the neighbor's house but quickly drew back. Lindell got the impression that she was fearful, maybe a cleaning lady working without a permit. There were rumors about a cleaning service that employed women without work permits from Poland and the Baltic states, who earned thirty-five *kronor* an hour. Rosén had written a memo after an investigation into the matter but nothing had been done. This female slave trade had a low priority. The clients moreover were well-adjusted Swedes in Sunnersta, Kåbo, and Vårdsätra.

Lindell walked up the stairs and rang the bell. The signal echoed inside the house but no one opened.

A strange feeling of foreboding came over her. It reminded her of an event several years ago when she visited a house in order to search for a hidden refugee. That time it had been just as forbiddingly quiet but in the end the door had been opened.

Lindell walked down the stairs and out into the garden. The place where Laura had burned the books was now a black gash surrounded by flattened grass. A few pages from a book had been blown into a bush. Lindell picked up a singed page and read a few lines. It was a poem, that much she could tell, and she guessed that the language was Italian.

She let go of the paper and it flew away between the bushes, fluttering nervously, lifting and landing in the fork of a tree about a meter above the ground. Lindell followed its flight and thought she recognized the tree. She didn't know much about plants but it was not your everyday tree, she could see that. The striped, arrow-straight trunk with the branches at sharp angles gave it an almost aristocratic appearance.

She walked closer and stroked the bark. Something told her she had seen a similar tree lately. Fredriksson should have been here, she thought, smiling.

She looked around, pulled on the ladder in the hopes that Laura would turn up. The garden really was run-down but it had a kind of charm that appealed to Lindell. Its wildness, the small rooms that were created in the midst of the overgrown vegetation, and the dark tunnels that led to dead ends reminded her of an unexplored jungle. At any moment you could disturb a strange animal who, as quickly as it had appeared, would disappear again into the wilderness. From the low-hanging tree branches, cold-blooded venomous snakes could unexpectedly attack.

Lindell forced her way through a couple of bushes. A cat came rushing past as if shot from a cannon and made her scream with fright. She shivered. The charm was completely lost and she tried to find her way back to the house. A twig was stuck in her hair, her shoes were damp, and she was cold.

Heavy clouds made their way across the sky and suddenly a strong wind blew through the trees, leaving the garden mysterious and gloomy.

Ann Lindell walked back out onto the street. A red Nissan Micra stopped in front of the neighbor's house and the woman she had spotted in the window stepped through the door, hurried down the stairs, and got into the car. She had a large sports bag in her hand.

Lindell memorized the license plate, walked back to her car, and called to find out who owned the Micra. It belonged to a bus driver with a Polish-sounding name.

Ann Lindell drove down Norbyvägen toward the castle and then took a right. Her thought was to drive to Alsike. She had taken the keys out of Fredriksson's bloody coat. That he had found a chess piece there didn't mean anything. Many people had chess sets in their homes. She seemed to recall they even had one in her childhood home in Ödeshög but she couldn't remember anyone who played chess.

She suddenly took a right at Artillerigatan. Without putting on her blinker and almost without braking she took the curve much too quickly and came close to crashing into an oncoming car.

It was a stab in the dark, the flash of the woman in the photograph and another in front of a bonfire, that made her perform the insane maneuver. At the Vivo grocery store, a couple of hundred meters from Laura Hindersten's house, she stopped the car and got out, consumed with an idea. The chance of success was minimal but it was worth testing.

There was a young woman at the cash register. She smiled when Lindell came in. Lindell introduced herself and asked if there was anyone around who had worked in the store about twenty years ago. The young woman looked perplexed.

"You mean here?"

Lindell nodded.

"Twenty years ago?"

A new nod. A polite smile doesn't always mean quick wits, Lindell noted.

"No, I don't think so. It's just mullah Ante and me here."

"And Ante?"

"He's twenty-five."

"Okay, do you know of anyone who might have worked here before, someone older?"

"Like you, or what?"

Lindell smiled.

"Yes, like me, or maybe someone even older."

"Sivbritt used to work here but she's retired."

"Then she's older," Lindell pointed out.

"She still comes in sometimes, pretty frequently actually."

"Maybe she lives in the area?"

"Ante!" the cashier yelled suddenly. "Do you know where Sivbritt lives—you know, the one who comes in all the time and tells us how to do our job?"

Ante emerged from the back of the store. He looked much older than twenty-five, probably because of his considerable beard.

"Sivbritt Eriksson, she lives on Birkagatan. I've delivered groceries to her home. Why?"

"What do you mean, why?"

"Why do you want to know?"

The cashier nodded at Lindell.

"It's her."

Ante looked interestedly at the newcomer.

"Has Nicke sent you?"

Lindell grew tired of this and explained that she wanted Sivbritt's address, and she wanted it right away. Ante reacted immediately, wrote it down on a piece of paper, tore it from the pad with a suave expression, and gave it to Lindell, who thanked them and hurried to the exit.

"While I'm here," she said and turned in the doorway. "I'm investigating a disappearance. It's an older man who went missing about a month ago, Ulrik Hindersten. Do you know who that is?"

"Your buddies have already asked us about it," Ante said.

"I'm asking you again."

"He was here sometimes but his crazy daughter is here, like, a lot."

"Crazy?"

"She's a real freak who asks for a sick amount of stuff."

"Like?"

"Cheeses and stuff," the cashier said and made it sound like a personal insult that Laura Hindersten wanted to buy more than bread and milk.

"Has she been here today?"

"Is she also missing?"

"Thanks," Lindell said abruptly and left the store.

Lindell knew where Birkagatan was. Several years ago, before she worked in Violent Crimes, she had been there to check on a reported case of domestic abuse. From what she could remember a woman was later charged with assault in a lesser degree. She had hit her husband in the head with a frying pan and thereafter thrown hot potatoes at him as he tried to flee from the apartment.

She parked directly outside the entrance, walked quickly up the two stairs, and rang Sivbritt Erikssons bell. It's sick how many Erikssons there are, she thought and smiled to herself.

After the third try she gave up. I thought retirees were home all the time, she thought obnoxiously, already having created a mental image of the whiny Sivbritt who disturbed young people in their work.

When she walked back there was a man next to her car. A white piece of paper was on the windshield, attached with duct tape. It looked like an enormous invitation to a funeral. The man surveyed his work with satisfaction.

"What the hell is this?" Lindell burst out.

"Read it yourself," the man said impudently, but drew back when he saw Lindell's expression.

She tore off the note and read, "You have repeatedly parked your car . . . " She glared at him.

"What are you talking about?"

"You can read, can't you?"

"Can *you* read?" Lindell said, fuming and pointed to a laminated notice that was visibly placed on the dashboard. "And secondly, I have *never*, I repeat *never*, parked in your damn parking lot!"

"Yes, you have, I write down all the licencse plate numbers," the man said and held up a notepad.

"Give me that! This is a punishable offense, do you understand that? You can be arrested for it. What's your name?" Lindell said, her voice now icy cold as she took out her notebook. "I'm with the police," she added.

The man ran away. Lindell stared after him with surprise.

"So you've run into Crazy Gudmund?"

Lindell turned around and there was Sivbritt Eriksson. Lindell knew at once it had to be her. Finally her luck seemed to have turned.

"Why is he called that?"

"It's simple: his name is Gudmund and he is crazy. A couple of years ago he was hit in the head with a brick."

Lindell started to laugh.

"I'm sorry," she said. "It's just that kind of day today."

The woman nodded.

"I know how it feels," she said, with a tone that made Lindell believe her.

"You're Sivbritt, aren't you?"

"Alice," Sivbritt said at once when Lindell showed her the snapshot she had found at Petrus Blomgren's.

"I can't remember her last name, but her first name was Alice. She died in an accident, fell down the basement stairs. Her husband disappeared this September and his daughter still lives in the house. She's some kind of an economist, I believe. Hindersten, that's what it was, I remember it now."

"You are a gold mine," Lindell said.

Sivbritt Eriksson looked noticeably pleased.

"What was Alice like?"

"A sweet woman, who didn't have an easy time of it, if you'll excuse me saying so. She always came in on Thursdays. That's when our meat came in. She was very particular, but knew what she was talking about. A good customer."

Lindell sized up the woman in front of her. About seventy, probably no taller than 155 centimeters, graying hair with a perm that was starting to grow out, a thin body, and that combination of reserve and complete frankness that Lindell had seen so many times in older people, perhaps above all in women.

Alice Hindersten may have been a good customer, but Sivbritt Eriksson was a good observer and judge of human character.

"Her place wasn't in Kåbo. She didn't really fit in. She knew how to behave, no question there, but she would have needed another kind of man, not one who buried himself in books."

"How could you tell she didn't fit in?"

"You can tell. When a woman has had to give up too much, well, then it . . . " Sivbritt Eriksson hesitated, ". . . it's not good. I mean, Alice liked to laugh but that man was like a walking migraine, all puffed up with his own importance. He kept people down, you could see it from a long way away. He didn't even have to open his mouth."

She stopped and Lindell was convinced she was thinking about her encounters with both Alice and Ulrik Hindersten.

"Alice was fond of veal," she continued. "It was for some special dish, Italian I think. It's hard to find good veal. Alice would rather pass if I didn't have a good piece, and then I would feel a bit ashamed but she was always so kind and said it wasn't my fault and of course she was right about that."

"I don't doubt it," Lindell put in.

"She liked to take walks. I often saw her walk by. I think she went to the Botanical Gardens each and every day. She took the girl with her. She was already dark as a troll back then."

"Are you talking about Laura?"

"They only have one. I remember Alice talking about new flowers that had bloomed. She was like a calendar. One day it was spring bulbs and the next day some primrose."

"Was she happy?" Lindell asked even though she already knew the answer.

"She was happy in the garden. I have been alone for fifteen years but we had a good marriage. Alvar worked at Ekeby for a long time before they shut down. Then he received his sick pension. I have lived here for over fifty years. Here in this building, I mean."

"When was this photo taken do you think?"

"Hard to say. Alice was a woman who didn't change. May I be nosy?"

"Of course."

"Why are you asking me about Alice? She died such a long time ago."

Lindell hesitated but decided to tell her.

"We are investigating the murders that you have probably read about in the papers. Alice's name has emerged in connection with them."

Sivbritt Eriksson clapped her hands over her mouth and stared at Ann.

"This is also about Ulrik Hindersten. He has been reported missing, as you know."

"Do you think he's been murdered?"

"There is nothing right now to indicate that," Lindell said.

Sivbritt turned her head and looked out the window and sat quietly for a long time. Lindell let her think in peace.

"Well, dear Lord," the woman said finally and looked at Lindell.

"I'm telling you this in confidence, you understand. I don't want you to mention this conversation to anyone."

"Of course," Sivbritt said. "Not a word."

"Did Alice talk about love with you?"

Lindell thought the question sounded silly but Sivbritt reacted like Lindell had hoped, with a meaningful silence before she began to speak.

It was three quarters of an hour later when Ann Lindell left. The last fifteen minutes she had been sitting on pins and needles but when Sivbritt Eriksson insisted on making her a cup of coffee Lindell felt she had to accept given everything that she had just received.

When she got into her car she gave the steering wheel a slap and drove whistling onto the street.

Crazy Gudmund, partly concealed in the garbage room, watched her vengefully and was convinced that the Eriksson woman was suspected of a serious crime.

"Breakthrough!" Lindell cried as she drove by the metal sheds on Karlsrogatan. She tried to restrain her excitement but the information that Sivbritt Eriksson had provided was the most sensational in the case yet. In one blow Ulrik Hindersten appeared as the key to all three murders. Was he also murdered, or the murderer? This was the question that clearly had to be put first.

In her inner map she drew in Jumkil, Alsike, and Skuttunge, extending the lines to Uppsala and the house in Kåbo. A connection was now established between Jumkil and Kåbo. Now she had to map out the connections between Jan-Elis Andersson and Carl-Henrik Palmblad and the Hindersten family. Ann Lindell was convinced such a connection existed.

The murders were no vendetta against the countryside, as many had believed. Neither the rental agreements, tractors, nor LRF had anything to do with the case. The three old men had qualified themselves to be brutally clubbed down in the eyes of the killer and everything most likely pointed right back to the rundown house in Kåbo.

"Motive, motive," Ann Lindell muttered as she drove past the Eriksberg Church.

Laura Hindersten was priority number one. She must have the answers. Of course she had denied knowing any of the three but Lindell was now convinced she had been lying. Or was her father Ulrik the spider in the web? In that case, where was the murderous professor?

She decided to return to the Hindersten house. The street was deserted and the driveway was still empty.

Ann Lindell parked on a side street and returned on foot to the house.

✦

Thirty-seven

The forensics department found no fingerprints on the chess piece that had been removed from Allan Fredriksson's coat. Ottosson had not expected there to be any, but he still sighed heavily when he received the news. He put down the receiver, then immediately lifted it and rang Ola Haver.

"Has he woken up?"

He listened to Haver with growing concern. Admittedly Fredriksson's neck and spine injuries were not as serious as they had initially feared but he was still basically unreachable.

"Have they operated on the arm?"

"They're waiting," Haver said. "He has to be stable first, they say. There's no bleeding in the brain but he has a severe concussion and from what I can understand the brain swells up. They may operate tonight."

"Has he said anything about the chess piece?"

"He's talking a lot of nonsense," Haver said in a quiet voice, "but from what I can tell he's been at Andersson's in Alsike. Wasn't Sammy going to go out there and check?"

"He called in," Ottosson said and Haver could hear in his voice that he was feeling under pressure. "He didn't find any other pieces, nor a chessboard."

"It seems a bit mysterious to only have one chess piece, don't you think?"

"You could say that. Säpo-Jern, Morenius, and Fritte the DA have been here," Ottosson said. "They're starting to get good and nervous. Silvia is arriving tomorrow."

"What do you think?"

"I'm as lost as all the others," Ottosson admitted.

"What does Ann say?"

"I don't know. She's disappeared."

"How do you mean?"

"I've called but she doesn't answer."

"She's probably having a cup of tea at the Savoy," Haver said, grinning.

"Perhaps," Ottosson said. "Give my greetings to Allan."

They wrapped up the conversation and Haver promised to call as soon as Fredriksson said anything of interest.

The big machine had been set in motion and that made Ottosson depressed. The decision had been made to reinforce the security around Silvia. On top of this she was not going to get to Uppsala by car, as previously planned. Instead she was going to land on the roof of the 85-building at the Academic Hospital and thereafter be escorted to the oncology division, and return the same way. Dinner at the castle had been cancelled and the governor was upset. He had been looking forward to hosting the queen. Now he had been cheated out of the prize of getting some positive press, for once.

The decision had been made at the National Police Heaquarters. A superintendent whose name Ottosson had repressed had called and briefly conveyed the news. A crisis group, with representatives from all thinkable areas, had been assembled and taken over. The national security force had been called in. Uppsala would for one day be a besieged city. All this on account of a recovered chess piece.

Ottosson knew he should go down to the large conference room, where a meeting was underway, but lingered in his office.

Perhaps the right decision had been made, perhaps it was an overreaction. At least the police chief had expressed his relief. Ottosson thought this mostly stemmed from the fact that he no longer had to shoulder responsibility for the state visit and Ottosson felt a similar relief. Others would take over.

As long as Fredriksson gets well, he thought, and slowly rose from the chair and walked out into the corridor where he immediately bumped into Berglund and Modin from Criminal Investigations.

"Have you seen Ann?" Ottosson asked.

Berglund shook his head. Ottosson kept walking. He heard Modin talking about bomb-sniffing dogs.

Instead of going to the conference room he went down to the cafeteria in hopes of finding Ann there. Ottosson had had the impression the last few days that she was unusually distracted. He was used to her shifting emotional states—it could be a roller-coaster ride in the space of one hour—but Ottosson knew her so well that he realized this time it was something out of the ordinary.

She no longer had the same spark. Ottosson thought there were problems with Erik and had cautiously asked some questions. But Ann had assured him that everything was great and the way her face lit up when she spoke about Erik made Ottosson believe her.

Was it the chess angle, that Lindell had so loudly and categorically dismissed, that had created this visible dissatisfaction in her and her al-most deliberate inability to cooperate?

Suddenly it hit him: it was love. Ottosson smiled broadly and some uniformed police officers gave him curious looks.

Obviously he had heard the talk going around the station: Lindell had been seen at the movies and on the town. Sammy Nilsson had also said something about the new technician, Morgansson. He and Lindell had been spotted outside a restaurant together. Ottosson thought that was less positive—police couples were not exactly an ideal combination.

He took out his cell phone and called her again. No answer.

✦

Thirty-eight

"You've had a visitor," the professor said when Laura got out of the car.

It almost seemed as if he had been waiting for her.

"A woman," the neighbor continued. "She seemed very anxious to get ahold of you."

Laura gave him a look of indifference.

"She even walked around the garden as if you were there."

Laura shut the car door. On account of all the garbage bags in the drive-way, half of the car was on the sidewalk. She opened the trunk. The pipe wrench lay in full view. Laura picked it up and weighed it in her hand.

The professor's smile faded.

"Don't go poking around in my life," Laura said menacingly.

Her neighbor stared at the pipe wrench and took a couple of steps back. Laura followed.

"Don't poke around in my life."

The professor backed up a couple more meters, looked around quickly as if to find help, but the street was quiet as usual. There was no one to be seen.

"Are you scared, you little professor-shit?"

"Calm down," he managed. "I haven't done anything to you, have I?"

"Not done anything?" Laura said furiously and charged at him. "You have talked behind our backs and spied on us all these years. Shouldn't that count?"

The professor fled while Laura laughed heartily.

"Hi Laura," a voice said behind her and she spun around.

Laura lowered the pipe wrench and concealed it behind her legs.

"He was threatening me," she said.

Ann Lindell nodded.

"Could we talk?" she said.

"Not today," Laura said quickly, "I don't have time."

"This will only take a few minutes."

"I don't have time!" Laura shouted.

The professor, who had been following this exchange from his front steps, suddenly became brave, ran down the steps, and stopped on the lawn with only the slim hedge between him and Laura.

"I'm calling the police," he said. "This can't go on. She's an embarassment to this whole neigborhood."

"It's not necessary," Lindell said.

"Necessary! If you only knew how we have suffered, year after year, with this crazy family."

"You old bastard!" Laura screamed. "You damned freak!"

"That's enough," Lindell said.

Laura's face was distorted with anger.

"I am a police officer. I'm here to talk about Ulrik Hindersten's disappearance. It's perhaps understandable that Laura is upset right now," she said and turned to the man.

"You're from the police?"

"Did you think she was from your illegal cleaning service?" Laura said. "She's here to talk to me and not to be accosted by some impotent professor."

"No, this is going too far! Did you hear what that Neanderthal said?"

"We're going in," Lindell said, and took Laura by the shoulders and led her like a hapless child toward the house. As they passed the car Laura tossed the pipe wrench into the trunk.

Lindell heard the neighbor yelling behind them, that he was going to report Laura to the police for unlawful threats and Lindell for incompetency.

"He employs an illegal cleaning service?" Lindell asked.

"The whole street does," Laura said flatly. "I'm the only one who does my own cleaning."

"And you do that with gusto," Lindell said.

Laura smiled at her. The tics in her face had stopped and her hand was steady as she put the key in the lock.

"You can sit in the kitchen for now," she said. "I just have to pee."

Lindell heard splashing from the bathroom. She looked around the kitchen with interest. The old cabinets with stainless steel handles and the low countertops bore witness to the fact that nothing had been renovated for decades.

There were newspapers, bundles of paper, and a dirty pair of panties on the kitchen table and up against the wall a dozen wine bottles arranged in double rows. Lindell thought they looked like a platoon of infantry soldiers on a march.

She picked up a pile of papers and read. The text was in German.

"This is from work," Laura said, who had snuck back in without a sound and was standing by the door.

"I'm sorry, it wasn't my intention to . . ."

"It's not secret. It's really boring."

Lindell was amazed that she could switch moods so quickly.

"I see that you keep to Italian labels," she said, indicating the bottles.

"Would you like a glass? We can celebrate a little."

"What's the occasion?"

"That I'll be free soon," Laura said and smiled. "I've met a man."

"Is that freedom?" Lindell said with a little laugh.

"His name is Stig and he is absolutely wonderful," Laura went on, ignoring Lindell's comment. "He's a colleague. We fuck. No, we don't fuck. We make love to each other. If you only knew."

Laura didn't look at Lindell. It seemed as if she was talking to herself. She walked over to the window and looked out. She grew silent but Lindell saw her lips still moving.

"He's mine," she said after a while.

"Congratulations," Lindell said.

"He's married but that doesn't matter. That can be solved. The essence of freedom lies in solving problems as they arise, don't you think? If you accept the fact that the problems are unsolvable then you become half a person. An impoverished person. Isn't that right?"

She turned to Lindell and looked at her for confirmation. Lindell nodded.

"For thirty-five years I have believed that everything was my fault. But it wasn't! Jessica is her name. She's no good for Stig. Jessica is no good. She . . . when everything . . . I've lived shut up here. Now I've paid all the debts."

"Are they getting a divorce?"

"Yes, I'm the person who's going to separate them. That has become my task. Stig is too weak for such things. He doesn't even dare talk to her. He says he has but I can see that he's lying. He is so scared! Just as I was. If you only knew how much he loved me. He's loved me for a long time. Maybe several years."

Laura smiled. Her features softened.

"Are you sure you wouldn't like some wine?"

Laura picked up a half full bottle from the counter. Lindell shook her head and at the same moment took out the picture of Alice Hindersten.

"This is you mother, isn't it?"

If Laura was taken aback she didn't show it. She didn't move a muscle.

"Yes, it is. My mother, Alice Henrietta."

"I found this photograph in Petrus Blomgren's house. He was murdered a couple of days ago. Why do you think he had a picture of your mother?"

"I've no idea," Laura said and sat down across from Lindell.

"I asked you earlier if you knew Blomgren but at that time you denied it."

The phone in Lindell's pocket rang but she ignored it.

Laura studied the photo.

"Wasn't she beautiful?" she said in a soft voice voice. "My mother."

"Did you know Petrus Blomgren?"

"No," Laura said.

"I think Alice and Petrus had a relationship."

Laura swallowed.

"I don't think so," she said, and Lindell could barely make out the words. "My mother was faithful. The letters!" she cried out suddenly.

She stood up and left the kitchen. Lindell heard the front door open and Laura ran down the steps.

She returned quickly with her handbag.

"Excuse me," she said. "I was just given some old letters."

"From your mother?"

"Yes, I visited a cousin and he had some old papers."

"Have you read the letters?"

"Yes, it was just family gossip but it was fun anyway. It was sweet of Lars-Erik to think of me."

"If we could return to Petrus. I think he and Alice went to Mallorca together. Do you remember that trip?"

"Of course, that was my mother's own little excursion, as my father called it. She had been operated on for something that spring and needed cheering up."

"What kind of an operation?"

"Something to do with her gall bladder, I think."

"But you didn't hear of anyone named Petrus?"

Laura shook her head again.

"How do you explain the picture?"

"Is he from Skyttorp or Örbyhus, this Blomgren?"

"No, why?"

"I was thinking perhaps he was a childhood friend of my mother's."

"But why would he have such a recent picture of her?"

"Maybe he was in love with her," Laura said simply and lightly, as if it were a trivial matter.

"If I can speak frankly," Lindell said, "then—"

"One should be frank," Laura broke in.

". . . I don't believe it. I am convinced that Alice and Petrus had a relationship. That you didn't know about it is one thing but do you think your father knew?"

Laura didn't answer. Lindell waited for a while before continuing.

"Your mother died shortly after she returned from Mallorca."

"My mother's death is personal and has nothing to do with anyone else. It is my grief. You can't sully it."

"I don't want to upset you but I need to clear this up. Do you think that Ulrik knew of Blomgren's existence?"

"In that case he never mentioned it," Laura said gruffly.

"No hints? No word after you had grown up? Some parents love to tar the other just to have the advantage or win the sympathy of the child."

"Ulrik isn't like that."

"How is he?"

"I don't know why you would be interested in that. Wouldn't it be better if you found him?"

"We're trying to, or rather, we have done everything. Your mother seemed very interested in gardening. You can still see that your garden was very beautiful once. While I was waiting for you I walked around in it. There is—for me at least—an unusual tree in your garden. It must be old, at least twenty or thirty years. It has several trunks. Do you know which one I mean? It has a striped bark."

Laura nodded.

"Who planted it?"

"My mother most likely," Laura said.

"I saw an identical tree outside Blomgren's house. Not quite as large, but it grows better here."

"You ask a lot of questions."

"That's my job."

"I also have a job," Laura said and gave a nod to the pile of papers on the table.

"Aren't you on sick leave?"

"Are you an insurance officer?"

Lindell smiled.

"Where did your mother die?"

"Are we going to dig her up as well?"

"No, I just want to understand how she died."

"I live with that knowledge every day."

"I know," Lindell said and wriggled out of her jacket.

She felt the tension and warmth rising in the kitchen. She couldn't figure Laura out. She was lying about Petrus Blomgren, Lindell was convinced of it. Behind the secure, swift replies there was a person who was on her guard.

"You don't understand anything about my family," Laura said. "My mother died. I was left alone."

"And your father?"

"He lived in another world. He simply happened to live here. There was a summer when I . . . was always swinging. I did lots of childish things, ran around barefoot, tied dandelions together, and everything I had never had time for. Ulrik read his books. It was a beautiful summer. He sat in a wicker chair and read. Sometimes he stood up and gave speed to the swing again. I was almost afraid I would go over the top but he just laughed. In the evenings we sat up late, played games, and listened to Verdi. Should we go down?"

"Go down?" Lindell asked.

"Into the basement. That was where she died."

Laura smiled sadly and for a moment Lindell hesitated. Something about this woman didn't add up. Lindell had seen it before, an unpredictable rage lurking behind the controlled surface.

She pushed aside her doubts and followed Laura into the hall.

"You'll have to excuse the mess," she said. "I can't afford an illegal Polish cleaning lady."

"That's allright," Lindell said. "I won't remark on the dust."

Laura pulled the door open and was about to walk down the stairs when she turned around.

"Wait a minute, I need to get a flashlight. The light down there isn't working."

Lindell peeked down into the darkness.

"Take this," Laura said and held a flashlight out to Lindell. "I'll get one more. It's probably in the kitchen," she said and left.

Lindell turned on the light. The battery was low and in the faint light she saw the contours of the steps and the little area at the bottom. There was the gleam of a large number of wine bottles. Most of the remaining space was taken up by cardboard boxes.

Lindell leaned forward to get a better view. On both sides there were openings that led to dark recesses. It smelled musty.

Laura returned.

"I can't find the other flashlight, but why don't you go ahead. Be careful, the third step is a little treacherous."

Lindell looked down. Laura nodded and smiled. Lindell took another step and let the flashlight illuminate her way. The third step swayed.

"Careful," Laura said behind her back. "It was that exact step that became my mother's death."

"Was she on her way up or down?"

"Up, I think, because she was carrying a jar of lingonberries."

Laura giggled and Lindell turned her head.

"Now you die," Laura said tonelessly and gave Lindell a shove in the small of her back so she fell headlong down the steep stairs.

✦

Thirty-nine

The red-haired nurse came walking down the hallway. She was talking to herself, unaware of the fact that Ola Haver was looking at her. She placed one hand behind her neck, leaned her head back, and stretched.

"Are you sore?" Ola Haver asked.

She looked up, startled.

"Yes, I know, I kind of blend in with the walls," Haver said.

"Maybe you're the secret police," she said and smiled.

Ola Haver immediately fell in love. This sometimes happened to him. It usually passed quickly but the feeling was equally pleasant every time. He saw it as a guarantee against boredom.

"You have to work hard," he observed.

"Everyone does, don't they?" the nurse said matter-of-factly. "How is your colleague?"

"He mostly mumbles stuff about birds."

"As long as there are policemen who are bird-watchers there's hope," the nurse said and fired off another smile.

"There are policemen for everything," Haver said.

"That's just it, isn't it?" she said. "For everything."

He got the impression she didn't like policemen. In another context he would have asked her to elaborate.

"I'm a nice policeman," he said and smiled.

"I'm a nice nurse," she countered.

"What a pair we make!" Haver said with enthusiasm.

She laughed and that was what he wanted, to hear her laugh.

"What do you think?" he asked and inclined his head toward the hospital room where Allan Fredriksson was.

"They'll probably operate tonight," she said.

"That means he'll definitely be gone for a couple of hours, won't it?"

"I'm sure you'll be able to get some coherent sentences out of him tomorrow morning."

"Well, we've never managed that before," Haver said. "That reminds me of the story of the patient who asks if he will be able to dance after his operation and when the doctor says there shouldn't be any problems the patient lights up and says: Great! I could never do that before!"

The nurse laughed again.

"Yes, I know. It's an old one," Haver said.

"Very old." She smiled and kept walking.

He returned to Fredriksson who was still sleeping. He went to the foot of the bed and studied his colleague's face, the way one can't do otherwise. Fredriksson's relaxed features gave an air of great calm. Haver suddenly felt uncomfortable watching him and walked over to the window and looked out. Traffic on the thoroughfare outside the hospital had intensified. A veritable stream of cars went by, people came walking along or half ran to the bus stop, and staff members in white coats jaywalked with an utter disregard for death.

As always when Haver was in a hospital he experienced a slightly sentimental sense of gravity and gratitude. Inside these walls, behind the windows to all of the hospital rooms, a struggle was going on. An army of doctors, nurses, subnurses, technicians, cleaners, janitors, and God only knows, were struggling on behalf of life. Like that nurse in the corridor, the red-haired one, who with her smile had probably assuaged the suffering of multitudes.

What is it that human hands cannot accomplish? he thought, almost devoutly and moved against his will. He twirled around and looked at his colleague in the bed. Allan Fredriksson returned his gaze.

"You're awake?"

Fredriksson nodded and his eyes were clear. Nothing remained of the earlier confusion.

"We were worried," Haver said.

Fredriksson smiled but also looked serious.

"Hospitals always get me down," he said.

"Still, you managed to get through this pretty well."

"What time is it?"

"Half past three."

Fredriksson shut his eyes and Haver sensed he was trying to remember what the time had been when he drove out to Alsike.

"Where did you find the pawn?"

"On a shelf in the hall. I saw it as soon as I came in. It's strange we missed it."

"We always miss something."

"No prints?"

Haver shook his head.

"Has the machine been set in motion?"

"You can count on it," Haver said. "You knew this would stir the pot, didn't you? The highest level of response with the National Guard, bomb squads, and the whole shebang. Ottosson almost shit his pants."

"What does Ann say? She was so grumpy about this whole chess thing."

"She's been swallowed up by the earth."

"The Savoy," Fredriksson said.

"I said that too, but she's not there. Otto actually called them to check."

"Have you checked with Blomgren and Palmblad?"

"Of course," Haver said, "there are no chess pieces there. But why did you go out to Alsike?"

Fredriksson told him about the lost cell phone and how on the way back to Uppsala he had caught sight of the buzzard and lost control of the car.

"I think Ann is up to something," he went on.

"What do you mean?"

"You know what she's like. I talked to her this morning and she was being all cryptic. It was like she was having trouble talking to me, as if she was hiding something."

"Like what?" Haver asked and sat down on a chair next to the bed. He trusted his colleague's tracking instinct and could imagine how he had picked up on Lindell's behavior. Haver also knew Lindell so well that he took her intuition seriously. It had brought success to many previous investigations.

"I don't know what it was, but it was something," Fredriksson said.

"Nothing concrete?"

"No, not at all, just hints."

Ola Haver dropped the topic.

"I'm going to call Otto," he said. "You'll manage now, won't you? They're probably going to slice you open tonight."

Fredriksson smiled faintly.

"Has Majsan been here?"

"She's been here the whole time," Haver said. "She's having a cup of coffee in the cafeteria right now."

Fredriksson shut his eyes as soon as Ola Haver had left the room.

✦

Forty

"Now you die," echoed in Ann Lindell's head. The words resounded again and again as she slowly floated up to the surface of consciousness. It was a long return, edged with a searing pain and confused words that circled like black birds above her head.

She took stock of the situation, how she had plunged down the stairs and landed among bottles and boxes. She had registered glass shattering against the floor and how everything at that point went dark.

Blood was trickling down one cheek. The birds shrieked. Her right shoulder was throbbing. "Now you die." She stretched out the uninjured arm and fumbled for the flashlight. The concrete floor was littered with slivers of glass. She cut herself and cried out.

The basement was dark. It smelled stale, raw, and moldy. There are probably a lot of vermin in this place, she thought groggily, and imagined long-legged spiders crawling over her body, and she dragged herself into a half-sitting position.

I'm not dead, she thought and the image of Erik appeared in her mind.

My phone, she thought, but she realized it was still pocketed in the jacket she had left behind in the kitchen. The first shock and surprise transformed into anger that she could have acted so clumsily. To be so damn right and act so damn wrong. But also because she had been pushed. The cowardly attack from behind, coated in small talk and that giggle just before the push, made her attempt to stand. She had to steady herself against the wall so as not to fall over.

"Pitch black," she muttered and felt her way along the floor with her foot in order to locate the flashlight.

The chance that it was still working was slim but it was her only source of light.

Thank goodness she had never been afraid of the dark, not even as a child. She remembered that time out in Gräsö Island when she had woken up in the middle of the night and not been able to fall back asleep. Edvard sleeping by her side. She decided to walk down to the sea. It was fall. It had been raining during the day, and there had been blustery winds but when she came outside the stars were out and the temperature had sunk.

That time she had thought her future was on the line. Would she be able to live with Edvard? Would she move out to Gräsö Island? The questions had woken her up. She walked to the sea. She knew the path well. The darkness was like a wall. The smell from the bay swept in with the northeasterly wind. Everything was quiet. Even the white birds were resting.

Her thoughts made her lose her way. She kept on going, unaware of her direction, preoccupied with her life-changing decisions, took a left instead of a right, became lost, and ended up farther and farther from the sea. Suddenly she came out next to an old hay loft. She didn't recognize her surroundings, she was shivering and felt more alone than ever. Lost, abandoned, even by herself, unable to think a single clear thought.

She wandered around in the November dark for several hours before she at last saw something she recognized. The road to Victor's house.

If she had imagined it was a matter of life and death that time, then Lindell was painfully aware that here, in Laura Hindersten's dark basement, there was a true threat to her life. It was suddenly clear to her that Laura had murdered the three men. Even if Lindell had only been able to confirm the link between the Hindersten family and Blomgren, there was a connection also to the other two, she was convinced of that.

If you have killed three times, a fourth is no great matter. Would she be the one? Would Laura return?

Lindell groped her way around. Her foot struck the flashlight. She bent down and picked it up, pulled the mechanism back and forth but it remained dark. The glass had been smashed. She shook it, and suddenly it started to shine. Only faintly, but enough light so she could orient herself.

She inspected the cardboard boxes and realized that they had saved her life. The door opening to her left led in toward what she believed to be a boiler room. The beam of light traveled over an old boiler. In one corner there was a bathtub. Wooden boxes with old junk were piled up along one wall.

She trained the light in the other direction. There was a narrow corridor that apparently ran the whole length of the house. There was an old rag-rug on the floor. It looked completely out of place. There were small nooks on either side. Lindell decided to search the entire basement and started with the boiler room.

It took her a quarter of an hour to go through everything. It was completely windowless. The most exciting thing about it was probably the wine cellar that took up an entire room in the part that Lindell figured out faced the garden. There were hundreds of dusty bottles that were clearly arranged according to vineyards. From what she could see all the wine was produced in Italy.

The light from the flashlight was growing weaker. She turned it off and ended up standing at the foot of the stairs. The ache in her shoulder had modulated into a smarting pain that made itself known whenever she moved carelessly. She had tested the strength of her arm but found that it was essentially useless. She could barely hold the flashlight with her right hand.

She turned it on again and directed the beam upward. She crept silently up the stairs, avoiding the third step from the top, and pushed down the door handle. The door was locked. She had not found any tools or objects that she could use to force the door.

The door and frame looked solid but the lock was not particularly complicated. With the right tools she could easily have picked it. But she had nothing. And her right arm ruled out more forceful methods.

She pressed her ear to the door but a deathly silenced reigned in the house. Had Laura left? Lindell started to sweat. There was still blood trickling down her forehead. Strangely enough she felt hungry. Good god how she longed for a cup of coffee and a pastry from the Savoy cafe. She sat down on the top step and tried to clear her mind, but all she could think about was that she had to find a way out. There was only one possibility and that was through the door. There must be something in the basement that could be used to pick the lock. A wire hanger, a bit of steel wire or . . . maybe an axe. The door was reinforced with steel but maybe—despite her handicap—she could break down the frame and part of the wall?

She got up, walked down the steps, and realized how close to death she had come. Then she searched the basement a second time. Time was running out. Soon the flashlight would go out for good.

The bins in the boiler room mostly contained old smelly men's clothes. Black beetles scurried around. Lindell tossed the clothes back and looked through the next bin, that seemed more promising. Here there were cables and cords, coupling boxes, and what looked like an old fuse box. She tried the strength of an old copper wire but it was too bendable to work well as a passkey.

While she searched, ever more desperately, she started to notice a pungent odor. She sniffed the pile of clothes. It smelled, but it was not the source of the odor, which was sharper, somewhat bittersweet. Deep down she knew what kind of smell it was. She didn't want to know, but the police in her took over. It felt like a game from childhood, "hide the key" it was called, and it was one of the few games where the whole family participated. Her father had taken a childish delight in hiding things that his wife and Ann had to try to find. Sometimes it was fun, but often too hard. Her father triumphed, gave them hints, and spurred them on to continue searching.

She finally determined that the smell was coming from a recessed area next to the boiler. It had a surface area of a couple of square meters. Big pieces of wood were piled into a high pile. Lindell started to pull the wood away, at first carefully with the thought that she didn't want to make any noise, then more violently. She threw the pieces of wood down behind her. The stench increased with every layer she uncovered.

Suddenly she reached black plastic. From what she could tell it was a garbage bag. The beam of light was growing weaker. A rat scrambled past and made her jump back. It wriggled in amongst the wood. She heard a rustling in there. If there was one rat there were usually more. She shivered. The flashlight went out but she managed to shake some life back into it.

On her guard against new surprises she stretched out, picked off more blocks of wood, and uncovered a larger area. Small pieces of plastic were gnawed through. She stretched out her left hand with trepidation. She felt the contours of a human body under the bag. It was a human hand. A human claw.

A new rat appeared. It was significantly larger and bolder than the first and it studied the intruder with sharp eyes. The tail was at least ten centimeters long and the fur was flecked with black. Lindell stared bewitched at the animal and slowly got to her feet.

What she had smelled was a corpse. She had sensed what she was going to find but the shock and the feeling of revulsion, above all when she thought about the rats' activities, made her stare mutely at the woodpile and the black wrapping.

Her own situation—alone in a basement with a rotting, rat-gnawed corpse, with a crazy mass-murderer one floor up and the awareness of Laura Hindersten's crimes and the fact that she was probably planning more murders—blocked her brain for a few moments. Laura's ice cold words "Now you die" returned. Lindell heard them repeated and she turned around as if Laura was standing behind her.

She backed out of the wood storage area and went as far away from the corpse as possible. She walked into the wine cellar, turned off the flashlight, and sank down on the floor with her back to the wall. For a moment she was tempted to take out one of the bottles and have a drink, but reconsidered.

A thought came to her: if I make it out of here alive I'm going to con-fiscate all the wine in this house. She started fantasizing about a wine tasting evening with Charles, Görel, and her husband.

What time is it? she thought suddenly. Erik needs to be picked up from day care. It must be four, maybe five. She let out a sob. He was go-ing to wonder where she was. The staff would be angry, then worried.

Did anyone actually know she was going to look up Laura? She had made the unforgivable mistake of not telling anyone she was coming here. This was her punishment for her lack of judgment, for not trusting her colleagues and keeping them in the dark regarding the photograph of Alice Hindersten.

She pulled herself up to her feet again and stood indecisive in the dark. Her right arm was dangling by her side. She didn't want to think it was broken, perhaps it had only been pulled out of joint. She had heard a story about someone whose shoulder was constantly popping out of its socket and who had learned to pop it back in again, but she realized this was not the right situation for medical experiments. She had to be grateful she was still alive.

Driven by her will to get out of the basement she walked up the stairs again. It wasn't so much the darkness that was frightening, nor the pres-ence of the rats and a stinking corpse, but the feeling of imprisonment that made her increasingly panic-stricken. The darkness she could bear, the rats she could fight off, and she would get used to the smell of the corpse, but the captivity was intolerable.

She banged on the door.

"Laura! Let me out!" she screamed, astonished at how terrified and desperate she sounded. "I know it must have made you angry when I talked about your mother but I'm just curious. That's all. We can talk about something else. Laura!"

She leaned against the door, breathed deeply, and tried to discern any sounds from the other side of the door.

"Laura! Listen to me!"

Not a sound. Not a sign that Laura had heard her. Lindell sank down on the uppermost step. She could hear the rats rustling in the woodpile. It appeared they had become more active since she had interrupted their macabre feast on Ulrik Hindersten's remains. She assumed it was he who was packed in plastic.

What kind of a person can kill her own father and then set out on a murder spree? Or was it the case that Ulrik was the serial killer and that he, after committing the three murders had in turn been murdered by his daughter? Or by a third person?

Ulrik Hindersten had been reported missing at the end of September and judging by the stench the body had been there since that time.

The rats may not have found the body immediately but Lindell knew that once they had gotten a taste of the professor it wouldn't take long until only the bones were left. Was it Laura's intention that the rats should take care of the work of destroying the body?

During this time Laura had burned the entire contents of a household and had perhaps murdered three people. Now it was her turn. Would even she be left to rot and eaten by rats?

She banged on the door. It was still completely quiet inside the house. Lindell walked down the stairs. Had she missed anything? She was struck by the thought that perhaps there might have been a boarded-up window somewhere.

She groped her way along the corridor when the door was suddenly opened and light fell on the boxes that had braced her fall.

"You didn't die," she heard Laura say.

Lindell stood absolutely still and didn't answer. She looked around for a weapon in the faint light, something to strike with. She wouldn't hesitate for a second to use violence if only she could come closer to Laura.

"Don't think I'm coming down," Laura said. "I just wanted to tell you I'm leaving now to go see my man."

Lindell walked out and placed herself at the foot of the stairs. Laura was standing in the doorway, lit from behind so that the light formed a halo around her dark hair. Lindell couldn't help noticing how beautiful she was.

"You have to stay here, as a punishment. I wanted to confuse you, but I did not want you to come poking around here. That bitch who took my report at the police station treated me like dog shit. Do you understand? She sat there behind her desk and—"

"Are you talking about Åsa Lantz-Andersson?" Lindell said, breaking into her rapidly flowing speech.

"Is that her name? She's such a nothing."

Laura started to laugh.

"Why did you kill your father?"

"Oh, you found him, did you? I didn't kill him. I strangled him."

Her voice echoed in the basement.

"Did he abuse you?"

"You've already asked me that."

"If that is the case then the repercussions will be much less severe. I'm sure you know that. Don't make it worse now. You will not be able to get off entirely but someday will be able to live your life as you please."

Lindell heard how hollow her words sounded but it was the only thing she could think of to get Laura thinking in a different direction.

"You must think I'm stupid."

Lindell shook her head.

"On the contrary," she said. "I think you're a smart woman."

Laura snorted.

"Tell me about your mother. Even if you don't think so maybe I'll understand. We are both single women. I have been thinking about you so much."

The silence made Lindell sweat. This was the moment of judgment. Either Laura would slam the door shut or she would start to talk. She kept her hand on the door handle. Lindell thought the strip of light on the basement floor grew thinner.

"Laura," she said and tried to keep her voice steady, "where does your rage come from?"

"I've grown up with the black death," she said and Lindell didn't know what she was talking about but hoped she would keep talking.

"Petrus Blomgren killed my mother, you know?"

"Indirectly, you mean?"

"He broke into her life. A farmer who thought he was some kind of Casanova. Do you realize how much pain he caused? He inserted a wedge in our lives, lured her away to Mallorca of all places, and then dumped her. He deserved to die, it's that simple."

"Jan-Elis Andersson, did he also deserve to die?"

"Did you find the chess piece?"

"We did," Lindell said and felt as if the air in the basement was running out. "Why a chess piece?"

"My father and I used to play chess in the cottage. That was when he taught me everything I know about chess."

"Which cottage?"

Laura told her about the only happy summer with Ulrik, when he was like a real father, and how Jan-Elis Andersson turned them out and put an end to the idyll.

"Why did you have to move?"

Ann was trying to keep Laura talking.

"He said he had to prepare the house for a relative but I know why he threw us out. He tried to feel me up. The second time I said I would tell Ulrik. That scared the old bastard."

"But why the chess piece?"

"When I was throwing out Ulrik's old things I found the chessboard and the box, and then when I drove out to Alsike I took a pawn with me. Like a reminder. A detail that was important to me. Did it confuse you?"

"Yes. We only found it today."

"How careless you are."

Lindell was prepared to agree. She thought of the photo at Blomgren's house. If Fredriksson had found it the first time they would perhaps have had a chance of stopping the murders of Andersson and Palmblad.

"So there was no larger scheme involving chess?" she asked.

"Why would there be?"

Lindell couldn't help feeling a certain measure of satisfaction. The chess theory had been plucked out of thin air. The threat against Queen Silvia was nonexistent.

"One of my colleagues had an idea," Lindell said.

Could she make it up the steps before Laura had time to close and lock the door?

"So Laura," she said and climbed a step at the same time, "why Palmblad?"

"Oh yes, 'The Horse.' Not that he looks like a horse anymore. It's strange what the years can do. I hardly recognized him, but he recognized me."

"Why was he an enemy?"

Lindell took another step.

"There are eleven steps left. You'll never make it," Laura said.

Lindell saw that she was smiling.

"You can think about it down there. You have plenty of time. Have a little wine. Acquaint yourself with Ulrik. He's better dead."

"There are rats down here."

"That's good company for Ulrik. He loved to kill mice."

Laura pushed the door shut and turned the lock.

✦

Forty-one

It's strange how quickly one's values can change, Stig Franklin thought, fastening the last straps on the tarpaulin that covered the boat. Only a few weeks ago this boat had been his all. During difficult moments at work the thought of the cruising yacht had been his comfort. It was his escape from melancholy. After he and Jessica quarreled he would turn his mind to contemplating the elegant lines of the boat, the beauty of the mahogany, or something he wanted to get for it.

He was still very fond of *Evita*.

"You're doing that at the last minute," a man observed as he walked by.

Stig, who was vaguely acquainted with him, nodded.

"Yes, but I did beat the snow."

"That's a good-looking vessel," the man said.

Stig nodded.

"If you have to go to the bottom of the sea it should be in that kind of beauty," the man went on.

Stig saw that the man would have liked a chat so he turned his back on him and pretended to be very busy with stretching the tarp even tighter.

The man watched him for a few seconds before moving on.

"Have a nice weekend!" Stig shouted after him and the man held up his hand without turning back.

He had bought the yacht cheaply from an alcoholic lawyer who had lost his docking privileges at the Gräddö Marina. Then he had renovated *Evita* for two years and put her to sea the same year he met Jessica.

And certainly, *Evita* was still the apple of his eye, but somehow he didn't feel the same joy now as before. Jessica had never been particularly interested in the sea. She became seasick easily and it was rare that he could tempt her out onto longer trips. They had gone to Gotland two years ago. After that holiday she had suggested that he sell the cruiser but he had just laughed and dismissed it.

Now it felt as if Jessica had won. All happiness had been swept away. Even the thought that it would soon be spring and that he would soon be taking the covers off *Evita* and putting her in the sea felt meaningless.

He studied the contours of the yacht under the tarp. He would be able to take her far away. The thought had been there. The Mediterranean, the Canary Islands, maybe even the Caribbean. Through the Panama Canal. Öquist, who had docked beside him at Skärholmen a few years ago had sold everything he owned and sailed away. Sometimes a postcard landed in his mailbox, the last time from an unknown harbor on the west coast of Africa.

Stig Franklin smiled to himself. Maybe it wasn't completely meaningless, with the boat, with life, simply because he no longer wanted to live with Jessica.

Maybe Laura would come with him? Hadn't she been talking about some harbor? To leave on his own was out of the question. The yacht needed at least two, ideally three or four on board. It would be too hard, and above all too lonely otherwise.

Uplifted by the thought of an extended boat trip—that suddenly felt more possible than ever—he walked to the car. Regardless of how things turned out with Laura, he was grateful to her. She had acted as a kind of catalyst, set his thoughts and his slumbering dreams in motion. He could see her before him, recalled her furious frenzy as they made love, and became horny all at once. It's not over for me, he thought, I'm still a man with force. Why would I settle for a boring and predictable existence in a house in Sunnersta?

The thought suddenly appeared preposterous. He steered the car as if in a trance, unaware of the traffic and the dramatic developments in the sky where the rain clouds were arranging themselves in dark columns.

He parked on the street. Stig felt like a young man. He got out of the car, let the door fall shut of its own accord, and locked it nonchalantly. His body was light as a feather, he walked with rapid steps toward the house and smiled to himself.

Perhaps it was his outfit that made him feel so good—his "boating gear" as he called the spotted and bleached-blue overalls and the checkered shirt that had been with him all the years he had owned *Evita*. They gave him a feeling of ease and freedom. He could almost smell the sea in the often-washed clothes.

"Never again a suit," he said quietly although he knew it was an untruth, but he liked it: saying the words, releasing the ties, and tasting freedom.

He turned into the garden and walked up the stone paved path, increasingly aroused, like an animal approaching its prey. He saw himself pulling down the suspenders and climbing out of the pants in one move, pulling Laura close and taking her.

The index finger that he used to press the doorbell was trembling. Laura opened at once, stared at him in amazement for a second, and then ran back into the house. Stig heard something that sounded like a scream before the sound of an opera boomed through the loudspeakers and filled the whole house.

"It's my way of celebrating," Laura said fervently and pulled him into the hall.

"Does it have to be so loud?"

His glow was going out as if the opera music was a bucket of water thrown over a fire.

"I'm on a high," she said. "I'm ecstatic."

He stared at her in wonder. Her unruly hair, glistening forehead, and glassy gaze bore out her words.

"Are you drunk?"

Laura shook her head.

"No," she said, "I'm just happy."

She danced around the hall, pulling him to her, letting go of him as quickly, ending up standing in front of him, her arms hanging at her side.

"Now we can travel soon," she whispered.

"What?"

The symphony orchestra in the living room thundered on with undiminished strength. The kettledrum rolls went through the house like waves of rumbling thunder. Laura's eyes were on fire. The strings burst into a showdown. Stig stood there paralyzed.

"Can't you turn it down?" he yelled.

Laura didn't answer, just grabbed Stig by the arm, led him to the kitchen, closed the door, and looked at him eagerly.

Even though the volume was somewhat lower in the kitchen the contrast between the peace at the shipyard and the chaos in the house was overwhelming. All his feelings of freedom and longing for Laura were blown away, but when she crept into his lap, put her arms around his neck, and pressed her body against his, the paralysis brought on by the music lifted and became a vibrating backdrop to his growing lust.

It's remarkable how she affects me, he had time to think before desire took over and made him tug at her clothes with impatience and excitement.

"You are a magical creature," he whispered and she nodded eagerly with her mouth attached like a suction cup to his neck.

He groaned with pleasure. The image of *Evita* returned.

"We'll go away together," he muttered and she moved his suspenders out of the way, unbuttoned his shirt, and pulled it down over his shoulders with surprising force.

"We'll go away together," he repeated as she licked his chest and nibbled his stiff nipples.

It was over in a few minutes in a crescendo that made Stig cry out and Laura beat her hands on the kitchen table so that glasses and bottles rattled, tipped over and rolled over the edge, and shattered into a cascade of slivers against the floor.

Laura swept her arms over the table and swept it clean. The smell of wine and desire mingled, and they sank exhausted onto the table.

Ann Lindell registered all of the sounds as she stood on the uppermost step. The sound of the doorbell, a man's voice and Laura's overwrought tone, the music that came crashing on, the banging on the table against the wall, the scream, and bottles shattering.

She could imagine what was going on up there. Despite her predica-
ment she felt a twinge of envy toward Laura. This must be the man she
had talked about, the married colleague. What was it Laura had said his
wife's name was? Jessica. Laura said something about it being her task to
solve the problem, to separate the two of them, that the man was too
weak and afraid for something like that.

Suddenly Lindell was convinced that Laura was going to murder Jessica. In light of what had transpired and in light of Laura's complete lack
of empathy her comment could not be interpreted in any other way. Was
the man in on this? Perhaps two people had been involved in the murders of Blomgren, Andersson, and Palmblad?

When the sounds of intercourse had ceased Lindell thought about re-
suming her attempts of trying to make herself heard, but realized the
senselessness of screaming to the point of exhaustion. She would not be
heard and perhaps it wouldn't matter anyway if the man was part of it.

Then it struck her: Laura turned on the music to cover her screams.
The man was unaware that Laura was keeping Lindell imprisoned in the
basement. The music could not be interpreted any other way.

She summoned her courage, started beating on the door with her left
hand, and screamed.

Stig Franklin stepped out onto the stairs. He carefully closed the
door behind him. The music was still thundering in the house. He smiled
to himself. The fact was that it worked with the music. After the initial
shock and displeasure over the volume he found that opera was a great
background for making love.

He checked the time. A quarter to five. Jessica usually came home
around five. Now is the time, he thought and walked swiftly to the car.

✦

Forty-two

Gunilla Uhlén, who was closing, had been alternating between concern and anger for the past fifteen minutes. Of course Ann was sometimes late but then she usually called to let them know. This time she hadn't said a word. Gunilla had even lifted the receiver to make sure the phone line was working. She had also dialed Ann's cell phone number but had not received an answer.

Erik was not one to whine but now he was starting to make noise. He had asked for his mother probably ten times during the past half hour. Now they were sitting together in the studio, painting—or rather, Erik was dabbing paint on an enormous piece of paper while Gunilla was listening for the sound of a car. At any moment the door would burst open and Ann would rush in, full of apologies.

Gunilla looked at the clock, stood up, walked into the office, and took out Ann and Erik's file. There were three contacts: Görel, the parents in Ödeshög, and Ann's supervisor at the police station. Görel, who also had children at the day care, was listed first. Gunilla dialed the number but there was no answer. The next name was Ann's supervisor. Gunilla hesitated, tried Ann's cell phone one more time without result, before she called the police station.

"Ottosson!"

The preschool teacher flinched at the sound of the gruff voice, but collected herself and explained that she was trying to track down Ann Lindell who had not picked her son up from day care. Ottosson interrupted her immediately.

"When should she have been there?"

"At four thirty. It's quarter past five now."

"I know what time it is," the policeman said sharply.

"Ann comes in late sometimes," Gunilla said, "and by the way I'd appreciate it if you didn't snap at me."

There was silence on the other end until Ottosson apologized in a regretful voice.

"We are both worried," he said. "I've actually been searching for her all afternoon. She hasn't called in at all?"

"No. I'm going to close up here now. I don't know what to do about Erik."

"I'll send a car over," Ottosson said quickly. "My wife can take care of Erik. They've met and get along well. If Ann turns up then call me immediately."

"Okay," Gunilla said, and now she was very worried.

Ten minutes later an unmarked police car pulled up in front of the day care center. Asta Ottosson stepped out. Gunilla and Erik were already bundled up and ready. Erik stared wide-eyed at the woman.

"Hi there Erik, my friend," Asta said, as she shook hands with Gunilla. "Why don't we go back to my place and do a little baking. You like cinnamon rolls, don't you?"

Erik nodded. Gunilla couldn't help but smile even though she had a heavy weight in her stomach. She remained standing outside the front doors a good while after Asta had taken the boy by the hand and trotted off to the car.

At the same time Ottosson was pulling out the big guns. News of Ann Lindell's disappearance was broadcast and information abouther dress, type of car, and license plate went out to all authorities. The search was immediately underway. The disappearance of an officer involved in a murder investigation wasn't your usual fare. Ottosson could easily imagine what an effect this kind of alarm would have.

Thereafter he called in Haver, Sammy Nilsson, Berglund, and Beatrice and told them the news. The silence that followed did not last longer than a few seconds but to Ottosson it felt like an eternity.

They stared at him with a mixture of consternation and disbelief, before Sammy Nilsson opened his mouth.

"She's been gone all day," he burst out.

"Not exactly," Ottosson said, "but all afternoon I guess. I've called countless times. No answer. Have left messages. I even called the Savoy. She has simply vanished into thin air."

It was simple with Ann Lindell. In the daytime she was on duty, always reachable with the exception of those moments when she retreated to the bakery cafe Savoy to think. Then she turned her phone off. In the evenings she was almost always at home. Ottosson had always gotten ahold of her the few times he had dialed her home number.

Everything spoke for the fact that the absence was not voluntary. Lindell was not one to stay away like this, but what clinched it was the fact that she had not picked up Erik at day care.

"What was she doing?" Sammy asked. "She must have said something to someone."

"You know what Ann is like," Haver said.

"We went our separate ways after we had visited Allan," Ottosson said, "and she didn't say anything at that time. We talked a little about the chess theory and she muttered something about it seeming unbelievable, but don't you also have the impression that she was keeping something to herself?"

Sammy Nilsson got up abruptly, took a few paces across the floor, and then sat down in Ottosson's visitor's chair.

"She found a photograph in Blomgren's house," he said. "The picture of a woman who apparently had a relationship with the farmer dude. We know he went to Mallorca with a lady. Maybe it's her. I think Ann is hunting down this lady."

"When did she find it?" Bea asked.

"Yesterday," Sammy said. "She didn't want to say anything because it would look bad for Allan who had searched the room."

"Did she say anything about . . ."

"No," Sammy said. "Not a thing."

"Damn," Haver said, "that she didn't—"

"Let's drop it," Ottosson said firmly, "what matters now is finding Ann and nothing else."

"And then this damned Silvia visit." Beatrice sighed.

The five officers discussed the possible directions that Lindell's investigation could have taken but since they were searching in the dark they only came up with speculation.

"Okay," Sammy said, "if we assume she's standing there with the photo in her hand. How does Ann think?"

"She went to see the neighbor, Dorotea," Bea said, "to see if she could identify the woman in the photograph."

Sammy nodded energetically.

"Let's call her right away. What's her last name?"

"I'll call," Bea said and walked over to the phone.

It was quickly done. Bea shook her head during the conversation. Ottosson looked at his watch.

"Sammy," he said, "search Ann's office. Ola, see to it that Alsike is checked out. Maybe she went out to Andersson's cottage. The same goes for the stables and Palmblad's relatives. Berglund will have to call Andersson's niece in Umeå. Ann may have contacted her."

He paused for a few seconds before he continued.

"Berglund, you've been at this a long time, what would you do?"

There was a note of pleading in Ottosson's voice that made the others start. They looked at Berglund, who had not said anything up to this point.

"We'll contact all the taxi companies and ask the drivers to keep an eye out for Ann's car. Maybe we'll even ask Radio Uppland to appeal to the public to do the same. It's a drastic move, I know, but we're fumbling in the dark. Ann is out there somewhere and we need to find her, and fast."

Ottosson and Berglund exchanged glances. Bea closed her eyes for a moment. Sammy Nilsson imagined she was praying. Haver drummed his pencil against the back of the chair.

"Taxi companies are fine," Ottosson said, "but the radio?"

"We can wait on it," Berglund said.

Sammy Nilsson sighed heavily.

"Can you please stop tapping like a woodpecker?" he said to Haver.

Sammy Nilsson turned on Ann Lindell's computer. He knew the password and typed it in: "Viola." He knew she kept a daily log of notes. Many times they had leaned over her computer screen together, discussing various cases. Her system of note taking was somewhat difficult to understand, with many abbreviations and words that did not always relate to the main text. It seemed as if she freely jotted down her associations even in the middle of her notes. Sammy had read some poems by a famous Swedish poet—at the urgings of his sister-in-law who had a fondness for the incomprehensible—and Ann's creations reminded him strongly of the cryptic, hard-to-interpret lines.

He opened this morning's document, created at 8:51, which consisted of three words: "Mallis," "Sorrow," and "Threat."

He understood "Mallis" or Mallorca immediately. That was where Petrus Blomgren had gone on vacation over twenty years ago. "Sorrow" and "Threat" were not as easy. Who felt the sorrow? Petrus seemed the most likely candidate. He had written a farewell letter. Did he also feel threatened? Sammy was struck by the fact that they had found the telephone number of a man who installed alarm systems. He had denied all knowledge about the farmer and that might have been true. Blomgren might have looked up the number in the phone book with the intention of calling but changed his mind.

Had Andersson and Palmblad felt threatened? Nothing they had turned up indicated this.

"Okay," Sammy muttered. This Petrus guy felt threatened, wanted to install a burglar alarm but instead decided to commit suicide because of his grief.

Who threatened him? The murderer, of course. The woman in the snapshot? He sighed. Ann had gone a step further. Her sleuthing had led her into a minefield and now she had disappeared. Had she been killed? Sammy pushed the chair back from the desk. He didn't even want to think the thought.

He studied Ann's desk. As usual it was covered in loose papers, transcripts of witness questioning, and files. It was a miracle that she ever found anything. Sammy maintained a very different level of order, he sorted and filed, threw out or archived material that was no longer relevant. Among the piles on the desk Sammy caught sight of files that pertained to cases they had worked on over six months ago.

He rolled closer to the desk again and started to look through the papers. A manila folder was lying on top. It concerned a man who had gone missing in September. Åsa Lantz-Andersson had written the report. Ulrik Hindersten, seventy, had disappeared without a trace from his home in Kåbo. Åsa had added a few notes. The man's daughter had called several times during the past month.

Sammy's cell phone rang. Before he answered he silently prayed for it to be Ann or at least a message that she had turned up, but it was Ottosson who reported that Ann had not been seen either in Alsike or in Palmblad's stables in Skuttunge.

Nor had any of their relatives heard from her.

"Are you finding anything?"

"No, Ann wasn't exactly the best in the world at keeping notes, she . . ."

He had said, "wasn't." To judge from Ottosson's silence he had also caught the use of the past tense.

"She's alive," Sammy said. "Isn't she, Otto?"

His commander was not able to respond immediately.

"Of course she is," he said finally.

They ended the call. Sammy got up and walked back and forth anxiously although his gaze kept being pulled back to the picture of Erik. It was an enlargement of a day care photo that Ann had pinned to the wall. The boy was looking right into the camera and laughing. He had some of Ann's features but the dark, curly hair had to be from the unknown father. Sammy had the feeling that Erik was looking at him and following his snooping.

He continued his search of the desk. Under several files there was a newspaper that had run a photo of Ann. Someone, probably Ann herself, had doodled horns and a goatee on her face and written in a speech bubble: "Kiss my ass."

Sammy smiled. Why not, he thought, and put the newspaper aside. If Ann really was gone for good he wanted to keep that picture.

✦

Forty-three

The driveway was full of leaves. It had been clean that morning. Stig Franklin's first thought was to get a broom and sweep them out onto the street but he changed his mind. Why should I care, he thought and walked into the house.

Jessica was half lying on the bed. She had piled a bunch of pillows at the head of the bed. A few reports that he recognized from the Hausmann deal were spread out over the floor.

"Have you been working?"

"Yes," Jessica said slowly, "I went home after lunch."

"I've been with *Evita*."

He could just as well have said he had been with Laura, or so he judged from her expression.

"Now it's all about other women," she said and he heard that she was trying to inject an ironic edge to her voice but she failed completely. She sounded miserable.

"I've had *Evita* just as long as you have been in my life," he said. "You are the one who has seen her as a competitor and not as an asset."

She said nothing but shook her head and sat up in bed. She was wearing a light-colored tank top that reminded him of summer.

"I've been thinking," she said.

Stig felt a tug in his stomach, fearing what would come next. Convinced he was making the right decision, he experienced this feeling as a solid mass in his body when he had left Laura's house but this now threatened to crumble completely. To himself he cursed his timidity and steeled himself for what was coming.

"I have too," he said with unexpected rancor. "I'm leaving you. Now. I don't want any fighting, I want us to be able to talk and separate—"

". . . in a clean way," she filled in.

He nodded.

"Is it Laura?"

"It's not just her," he got out, suddenly overwhelmed with sadness.

Their life together suddenly appeared so trivial. Even splitting up became petty.

"It's not about you," he said.

"Stig," Jessica said, "do you know what you want? Is it freedom?"

He nodded and let out a sob. Damn, he thought exasperatedly, she makes me feel sorry for myself.

"Don't treat me as if I'm underage," he said. "I can make my own decisions."

She looked closely at him as if to take measure of his steadiness.

"Okay," she said. "We'll sell our shares, rent out the house, prepare *Evita* for a long-distance trip, and set off."

He stared at her. He could hardly believe his ears.

"We'll be able to scrape together a decent amount, especially now when it looks as if the Hausmann deal will go through. I don't need any of this," she continued and made a sweeping gesture.

"Then what is it you want?" he whispered.

"Don't you think I have dreams too? I have been struggling like an animal to build up our life, you know that. We have done it together so I'm not complaining. I saw it as our project. Now you're getting off because Laura . . ."

"This isn't just about her. We aren't really living. All our so-called friends at all our respective dinner parties whine about not having enough time and that they should really devote themselves to living instead."

With each word he raised his voice. By the end he was snarling.

"Look around you! No one we see lives a dignified life. I don't want to be like this anymore."

"I'm not letting you go," Jessica said calmly. "Not to a completely deranged lunatic. I care about you more than that."

It wasn't her self-possession that frightened him but the very fact that she was speaking to him.

"She's not crazy."

Stig sank down onto the bed. He felt Jessica's gaze on the back of his neck. It felt as if a giant glacier was forming in his insides and freezing his internal functions.

Jessica inched herself closer and put her hand on his shoulder. He flinched and became terrified that she was going to hug him. But instead she stood up, crawled clumsily out of the bed, and left the room.

He heard her in the living room. It sounded as if she was moving objects around, picking up.

"Come out here and look," she called out, but he did not stir from his spot, disturbed by her calm. It would have been easier if she had screamed and yelled.

The sound of her bare feet on the floor as she approached the bedroom reminded him of their Åland vacation the first summer they had spent together.

She appeared in the doorway.

"Come," she said and vanished again.

He got to his feet and followed her. She had placed herself at the window. The Italian glass vase that they had bought in London, the eighteenth-century goblet they had bought at an auction in Helsinki— a real find—were both placed on the couch, and several paintings were leaning against the back of it.

He looked bewildered around the room.

"These are worth at least four hundred thousand, perhaps half a million. You know what we paid for Liljefors alone."

"Take it," he said. "I don't want anything."

He stared at a grotesque painting by Lindström. A distorted face in red and yellow with thick layers of paint. He hated it.

"We'll sell this," she said.

"But you love the paintings."

She shook her head.

"We'll sell them and start over. I want to. Do you remember what we talked about in the cottage at Kökar?"

Something in her voice made him look at her as if he was seeing her for the first time. Maybe it was because Jessica was also thinking about that summer. Afterward they seemed like the happiest weeks of his life.

"We can sail there," she said.

She's tricking me, he thought, but there was nothing of the calculating expression in her light face that he recognized so well from when she wanted to tempt him into an argument from which she would emerge the victor. There was no aggression, but also no submissive pleading. It was as if her features were smoothed out, milder. She suddenly resembled a young girl, unscathed by years of tiring fights.

"Do you really want that?" he asked.

"Yes."

"Why this turnaround? All this," he said and held out his arm, "that was so important."

"I have also been thinking," was the only explanation she gave him.

He tried to evaluate her metamorphosis. Jessica was not the one who threw out claims without first having worked them out carefully. The fact that the old Jessica never bared herself in this way convinced him she was being genuine, and he was suddenly touched by her courage. He knew what it must have cost her in self-esteem and pride.

"I need a beer," he said and went to the kitchen.

He took down the bottle opener that was hanging above the counter but dropped it into the sink. It hit a glass that broke. It was not a valuable glass but the sight of the shards made him cry. He leaned his forehead against the cupboard and tried to be clear about what was happening. Jessica's suggestion of leaving the company and setting out on the boat was too big. Even his own wild plans seemed harmless in comparison with a life reorganization on that scale. What had she been thinking? It remained a riddle to him.

He picked up the opener and managed to get the bottle cap off, took a few sips, and then went back to the living room where Jessica was waiting in the same position as when he had left.

"Why?" he asked again.

"Because I love you," she said, as if it were the most natural thing in the world.

"And you tell me this now? First now, after years of coldness? You mentioned Åland but do you remember what that was like? How we made love and talked. Talked! About everything and nothing. Do you remember the old graveyard with the crosses that stood piled up against the wall? The scent of thyme from the sand dunes and tar from the church roof?"

"Of course," Jessica said.

"How moved we were by the simple crosses and the inscriptions. You said something about that fisherman's wife."

She nodded. Stig couldn't continue.

"Of course I remember," she said. "That's why I want to go back there. Maybe we'll recapture that feeling and find our way back to those words."

He looked dumbfounded at her. She was crying. He saw that she didn't want to, but she couldn't stop the tears.

"Jessica," he whispered, paralyzed by a mixture of guilt, bitterness, and tenderness.

Lindström's grotesque face on the couch grimaced at him. The anxiety communicated by the picture became his own and suddenly it struck him that he never wanted to sell it.

Jessica advanced several steps. Stig fled to the bathroom.

Jessica had scrubbed it. It smelled of lemon. He stood in front of the mirror and for several minutes he studied his image. His anxiety felt like a pole thrust into his stomach. He knew he had to make a decision. A decision that would influence the rest of his life.

He took off his clothes. The overalls and the shirt landed in a heap at his feet. He pulled off his socks and his underpants.

"Who is Stig Franklin?" he asked the mirror.

He heard Jessica walk past, how she put on the kettle for tea and took milk out of the refrigerator. He sank down onto the toilet lid and held his head in his hands.

"How is it going?" Jessica asked through the door.

"I'm going to take a shower," he said.

"Would you like some tea?"

"No thank you," he replied and stepped into the shower stall.

When he stepped out of the shower a quarter of an hour later there was a suitcase in the hall.

Jessica was sitting in the living room with a cup of tea and a few rusks.

"Have you packed?"

"Only the essentials," she said, picking up a rusk. She spread marmalade on it, looked at him, and smiled.

Stig had only slipped on a bathrobe and regretted that he had not dressed properly. Now it seemed like she was the one who was leaving him and not the other way around. First she was going to drink a cup of tea, then stand up, take her bag with "the essentials"—whatever that was—and leave the house.

He walked to the bedroom and quickly pulled on a pair of pants and a shirt. When he returned she had finished her tea.

"I want you to unpack," he said.

The silence in the room was deafening. They looked at one another. There was no triumph in her voice when she finally answered.

"Allright, I'll stay."

She didn't ask him why he had changed his mind, made no attempt to get up and throw herself in his lap or venture any words of reconciliation, simply a dry observation that they were still a couple. What he was grateful for was her passivity. It was as if she could tell that if she made a big deal of the whole thing then Stig would have fled.

He poured himself a cognac. They sat quietly, Jessica on the couch and he in an armchair. He knew that the silence could only be broken slowly and with great care. For a long time they would have to walk across new ice.

He thought about Laura, about her suitcase and the decision to leave the country for Italy. She had shown him the airline ticket to Palermo, told him which hotel she was going to check into, and that he could come later.

She was going to leave on Saturday morning and then wait for him there. An old song about longing came back to him. It was about Italy, wasn't it? He only knew the fragment of a stanza: ". . . where small lemons grow . . ."

Then, a couple of hours ago, the thought of spending days and nights with Laura at a romantic hotel by the sea had seemed fabulous. Granted it is not particularly warm in Sicily in November but the air in the mountains is fantastic, there are few tourists, and the wine is excellent, Laura had explained.

Can I ever trust myself again? he wondered and glanced at Jessica. Can she trust me? He was unable to feel real joy. Not yet, maybe it would come. It felt as if he had completed a terrible training session, run a marathon, or wandered thousands of miles through the desert under the burning sun. The exhaustion was total, both physical and emotional.

He felt as if he could go on now that he was cleansed. Of course he had heard friends talk about similar conflicts, emotional and mental cleansing rituals, but he had not understood how arduous they could be.

Jessica was lost in thought. He knew she was keeping tabs on him and that she would continue to do so for a long time.

What he was dreading most was the conversation he would have to have with Laura. Was that what Jessica was waiting for? He suddenly stood up and left the room without a word, closed the door to the study, and walked over to the phone.

When Stig was gone Jessica made two calls from her cell phone. One was to the lawyer who took care of the firm's business. They only exchanged a few words, as if speaking in code. The second call went to Lennart Öhman. He was still at the office.

"It's me," Jessica said in a strained voice. "Whatever Stig may tell you, it's not true. If he talks about any changes, wants to sell, or talks shit about Hausmann, then don't pay any attention. Listen but don't talk back too much."

"But—"

"Don't interrupt me! Stig is going through a crisis but everything's going to be fine. First we'll finish with the Germans and then continue on with Paris. Have you heard anything?"

"Philippe called. He thought things would work out in Lyon."

"Great! As I said, keep up appearances and don't do anything until you have spoken with me."

"But—"

"I have to go," Jessica said and hung up.

When the doorbell rang twenty minutes later Stig realized it was Laura. He gave Jessica a quick glance and saw that she was thinking the same thing. As he slowly rose up from the armchair he could see Laura's red car in the driveway through the window.

The question was if he was going to open the door or not. Letting Laura in could result in anything. On the other hand, if he didn't open then she could make a scene outside the house.

Their phone call, when he told her his decision, was short. At first Laura laughed and called him a coward, then she became threatening and finally hung up.

Now the doorbell was ringing nonstop.

"Open it," Jessica said.

He walked over to the door. He could see her before him, the implacable Laura, who had been an asset in the negotiations with Hausmann but who on other occasions had made him and the others in the office wary and scared. It felt as if he was standing before his executioner. He heard Jessica leave the living room and walk into the study.

Stig threw open the door, gripped by a sudden wrath. Laura was standing outside, her hair framing her face like a dark halo. Her features were almost unrecognizable, her mouth a line and her eyes black with hate. She was holding a pipe wrench in her hand.

For thirty seconds, perhaps more, they stood there quietly with only the threshold between them.

"I want to talk to Jessica," Laura said finally.

"There's no point," Stig said and was surprised that he even managed to open his mouth.

"I'm going to kill that whore," Laura continued and made an attempt to step into the house.

Stig made himself wider, put his right hand up against the door frame, and prepared himself to stop her.

The blow came unexpectedly. Laura swung the pipe wrench and brought it down on his arm. It was not a hard blow but his knees buckled and he took a step back. He registered Laura smiling before she forced her way past him.

She saw the suitcase in the hall and turned around.

"Is it yours?" she asked.

"What the hell are you doing? You've taken my arm off!"

"I don't think so," Laura said calmly. "Where is she?"

At that moment Jessica opened the door to the study and walked toward them.

"Watch out, she's armed!" Stig yelled.

"Laura," Jessica said. "It would be best if you left."

Stig could not fathom how Jessica was able to retain her calm. It seemed as if Laura was taken aback for a few seconds at her unexpected entrance, before she went on the attack.

"It's you, you devil," she snarled and rushed forward, raising the pipe wrench and striking.

Jessica threw herself to the side and the wrench struck a painting behind her back. It was one of the first paintings they had bought, one by Nils Enar Eskhult. It depicted a blooming garden. The metal tool crushed a flowering apple tree in the middle of the picture. Slivers of glass spilled over the floor.

Laura lost her balance and Jessica sprang to the side, lifting up a chair and using it like a shield. Stig stood frozen to the spot.

"This isn't happening," he said and stared at the woman he had made love with only a few hours ago, and with a passion that he had not thought possible.

When Laura again rushed forward with her weapon raised above her head, like a runner with the Olympic torch, Stig's passivity was broken. He thrust his leg forward and tripped Laura so she tumbled headlong onto the floor and dropped the pipe wrench. Stig threw himself over her, gripped her wrists, and pressed her body to the floor.

Laura's body went completely limp and Stig was afraid he had injured her with his violent attack.

"Let go of me," she hissed.

Her eyes shone with panic.

"You damned lunatic!" he yelled.

"No one is allowed to hold me down!" Laura screamed. "I'll die!"

"I don't think so," Stig said and pressed harder when he felt her try to get up.

"I'll die," she whispered.

"Let her go," Jessica said. She had picked up the pipe wrench from the floor.

"Never," Stig said.

He felt Laura's body working under his own, heard her heavy breaths, and saw how she tried to bite his arm. Suddenly and for a few moments he relived their last tryst. Revolted by his own reaction he loosened his grip a little.

"Let her go," Jessica repeated and Stig got to his knees.

Laura remained lying on the floor. The only thing they heard were her panting breaths. Jessica looked at Stig but he avoided her gaze. I've fucked this woman, he thought and had a bitter taste in his mouth. I've cheated on my wife with her, planned to run away with her. Shame made him get up quickly and direct a kick against the body at his feet but he stopped himself at the last moment.

"It's over now," was the only thing Jessica said, and he knew that she had sensed what he must be thinking.

Laura let out a sob and then started to crawl to the door. Stig thought she looked like a wounded animal who was trying to drag herself away from a fight.

When she reached the door she turned her head and looked one last time at Stig before she picked herself up and on unsteady legs disappeared from their view.

Jessica walked over to the door, looked out, and then closed it very carefully.

"She's crazy," Stig said.

Jessica simply nodded and she didn't cease to amaze him. He wanted to hug her but knew it would be a while before that happened.

"Lock the door," he said. "I have to have another cognac."

"Pour me one too," Jessica said and only now did she put down the wrench.

✦

Forty-four

The flashlight gasped one last time and then went out for good. However Ann tried it remained dark. She tossed it away and curled up in the wine cellar.

The rustling of the rats became louder. It was as if Ann's rearranging of the wood drove them to gnaw even more eagerly on Ulrik Hindersten's body. Ann also thought the smell of rotting flesh had grown stronger.

Her hand fumbled over the bottles of wine. They tempted her. She longed intensely for a sip of red wine. She sneezed as a result of the dust she had disturbed. The rustling died down for a few seconds. The rats were aware of her presence, they heard her and perhaps with cold calculation counted on the fact that a new feast awaited them.

She had been cold for the past half hour and regretted the fact that she had not gathered up some of the old clothes she had seen. Now that the light was definitely not functioning she was hesitant to move around in the dark basement. She told herself that it wasn't because of the rats, but the fact was that her terror was building minute by minute in the pitch black and stinking cellar.

Wine was her only friend, the only thing she could perceive as positive. But she was not allowed to drink it. When Laura returned, Ann had to be in good shape. She did not count on being able to free herself with physical force; she assumed the only possibility was to talk herself out of the basement and then she could not be slurring her speech. And above all, her thinking had to be clear.

It struck her that perhaps Laura would not be coming back at all. That she had left the house for good. Ann had seen the suitcase in the hall. The sudden insight that she was going to be abandoned made her jump to her feet. Instinctively she groped around with her hand in front of her without knowing what she was going to do—it just seemed wrong to sit there completely passive. She thought she had tested all the possibilities open to her. Now she could only hope that Laura would return.

Only seeing a hint of light if Laura was going to open the door, and even if Ann had to stand at the foot of the stairs, a glimpse of light was so enticing that she cautiously made her way out of the wine cellar and haltingly made her way closer to the staircase even if this meant she drew closer to the rats.

She had heard that your eyes grew accustomed to darkness and that you would start to see partly after a while but it wasn't true. The darkness was as compact as before and she regretted having wasted the batteries in the flashlight as she had looked for a way out.

Her thoughts and yearning for Erik were the worst. At a few points she had sniffed her right shoulder. When she carried him he would rest his head there and sometimes his scent lingered, but now she picked up nothing.

Does terror smell? It must be sweat in that case, she thought.

She ended up standing by the staircase, crouched down, and brushed her hand over the first step. If I sit at the very top, she thought, and hold a piece of wood in my hand I can hit her as soon as she opens the door.

In the midst of her misery she laughed at the thought of getting free. The rats quietened again. They were apparently sensitive to sound. God, how she hated rats. Were there more detestable animals?

The closer she got to the woodpile the more it stank. In order to control her revulsion and urge to vomit she tried to imagine which state of decomposition the corpse was in. Ryde could have informed her. He could have given her a long lecture about the various decomposition pro-cesses of the human body depending on temperature and other factors, if he was in the mood. Otherwise he would simply snort.

She recited the names of her colleagues while she searched for a weapon. She had thrown some logs to the side and after a while her foot bumped up against a heavy piece of wood, which she quickly bent down and picked up.

She crept carefully up the stairs and sat down on the top step, ex-tremely pleased with her new position, raised above the rats and within striking distance of Laura.

Normally she didn't hate the criminals she came into contact with, even if she at times had wanted to castrate some of the rapists she had arrested. But she hated Laura without reservation. Not because she had killed her fa-ther and most likely three other men but because she had robbed Ann of her freedom in the most ignominious way. The feeling of having been tricked probably played into this, but Ann convinced herself that Laura was an evil person through-and-through who deserved to get a piece of wood in the face.

Hell, how she would strike! That witch would get a real bonk on the nose. Then down into the basement with her and only after a good long while would Ann alert the rest of the police corps. Red alert. Bring the bitch to jail. Lock her up. A cell. Under lock and key. High-security prison. Rats. Bleached bones that are raked away after fifty lonely and painful years.

Thoughts of revenge were the nourishment to keep Ann's spirits up, at least at such a level that the anxiety did not completely get the upper hand.

"Erik," she said softly.

Why do I expose myself to this? she thought and the anger at herself that had been lurking beneath her venting at Laura broke out. She had acted in such an amateurish manner. She had broken her own ground rule: to always maintain contact.

She could hardly keep still in the darkness. The air seemed more stale and smelly for every minute that went by. She had the strange feeling that the stench of Ulrik Hindersten would follow her for the rest of her life, seep into her pores and constantly make itself known.

Perhaps it was her own aching arm that made her think of Allan

Fredriksson. Bird-watching was for sissies. She shook her head in the dark. It was envy, nothing more. Fredriksson had an interest outside of his work. Ann felt as if she didn't have anything, except caring for Erik. Not mushroom-picking and bridge, like Sammy; or gardening, like Bea, with her flourishing vegetable beds that she was always talking about; or Ottosson with his summer cottage where he happily pushed a lawn mower around in shorts and a straw hat.

Ann was like a robot with three stations: her home, day care, and the station. She snorted when a thought of Charles fluttered by.

She retreated into self-pity and nodded off with her head against the door.

✦

Forty-five

As if by a miracle Laura Hindersten arrived at the house in Kåbo without crashing or driving off the road.

She felt empty, like a shell. It felt as if the last ounce of humanity had drained out of her. She regarded her surroundings with a dull gaze, without really taking in what was happening around her. She might as well be driving on the moon. Everything was strange. Even her friend, the car, that she during the past few weeks had set such great store in, was like an unfamiliar object.

She parked on the street, didn't cast a glance at the professor's house but walked straight onto her property. There, she ended up standing like a zombie in front of the door before it occurred to her to get out her keys and open it.

Somewhere she understood that Stig had rejected her but the memory of what had transpired in his house was diffuse. What had happened? What she recalled most clearly and with the greatest degree of pain was that he had pinned her arms and legs and held her to the floor. The pressure on her chest had been unbearable. It was as if something broke inside.

She walked into the kitchen and sank onto a chair. Slowly fragments of the events returned. She remembered that Jessica had been holding the

pipe wrench in her hand. It was confusing, as if their roles had been re-
versed. The tool belonged to Laura. She looked around the kitchen as if
she would be able to find the tool there. Her gaze fell onto the letters on
the table. She hadn't read them yet. She reached out for the bundle and
loosened the string, picked up a letter and started to read.

> *You can't imagine what beautiful landscapes we have seen. I would
> love to settle down in Tuscany if only Ulrik could do it. Laura was
> quite whiny, sometimes obnoxiously so, on the trip. She complained of
> the heat and I can partly understand her, it was so terribly warm, but
> it is as if one's life spirit is awakened by the heat. I can tell from the
> people here that they are really alive. You should know how romantic
> the Italians are! I am constantly complimented, while Ulrik walks
> around like a prehistoric monument.*

Laura sat there with the letter in her hand. Certainly she remembered the
heat and the crowds in Florence, how they had forced their way through
the throngs to the palaces and the churches. She had thought she was going to suffocate.

She took out the next letter. It was from October of the same year.
Mårten had offered to come into town and help out with the garden but
Alice had declined.

> *I don't think Ulrik would appreciate it. You know how touchy he is.
> He doesn't want to have a debt of gratitude to anyone, especially no
> one from our side of the family. Sometimes I dream that I am still in
> Skyttorp. What would my life have looked like then? How are Jan and
> Martin? And Lars-Erik. You have to write and tell me. I want news. I
> love to get letters. The few times Ulrik sees your letters he stares at
> them but he doesn't dare say anything.*

Laura put the letter down and looked out the window. The branches of
the apple tree were bare. She mechanically took out a new letter.

> *What a spring! The lilacs are so early. They will have finished flow-
> ering when the schools let out. The girl is being difficult. A couple of*

weeks ago they called from school and complained about her behavior. I reprimanded her severely but it didn't help because they called again today. She harrasses her schoolmates, calls them names, and teases. At home she is all smiles, pretends to listen and understand, but it is all an act. I don't know what to do. Ulrik is no great help. He is the same way. The situation at his work is worse than ever. He makes trouble over everything, with everyone. Sometimes I think he is crazy.

Laura forced herself to unfold the next letter.

If Laura were not so little I would immediately leave Ulrik. The problem is that he is unable to control the girl, who is becoming more unruly by the day. I have met a man again. Yes, I know what you are going to say, but you would like him. His name is Petrus and he is a farmer, or has been, and you can tell from his straightforward manner. Ulrik hired him once to help out in the garden. He referred to Petrus as "our man." If he only knew! This time it is not only the lust of the flesh but I am in love for real, but again Laura is the big obstacle. I cannot escape. I don't know why fate—I no longer believe in God—led me to Ulrik. Of course I was charmed by his fancy language and manners but I should have seen through the facade. Then Laura came along and you know how I hesitated to the last minute. You advised me to keep the child, but Laura has become my ball and chain. You think I am unfair to her. She is my love but not my life. Otherwise I have received mostly good advice from you. You have been the rock I can lean on in difficult times. I know that you wanted me and many times I have regretted the fact that I didn't yield to you but you know why and we have talked about it so many times, that it would be hard for me to share a bed with you, my beloved little sister's husband.

Laura was unable to keep reading. She crumpled up the pages in her hand and swept the other letters onto the floor.

Ann Lindell woke up with a start. She squeezed her piece of wood and listened with her ear pressed to the door. It was deathly silent in the house and she thought it was perhaps the scuttling and rattling of the rats that had woken her. But then she heard a scraping sound, as if someone was pulling a piece of furniture along the floor.

Had Laura returned? Ann didn't know how long she had been gone. Ann had heard the phone ring, and a distraught Laura. Then it had not taken long before the front door was slammed shut.

Ann listened intently but heard nothing more. She rose warily to her feet. This is the moment of truth, she thought and the terror gripped her again. She had to get out of the basement! The dark, the rats, the stench, and above all the fact that she was locked in was suffocating her. It felt as if the air was running out. She drew a deep breath and hyperventilated. Nausea shot up, she burped, and noticed a sour taste in her mouth.

"Laura, open up!" she screamed in a shrill voice that she didn't recognize as her own.

No reaction.

"Talk to me!"

She started to cry.

"Laura!"

Her screams echoed in the basement. The rats froze. She dropped the piece of wood that clunked down the steps.

The compact silence that followed was suddenly broken by something that sounded to Ann like tin cans rattling against each other. Thereafter there was intense movement. Laura must be walking around the house and her heels smacked against the parquet floor. She appeared to be in a great hurry. The steps came from the right, then from the left. For a while Ann thought someone was walking around on the second floor. The tapping of steps went past the basement door. A door was shut and then the taps returned.

"Laura!" Ann screamed.

There was silence for several seconds, then Laura continued.

She doesn't care about me, Ann thought. What is she doing? Watering the plants? But Ann didn't remember seeing any. Why is she running around in this way?

Then everything was quiet for a few seconds before Lindell heard a poof, followed by swift steps across the floor. The front door opened and shut. It was quiet for a couple of seconds before Ann started hearing a sound she couldn't place. It sounded as if a great many people were in the house tittle-tattling, whispering secrets to each other. The sound intensified and became a whining, low-level roar.

She listened for a few seconds before she understood what it was: Laura had set fire to the house.

✦

Forty-six

After the group communication that Ann Lindell was missing there was a restless atmosphere at the station. There were those who connected the disappearance with the impending visit by the queen. One of these was Säpo-Jern. He claimed with deliberation that it was very likely that Lindell had found a significant lead and either been stopped or had been stopped from communicating with the outside world.

He expressed annoyance at the crime team's apparent lack of ability to communicate with each other.

"How is it possible that no one in Violent Crimes knows what their colleague is doing?" he asked rhetorically in a small-scale conference in Ottosson's office.

If you only knew, Ottosson thought but held his tongue.

"We don't have time for an internal investigation," he said curtly and tried not to show his irritation at Jern's insistent voice or his own concern for Ann.

He had been pondering this, tried to remember something that Ann had mentioned over the past few days and that could bring them forward in their search. Often she tried out a new idea on him. It could be a new angle of a problem or a stab in the dark. Ottosson had become increasingly good at reading the various nuances of Ann's work method. In fact, this was one of the things he had appreciated most in her. He felt a bit flattered that she showed him the confidence of sometimes presenting completely bizarre ideas and impulses, which in many of their colleagues would have elicited snickers and perhaps future teasing when it became clear how insane the idea was.

But Ottosson could not think of anything that explained her disappearance. For a while he speculated that she may have had an accident. Perhaps she had driven off the road and sat unconscious in the car, which was hidden by vegetation. It had happened before that people had been trapped in their cars. He recalled an accident involving one car on the E-4 the driver had been able to call the emergency number on his cell phone but the ambulance and fire department had not been successful in locating him. The driver saw them pass by him and despite his injuries was able to guide them to the right place. That time there was a happy ending.

Ottosson could see Ann's car in his mind, driven into a bush or against a tree, with Ann hanging unconscious over the steering wheel or thrown through the windshield. She was sloppy about her seat belt.

He quickly got up. She must be alive, he thought and was gripped for the first time during his long police career by what most closely resembled desperation.

"What is it, Otto?" Berglund asked.

"To hell with this!" Ottosson burst out, and Jern, who had continued his litany of the inadequate routines at the crime squad, stared at him with astonishment.

"Out and look for her, god damn it," Ottosson went on in an agitated voice, "instead of sitting here and kvetching like a little old lady!"

Bea, who had also been listening to Jern's tirade with growing anger, gave a chuckle.

"While you're at it why don't you harrass some Arab in town," she threw out. "Maybe al-Qaida is involved."

Jern gathered up his papers and left the room without saying a word.

Sammy Nilsson devoted himself to Ann Lindell's office with minute attention to detail. He had wolfed down a sandwich and a cup of coffee in the cafeteria and was forced to attend a short briefing, but otherwise he had spent all his time at Lindell's desk.

He thought it was possible the answer would be found there. Looking aimlessly was nothing for Sammy Nilsson. The problem was that Lindell left so little behind: scattered notes, incomplete reports, and terse theories jotted down in a notebook.

For a while he was angry at Ann. The lack of an organizational system in her office made him wonder how she could function at all as a detective.

Sammy Nilsson flipped through the transcript of the questioning of Ulrik Hindersten's daughter and Lantz-Andersson's own comments. It was very brief. Nothing had emerged that could explain the disappearance. What perplexed Sammy was the fact that the file lay on Ann's desk to begin with. Why was she interested in a missing person's report from September? He could not recall having talked about this Hindersten, but he sensed what Ann's thinking had been. Three men around seventy years of age had been murdered and here there was a fourth man of the same age, missing without a trace.

He had called Åsa Lantz-Andersson but she had gone home for the day and when he tried her at home her husband said his wife was out for a run. Two, three times a week she ran a ten-kilometer trail in the forest. She had just set off.

Then go catch up to her, Sammy thought. He asked the man to make sure Åsa called as soon as she got home. When he had put the phone down he started calculating how long it would take to run ten kilometers. Forty-five minutes he decided and looked at his watch. It would be at least half an hour until his colleague called back.

He flipped through the folder again. The daughter's name was Laura Hindersten. She was most likely unmarried since she had the same last name and address as her father. The street where they lived he couldn't place exactly but he knew it was in Kåbo.

Ulrik Hindersten was retired but had been an associate professor in Italian literature. Sammy re-read the sentence.

"Italian literature," he muttered, got up, took out his cell phone, and called Berglund.

"Hi, where are you?"

"In the bathroom," Berglund answered drily. "Do you want to hear me flush?"

Sammy heard flushing water in the background.

"Hey, Berglund, didn't you say something about Jan-Elis Andersson being a farmer with a flair for languages? What did you mean by that?"

"I saw an inscription on the side building," Berglund said, and now his voice was serious. "If you remember, there was a smaller cottage a little ways off."

"In what language?"

"I think it was Italian, why?"

"Then I was right! Do you have any idea what it said?"

"Not in the least," Berglund said and Sammy realized he had left the bathroom because now there was no echo in the phone.

"Can you come to Ann's office?"

Berglund arrived after half a minute.

"Why were you asking?" he said as soon as he came in.

"I had a vague memory of you talking about something Italian," Sammy Nilsson started, and then summed up the case of the professor who specialized in Italian.

"The connection is tenuous but . . ." Berglund said.

"But . . ."

". . . but interesting," the old criminal investigator went on. "You think there may be a connection between the professor and the farmer in Alsike?"

Sammy Nilsson nodded and told him about the file he had found on Lindell's desk.

Berglund eyed the first page.

"Kåbo," he said.

"Do we know anyone who speaks Italian?" Sammy Nilsson asked.

Berglund shook his head.

"But that can be arranged," he said. "Should I call Örjan Bäck? He knows these things."

Sammy Nilsson nodded. In his thoughts he was already in Alsike to check the inscription, which according to Berglund appeared on the wall of a farm building some thirty meters from the murdered Andersson's living quarters.

"Another idea would be to call Andersson's relative in Umeå," Berglund said. "What was her name? She may know if there were any ties between the professor and her uncle."

"Lovisa Sundberg," Sammy Nilsson said. "Let's do that. Damn that I didn't think of it."

"We're all exhausted," Berglund said.

"Do you think Ann has called her?" Sammy Nilsson asked.

"No, she hasn't been in contact with any of Andersson's or Palmblad's family. I've checked."

Ottosson called home to see how things were going with Erik. As he expected there was no problem. The boy had eaten and was right now playing with one of Ottosson's grandchildren, a girl about Erik's age. Asta had nothing but praise for his calm and social skills.

"You can tell he has learned from day care how to be around people," she said, which surprised Ottosson somewhat. Asta was not the one who usually had anything good to say about the communal childcare services and he couldn't help pointing it out.

"You don't understand all that," Asta determined calmly, "but I will try to explain it to you one day when you aren't so stressed."

They finished the conversation and Ottosson really did feel stressed. The worst thing was not being able to do anything, not even pretend to look for Lindell. What would that even look like? Should he walk around on streets and squares and call out her name? Suddenly he understood the frustrations of relatives of missing people. They could be a complete pain during an investigation, call all the time and nag, suggest various approaches, and sometimes threaten to file a complaint with the Parliamentary Ombudsmen or go to the papers and say how passive the police were being.

There was a knock on the door. Sammy Nilsson came in. Ottosson thought he looked as eager as a playful boy.

"I think we have a connection between Andersson and a missing professor in Kåbo," he started without introduction. "I called Lovisa Sundberg and she confirmed that the uncle had rented a cottage to the academic about twenty years ago. It was the same cottage she lived in later for a while. She couldn't remember his name but she recalled that he worked with books and was unpleasant. I think it was Ulrik Hindersten."

"And?"

"This is what Ann is doing. I am absolutely sure of it. Berglund saw an inscription in Italian in Alsike. Everything adds up. He's a professor of Italian or something."

Ottosson couldn't help smiling in the midst of the misery. He now remembered that Ann had said something about a missing professor.

"Okay, take this slowly and from the top," he said and pointed to the visitor's chair, grateful to have someone to talk to.

✦

Forty-seven

Ann Lindell listened, fascinated against her will, at how the murmuring sound grew and became a rumble. At times there was a sharp bang as if shots had been fired. She put her hand on the door. It had not yet become warm.

What kind of chance do I have? she thought. The house is made of wood and will probably burn like kindling. She guessed that Laura had set fire to several places at the same time, remembering how she ran around before she left. Maybe she was even calculating enough to have opened a window to increase the air circulation.

The door was still cold. Lindell was standing there with her left hand pressed against it as if she was being sworn in as a witness in the box, when smoke started to filter in at the threshold. She didn't see anything but detected the acrid smell and realized that if the fire didn't get her the fumes would.

She had on occasion seen people who had died of smoke inhalation. They fell peacefully into a slumber. She particularly remembered a woman who had died in a smoky apartment fire in Knivsta. She had looked almost pleased as she lay there on the bed. The only thing that hinted at death were streaks of black soot at the corners of her mouth. No, Ann corrected herself, it was in Vassunda she lived. The woman had a dozen stuffed animals in her bed but had lived alone for many years. Not even the neighbors could give her first name. She was thirty-five years old and known to all as "Subban."

Ann started to cry. Warmth was spreading to her hand. The smoke made her cough. She removed her hand from the door and walked with halting steps down the stairs.

There was a roar in the floor above her and she tried to imagine what it looked like. A sea of flames, devouring everything in its path.

She found her way to the store of wine, pulled out a bottle, and struck it against the shelf. The bottleneck broke off and wine ran out over her hand. The scent indicated a bold red wine. She carefully fingered the jagged edge, poured out a little wine into her almost unusable right hand that she had formed into a little cup and slurped up a sip. It was strong. Maybe it was the Amarone that Laura had talked about.

She sipped a little more from her hand, then grew more daring and put the broken bottle to her mouth and drank. One floor up there was an explosion and it was as if the whole house swayed. Ann guessed that it was a window being blown out and knew that the fire would transform into a roaring, thundering inferno.

She drank a little more wine and already felt the effect of the alcohol. She had drunk maybe a quarter of a bottle and that was usually enough so that she would feel it.

She thought of the fact that she wasn't alone in the basement, but the rats were probably fleeing now and leaving her alone with Ulrik Hindersten. He would sort of die a second time.

A crackling sound made her peek out into the basement corridor. At the far end part of the roof had started to give way and sparks were flying around. Ann thought that must be what fireflies looked like. She took another sip of wine and emptied the bottle, reached for another but changed her mind and let it glide back onto the shelf.

"I don't want to die," she said straight out into the dark.

The fireflies danced.

"I don't want to die!" she screamed. "Erik!"

She was overcome by a violent rage. If Laura had been in front of her she would have killed her with a bottle of wine, she was sure of it. This wasn't fair! Her earlier calm was completely gone. It was as if she knew deep down that, in spite of her situation, she was going to wake Erik up the following morning, drop him off at day care, and then have a morning meeting with Ottosson and all the rest of her colleagues. Just like every other day, one indistinguishable from the next.

The fire had meant a change that she unconsciously had regarded as positive. Now she realized the full extent of the approaching catastrophe.

The fire changed the situation, but for the worse. To be locked in was bad enough, to fry to death was worse.

It was only now that she started to actively plan for her survival. Soon even greater parts of the floor joists would give way and that which was the basement ceiling would cave in. She would be buried by burning timber.

Even though she didn't want to face up to how badly things looked, she was forced to try to estimate how far along the fire had progressed. The ceiling was now burning in several places. Wood shavings that had caught on fire and were whirling around gave the illusion of fireworks.

It occurred to her that somewhere in the basement she had seen a bathtub. It was probably in the far end of the basement where it was burning the most. She went down on all fours and crawled along the corridor. With the help of the light from the fire she caught sight of the recessed area where she believed the bathtub was.

A beam that collapsed tore down large amounts of wood shavings that immediately caught fire. The heat became more intense. She kept crawling. The tension, or perhaps the wine, made her vomit. She crawled, vomited, coughed, and crawled on.

In the narrow recess she saw the bathtub. It was an older model, heavy and awkward. Would she have the energy? After having kicked away a piece of plank blocking the entrance she grabbed the tub with her left hand and tried to drag it toward her. It was heavier than she had imagined. The heat singed her cheeks and bare arms. On the floor there was a rag that she draped over her head and she tried to turn the tub so she could pull it farther.

She turned around in order to assess her options. It was burning behind her now. A rat ran past, then another. They were leaving their feast and running toward certain death.

With her last ounces of strength—she had to use her right arm and the pain was brutal—Lindell managed to tip the bathtub on its side and pull it out of the recess. Then it suddenly came to an abrupt stop. One of the legs had caught in the door opening. She laid down on her back and braced herself with her foot while she tugged with her left arm. The tub came loose.

The fire was spreading quickly. New areas were burning and Ann was having a harder time being able to stand the heat and smoke. She pulled the tub, on its side, all the way to the wine cellar. In this part of the basement the heat was not quite as bad. She reached in and grabbed a bottle of wine, smashed the neck of it and let wine run over her face and chest. It was a white wine. She licked her lips. Before she tossed the bottle to the side she tried to read the label. She thought it said "Peter Pan."

Now larger and larger pieces were tumbling down from the ceiling. Soon the whole basement would be on fire.

✦

Forty-eight

Sammy Nilsson became increasingly impatient. The interpreter had still not arrived and Sammy set off on his own. He wanted to see the inscription with his own eyes. He drove south on Kungsgatan at a death-defying clip. At the traffic lights shortly before the Samaritan home he took a risk and drove against a red light. He almost crashed into a city bus that was coming out of Baverns Alley.

"Damn farmers!" he yelled for no reason.

The bus driver gestured, car drivers beeped, and Sammy sped up. He had his first doubts as he drove over the Fyris River bridge. Was he doing the right thing in hurrying out to Alsike?

At the crossing with Rosendal some fire trucks came trundling along. Sammy was forced to stop, tried to finesse his way past a truck, but the driver discovered his maneuvering and with a huge grin pulled up a few centimeters and blocked the gap.

The blaring of the fire trucks could be heard long after they had disappeared in toward the city.

The light turned green and Sammy turned left, but then realized he had taken the wrong road. He should have taken the old Stockholm Road, of course. Now he would have to drive through Sunnersta and over Flottsund.

"Shit, shit!" he yelled.

He drove off to the side, looked in the rearview mirror and in line with the Skogskyrkogaarden graveyard made a U-turn with screeching tires. It was ridiculous to waste time on Alsike. The barn with its Italian text would still be standing. He cursed his stupidity.

Instead he headed to Kåbo. If the missing professor had anything to do with the murders then that was where he would have to start looking for Ann.

Seven minutes after the alarm had sounded the first fire truck arrived. It was a pump truck with five firefighters. Thereafter came a ladder truck, and command car.

"There it is!" a man on the street cried out and pointed at the Dream House, as if there was any doubt where the fire was.

"Step aside," the fireman who had been the driver said. "I'll connect the hydrant!" he yelled.

Hoses were being rolled out at high speed. Within a minute the firemen were dousing the house with the water they had in the truck. Flames were coming out of all of the windows in the lower story. The windows one floor up were still intact. Smoke was rising from the seams in the metal roof, and a thick pillar of it was coming out of the chimney.

After a couple of minutes the approximately two cubic meters of water in the car were gone but by then the driver had connected the fire hydrant to the truck's pump.

A patrol car was in place. One of the patrol officers, Hjalmar Niklasson, was speaking to the neighbor. It was the professor.

"Who lives in this house?"

"The professor, but he's missing and so is his daughter."

"Are they at home?"

"The professor is missing," the professor repeated.

"What do you mean?"

"He disappeared about a month ago."

The officer knew who he was talking about. He had taken part in the search for Ulrik Hindersten.

"And the daughter?"

"She took off a little while ago."

"Do you believe the house to be empty?"

"Yes, I guess so," the professor said, "but . . ."

"Were you the one who called in the alarm? Two residents, are you certain?"

The professor nodded. He had his gaze fixed on the firemen.

"Will it spread?" he asked, but the officer had already left.

Niklasson's colleague came running. This was somewhat difficult since Åke Wahlquist was twenty kilos overweight.

"Don't we have a fourteen out on Lindell, from the crime squad?" he panted.

"Yes, why?"

"I think it's her car that's parked around the corner. I slowed down when I caught sight of it and . . ."

Niklasson pulled out his phone.

"Are you sure?" he asked Wahlquist, who nodded.

Ottosson received the news on his cell phone. He was discussing the Italian lead with Berglund; the interpreter was on her way. Berglund was going to give her a ride out to Alsike in order to have her decipher the inscription on the side of the barn.

"A patrol unit has located Lindell's car," Ottosson said.

"Where?" Berglund asked.

"Kåbo. They didn't say which street but it intersects with Götgatan. There's a residential fire there somewhere. 'Tiny' Wahlquist . . ."

Berglund ran. He had a feeling he knew what was burning.

Ottosson watched the back of his colleague as he ran from the room and Ottosson was filled with a mixture of pride and a great anxiety. Pride for what he for a second had observed in Berglund's face before he ran off. Ottosson knew Berglund would go through hell and high water for his coworkers. It was not only because of collegial loyalty, it was something more. Not love in the regular sense, comradeship sounded too army-like, and friendship too trivial. Trust was the word Ottosson thought was closest to describe the ties that knit the good officers together.

But above all he was worried about Ann. Berglund's expression had illustrated what could be thought to have happened. The unthinkable was thinkable and now perhaps even likely.

He snapped up his jacket and left the room.

When Sammy Nilsson reached the flaming house he spotted "Tiny" Wahlquist, who was waving for him to come over. Next to "Tiny" there was a man of about sixty.

"This guy has a little info," Tiny said. "He's a neighbor and he saw a woman, about forty, who was with Laura Hindersten—the woman who lives in this residence." He pointed to it.

"She said she was a police officer but she sure didn't look like one and she behaved more like a thug," the neighbor said.

"Is this the one?" Sammy held up a picture of Lindell. He had been carrying it around in his pocket ever since the report on her disappearance was disseminated.

The man nodded.

"Is she wanted?"

"Shut up," Sammy Nilsson snarled. "Ann is the best officer we have. When did you see them?"

"This afternoon," the neighbor said meekly. "She went into the house with Laura Hindersten."

"Have you seen her leave the house?"

The neighbor shook his head. Now he was pale, suddenly aware of the seriousness of the situation.

"Jesus Christ," Tiny said.

Sammy drew a deep breath and looked around. A fire commander was stationed a little ways up the street and Sammy ran up to him. They vaguely knew each other from before. Sammy thought his name was Eddie Wallin.

"Hi there," Sammy said. "It turns out we may have a fellow officer in the building."

He was near tears but did everything to sound collected.

"What the hell are you saying? You see what this looks like. We don't have a chance of going in yet," the fire commander said and gestured with his arm to some smoke divers who were standing at the ready.

✦

Forty-nine

Ann Lindell leaned forward with her healthy hand on one knee and rested for a few seconds. The fire thundered overhead. It occurred to her there might be water in the basement. She had seen an old washing machine and stainless steel rinsing tubs in one of the areas but realized it was too late to make her way there. And what could a thin stream of water do against a raging inferno?

She took out another bottle of wine and did the same thing as before. This time it was red wine. It helped for the moment but the heat was starting to get so unbearable that soon no wine in the world would help her. She would be poached in wine.

She drew farther back into the wine cellar. The floor, walls, and ceiling were lined with brick. She guessed that Ulrik Hindersten had had the area reinforced in order to maintain the right temperature for the wine. This played to her advantage in the short term but she knew it was only a matter of time before the bricks started to rain down.

She turned the bathtub upside down and put some bottles of wine on the floor. She wet a rag with wine and draped it around her face, lifted the side of the tub, and crawled in under it. Now it was dark again. If she had felt the basement was bad the tub was a veritable prison cell by comparison. She lay on her left side with her legs pulled up. There was hardly enough room for her. Her arm ached and the effort of moving the tub had brought her close to fainting. Even so Ann experienced a measure of calm. When they found her they would know she had done what she could. She had not given up. Ottosson, Sammy, or perhaps Bea would tell this to Erik one day when he was old enough to understand.

She sucked a little on the rag. The taste of wine reminded her of all the evenings she had spent at home on the couch. Would she have been able to live differently? The thoughts hooked one into the other, memories from her childhood in Ödeshög mingled with love nights with Edvard in Gräsö.

"Water," she mumbled and thought about the late nights they had rowed out into the bay. Edvard loved to fish and became childishly happy every time he caught something. What was he doing now? Her sadness about how her life had developed and her longing for the only man she had ever loved made her tremble with sobs. She could still clearly recall the image of his face although it was said that an absent loved one's features became more blurred with time. That wasn't the case. The pictures of Edvard and Erik were there, every wrinkle, expression, and glint in their eyes were clearer than ever. The same went for their voices, laughter, and variations in pitch.

Her head sank down to the brick floor that still felt cool. The smell of wine took on an increasingly smoky note.

She muttered words of love and was slowly rocked into unconsciousness.

✦

Fifty

The smoke divers prepared themselves. They struggled into their suits and pulled out hoses of a slightly smaller dimension than the ones used from the outside.

The fire was no longer burning as intensely. All of the cubic meters of water that had been dropped over and into the house had had an effect.

Firemen on the ladder had punched two holes in the roof and sprayed in water. In the basket of a crane two men were systematically working on the west wing where the fire was most intense.

Ottosson and Berglund had arrived. They stood as close to the house as they were allowed but were not able to be of any assistance at the moment. Berglund had broken a window in Lindell's car and searched it but had not found anything remarkable.

"Could she be in there?" Ottosson asked for the third time. He stared at the remains of a curtain fluttering in the window.

"Why haven't they gone in yet?" he asked himself although he knew the answer.

Eskil Ryde from forensics came zooming along in his old Mazda. He got out, appraised the situation, and then turned to Ottosson.

"May the dear Lord have seen to the fact that Ann is not in there," he said and returned to the car as quickly as he had come.

Ottosson took a few steps closer to the house. Wallin, the fire commander, came forward.

"You should watch it, Otto," he said. "Objects can come flying."

As if in illustration to what he had just said, a gutter pulled loose from its moorings, swung out from the wall like pendulum, and hovered there for a few moments before it crashed to the ground.

"Could someone survive in there?" Berglund asked.

"To be honest, I think it would be tough," Wallin said.

"Have you put the word out on that Hindersten?" Ottosson asked. Berglund nodded.

"She has a brand new red Ford, bought only a few weeks ago," he said.

"The neighbor thinks she had a packed suitcase in the car with her," Ottosson said.

"There's a national alert on her," Berglund said.

"Good," Ottosson said.

Three smoke divers went in, Sven-Olof Andersson, David Näss, and Ludde Nilsson, who was the team leader. He placed himself by the door and was the one who maintained contact with the commander outside.

The smoke divers communicated by radio. Näss first checked the kitchen, which was relatively unharmed but covered in soot. The floor timber had burned as well as the linoleum floor.

He looked over his shoulder and saw his colleague peek into a bedroom. They stayed close. Näss quickly checked the area behind the kitchen table and then joined Andersson in the bedroom, which was burned out. An iron rod that he assumed had once been a floor lamp had bent from the heat. Of the bed only four bed knobs remained.

The next room was also a bedroom with damages similar to the first. They could not see any remains of a person in here either. With their experience, they could often form an understanding of what had happened from a cursory glance around a room. That which looked like one big burned-out hole to others could tell the smoke divers a great deal.

They kept searching. The next room had apparently been a living room, that bordered the dining room.

"There's so damned little in here," Andersson said over the radio.

Näss nodded. In all its sootiness and with water running down the walls, the room looked naked. They checked every nook and cranny but found nothing of interest.

They walked back into the hall. Andersson pointed to the basement door and Näss nodded.

The door was locked. The color had peeled off and curled up and revealed that it was made of steel.

"The crowbar and axes," Näss said clipped. "We're going to force the basement door."

Ludde Nilsson forwarded this message to the commander. After half a minute both of the smoke divers could let loose on the door hinges. It was over in ten seconds and then they directed their flashlights into the basement. The stairs were made of wood and were still burning. Andersson sprayed water down and the flames on the steps died with a hissing sound.

"Ladder," Näss said, "four meters."

When they had received the ladder they went down, Näss in the lead. Adrenaline was pumping through his body. He let the beam of light play along the walls. It was smoking and burning, above all in the west part of the basement. Andersson came down after him and sprayed water in that direction.

Näss examined the ceiling. He reported to Ludde Nilsson and told him about the damage, that there was a great deal of smoke and that the risk of collapse was great.

"We're going in," he said and sensed in a spooky way that something terrible had happened in the basement. Every time he had this feeling at the scene of a fire the load of compressed air on his back felt heavier. The twelve, thirteen kilos felt twice as heavy.

"We have something here," Andersson whispered, and confirmed Näss's feeling. They walked together, first to the right and discovered the remains of a rat on the floor. It was half burned up. A little farther forward there were two more.

The water they sprayed created clouds of steam and together with the smoke this made it hard for them to pick out details.

They started to search through the basement systematically.

———

"Ludde, we have a body," Näss said.

"Any resuscitation required?" the team leader inquired, although he could tell from his colleague's voice that there wouldn't be.

"Most likely negative," Näss said.

The fire commander, Eddie Wallin, received the information. He looked over at the two police veterans. They were stamping their feet, silent, waiting for news. They had probably seen and heard everything, the commander thought, but hesitated in going over to them. Ottosson met his gaze and understood him at once. Tears, that seemed to have been lying in wait, started to run down his cheeks.

Berglund turned around and looked at the commander who was shaking his head. Berglund put his arm around Ottosson's back. He knew what Ann meant to the old fox. Ottosson held a hand to his chest and Berglund feared he was having a heart attack.

"How are you doing?"

"Think of the boy," he wept, and stared with tear-filled eyes at the ruins of the house.

"Let's go to the car," Berglund said. He had never seen his colleague cry before.

This was the worst. This wasn't something that got better with practice. He hated it. He could take all the physical exertion in the world, strange passageways, collapses, and everything a smoke diver had to withstand, but the sight of a dead person in connection with a fire always made him weak in the knees.

Sven-Olof Andersson bent over and started to tear off the plastic bag. He knew about Näss's weakness and urged him to check the boiler room.

The plastic had been gnawed away in many places and Sven-Olof quickly perceived that it was a male body. The rats had eaten through the fabric of what he took to be a pair of pyjamas and had gnawed the man's shoulder.

He tore away more of the plastic and discovered that one ear had been eaten clean away.

"Ludde! What we've found is a man," he said.

"Repeat!" the radio crackled.

"This is an older man who has been lying here a good while," he said in a louder voice. "The rats have had a party."

Näss came back and stood behind Sven-Olof Andersson's back.

"This isn't the female cop?" he asked.

"This is no female," Andersson said.

What they've found is an older male," the fire commander screamed at Ottosson and Berglund.

It was admittedly unprofessional to scream out such news at the scene of a fire but it was a spontaneous reaction. Afterwards he received numerous reprimands.

Ottosson hurried over.

"What the hell are you saying, Eddie?"

"It's an older man, probably dead for a long time."

There was nothing they could do to help him so they left the body and continued their task of searching the basement.

"Look at this," Näss said, who was happy to leave the dead man behind.

Andersson looked at all the wine bottles. At the same time there was a loud boom behind them and part of the ceiling fell in. Näss immediately straightened his helmet and looked up at the ceiling of the wine cellar. There was an upside-down bathtub on the floor. The smoke divers exchanged looks. Andersson bent over and lifted the tub. A lifeless hand fell out onto the floor.

He wrenched the tub aside. Näss's flashlight illuminated Ann Lindell's twisted body. Andersson leaned over her.

"She's alive," he said.

"Start rescusitation of middle-aged female," he said, as he checked her for possible external injuries.

Satisfied with what he observed he slid his hands under her neck and knees.

"I'll take her up right now," Andersson said and lifted Lindell.

With Lindell hanging over his shoulder he balanced up the ladder.

Näss climbed behind him and helped him balance the load. The police-woman's hair billowed out over his helmet.

The ambulance personnel were poised and started breathing resuscitation as soon as Andersson laid her on the stretcher.

Ottosson pushed his way forward and fell down on his knees next to Lindell.

The smoke divers returned to the house.

"And we're lifting," one of the emergency technicians said.

"Will she make it?" Ottosson asked.

Eddie Wallin shot him a look as the ambulance drove off with sirens blaring.

✦

Fifty-one

"You came back," Lars-Erik Jonsson observed.

He had been watching television when he heard a car drive up into the yard. He had sensed it was Laura.

She dragged a suitcase into the hall without saying anything.

"Would you like some coffee?" Lars-Erik asked.

She looked around as if it was the first time she was seeing his kitchen.

"Could you turn off the television?"

"Of course," Lars-Erik said and hurried into the next room, turned off the TV, and returned to the kitchen.

Funny how much nicer it is to put in several measures of coffee, he thought and chuckled.

"We're cousins," Laura said.

"That we are, and that's nothing to scoff at," he said and turned on the coffeemaker. "Please have a seat."

After having filled the coffeemaker with water he sat down at the kitchen table. Laura looked at him inquiringly as if she wanted to establish if there was anything hidden behind the casual words. He had the feeling that she regarded him as a country bumpkin, a real cousin from the country, and suddenly felt embarrassed.

"How is everything? You look a little down in the dumps."

She shook her head.

"It's been one of those days," she said finally and sat down across from him.

"Well, everything is calm here," he said.

"Why did you give me the letters?"

"Have you read them?"

She nodded. If only she wanted to talk more she would probably feel better, he thought.

"I only read the first few," Lars-Erik confessed. "If I can be completely honest it got too hard."

Laura regarded him with an amazed expression.

"It's strange that they corresponded for so many years," Lars-Erik said and started to put out cups and saucers.

"My father could hardly write," he added with a grin. "He was a real practical type, if I can put it that way, thought all that stuff with gatherings and talk got to be too much. He often drew back, never took part in associations or anything. Well, he was part of the Construction Workers' Union, of course, but that was so he could collect unemployment if things looked bad with work. And that happened from time to time. We on the other hand thought it was nice, because then he was home."

Lars-Erik paused but kept going when she didn't jump in.

"And the road association. That was obligatory of course. He—"

"Do you have any wine at home?"

He got up halfway then sank down just as fast back on the chair.

"I put on some coffee. Maybe you want some cognac?"

"Did you know about this thing with Alice?"

"What?" Lars-Erik asked and took a bottle out of a cupboard.

"That she had many men."

"What are you saying?"

"You don't need to keep up appearances any longer," Laura said.

He sat down, put out two cognac glasses and a bottle. His gaze lingered on the bottle as if there was something in it that could explain Laura's state of mind.

"I didn't know anything about it," he said. "Alice and you lived your life and we ours."

"But surely you must know that Mårten and Alice fucked?"

He winced.

"I don't believe that. My father wasn't like that. Alice was married."

Laura let out a laugh and rose up from the table. One of the glasses tipped over but Lars-Erik immediately turned it back up. Laura poked her head in the other room, then turned around and looked at the back of her cousin's head where the thin neck hair stuck out like a brush.

He looks like an old man, she thought, as she raised her right hand and made a fist. He poured out two drinks and turned around with a smile on his lips but stiffened when he saw her expression and the raised fist.

"What is it?" he asked.

She lowered her arm.

"She probably fucked everybody," she said.

"Did it really say that Father and Alice, that they . . ."

"Not exactly," she admitted.

"It's a lie," Lars-Erik said calmly. "Mårten never spoke between the lines. When he talked it was direct, unveiled, and never with hidden intentions. You are welcome to come here, I am glad to see you, but you are not allowed to speak ill of my father."

"Cheers," he said and raised his glass. "Let us forget about the past and think about the future."

"I caught her in the act," Laura said. "It is so ugly. She became ugly. Ulrik knew but he shrank down to a little shit. Then when I called that bastard he cried."

Laura let out another laugh.

"Who did you call?"

"I caught up with him. He said he was tired of living. Should he be allowed to take his own life without punishment? Would that have been right?"

Lars-Erik had been sitting with the glass in his hand. Now he moved it up to his lips and drank.

"But he ruined everything," Laura sobbed.

"Have a little cognac," Lars-Erik urged.

"She fucked everyone," Laura mumbled and sat down at the table.

"Alice was unhappy," Lars-Erik said, "you can't blame her for everything."

Laura stared at him, raised the brandy snifter, and threw it onto the wall above the sink so the glass sprayed over the kitchen.

"I don't want alcohol," she said, "I want . . ."

She leaned her head in her hands. Lars-Erik stretched out a hand and patted her on the cheek.

"You aren't feeling so well," he said tenderly. "Maybe you should rest a while and then we can talk more tomorrow. Maybe you're tired? I remember a time when we were picking lingonberries up on the heath. Do you remember? You were tired and cheated, put moss in the bottom of the pail. How Father laughed. He said you were like a forest troll. What could you have been, twelve, thirteen? Father was pretty funny about that. The berries and everything. He wanted me to tag along. He always said it was so we could check out the elk trails at the same time. Janne also came along. Martin was probably out with some girl. I remember how quick Alice was. It was the same with my mother. They had that in the blood. Their arms went like sawmills. Do you remember? I sometimes go up there when it's all red with lingonberries and then I think about you and . . . well, you remember . . . how it was."

Lars-Erik finished with a sigh. Laura had removed her hands from her face and looked at him.

"Alice died with a jar of lingonberries in her hand," she said. "They said I wasn't supposed to look but I knew what she looked like. Like a whore with her ass in the air and that farmer going at her from behind."

Lars-Erik's dismayed expression made her laugh.

"Of course I remember the heath. I wished I had died there. That everyone had died. Ulrik asked me once how I was doing. *One* time. It was at the cottage. He had grabbed me and Ulrik saw the marks."

"Ulrik grabbed you?"

"Not him," Laura said and drew her breath. Panic was shining from her eyes.

"Laura, maybe you need help? I don't get all this but that you've had a hard time of it, I understand that much. You are welcome to talk with me, but maybe you need someone who's good at this kind of thing."

"You're sweet, Lars-Erik," she said and took his snifter, drained it in one go, and poured another glass.

"I think about Alice," he went on, "such a life-loving person. To die like that. It's so pathetic. On the stairs."

Laura took a sip of cognac and grimaced. Lars-Erik thought she was going to throw the glass against the wall again.

"And if I was the one who did it, what difference does that make? I knew even then . . ."

"What do you mean?"

Laura drained the glass again.

"She laughed at me. Do you understand? She laughed. I just wanted her to be like a mother should be, but in the end she didn't care. She didn't even pretend. She laughed at me. I asked her to stop, to be a mother."

"You've had relationships yourself and know how hard everything can be!" Lars-Erik burst out. "It couldn't have been easy to live with that block of wood."

He poured out a cognac and drank, setting the glass down on the table heavily.

"She was unfaithful," Laura said, "and it was just as well that she died."

"You can't kill everyone who's unfaithful!"

"Don't yell at me. I'm warning you, don't yell at me!"

Lars-Erik drew a deep breath.

"She tripped. I can't help that, can I? She said something about lingonberries and laughed. They were his lingonberries. I wanted to smash the jar."

"But, Laura . . ."

"She was my mother and she let me down. She was like an apple that is rotten on the inside. You only saw the outside. But she burst in the end."

"Oh dear God."

Laura's face crumpled up. It was as if a great weight had landed on her. Her shoulders were pulled down and her head fell forward.

"Will you come with me?"

"Where to?"

"I know a place. A restaurant by the sea."

Laura didn't notice him shake his head. Lars-Erik thought she had changed into a little old lady.

"Can't we go there, just you and me? We can have a good life."

"No, Laura. Stay here for a few days instead and get your strength back."

Lars-Erik made up a bed in his father's old room. He walked past the suitcase in the hall but didn't know what he should do with it. If he carried it up it would give the impression that he expected her to stay longer.

Laura was still sitting in the kitchen.

"It's time to get ready for bed," Lars-Erik said.

He had been standing for a while looking at his cousin, how she poured out another glass and downed it.

She got up on unsteady legs and walked over to the window. Her face was reflected in it. She smiled and started to recite a poem:

"When evening drives away the shining day
And our deep night to others brings the dawn
Sadly I gaze upon the cruel stars
That formed my body out of sentient earth
And I do curse the day I saw the sun
Until I seem like one reared in the wood."

"Beautiful," she said and turned around, "Stars are cruel. They shine, beaming toward me, but so cold, so cold."

The silence in the kitchen lasted several minutes before she let out a sob.

"That is what I have received. Poems."

Lars-Erik walked over to her and put his arm around her shoulders.

"Do you want to make love to me?" she asked abruptly.

Her breath was sweet and strong from the cognac. Lars-Erik caught his breath.

"I don't think that would be so good," he said. "Let us be friends."

"Friends is good," she said, still turned toward the window.

Lars-Erik woke up, as he usually did, shortly before six. It took a while before he remembered he had a guest in the house.

He tiptoed down into the kitchen and closed the door behind him, turned on the radio and started to make his breakfast. He always ate porridge with lingonberry jam.

Radio Uppland started their transmission.

"Violent fire in Uppsala . . . may have a connection to the serial killings the past week . . . earlier missing man found dead . . . female police officer seriously wounded . . . Radio Uppland is on location in Kåbo."

Lars-Erik put down the package of oatmeal and stared at the radio. The agitated voice on the radio gave an account of the house that had burned down.

"The owner of the house, an older man who had been reported missing a month ago was found dead in the basement. It is unclear if the man's death was caused by the fire. In the basement there was also a female detective inspector, who has been leading the investigation into the three murders that have shaken Uppsala. She is injured and her state is reported as serious but not life-threatening. According to the information that Radio Uppland has been able to gather she was badly injured from the smoke. A thirty-five-year-old woman who is believed to be connected to the fire is now wanted by the police. She is driving a red Ford Fusion. There are facts indicating that she is connected to the murders."

Lars-Erik walked over to the window and looked out.

The radio announcer continued with the report but Lars-Erik did not need to hear more. He sat down at the table where the glass and the bottle still stood.

He didn't want to believe it was Laura they were talking about but everything fit. He looked around the kitchen, discovering glass slivers on the floor and got up, unsure of what to do.

Radio voices went on about the events that had taken place yesterday but he only sporadically registered what they had to say.

The suitcase was still in the hall. He walked over and checked the address label where it stood. "Associate professor Ulrik Hindersten— Uppsala University."

He looked up the stairs, turned his head, and saw the telephone on the wall in the kitchen. He walked over and lifted the receiver but immediately hung up again.

The stairs creaked as usual even though he was trying to walk as soundlessly as possible.

If she had only come earlier, he thought and stared at the closed door to the room where she was sleeping.

In order not to wake her, he pushed the door open gently and peeked in. The bed was empty. It had not even been touched. The blanket at the foot was wrinkled so Laura had perhaps sat there for a while during the night.

She had turned up so unexpectedly that in a way he was not surprised to find that she had left.

He walked out of the room and went down, checked the parlor and the TV room before he walked out into the yard. The car was still there. He felt the handle. It was unlocked. A few clothes and a purse were in the backseat.

The wind was sharp and the clear weather during the night had made the temperature fall below freezing. The lawns were white.

He called out her name and checked the storage shed, woodshed, and garage but could only establish that Laura was not on the farm.

He wondered if he should walk over to the early riser Egg-Elsa and ask her if she had seen Laura. But he sensed where she had gone, so he went back in and lifted the receiver again.

As he was describing the way to the police officer in Uppsala he thought about Rose-Marie, that he had done the same thing before her first visit to Skyttorp.

After the call he fetched his fleece jacket and walked out into the yard again. Now Egg-Elsa had made a fire. Smoke was coming out of the kitchen.

From the thin fir forest to the east there came a call from a wood-dove that had apparently decided to stay for the winter.